THE PEN

HERB SCRIBNER

[signature]
9/21/2016
May the Pen Serve you well!

Copyright © 2016 Herb Scribner

All rights reserved.

ISBN: 1535340924
ISBN-13: 978-1535340922

REVIEWS OF *THE PEN*:

"Friends and foes are not who they seem to be in this debut fantasy by Herb Scribner, but they are all tested beyond their limits in this epic story of bravery."

— Jacqueline Sheehan, New York Times bestselling author

"Herb Scribner's novel *The Pen* takes off with a bang, catapulting the reader into an epic sci-fi journey that draws you in and leaves you eager to uncover each mystery the characters encounter right along with them. This fast-paced tale both is surreal and fantastical, while constantly remaining inseparable from its great unifying themes of friendship, bravery, and the triumph of the human spirit. Scribner has cleverly crafted an out-of-this-world setting filled with characters you will cheer for and plot twists you'll never see coming. This book is for every reader who has ever dreamed of setting out on a wild and magical adventure."

— Allison Floyd, author of *A Wider Universe*

HERB SCRIBNER

To my mother, who never let me forget about this book.

CONTENTS

	Author's Note	i
	Prologue	1
1	The Pen	11
2	The Blizzard of Lexington	73
3	The Hut	149
4	Home	193
5	The Battle of The Pen	279
	Epilogue	367

AUTHOR'S NOTE

Thank you, dear reader, for taking the time to read this book. You deserve an acknowledgement over any other. I hope you enjoy the book and come back for more. There will always be more.

I'd also like to thank Jackie Hicken, cover-design extraordinaire and my unbelievable editor. Without you, none of this would be possible. We met really through fate, and I could not thank the world enough for bringing us together.

Again, thank you, Mom, for everything you've done for me. You put up with my rants about this book and the forthcoming ones. I couldn't have worked through the stories without you. And thank you for reading so much. My love for books and the written word would not have been possible without you.

Thanks to my sister, Jean, who helped me with some confusing parts of the books and for always asking me when it was coming out.

I also have to thank my grandmother for always believing in me and spreading positive vibes to her friends and the heavens above.

Thanks to Coach Mike for buying me The Pen that gave me the idea for this story.

I also extend gratitude to Payton and DeGroote, who helped me through the writing and test reading process. Your advice, both lengthy and short, helped me through the writing process.

Also, thank you to KP, Nick, and Leona. Without you, Kevin, Richard, and Feona wouldn't exist. You all helped this story grow in more ways than you know.

I have to thank all the influential English teachers who helped this process, including Mrs. Morin, Mrs. Smith, Mr. Everett, Mr. Hahn, Mr. Dragon, The Czar, and the Literary Treasure Trove Troll.

There are also my inspirations to consider, like authors Stephen King, Justin Cronin, Dan Wells, Dennis Lehane and Gillian Flynn. I also earned a lot of motivation from music done by Eminem, Drake and The Killers.

And at last, I'd like to thank the Irish girl I had a crush on in middle school, who, in sixth grade, gave me the best words of motivation someone could ever give: "Herby, you're like the sk8er boi in that song. None of the girls want you now, but one day you'll be successful and we'll all regret it." Thank you for that, and I'm glad I found a way to work you into this book.

PROLOGUE

I

A woman cried for help.

Richelle Ewings turned her head toward the sound of screaming and only saw flames, large, ominous orange and yellow flames, eating away at the side of the toppled-over bus—the one Richelle had been on just moments earlier.

She remembered the crash, sort of. She had been sitting in the aisle seat, next to a man whose arms covered both armrests, when, almost out of nowhere, she was shoved against the window. The last thing she remembered was looking out of the driver's window and seeing trees.

Since that moment, all she heard was noise. Screams, in particular.

"Help!" cried another girl off in the distance.

Richelle jerked her head toward the sound of the girl's voice. Should she go and help? She didn't know any of these people. No matter. Richelle ran past the bus' charred bits and pieces, through some trees, to find the crying girl standing next to a man who lay on the ground in a patch of dirt, surrounded by trees. Another man, who seemed to be the same age as Richelle, stood by.

"What's wrong?" Richelle asked, yelling over the roaring flames behind her.

"He fell out of his window and landed here," the girl spoke.

"Umm, OK, look, I'll go look for some help. Stay right here!"

The man grunted in pain. Richelle ignored it and was about to head off, but as she turned around, she bumped right into the other man. He was just as tall as her, with brown, curly hair. His face was a pale white, with sunglasses covering his eyes. He wore a black T-shirt with a skull in the middle. Jeans covered his legs and mud covered his jeans.

"What's wrong, sweet thing?"

"Are you a doctor?" she asked.

"Not officially. Still in medical school, last I remember."

"Well, there's another guy, about our age. He's laying on the ground there, can you–?"

"Help him? Sorry hunny, but, Grant Revel didn't take a trip just to—"

There was a flash of green from the sky. It illuminated everything overhead, turning the grayish clouds into a pale pastel green.

"What the hell?" Richelle asked.

After a large crack and a boom, the light disappeared.

"What just happened?"

II

Grant hunted through his surroundings. What had just happened to them? What was going on? What had that light been? They stood there pondering before they turned their attention back to the man on the ground. Richelle bent down and examined him. She was no doctor, but she could probably tell what was wrong. The man bled from the ears and top of the skull. He looked awful. And if he wasn't dead yet, he would be soon.

"Don't waste your time! He'll die!" Grant yelled over the roaring flames. Richelle saw the seriousness in his eyes.

"We can't just let him die!"

"Well, you're gonna have to! Don't waste your time and energy! If he ain't dead yet, reaper's here for him!"

"You're a doctor! Help this guy!" Richelle pleaded.

"Why would I waste my time?"

"Because that's what doctors are supposed to do!" Richelle yelled back. "Do no harm!"

Richelle and Grant's faces were red from the heated argument.

"Hey!" called another man, approaching the scene. He was a little taller than Grant and wore a light blue collared shirt and tan shorts. His shirt was covered in a little bit of dirt and splashes of blood. His hair had probably been spiked at one point, but was now completely messed up from the crash.

"And who the hell are you?" Grant asked.

"Name's Thomas. What's going on here?"

"We're just relaxing man, just hanging out," Grant said sarcastically.

"Quiet," Richelle said. She turned her head from Grant to Thomas. "This guy's hurt. He fell out his window, and douchebag behind me won't help him, even though he's a doctor."

"Are you kidding?" Thomas asked.

"Piss off," Grant spat.

The guy on the ground yelped in pain. Richelle, Thomas, and Grant all turned toward him and the girl with dark brown hair, who still stood beside him.

"Stop arguing and help him!" the brown-haired girl yelled.

"Who the hell are you?" asked Grant, angered that this girl was telling him what to do.

"I'm Jupiter!" she cried. "And he's dying!"

"Help," the man on the ground croaked.

"Help him!" yelled Richelle.

"Why? He's going to die!" Grant argued back.

"Stop fighting!" yelled another voice.

"Oh great, red-head wants in!" Grant shrugged.

Richelle turned to Thomas. "Can you do me a favor? Round up whoever else there is to help us. We need everyone to tell us their jobs. Hopefully there's another doctor," said Richelle, glaring at Grant.

"All right! Give me a sec!" Thomas ran into the woods to find other people.

He came back moments later with some men and women he had found deep in the forest. They all hurried back to the crash site. The bus lay on its side, in burning, churning, flames, while Richelle, Grant and Thomas stood around the bleeding, and possibly dying, man on the ground. Patches of trees surrounded the group, save for the barely measurable open circle of dirt where everyone was.

"This is it," Thomas said.

"That's it?" asked Richelle, noticing there were only eight—or seven, if the man on the ground died—who had survived a bus crash of over forty people. "No matter. All right, are either of you a doctor?"

"No," two of the men said together.

"Dammit!"

Thomas turned to Grant and pulled on his shirt. He shoved him up against a nearby tree. "Why won't you help him?" Thomas yelled. The rest of the group focused their attention on the two struggling men, with the fire of the bus still crackling in the background.

"He'll be fine. He fell out the window and hit the ground. He's got a concussion, nothing more," Grant spoke, shoving Thomas off of him. The rest of the group eyed Grant, wondering what had just happened.

"Why didn't you say that earlier?" shouted Richelle.

"Simple, doll. If I had said he had a concussion, you all wouldn't have come together so we could get a count. Now we know who survived. We're all here now. Your bus driver will wake up in about an hour. I suggest we put out that fire before—"

They all felt themselves shoved back by a force so strong it could only be nefarious. They want sailing back, slamming against nearby trees. Grant collapsed down to the dirt below.

Pieces of the bus sailed in the air and crashed into the ground. Broken shards of metal covered in flames pierced the dirt. Flaming parts of the bus littered the ground, and the fires went out almost immediately.

"Is everybody all right?" Richelle called.

She scoured the area quickly. The entire group nodded and looked fine. What about Grant? She looked for Grant and found him kneeling next to the now conscious bus driver.

"Grant?" Richelle called, walking up to him. She looked down as Grant wrapped his shirt around the bus driver's gut.

"What happened?" Thomas said, hobbling over to the scene.

"We've got a problem now," Grant answered. "A shard of fire fell into this man's gut. Without any medical supplies, he'll die."

The group all glanced at each other, scared. What was going to happen now? Grant looked over, hoping that the whole bus hadn't exploded, but it had. The first-aid kits, the luggage, the food, everything. Destroyed. Grant turned his head back down to the bleeding and dying bus driver.

"Great."

III

Grant Revel paced around, pulling his hair so hard he wished he could rip it out. He had already tossed his sunglasses to the ground in anger. Richelle and the rest of the group watched, wondering what was going to happen to the bus driver. He had a concussion and a metal shard in his gut. Grant's shirt had covered the shard and the wound had stopped bleeding for the moment. But without alcohol, or any other type of medical product, the driver would be dead by nightfall.

"Grant?" Richelle asked. The curly-haired man had been pacing for at least ten minutes now.

"I'm thinking!"

"What can we do?" Jupiter asked.

"Leave me alone. That's what you can do."

Jupiter stepped back, embarrassed. Thomas stepped up to defend her. "Hey, Grant. Why don't you—"

"Why don't you shut up and let me work?"

"You don't have to be this mean," Thomas replied. Grant turned toward him with glaring eyes.

"You don't even know me."

There was a deep pause as Grant and Thomas' eyes met, flames burning within them.

Breaking the silence, the bus driver suddenly yelped in pain. He had just woken from his unconsciousness.

"Great," said Grant again, getting down on his knees next to the driver. His bloody shirt had a label sewn on it with the name Jordan written out in cursive. Grant grabbed hold of Jordan's face, trying to calm him down. "Hey. Hey! Shut up!"

"Grant!" yelled Richelle.

"Shut it, princess!"

"Hey, big muscle guy!" Grant yelled, nodding over at one of the other men—Chris. "Go get me a large stick so I can knock this guy out."

"You aren't actually going to do that?" one of the women asked.

"Bet he would," another young man replied, now getting into the conversation.

"Who are all you people? Tommy, get these idiots outta here! I need space!" Grant yelled.

Thomas thought over the decision at first, but then ushered everyone away. Thomas told them all to go look for medical supplies, food, or water, if they find it. They ran off as Thomas came back to Richelle, Grant, and the bus driver.

"All right, I sent them all off looking for stuff," Thomas said.

"Good, good," Richelle replied.

Grant sighed. "They better hurry back. Otherwise I'm gonna have to kill this guy if he doesn't shut up!"

The driver was still screaming, louder than before. He hadn't calmed down.

"I still don't get how you got a job as a doctor," Thomas spoke.

"You don't know the half of it," said Grant, looking over at Thomas, who was now kneeling on the other side of the driver.

"How long till he dies?"

"Well, judging by the temperature of the air and the way the damn sun is hitting my back, we've got about three hours till dark. So judging by his condition . . . I'd say within the next 20 minutes," Grant explained.

"You're not serious?" Richelle asked.

"I'm serious as a heart attack, my dear. I don't have anything to really stop the bleeding."

"What about the shirt you put around him?" Thomas asked.

"He's bleeding in the gut. The shirt will only hold temporarily. But the blood will soak through the shirt and he'll die. I need some alcohol, stitches, SOMETHING," Grant complained, his hands on the driver, trying to keep him alive.

"Stitches?" Richelle asked. Grant looked up at her and nodded.

Richelle reached into her pocket of her jeans and pulled out a small sewing kit holding a tiny piece of linen and a small amount of thread—denim-colored, and only enough to patch a pair of jeans. She tossed it over to Grant, who caught it and looked at it with amazement. He didn't smile, but only stared at Richelle with an angered expression.

"Had to fix a hole while on the bus," she explained.

"Thanks."

Grant looked down at Jordan and took a deep breath. He did this before all of his surgeries. Grant unwrapped the shirt from Jordan's gut and watched pints of blood gush out. He looked at the burnt shard of metal. This was his first task. He had to somehow take the shard out and cover the wound before too much blood spat out. Grant looked over at Thomas.

"Tom," Grant began, "I need you to help me. I'm gonna pull this shard out of his gut, and you gotta cover it with the shirt, got it?"

"Yeah, I got it."

"Good," Grant said.

Grant reached down to the shard. He grasped his hand around it and told Jordan that this would be painful. Grant waited three seconds to ready himself for some serious screaming. The three seconds ended and Grant ripped the shard out of the driver's gut.

The driver shouted wildly, blood gushing and spewing everywhere.

Thomas stood there in a state of stupor. He had been a farmer for most of his life, but he had never seen such a disastrous thing as this. He saw a man, a grown man, crying in pain, while blood poured out of him and stained the dirt below.

Thomas snapped back into real life and tossed the shirt on top of the driver's gut. He wrapped it around the back of the driver and tightened it as much as he could. But it was no use. Thomas could see the blood was soaking through the shirt. The shirt was probably bought at some lame concert.

Grant looked down at Jordan, suffering and in such pain. He had never been in such a situation as this. Grant had never had to repair a person without any medical supplies. The likelihood of Jordan living was slim to none, and Grant reminded himself of that. He needed to remind himself that if Jordan died, he couldn't blame himself.

"All right, he's gonna die really soon if I can't patch him up. We don't have any water? None whatsoever?" Grant asked.

Both Richelle and Thomas shook their heads.

Grant sighed. "He needs some kind of liquid to keep him going. He'll be dehydrated when I'm done, which wouldn't be good."

"What can we give him?" asked Richelle.

Grant shook his head and shrugged. He was out of ideas.

"HEY!"

The people who had been ushered away came running from the forest. Each of them had something in their arms. One of the girls had a broken first aid box, a man had a cooler, another had bandages in his hand and the last had a backpack. They all charged down to the spot where Thomas, Richelle, Jordan, and Grant were. They ran and threw the stuff to Grant.

The last man even tossed his cooler in the patch of sand they were in.

"What do we got?" asked Grant, walking right over to the cooler. He opened it and saw stacks of old beer cans. He looked shocked when he first saw it but then nodded because it could help. He grabbed a can, opened it and ran back over to Thomas.

"Uhh," started Chris, "we got some beer, some first aid crap, and a backpack."

"Right," Grant said. He snatched the first aid kit from the young woman. He opened it and saw some Band-Aids and some other stuff for young kids. "Oh, well, I didn't know we were kiddies!" yelled Grant at the crying bus driver. Grant left it though, and grabbed the shirt and tore it off of Jordan's gut. He dripped the alcohol onto Jordan. The sting knocked the driver out.

"Will he be all right?" Richelle asked.

"I dunno. We'll have to wait till tomorrow."

IV

Most of the survivors relaxed around the blazing campfire that they had made that night. Chris smoked a cigarette nearby, blowing a puffy haze to his right.

Grant also had a cigarette in his mouth and blew it away into the wind. Everyone sat around the fire in silence. The crackling blaze and the noises of animals of the night roared around them. They didn't know what to say to each other. Here they were, stuck in the middle of a forest, with barely any supplies. The only type of drink they had was old beer.

"All right," started Richelle, leaning closer to the fire. Everyone turned to face her. "People should be here in the morning, and hopefully they can get the driver some help."

"Yeah, right," Grant said.

"Hey, Grant, if you're gonna be negative, then just leave," Richelle said. Thomas looked over at Grant as well, who took a drag of his cigarette and then threw it to the ground.

"Look, Jess. I wanna get out of here as much as Saturn over there—"

"It's Jupiter," the brown-haired girl said.

Grant ignored her. He leaned back against a tree. "As I was saying, I want out. But no one is coming for us."

"Why are you saying that? Hope is the only thing that'll get us through all of this," Thomas said, uninterested in Grant's negativity.

"Did any of you look up at the sky?" Grant asked, pointing up. The group followed Grant's finger and looked to the stars.

But overhead, they didn't see a dark blue sky with white stars and a moon like they expected. Instead there were two moons, both of equal size, hanging there—like two apple slices. The group stared upward in confusion, unable to believe what they were seeing. Richelle looked up at the sky, too, intrigued.

"Tomorrow we should explore the area," she said, still looking up.

"Why's that?" another of the men, Brent, asked.

"Because we're not on Earth," Grant answered, his eyes fixed on the two moons hanging in the sky.

PART I: THE PEN

CHAPTER 1

I

Jake Serent hated bacon.

Well, maybe it wasn't the bacon that he hated. Maybe it was the smell. It reminded him of his childhood, when he'd wake up during a sleepover at his cousin Kevin's house and the first thing he'd smell was bacon. Sometimes burnt, sometimes a little fatty. But always bacon. It was Kevin's favorite breakfast food, after all, so of course that's what they ate.

Everybody loved Kevin.

Funnily enough, Jake smelled bacon, of all things, as he walked into Friendly's with Kevin on the same day his teenage cousin disappeared.

The two laughed as they entered Friendly's, Jake behind Kevin, the smell of fresh grilled ground beef and iceberg lettuce everywhere. When Kevin entered, the high schoolers, who had just came from a South Hills Tigers football preseason victory, roared and cheered. Jake had forgotten about the game. He'd never been invited to one, which made them easy to forget. Swarms of girls ran over to Kevin, hugging and attempting to kiss him. They loved his handsome James Dean charm. Jake stood beside Kevin and got no action at all. It was probably the mushroom haircut that went out of style in the 90s.

Kevin pushed his way through the crowd and Jake followed.

"Kevin! You're back, man. Great to see you," one of the linebackers said.

Kevin pounded his fists. "You know it, Nick, you know it. How's things?"

Nick shrugged. "Just surviving."

The two cousins sat down at a table, where many girls squished next to Kevin. As more people shoved their way into the booth, Jake got closer and closer to the wall. Kevin, meanwhile, flirted his best game and ignored Jake.

Jake ordered the usual for Kevin and himself: two orders of chicken fingers, fries, and root beers. It was the same meal that the two cousins had gotten since they were eight years old.

"Hey Kev! You plan on skateboarding again?" a random kid asked off in the distance.

"Nah. I'm just here with my pal Jakester," Kevin said, pointing over to Jake.

"How long you gonna be here?" asked a girl. It was Colleen. Jake recognized her from English class.

"Not long. Jake and I are going to Vermont for five days. Then it's back to the orphanage for me. Back to Lowell, probably. Assuming I don't get caught by police along the way," Kevin said with a wink.

Kevin laughed, and the crowd followed his lead. Jake gave a courtesy laugh. Sure, it was funny to everyone else, but Jake didn't find all of Kevin's jokes funny, especially ones that poked fun at his family history.

The orders came. Jake shoved fries in his mouth—he hadn't eaten all day—and slurped down some root beer. Kevin, meanwhile, teasingly fed some girls—a pair of sexy seniors—his fries. Jake looked down to the green and red carpet, not wanting to watch his cousin get further than he had with the girls at his own school.

Jake lifted his head a second later and saw a tall, black-haired teenager enter the restaurant.

Shelton Reclard.

If Jake could see auras, he knew Shelton's would be the darkest shade of black. The boy, who shot daggers of hate at everyone in the diner with his eyes, was dressed in a black hoodie and dark jeans. His arm was wrapped tightly around his girlfriend Feona's thin waist.

"Look who just came in," Colleen whispered to the group.

Jake didn't look. He already knew what was coming.

"What a nerd," Kevin said. "Dude is so goth."

"How do you know that, Kevin?" Colleen asked. "It's not like you go to our school anymore."

Kevin nodded over to Jake. "My cousin told me. This dude is a nobody."

Nick, the linebacker, leaned in close. "Heard he's got some girlfriend who likes to get a little freaky. One of the dudes on the football team says she's got some weird stuff going on in her basement."

The people in the group shook their heads in unison and looked away.

Jake, meanwhile, watched as Shelton sat down next to that gothic girlfriend and glared at the world as though it had wronged him. Jake and Shelton's eyes locked for a second, but Jake looked away only to see Kevin making out with Colleen. He turned, then, and gazed away at the windows. He had nowhere to hide and nowhere to look.

Kevin stood up out of nowhere, tugged at Jake's shoulder, and left the booth. When they were away from the booths, Kevin coddled Jake's head under his arm. Jake smelled the cheap body spray that Kevin had put on this morning.

"You OK?" he asked, letting go of Jake.

"Yeah, I'm good," Jake replied, brushing his hair back the way it was before.

Kevin raised an eyebrow. "Are you sure? Man, you always get like this when I'm in town. Enjoy the moment, man. Just chill, relax, ease up. We're all having fun here."

Jake looked at the carpet again and then back at Kevin. "Yeah, sorry. I'm just tired from work. Kind of want to get out of here."

Kevin smiled. "All right, yeah, let's get out of here. We'll go pay and then go do something else, all right?"

Jake nodded.

"Ahh, crap! I forgot that I was supposed to meet up with my grandma tonight!" Kevin slapped his leg. "She's going to kill me if I don't show up. Meet up later at the library for the draft?"

Jake nodded, though he was a little upset Kevin had forgotten that the two had planned to make their fantasy football draft selections together tonight. "All right dude, yeah, sounds good," he said. "I'll get going. Call me when you're heading over?"

"I'll call you," he answered. "You don't mind paying the check?"

Jake was already planning on it. "Nah man, I got it."

"Thanks," Kevin said, slapping Jake's arm. "I owe you one."

Jake knew Kevin owed him something closer to 100 than one.

Kevin pushed open the door to Friendly's and left, jumping on his skateboard and riding away. Jake sighed and turned back to go and pay for the meal. As he arrived at his table, he saw that all the seats were now filled. Nick shoved Jake away.

"Get outta here, loser," he said.

"I've got to pay my bill," Jake said.

"Then do it," Nick said.

Jake reached into his pocket and retrieved his wallet and a $20. He went to throw it on the table, but Nick ripped it from his hand and buried it in his own pocket. Jake stared at the large, muscle-built star linebacker of the town football team, rage building inside of him. All he wanted to do was punch the guy right in the face.

But he knew that starting a fight with Nick the linebacker would be like throwing fruit into a blender. He'd turn into a smoothie.

"Well, pay your bill and get out of here," Colleen said.

All the rage disappeared from Jake. Instead, his face turned a bright red. He saw the jocks and seniors smile and start to giggle.

Jake reached into his wallet again and dropped another $20 bill on the table. He turned and left the restaurant with his head down, the smell of bacon trailing behind him.

He had no idea that Shelton was still watching him.

CHAPTER 2

I

"So, how was Friendly's?" Jake's mom asked as mother and son settled down for dinner.

Jake stared down at the green glob on his plate, unsure of what his mom had cooked.

"It was OK," he said.

Jake slid his phone out of his pocket and hid it under the table to check the time—5:49 p.m., 11 minutes till draft time. No texts, calls, or notifications from Kevin.

"Hey! Phone away," his mom commanded.

Jake made sure the sound was on before he slid his phone back into his pocket.

"Sorry, Mom."

"How was Kevin?" Mom asked.

"He's the same old person. I don't know why, but he left Friendly's a little bit early. Maybe I ruin his popularity. I mean, the dude is more popular than me, and he doesn't even live here."

"Oh, it's OK, hunny," his mom said. "I'm absolutely positive he had a real reason to leave."

"Yeah, whatever," Jake said.

He pushed his plate away and walked up to his room without another word to his mom. He threw open his bedroom door, where the red strobe light he had gotten for his sixteenth birthday blinked, and slammed the door closed behind him. Jake crashed onto his pillow top mattress and stared at the ceiling, thinking of Kevin and his cousin's immense popularity. The strobe light flickered.

Jake checked his phone again. 5:53 p.m. Seven minutes till draft time. Where was Kevin?

"Of course," Jake said hopelessly.

Jake opened up one of his social media apps and saw something he didn't expect: a status update from Kevin.

[Kevin Keys]: drafting for fantasy with my best bud Trevor. Hopefully this year goes better than last!!]

II

The screeching wheels of his cheap skateboard made Jake's ears bleed. The board wiggled and waggled from left to right as he soared down his town's main road in the white turning lane. It didn't matter to Jake that he had already missed his own draft picks. Kevin had lied to him and had gone to Trevor's house instead of his for the draft. He needed answers. Maybe Kevin had wanted Jake to go to Trevor's too?

As Jake reached a side street, he swerved around the corner and stopped before the incline that led to Trevor's neighborhood. Jake tapped the end of his board, hoping to catch it with style. He fumbled the board and watched as it went sailing through the air. It landed in the middle of the road just as a red Hummer H2 drove by and smashed the board into pieces.

Forced to run the rest of the way up the hill, Jake panted harder and harder as his destination—Trevor McGaven's house—neared.

"Hey Trev, open up!" Jake yelled as he pounded on Trevor's door. No one answered. He thought about turning away, but he noticed Kevin's skateboard leaning against the garage door. His cousin was here.

Jake pounded again, twice as hard. His hand began to glow red.

Jake thought of his next step—to smash open the door. He took a few steps back, realizing all the problems a broken shoulder could give him. Regardless, he sprinted toward the door.

Just as he was about to clash with the red wooden door, it flew open, and Jake stumbled through and crashed on Trevor's off-white tiles. With Trevor hysterically laughing at him, Jake stood and regained his balance. He looked up and saw Kevin sitting relaxed on the couch. There was a haze in the air.

Jake saw Kevin's hand, holding something that looked like paper between two of his fingers. Smoke came up Jake's nose and he coughed. The air smelled like skunk. He coughed again. Kevin lagged a little bit, and it took him a few seconds to realize Jake was standing in the doorway. Kevin, now wide-eyed, dropped the small piece of something. Trevor took one last puff off the thin cigarette and threw it to the ground.

Taking all this in, Jake shook his head and headed out the door into the setting sun.

"Yo Jake!" yelled Kevin, who came running out of the door after him.

"Jake!"

But Jake, ignoring his cousin, stormed away across Trevor's fresh summer grass. Kevin stopped him as he grabbed his cousin's shoulder.

Jake turned and shoved Kevin, who fell back into the grass. Kevin yelled something that Jake couldn't hear and tackled Jake to the ground to get him to stop. But Jake rolled Kevin as the two tussled for dominance.

Trevor burst onto the scene, holding a black bat with red logos down its center. He wound up and hit a grandslam across Jake's back.

The grass was implanted as Jake fell over. He cried out as his back burned from the strike. Kevin hopped up to his feet. Trevor went to hit Jake with the bat again, but Kevin grabbed the weapon and shoved Trevor away.

"Come on man!" Trevor yelled. "One more!"

"Nah man, we're good, we're good," Kevin said, saving Jake from more pain.

Trevor and Kevin both left Jake writhing in pain.

III

"Are you OK?"

Jake's eyes opened and he had an up-close view of his mom, who might as well have been holding a piece of meat over his head. He looked over at the window. The sky was a midnight blue. White stars hung under the mask of the night sky. Jake saw the stars better than he'd ever seen them before.

"Where's Kevin?" Jake asked. His mother pointed upstairs in the direction of Jake's room.

Jake sprang into action and ran up the stairs of the house, his shoes thudding against the hardwood floor of a house constructed in the early 20th century. He swung open the paper-thin door of his room and saw Kevin now laying in the bed, fully awake and playing coy. Jake walked around the room, the brown wooden floor thudding and the white walls blankly staring down at them.

"Get out of here, man," Jake said with ease. Kevin jumped up.

"Shut up Jake. Look, I need your help."

"What?" Jake asked. When he saw Kevin was already moving, Jake brushed hair out of his face and approached the conversation again. "I'm not going to help you after what just happened. Forget it."

"This big thing's going down man," Kevin said, off in his own little world. "We're all gonna skate on the highway, and then go to an insane party later. It's the roof stunt from last year but better! But I'm not allowed to be out late right now. Gram's rules. Can you cover for me? If she calls and asks where I am, make something up, please?"

"No, I won't help you," Jake answered. "Not this time. You're on your own, man."

Kevin put one leg out the window and brushed away his steaks of hair that had been dampened by sweat. His other leg was still in the room. "Jake, dude, serious. I know I owe you a ton of stuff, but come on. This is supposed to be awesome. Don't be such a nerd. Please, please, please cover!"

"No man, no! You didn't try to talk about you smoking or anything like that, you just got in a fight with me, and didn't even protect me when Trevor hit me with the bat!" Jake yelled.

Kevin shot a stern look over at Jake.

"Look, Jake, if it weren't for me, you'd be the biggest loser in town. But because of me, people at least know you as 'Kevin's Cousin,' and that's better than being known as a nobody. I've gotten you so many girls and gotten you out of so many fights. The least you can do for me is cover," Kevin said with venom.

Jake mouth found no words, while his eyes found the floor.

Kevin hopped out the window as a pack of wrapping papers fell out of his pocket and onto the bedroom floor. Kevin snatched the papers up, climbed along the roof, hopped down to the street, and grabbed his skateboard from Trevor, who had been waiting for him.

Jake watched Kevin skate down the street in the direction of the highway. He stepped away and checked his phone again. It was 9:03 p.m.

His shoes went thudding again as he opened his bedroom door and went back downstairs. Without a word to his mother, he searched the ground floor for his wallet, which was waiting for him on the kitchen counter.

"Mom, can I have a ride?" he asked.

"Yeah hunny, where to?"

"The highway. Kevin's about to do something really dumb."

IV

Jake and his mom hopped in the car. His mom pushed the pedal harder as Jake rushed her to get to the highway. He reiterated over and over that Kevin was in danger. Jake couldn't take anything that was going on. The radio, blaring some bubble-gum pop song, didn't stand a chance against Jake's rage. He shut the radio off without a care for his mother's concern. He needed time to think. What was he going to do when he confronted Kevin? All he wanted was for his cousin, his best friend, to not die because of a stupid highway stunt.

Jake spent so much time thinking that he didn't even realize it when the car came to a stop. His mom parked on the edge of the highway, just a few feet behind Kevin.

"Do you want me to go with you?" his mom asked.

Jake shook his head. "Probably better if it's just me, mom. I'll be back in a minute."

Without another word, Jake stormed out of his car and jogged along the highway, where he saw little specks in the distance. An orange fire was lit with roaring flames. His mom was too far away to see anything.

Jake heard Kevin's laugh. He surveyed the people up ahead and picked out Kevin, who was doing skateboard tricks along the highway roads.

"Kevin!" he yelled.

Kevin, Trevor, and the rest of the group exchanged a few words between each other as Jake approached. Jake could see they were getting a little nervous, worried that something was about to happen. Kevin and Trevor eased out of the crowd and then jogged toward Jake. They tossed their boards to the ground and rolled the last few feet toward him. The rest of the group disappeared into the roadside forest.

Jake wasn't sure about what he saw at that moment. He was unsure, but sure. Something happened that bewildered him, but yet it was totally believable. It was something he never expected to see and yet he saw it. It was like the first time anything major happens in your life. You know it can happen, you want it to happen, but you still can't believe it when it does.

The sky was midnight blue and the flames in the distance flickered. The August crickets chirped and the wind made the browning leaves tussle. Kevin and Trevor hurried toward Jake on their boards, their skateboard wheels scratching against the highway road.

But then everything went quiet.

Jake watched Kevin and Trevor disappear into thin air.

CHAPTER 3

I

    Jake Serent hated the rain.
    And unfortunately for him, it had rained every day for the last two weeks—ever since his cousin had disappeared. From his window, Jake watched sheets of rainwater splash on cars and soak the streets. Autumn leaves from the dead trees were damp and sticky on the ground, and the air reeked of wet dog.
    Jake hated all of it.
    Jake knew for sure that his cousin was not coming back. Though he didn't want it to be true, he knew it was. He had been gone for two weeks, after all. And the worst part about it was that Jake had been there when he disappeared, and he couldn't tell anyone what he saw. No one would believe him; people didn't just disappear from reality. He would easily be committed. And if he weren't sent to the loony bin, his social status would drop well into the red. There was no easy way out, except for keeping his mouth shut.
    Kevin wasn't the only one to disappear, either. Trevor had, too. And two missing teens isn't a story that gets underreported. Jake had read some news stories on his phone about how his missing cousin had been kidnapped or had ran away, but only Jake knew the truth. He just couldn't remember it. Somehow his mom and the other teens on the highway hadn't seen what happened, either.
    Two weeks after his cousin disappeared and with only a day or two to go until school started, Jake sat alone in his room with his cell phone on the table next to him. The screen stayed black. Rarely had it buzzed or lit up in the last two weeks. Kevin had been his main source of social life. Now, like Kevin, that was gone.
    Jake rested in a black leather chair in the corner of his room, twisting it

ever so slightly by pushing his feet on the ground and looking out the window at the storm. The few cars that drove by were barely visible through the silver sheets of rain. Jake bent his head and rubbed his eyes. Another day. No friends. No family. No school. No nothing. All alone.

His phone buzzed against the table.

Jake leaned over to see the highlighted screen, where a message notification waited for him.

+102511: [It stands near you . . . It's outside the library . . . Go and get it . . .]

Jake swiped right on the message so it would open up in his messaging app. He stared hard at the kelly green bubble, trying to make sense of it.

Jake typed his reply.

Jake Serent: [Who is this?]

+102511: [. . .]

The number stopped typing.

Just as Jake was about to type another response, his phone went black and shut down completely.

Searching for answers, Jake glanced out the window at the rain again. He didn't understand the message, nor did he have a clue as to who it came from. That number wasn't American or European. Could it be from somewhere else in the world?

But the message, regardless of its oddity, intrigued him. Something about the message called out to him and tugged at his mind. He couldn't shake the feeling that he was supposed to listen to the message and follow its orders. Yet again, he felt sure, yet unsure.

Jake dashed downstairs and slipped on his pair of gray—once white—basketball sneakers. When his shoes were tied up, he walked over to his closet and pulled out an orange hoodie, slipping it over his red T-shirt and feeling the fuzzy inside slither against his head. He bounced out the door, the hood shielding him from the rain. He didn't have hope for his khaki pants. He knew they'd get soaked.

Jake braved the rain and walked toward the library, on a mission to find out what this mysterious texter was going on about.

As Jake walked through the thick, rapidly pouring rain, he thought more about the message, unable to rid himself of that feeling that this 102511 number and Kevin's disappearance were somehow connected. His cousin disappears into thin air, and then less than two weeks later he gets a message that's completely out of the ordinary? They had to be connected. It was a gut feeling, really. He was sure, yet unsure.

He continued on toward the library, the ominous rain still pouring.

II

"So, we meet again," Jake sighed when he reached the library. He had already spent the whole summer volunteering there, and now he was back. It was hardly ideal. Anyone ever heard of a day off?

The rain poured onto the library, turning the building's plaster gray exterior into a muddy brown, and it reminded Jake of an old, classic horror film. Goosebumps bubbled around the hair on his arms. Jake pulled his hood up and searched the building for answers, expecting something big or something phenomenal to happen.

But all remained still in the storm.

"What a waste," he said, turning to leave.

"No," a voice said through the silence.

"Who the—" Jake began, but stopped.

"Thank you for coming, Jake Serent," the voice said, deep and foreboding. "Please, pick up my Pen."

Jake ran his hands through his hair and felt the cold, hard rain pound on him. Where was the voice coming from? Jake narrowed his eyes to the sky as the voice continued.

"Listen to me," the voice said. "My Pen is buried in the grass to your left. All you need to do is pick it up and bring it to me."

"Your what? Your pen? Wait, what?"

"My Pen," the voice confirmed. "On your left."

Jake looked to the patch of damp grass on his left, but he didn't see anything resembling a pen. He bent low to inspect it further, feeling his shoe slip into the squishy grass. When he stepped again, he heard a crack and slipped forward, face first. His head sank into the mud. He tried standing up, but it took him a few seconds, since his hands slid against the soupy mud below. He threw some of the brown goo away from his eyes and looked down to see a small purple rock poking out of the ground.

Only it wasn't a rock.

It was a pen. The Pen.

When he pulled it out of the ground, he noticed The Pen was bigger than any other he had seen in school. It was about the size of a roll of quarters. It was mostly purple, save for the six cubes—purple, blue, light blue, green, yellow and red—that went from the top to the purple grip, which hovered above a platinum silver tip. Blue ink stains rested on the sides from past use.

The purple cube had two swords clashing together, like some sort of battle, on two of the four sides. A knight's helmet embedded on a flag rested on the other two faces.

He saw the second cube—blue, with an axe on two of the four sides, and a bow and arrow on the other. Both were gray.

The third cube was baby blue with a castle wall and tents on it. What was this? Jake thought that it might represent ice, or something close to it.

The green one was the simplest of them all, with two horses—one

THE PEN

black with a red muzzle and a red saddle, and the other white with a blue cape.

The next cube was yellow with a Brahman bull's head on it. On the other sides, treasure chests sat open, revealing gold.

And the final cube was red with a wizard who wore a baby blue cape and hat, coupled with a crest of a lion.

"What the—?"

"Now, Jake, bring me The Pen," the voice requested.

"But I don't even know who you are, or where you are," Jake said, searching the skies. "Beam me up?"

"This doesn't have to be complicated, Jake," the voice said. "It's simple. Walk up those steps, open the doors to the library. Walk in and hand me The Pen."

Jake looked to the door of the library with an eye of contempt. The wind howled and the rain slapped against the tall glass door. Could he even get through the door if he wanted to? Since it was a Sunday, the door would obviously be locked. Other than breaking the law, there wasn't really a way for him to get inside.

"Listen, Jake, if you bring me my Pen now, you'll avoid doing many things that you really do not want to do. You will meet people who will cheat you, people who will betray you, and people who will destroy you. Save yourself the trouble," the voice pleaded.

Jake rolled the tip of The Pen with his fingers. None of this was making sense.

"You will escape all death, all chances of death, and all types of pain if you just bring this Pen to me," said the voice.

"Huh?" questioned Jake.

"Please, Jake, bring me this Pen now. I'm trying to help you. You will not regret it."

"I won't?"

"No, Jake. Betrayal, hatred, fighting, pain, and suffering all lay ahead for you, unless you bring me my Pen now."

Jake whispered to himself, "You're going crazy, Jake."

"You're not crazy. You really should listen to me, Jake," the voice insisted.

Jake flicked The Pen on.

"Jake," the voice said, "I have something you want."

"What is it?" Jake asked.

"Your cousin," the voice said.

Jake's eyes shot up to the sky.

"Jake, your cousin, Kevin, is here in my world. People can enter my world from many different places. The library, a corner market, their closets, even the highway. That's right, Jake, Kevin's here. He disappeared here! I know you've been searching for him. Your search is over. If you want to see your cousin again, and escape pain, and betrayal, and all of that, I advise you to step through," the voice said.

Jake's eyes questioned the library. He looked down at The Pen and figured this was a good idea. All he had to do to get his cousin back was walk through the library doors and hand some random person—some random voice?—a pen. No big deal.

Jake didn't have time to answer the voice. He blacked out instead.

III

Jake's eyes opened and he was still out in the rain. His body was drenched, his clothes choked his body, and his face was frosted with mud and slivers of grass. Everything smelled like dirt and wet leaves. The sky was still a dark gray, so Jake had no idea how much time had passed since he blacked out.

"What the heck is happening?" he asked himself.

Something poked at Jake's back. He turned and saw Richard Lyons—short, pale and pimple-faced—standing there, his head mostly covered by a hoodie that referenced some 1994 video game Jake had never heard of.

"You all right, Jake?" Richard asked through the rain. "I was walking out to my car to go pick up the latest version of Halo and saw you laying here. Thought I'd see if you were all right, buddy. You know me, just, always in a rush."

Jake was slow in hearing everything Richard spat out.

"What?" he asked, still not in the conversation.

"The new Halo. It came out a few days back. I was going to go buy it and saw you sleeping here. You know it's raining, right? Of course you know. Reminds me of *Rain Storm*, actually, that game that came out last year for Playstation only. Did you play that one?"

"Oh, mine's still on backorder, dude. How is the game?" Jake asked, pretending to care about the conversation.

"Great, finished it in a few days. It's great, yet hard."

Jake nodded his head.

"By the way," said Richard, reaching into his pocket and pulling out The Pen, "I found this with you, so I kept it in my pocket. Nice looking Pen, dude. I swear I've seen it somewhere before."

Jake took The Pen in his hand, felt its edges, and smiled. For some reason, he was happy to have it back in his possession. Jake wasn't sure why—it was only a Pen he found moments ago that he had very little understanding of. But there was something about it—a gut feeling.

Still holding The Pen, Jake looked to the sky for answers. He remembered the voice and how it desperately tried to get Jake to bring The

Pen back to him.

"You all right, dude?" Richard asked again. "I mean, you look like you've seen a ghost. Well, not the Halo kind of a ghost, but a ghost."

Jake ignored the joke. "Richard, can you give me a ride?"

"Sure, where to?"

"Shelton Reclard's house."

CHAPTER 4

I

Shelton Reclard's room was dark, with monochromatic navy blue walls, windows, and door. His soft mattress lay flat in the center, and a TV and cheap video game system rested in the corner. Behind the bed was a closet that held his clothes and colognes, and his most prized possession, a mirror his grandfather had given him when he was barely old enough to speak.

Sitting on his bed, wearing his typical outfit of dark blue jeans and a black hoodie, he fell into the arms of his girlfriend, Feona Griswold, a red-headed princess who ruled his world and his bedroom.

"I love you babe," he said, as his lips splashed against Feona's. Her tongue licked the outsides of his lips.

Shelton's kisses continued as he moved his hands more and more. She hopped onto him. He felt her legs and then moved his hands up her side under her hoodie, cupping her breasts.

There was a knock at the door.

Shelton let go of his girlfriend. He glanced at the door. It was closed, but Shelton already knew who was on the other side. It was a gut feeling. He swallowed hard and adjusted his clothes to a more professional position. He swerved around to see Feona fixing her hoodie to cover her body.

"I'm gonna go use the bathroom," she said. Her voice was a tad too whiny for Shelton's liking, but she had a body of a mermaid.

"Sounds good," he said. "Take your time."

Feona shot him a questioning eyebrow before she turned around the corner of the door and disappeared into the bathroom. When she was gone, Shelton breathed a heavy sigh of relief to calm his nerves. The knock had frightened him.

"Ah, Shelton, sorry to interrupt you."

THE PEN

"Ah!" Shelton exclaimed, jumping. He held his chest and turned to his right, where he saw a thin purple outline of a man, which looked similar to a wad of floating gas.

"You," he said.

"Me," the voice said.

"What are you doing here?"

"Someone has finally found The Pen," the purple outline said.

Shelton's eyebrows jumped. "We finally have our next Holder, then?"

The spirit nodded. "And I believe you're familiar with him. His name is Jake Serent."

"I know him," Shelton answered, flipping through his school yearbook in his mind. "Kind of a loser. Odd choice for a Holder."

"He has motive to come to my world," the spirit said, ignoring Shelton. "His cousin, Kevin, is also here."

Shelton remembered the bond Jake and Kevin had from high school, and knew Jake easily had motivation to go to Discis, since Kevin had disappeared just a few weeks back.

"Well, good," Shelton said. "So he should just return The Pen to you easily, right?"

The spirit shook his head. "He declined my request earlier. There's no telling what he's going to do next. He has motive to come here and he's . . . different."

"What should we do?"

"The boy will come here. I have foreseen it. Be stealthy, and make sure he doesn't get hurt," the purple blob instructed. "Make sure he survives at all costs and brings me my Pen."

"Understood," Shelton said. "Creator."

"And there is another piece to this puzzle," the spirit said. "Remember Moss?"

"Yes, Moss," Shelton recalled. "Does the pirate still have The Orb?"

The Creator nodded. "Yes. And not only does the pirate still have The Orb, but he is waiting for Jake. He is the man who knows the land too well and will lead Jake to my Palace," The Creator said. "He is a part of the prophecy."

Shelton searched the ground, and when he returned his gaze to the spirit, his eyes were stone-black.

"We kill Moss, then."

"My Master would be very pleased if we got him The Orb back," the spirit said.

Chills ran up Shelton's spine.

He went to reply, but his mom's voice screeched through the halls. Shelton darted out of the room, past the spirit, and into the hall so he could find his mom.

He didn't think to keep Feona from entering the room.

II

Shelton wasn't alone when he got back to his room. His face was dark with displeasure, since the kid behind him, with greasy brown hair and a face peppered with pimples, rambled on and on about anime characters from some manga comic book. Shelton didn't remember his name, but knew he was one of the kids who sat alone at lunch. Jake Serent followed behind him. The spirit had been right all along.

"This," Shelton started, "is my room."

"Cool," the boy—whose name was Richard—said, moving over to Shelton's video game system in the corner.

"What's that?" asked Jake, pointing to the corner of the room.

Shelton, wide-eyed, approached the corner, where a phrase hung in the air. Letters were written in red cursive as though they had been scrawled in blood.

The words across the air read:

"NO DISTRACTIONS."

"Oh my god," Shelton said, getting off his knees and laying back against his bed.

Jake got up and walked over to Shelton. "What happened?"

"He killed her."

"Who did?" Jake asked.

Shelton smirked. "Your newest enemy. The Creator."

III

"OK, you want to see your cousin Kevin right?"

"Yeah," Jake answered, watching Shelton move from one end of the room to the other.

Richard cocked his head from the corner, unsure about what was happening but still vaguely interested.

"Well, it is easy to get your cousin back, but it will take work, if ya catch my drift," Shelton said. Jake didn't get his drift at all. "Right, you don't get it. Well, if we do this right, we'll be able to open the doorway to Discis, where your cousin is."

"Wait, Discis? What the hell is a Discis?"

Shelton shook his head. "Discis is a where, not a what. It's a planet way off in the galaxy. Your cousin is there, right now. You want to see him again? We have to go there and find him."

Jake didn't understand. "I'm not sure I want to be heading off to another planet right now. I've got family, friends and, well, no money for a bus fare."

Shelton sighed. "Jake, why did you come here?"

Jake pulled The Pen from his pocket. "I found this."

Shelton smiled when he saw The Pen. It was something he only heard ghost stories about, not something he thought he'd actually see.

"Wow, it's real," he marveled, moving closer to Jake. "The Pen is real."

Jake shot Shelton a questioning look before the dark-haired teen rubbed away his astonishment and refocused his attention to Jake. "Anyway, the point is, that Pen is from a planet called Disics. And the man who wants it back—that voice you heard—is from Discis. And your cousin, he's in Discis. All of this is connected. You want to see your cousin again? That's where we need to go. I know it's a lot to handle right now, but I can explain more as we get going."

"Psychos," Richard said, moving closer to Jake and Shelton, who ignored the crater-face.

Jake was still unsure about all of this. None of it seemed real, like it was one big dream that he had yet to wake up from.

Might as well embrace the dream before his eyes opened.

"How do we do it?"

"We scry," Shelton replied.

"Scry?" Jake asked.

Shelton stood up and walked over to his closet. He pulled down a thin black mirror with silver characters etched around the edges from the top shelf. He wiped the dust off the cover sheet and presented it to Jake.

"This was my grandfather's. He gave it to me when I was a kid. It's a scrying mirror, which shall take us from here to Discis. Magic. Druid magic, specifically. Again, confusing, and I don't expect you to understand right now. Just go with it."

Jake nodded. "Shelton, look, I get it. But why are you helping me? We barely know each other and I'm pretty sure you hate every human in the world."

Shelton glared at Jake. "He took the love of my life. The only thing I want to happen is to see him suffer. To die a most painful death. He said no distractions. Well, I'm not going to let anything distract me from slitting his throat."

"Who?" Jake asked, sitting in a big chair in the corner of Shelton's room. Richard followed, sitting down on the armrest.

"Remember the voice you heard?"

"Yeah," answered Jake.

"Well, that was the man The Creator. He is from Discis. In the beginning of his life, he was but a farmer in the beautiful land run by two

Empires. He led a rebellion group that was unclaimed by either empire, and soon there was a world war in Discis. Eventually the Creator turned on his own people and wound up being the mastermind behind everything. From there, he had ultimate powers to create anything he wanted because of The Pen. He pushed the northerners south and had the entire northern region to himself, to do whatever he wanted.

"But for some reason, and I'm not really sure why, he lost The Pen. So he wants you to head to Discis and give it to him," Shelton said.

"I don't feel like getting involved in another world's affairs right now," Jake said.

Shelton waved the idea away. "You won't. Look, you want to see your cousin again, right? And I want to kill The Creator. Let's both go to Discis, save your cousin, and then I'll go finish off The Creator. Mutual interests."

Jake massaged his chin and looked out the window. He thought of his mom and his family and the world he'd leave behind, at least for a short while. But when he remembered that eventually he would return home, hopefully with his cousin, he nodded.

"Let's do this."

IV

Shelton laid his back against the back corner of his room, where Feona had been. All he wanted was to get to Discis and take his revenge on the Creator.

"So, wait," Richard said, walking over to the other two boys. "What are you guys doing?"

"Ugh, just trust me," Shelton said. When he saw Richard wasn't swayed by such an easy answer, he continued, "We're going to scry. Druid magic. It's apparently Shelton's thing. Long story. But we should end up in Discis. Just not sure where."

"There is another option," Jake began. "There is a library, where the Creator's voice told me to go. Why not just—"

"Sorry Jake, but the library is where he expects us to go. Loopholes are the only thing that will work now. Calling upon the spirits will get us where we need to go. And it's the last thing the Creator would expect. Then, we find Moss and he will guide us forward."

V

The 16-year-olds all sat on Shelton' bed. A soccer game played on the TV in the corner. Shelton didn't have much interest in soccer, but he had interest in getting revenge on the Creator, and soccer calmed his mind. He needed a still mind if he was going to make this work.

"All right," Shelton said at last, rising from the bed. "It's time." Jake and Richard turned their heads and stood up too. "Not you Rich; you're not coming. Can't chance it."

Richard sat down and the bed bounced a little. He pulled out his iPhone. "Whatever, I've got to go buy a video game anyway."

A few feet away, Jake and Shelton gathered around the mirror that Shelton then placed on the floor. The magic-user let out a sigh of relief. "OK, here we go. You ready, Jake?"

Jake thought of his mother, his sister who was away at college, and the rest of the people he'd leave behind. He turned back to Shelton. "We'll be back soon, right?"

Shelton nodded. "Shouldn't take more than a few minutes."

Jake nodded. "What do we do?"

"I'll recite a spell. It should awaken some magic and get us there," Shelton said. "If they answer me, things are going to get nutty, so hold your ground."

Before Shelton could recite the spell, the TV shut off. The lights in Shelton' room dimmed. The rain picked up and the windows blew open. The rain shot at the faces of all three boys. It stung and stabbed.

"It won't shut!" Shelton exclaimed. Jake and Richard jumped up to help, but the windows wouldn't close.

The wind picked up and soon a mass of air swirled around them, a big silver tornado wreaking havoc in the center of the black mirror. Jake turned his head as the tornado sucked The Pen from Jake's pocket. It yanked harder and harder, and The Pen finally came out and fell on the floor.

Richard saw The Pen and knew to get it and protect it. So Richard, redirecting the strength he was giving to the open window, jumped flat on The Pen. The Pen bounced up, still headed for the tunnel of silver rage, but Richard held it down. The tornado caught him and started to drag him in.

Shelton released the window as Jake did, and they pulled on Richard's leg. The tornado yanked harder, dragging Richard closer to the tornado.

Shelton, wide-eyed, ran over to the mirror and tried slamming the tornado down.

Nothing worked.

"The panel is open! Hold on!"

And then the tornado pulled harder and Shelton, Jake, and Richard went through it, disappearing from Earth.

CHAPTER 5

I

Waves of molten hot lava crashed together, surrounded by the cavern walls of the volcano. The yellow, orange, and red river of steaming hot soup flowed around black boulders that lay dormant and still. Short sun-colored waves brushed against the rocks and spilled on top, spitting out steam and hissing as they hit the cooler air.

And from the volcano's gaping top came three boys—with nothing to stop them.

II

Jake Serent should have died when he fell into the volcano, but The Pen kept him alive.

The steam should have melted his face right off. The flames below should have turned his eyeballs into sloppy goo. The toxic gases should have clogged his lungs. His body should have been incinerated. He should have splashed into the lava almost immediately after falling into the volcano's caldera.

But he was still alive, and he knew it was because of The Pen. He just didn't know how The Pen had saved him or how much time it had bought him.

His eyes were closed when he first entered the volcano's mouth, but he could feel the fierce heat. When he opened his eyes, he saw orange and yellow surging below.

Jake had nowhere to go. Nothing to grab on to. Nothing.

He turned his head and saw Shelton and Richard, both unconscious and heading toward their own deaths. He yelled, trying to wake them, but nothing could be heard over the raucous noise of the splashing hot lava.

Jake realized, as he continued to fall toward the lava, that his life was coming to an end. He would die here, nothing but ashes in a swimming pool of lava.

Memories flashed before his eyes. He thought of his mother, whom he had left to embark on this brief and fatal adventure. He remembered his cousin, who was the whole reason behind this quest. He thought of the world he left behind and how he'd never see it again. His life was over.

Something in his gut told him to look—to ask for help.

In end-of-life desperation, Jake searched his pockets as he plummeted into the volcano's soup below. Maybe he had something that could help him.

And he did: The Pen.

He slipped it out of his pocket. Only a few feet from the lava, Jake maneuvered his body closer to the wall of the volcano and whispered, "Hold my weight."

A purple light glowed around him. It had been the entire time, Jake realized. But only now it glowed like a lantern in the night.

The swirling purple light caught Jake in his fall and held him in the air. Jake, hanging in the air, stabbed The Pen into the side of the tunnel that was nearest to him. He grasped onto The Pen with one hand and hung loosely.

It held his weight, like he had asked.

He held on to The Pen for dear life, his feet dangling a safe distance away from the lava. He could feel the lava's heat on his leg, but it wasn't strong enough to burn his clothes. He smiled.

Suddenly Richard flew past him, his eyes shut and his body motionless. Jake reached out to help, but it was too late.

Richard splashed into the lava below.

III

Jake hung with one hand latched around The Pen, which dug deep into the rocky surface of the volcano's interior. The winds pushed him, swinging him back and forth. His body tingling with fear, he gazed downward and shouted for help.

But Shelton had someone else to help. Floating in mid-air, surrounded by blue, jagged electric sparks, he moved toward the lava below and then disappeared completely as he dipped into the yellow soup.

Shelton spotted Richard floating in the lava, his body still together and intact. Something had kept him alive. For now.

"Weird," Shelton said.

He tugged Richard's arm and pulled him up through the lava. Surrounded by blue again, Shelton emerged from near the lava, holding

Richard's flimsy and lifeless body. Jake couldn't understand how, so he chalked it up to Shelton's magic. It had more power than he realized.

"Jake," Shelton started, from below, holding Richard in his arms. "I need you to jump down to that black rock."

"What? That's suicide. I'll die," Jake said, still swinging on The Pen, his face a mix of ash, sweat, and steam.

"You won't, you'll be fine. Trust me. Jump down to the rock. Please!" Shelton noticed the fear in Jake's face as fire shot out of pear-sized holes on top of the boulders.

Jake took a deep breath and then ripped The Pen out of the volcano, soaring downward toward the rocks.

At first he headed for the lava, but he twisted mid-air and went in the direction of the rock, hoping he'd land there. Hope was all he had now. And The Pen.

He lost the ability to breathe when his back cracked against the rock next to the raging fire. With tic-tac pebbles and chipped rocks digging into his back, Jake couldn't turn over. But he used the little upper body strength he had to push against the rock and turn backside up. He pushed himself to his feet and, as soon as he was on one knee, the rock shook, and he fell back down exhausted.

Shelton was happy with Jake's inability to stand.

"Jake! Remember, stay down!"

Jake held himself down as Shelton floated down from above and landed softly on the rock, still holding Richard. He put Richard down on the rock's flat surface, next to a boulder that spat fire.

Jake tried standing up, but Shelton put his foot down on his back. "Not yet. I need concentration if I'm going to save his life."

Jake decided to stay down. Shelton raised his arms high into the sky and hummed. It was a familiar tune. Trying to figure out what the song was, Jake closed his eyes and searched through his head like an internet lyric website, remembering almost every song he knew. But this one Shelton was humming? It really bothered him that he didn't know what it was. It will probably mean something later on, Jake thought.

"I still can't believe this is happening," Jake said to himself.

Alternate worlds were not what Jake had expected to see today. Right now, he was trying to remember what it would be like to be vacationing in Vermont, like he was supposed to. But Kevin's "death" brought too much pain. Hopefully, when Jake proved all of this was a misunderstanding and Kevin wasn't dead, he could go back there with his cousin.

According to Shelton, Kevin was alive in the world of Disicis, with a man named Moss.

Moss.

Jake rolled his eyes over and saw Richard rising from the rocky surface surrounded by those blue sparks. Shelton was floating in the air now, humming the tune again. Richard lay in Shelton's arms as the black-haired boy hummed. *Humming what, though?* Jake thought. What in the heck was this song? He listened to Shelton.

Jake heard himself sing words that he had known all of his life, and yet they were completely new to him.

"We have a chance to feel the night," he sang, "to feel our faces and go to places that we never knew were alive."

Shelton heard Jake below.

White light erupted from the lava.

IV

A rocky hand came from the red and orange molten rock, black with orange veins running through it, its blood steaming lava. White light surrounded the hand as it ascended from the orange river.

As Shelton's eyes opened, he watched a full body emerge. Its bones and skin appeared to be made of black rock, and veins of orange lava spread throughout like a spider web.

Shelton flew fast down to Jake.

"Jake! Nice going, dumbass!"

"Why? What is it?" Jake yelled over the roaring that erupted from the hollow mountain.

"It's called a Vetex, a monster that the Sluronnano created a few centuries ago to keep people out! The song you were singing must have woken it up! Great going!" Shelton yelled. "This must be why no one survives this fall."

The Vetex roared, shaking the inner walls of the volcano. Horns came from its ears and its bloody eyes. The Vetex barely fit within the volcano's walls, its hands reaching the top of the layer just near opening.

Jake asked Shelton for help with his eyes.

"Our only chance to make it out of here is to get out of the tunnel!" Shelton yelled, pointing at the top of the volcano.

"Where will it lead us?" asked Jake, the monster roaring like a caged lion.

Shelton ignored him. "You still got The Pen?"

Jake felt his pockets. "Yeah! Why?"

The Sluronnano volcano shook.

Jake ripped The Pen from his pocket and looked at it as the volcano shook again. The Pen nearly slipped away, but Jake held onto it with his hard, sweaty hands. He turned to the Vetex, which roared and pushed through the lava with ease. It was hungry. Hungry for humans.

Jake had that feeling again—one he couldn't shake. Something was telling him to do something he wouldn't otherwise have known to do. He raised The Pen and pointed it at the Vetex: "Disappear!"

A gleaming purple light shot from the tip of The Pen and splashed over the monster.

It disappeared, leaving nothing but sparks in its wake.

But the volcano continued to vibrate. The pulsations shoved Jake down on all fours. Shelton grabbed him by the neck and dragged him upwards, all the way to the volcano's mouth way up above. As they flew, Jake's glance snapped toward the top of the mountain. And, to his surprise, glass began to move from one side of the volcano's lip to the other, apparently intent on locking them inside the volcano.

Without hesitation, Jake pointed The Pen up at the glass. He whispered something to himself, and then another deep purple light shot out of The Pen, creating a rope that slithered out past the glass to the other side of the volcano. He put The Pen back in his pocket and grasped the rope with his free hand and began tugging his way up, one foot at a time. He had never been the best at rope climbing during gym class, but when it came to life or death, he was a champion.

Shelton was about to grab the rope, but then he remembered Richard, sprawled out on the rocky ground near a set of exploding boulders. A wave of lava sprang high up and headed toward Richard.

Shelton, without wings, flew down at full speed, leaped onto a rock and grabbed Richard's arm. He bounced off the rock as it exploded in a mess of fire and lava.

Shelton jumped to another rock. He gathered up all his strength, flew like a bird over to the rope and climbed, holding the pruned Richard in his left hand and climbing with his right.

Jake inched closer to the top of the closing volcano. He looked down at Shelton, who nodded to push on. Jake climbed his way to the top, where the mirror was just about shut. *Just enough to get me through*, Jake thought.

He held onto the glass edge and pulled himself through the side of it. He collapsed onto his right, laying flat against the rocky surface.

"Shelton!" Jake yelled.

Shelton was still below. He let go of the rope and fell toward the lava.

But then he stopped and floated back up.

The closing glass only left enough space for one body to pass through, not two. Maybe Richard could fit if he was pushed, but both could not fit through at once. The glass nearly closed, Jake put his hand in, hoping to grasp Shelton's hand, but he got nothing but steamy air. He pulled his hand back out of the volcano, the cool rush of nighttime air cooling his body.

The glass covering closed.

Jake saw Shelton a few feet below on the other side, trying to push his way through. Lava splashed and rose from below toward Shelton and Richard.

Jake hunted around him and saw a boulder about twice his size waiting for him. He knew he wasn't strong enough to lift it himself.

But he wasn't alone. Not anymore.

Jake put his hand in his pocket, grasped The Pen, and yelled: "Lift!" and the boulder ascended into the air.

Jake pointed The Pen at it and took control of the boulder. His head and body tight, his heart racing, Jake pointed the rock at the glass and the boulder went speeding down.

Bits and pieces of black glass scattered everywhere.

Holding Richard still, Shelton dodged all the glass that rained down on him. He flew out onto the rocky surface where Jake waited on his knees, breathing heavy and sweating bullets. Both of them panted harder and harder as Jake realized The Pen had taken some strength and adrenaline from him.

Shelton rested his free hand on Jake's shoulder and laughed. Shelton's other hand waved Richard down onto the ledge near them. Jake and Shelton looked down at the boy.

"This kid," Shelton said, shaking his head in amusement.

"Yeah, he missed all that fun," joked Jake, out of breath. Shelton nodded. "Can you bring him back?"

"I hope so."

CHAPTER 6

I

The midnight-blue sky and polka-dotted stars hung over the world as Jake and Shelton made camp about a mile away from the volcano. Richard's body–which Jake had carried the entire way there—rested by the side of the fire. Shelton and Jake had stored a pile of twigs, logs, and branches next to the burning flames.

Jake bent his head and fiddled with The Pen, twisting it in his fingertips.

"So is this the place you were talking about?" Jake asked, still staring at The Pen. "Wherever we are, it looks like Earth, except there are two moons." Jake had observed this a few hours ago while finding the campsite. "And it has a dark feeling to it."

Jake finally took his eyes off The Pen and looked over at Shelton, whose eyes were shut.

"We are in Discis, Jake," Shelton confirmed.

"So what do we do from here?" asked Jake, getting up to add more twigs to the fire.

Shelton waited a beat before answering. "First, we wake Richard, or at least try and bring him back to life. And then we have to find the Krowian Desert, where Moss awaits us," he said with authority.

"Who is this Moss?" Jake asked.

"Moss is a pirate of this world," Shelton began, rubbing his hands together with his eyes locked on the fire. "His family came from a part of the world once called the Unknown Islands, though Discis folks are still unsure if those islands even exist—hence why they're unknown," Shelton explained. "When the Creator took over the world back a long time ago, he double-crossed the pirates. And it was sort of my fault. Without getting into too much detail, I told the Creator where the pirates were. Anyway, since then, Moss decided he wanted to get revenge on the Creator and anyone else who aligned with him. So Moss and I don't exactly have the greatest history, since, as you know, I used to work with The Creator."

Jake nodded. If he were being honest, he didn't fully trust Shelton either. Shelton had an absurd amount of knowledge about Discis and had worked with The Creator up until this point. And if Jake was supposed to call The Creator an enemy, wasn't his enemy's friend also an enemy?

Shelton ran a hand through his hair, wiped his face clean, and shifted his gaze back to Jake. "It's going to be hard convincing Moss that I'm on your side. He still hates me for everything that happened years ago."

Jake extended his fist. "I got you."

Shelton pounded Jake's fist and, for the fist time in what seemed like forever, felt like he had a true friend.

II

After sleeping, Jake woke up to see one of the two moons glowing bright pink and the other a pale dark blue that barely made itself present against the backdrop of the near-black sky. Jake, funnily enough, wondered what time it was. He should be heading to work or school or something, right? Or making breakfast for him and his mom? Running down to the local gas station to buy his mom a pack of cigs?

But there weren't any clocks nearby. And he doubted that people on Discis—if there were any, since they hadn't seen any yet—counted time the same way as people of Earth did.

Jake remembered hearing in science class that planets had different times. Of course, that was the easy way of putting it. But he had heard that your age on one planet might not be the same as the other—that planets move on without you if you leave. It was entirely possible his world had left him behind. It's possible he was already older than he had been when he left. He had come to Discis 16 years old, but could very well be 61.

On his left, Shelton lay on his back, sleeping away. Richard, dead and lifeless, it appeared, was on Jake's right. A bird screeched in the distance. Jake followed the sound and noticed a deep green forest nearby.

He lifted himself up and decided to stretch his legs. His shoes made imprints in the grass as he walked toward the nearby forest. When he reached the tip of it, he looked in, and through the trees he saw twigs, logs, and moss planted everywhere, choking each other. The sun slanted through to illuminate the patch of verdant majesty.

Before Jake could take a step into the woods, Shelton grasped his shoulder.

"Hold up, cowboy." Jake turned around. "The desert's that way." Shelton pointed to his left. "We have no need to go through the woods, because we have no idea what's in it."

Jake followed Shelton back over to the campsite. Moments later, Shelton stood over Richard while Jake sat down on a log and thumb-wrestled himself. His eyes followed Shelton, who picked up Richard and rested him on another log.

"Hey Jake, do you have anything of Richard's? Like a ring, watch, or anything he might have been wearing?"

Jake searched the ground for answers, but found none. He raised his arms in the air before slamming them back down against his leg.

"Right, OK," Shelton said before he felt around Richard's pocket and, lo and behold, found a card—purple with a red trim. The picture on the card's front face showed a female warrior, dressed in all gold, in the middle of battle.

But Shelton ignored the card's face and placed the card on Richard's forehead and closed his eyes. He hummed again. Jake recognized the sound, and decided it would be better not to sing along this time. When Shelton finished humming the chorus of the song, Richard's eyes popped open and the boy sat up stiffly. The card that was on his head had fallen off and floated away with the wind.

"Where am I?" he asked, touching the blood on his lower lip.

"Discis," Jake said as he patted Richard's shoulder.

Richard wasn't sure what that meant.

"Welcome Richard! Are you tired? Do you need a vacation? Well, then, come on down to Discis! We have things such as unknown deserts, pissed off politicians, volcano monsters, and a Pen that can save the world!" Shelton smirked at his joke.

No one else did.

Jake patted Richard on the shoulder again. "Good to see you, man. Happy you're alive."

Richard grinned. "What a time to be alive."

Now that their friend was saved, Jake fixed his gaze on Shelton. "So, should we get moving toward the desert? Or whatever you said."

Shelton nodded. "We'll need to get up on high ground to see if we can spot the right direction. I know it's to our north, but I'm not sure exactly where. We go too far West and we'll end up somewhere we don't want to be."

The three boys looked over to the forest and saw a mountain waiting for them in the distance.

"No," Jake said. Richard agreed.

"Then where?" asked Shelton, scanning the lands away from the forest.

Jake saw only an endless amount of grass nearby and another set of mountains way off in the distance, so far away that they were nearly invisible. Before Jake said anything, The Pen vibrated, and Jake mistook it for a text message. He reached into his pocket and pulled The Pen out. Oddly enough, The Pen was surrounded by a purple light.

The Pen, vibrating harder than ever, soared out of Jake's hand and landed on the dusty ground below. It spun around for a moment or two before stopping, its tip pointing toward the grassy plains ahead.

"The Pen speaks," Shelton said.

Jake bent down, picked up The Pen, and started walking.

III

Moving through the tall grass was not easy. After all, each strand—green, with an electric blue tip—was about knee-high. Jake felt pain on his knee from a slight cut, which he probably had gotten while in the volcano, each time one of the strands brushed against his leg. Blood trickled down his knee, but Jake wiped it away without much concern.

The boys' steps made imprints in the grass, mostly from Shelton's hard black boots, which slowly churned away at his energy and tired him out, as they walked on. Thick boots through thick grass is just failure waiting to happen. It didn't help matters that it was hot. Shelton's dark, blue hoodie, which he had taken off now, hadn't done him any favors, either. Sure, he loved the color black and many forms of dark blue, but that wasn't a good thing in this part of the world, which often, at least back in the old days, embraced whites, taupe, and yellows.

"How much longer?" Jake asked. "We must have been going for—"

"Three hours," Shelton interrupted.

"Three hours? Are you saying that we've been going three hours in the blistering heat, trying to get to a desert? Come on, dude, this is bad. Can't you like, teleport us?" Richard asked, now only wearing a red wife beater.

"First off, teleporting is hard and I would most likely die by trying it, given all the energy and strength I used earlier to save your lives," Shelton said, mulling over options. "Also, you think this grass is bad?" He laughed. "There's a land, about 8,000 miles away—if that—full of grass that goes for more than the length of Russia. And you call this bad?"

"Oh yeah," Jake said, "I forgot you lived here. What was that like?"

Shelton shrugged. "It was great. Even better once the Creator took over."

"Really?" Jake asked, now curious.

"Yeah. World finally had peace, and I got to work front and center with it."

Richard raised an eyebrow. "Wait, what? You worked here?"

"Well, I used to live here, and once The Creator took over, he asked those who would help him to, well, help him. So I signed up and I got to travel the world and see everything. The Creator sent me on a special mission to Earth to help him get back his Pen. He said I'd have to wait until the next Holder came to be before I got to make any moves," Shelton explained. "Not the best job in the world, but, hey, I was young."

Jake raised an eyebrow. "How is this possible? You're our age. How did you live so much time in Discis?"

Shelton's face turned into deadpan. "You'll come to find, Jake, that time moves slower here."

Jake's suspicions about time were confirmed. He paused in his step and looked straight forward, where the colossal purple mountains, tipped with cream-white snow, waited far off in the distance.

"I'd say we got another ten miles or so," Shelton said.

"And then?" asked Richard.

"We'll reach the desert and find Moss. Once we find Moss, we'll rest." Jake nodded as he put The Pen away in his pocket and led the crew forward.

Shelton grinned. "Yeah. Moss. Rest. That's a good joke."

Jake felt his stomach drop. Maybe Moss wasn't the hero and savior he thought he'd be.

IV

There was no rest. At least Shelton was honest. Time was short to Shelton; he didn't know why, but there was a feeling inside of him that they didn't have a lot of time to do this. He imagined Moss had been waiting for ages to meet Jake.

With the sun down, the night sky was just about up. Stars hung in the sky, making Jake remember home. He missed home. It seemed like forever had passed since Jake had actually been in the "real world"—which he felt he left back on the day Kevin disappeared.

Sorrow and sadness came back to Jake. He missed his cousin. Right now, they would probably be up in Vermont, playing video games or going swimming in the lake by Kevin's grandma's little cottage. But things took a turn for the worst that night when Kevin went skateboarding on the highway. The pain of the night rushed back to Jake. An image of what he saw—or didn't see?—floated in his brain. He could see Kevin, skateboarding, riding, heading toward him, when—

"How much more?" asked Richard, holding his rumbling stomach.

"Jake, use The Pen," Shelton answered.

"Does this Pen ever run out of ink?" asked Jake, still walking through the endless blades of grass. "Or how does it work?"

"From what I've heard, no," Shelton said. "But if I remember correctly, you can only use it in certain circumstances. I don't know anything more about it, but I've heard there are restrictions." When he saw Jake's displeasure with not getting a real answer, Shelton shrugged. "Probably best for you to only use it when you need to, then. Now wouldn't be a bad time."

Jake hesitated a little, thinking ink could run out or about the restrictions. Then he took The Pen out of his pocket.

"Show me the miles we have left," he whispered to The Pen.

Much to his surprise, a silver line shot out of The Pen, turning into a chain that shot off into the distance. The Pen then burped out a silver round sphere. On it read the letters, JS.

"Woah," Jake said.

He pressed a small purple button on top and the sphere popped open, revealing some sort of map. There were two lands separated by a body of water. But Jake didn't get a long time to look at the map, for it automatically zoomed into the northern part of land, specifically a vast sand-colored area, with the words Krowian Desert written on it. Jake eyes fell upon a purple blinking dot, which he imagined represented their group. It couldn't have been too far from the desert, maybe a mile or so.

"Guys, we are almost there," Jake said. He slipped the map into his pocket, hooking the chain onto his pants. The three ran forward.

V

Their shoes rustled through the tall grass. Running was the only thing left in their minds at the moment—running to Moss, running towards rest.

Shelton's thick black hair waved through the wind. "There!" he yelled. "There! The desert! There is the Krowian Desert!"

The grass thinned out as they approached the sand, the strands fewer and farther between. About a minute or so later, specks of sand invaded the grass's territory, increasing until all the green had become a pale dust.

When Shelton and Jake halted before the sand, which looked cold due to the sun no longer shining, Richard went speeding into the sand. He stopped, skidded, and turned back to the other boys.

"What's the hold up?" Richard asked.

Jake didn't know. He felt compelled to stop. But when nothing happened, he picked up pace again.

The three boys ran for the man named Moss, the smell of dust and sand flying up their noses.

CHAPTER 7

I

Geoffrey Moss—a rugged man with aged eyes and a sun-kissed beard—sat cross-legged in the desert. His olive green pants collected the sand and his cape hung loosely on his neck, waving with the wind. He searched through his oatmeal-colored sack, which was stocked with maps, a compass, a combination of some liquid that had dry bits of food swimming around in it, and The Orb, one of the most powerful weapons in the universe, which he had stolen years ago.

Moss's black glove, which he had worn for over three decades and which was once his father's, ran through the sand. He drew a straight line and soon crossed another line through it to make an X. He dove his finger into the center and twisted it so wide the edges sand fell into the newly-created hole. It was one of the few ways Moss cured himself of boredom.

"What's the hold-up?" Moss heard from the distance. He cocked his head to the right and stood up, his boot dipping into the sand. He kicked off whatever sand covered his boot and, as he had done for a long time now, stared out into the desert, where trio of dots were rushing toward him.

"Here they come," he said with a rare smile. Joy filled his heart. After months and months of waiting, the destiny that Moss hoped for was happening. A warming sensation filled his heart and he burst out laughing. He held his chest, covering the torn up white cloth under his cape.

"One wears red. Another wears white. The last wears black."

The wind picked up.

II

When Moss saw the three boys clearly for the first time, he knew that the one in red had The Pen. He was brimming with glee.

THE PEN

A few minutes later, the three boys came within a foot or two of Moss and each of them slowed. Shelton Reclard's eyes did not move.

"Moss?" Jake asked, panting.

Moss nodded, but his eyes had found something else to distract him.

Jake, happy to find rest, laughed. "Do know Kevin? My cousin?" Moss nodded again, but his eyes were locked on something else. "Where is he?" Jake asked, a smiling filling his face.

Moss shook his head, as if he cared about this Kevin when one of the boys standing there was his greatest enemy.

"And you're with this traitor?" Moss spoke, nodding over to Shelton. Now Moss's silence made sense. "This man sold his soul to the Creator himself. And you're with him?"

"Told you he wouldn't trust me," Shelton said, waving his hand. "Moss here is jealous because he couldn't get a seat with The Creator. Eh? Mossy-boy?"

"You were a part of the greatest evil that's ever happened to this planet," Moss reasoned. "Because of you, hundreds of thousands, maybe millions, of people lost their homes and were banished to the South. You destroyed us when you joined him! I should kill you for showing up here."

"Can't do this without my help, though," Shelton said, brimming with confidence. "You need me more than ever."

Moss turned his head toward Jake, ignoring Shelton, and smiled at him. "Truth is, I did meet your cousin Kevin and his friend. But, they, uh, ran from me when they met me."

Jake opened his eyes wide. "We need to find him! We have to find him now!"

Moss gazed back at the desert—just endless miles of sand going on for an eternity, with an occasional bush or two to give wanderers some hope.

"Well, they ran due north, which means that we could catch them," Moss said, moving his finger in the air, as if he were doing a math problem. "Yes, I suppose we can."

"Got any food? Or water?" asked Richard, who was still panting from running.

"Water? No. None at the moment, unless you're fine with some dirty water with some bits of pesana in it," Moss said.

"Pesana?" Richard asked.

"Pepper," Shelton whispered.

"No thanks, I'll die first," Richard said.

"Have it your way," Moss said. "Tonight, we will rest. And in the morning, we'll get on our way to find your cousin."

III

Before they could start their move throughout the desert, they slept.

While Moss was turned over trying to sleep, Shelton and Jake threw sticks into the campfire. Though it was easy for them to make a fire, it was more difficult trying to strike up a conversation. For the most part, they talked about Moss and finding Kevin. That was the only thing Jake wanted at the moment: his cousin.

"Something bothering you, Jake?" asked Moss, who was still rolled over on his side. They had thought he was asleep, but he was clearly awake.

Jake paused at first, but then begrudgingly answered. "Yeah. See Moss, I don't know. It's complicated."

"I've heard a lot in my time Jake, and I've been through even worse. Let me hear it."

"Right. Well, if we find Kevin, will I be able to bring him back to the real world?" Jake asked. Was "real world" the right choice of words? Wasn't this all real? "Because that's all I am here for. After I get Kev back, I'll give you and Shelton The Pen so that you can both figure out what to do with it. I'm only doing this so I can get my cousin back. And, I just don't know if there's going to be an easy way to do that."

Moss leaned over and fixed his eyes on Shelton. "You haven't told him?"

Shelton shook his head. "Waiting for you boss."

Jake leaned forward. "Tell me what?"

After a heavy sigh, Moss sat up, ready to tell Jake something he needed to hear.

"Jake, listen to this story very carefully," Moss said, putting his hands together. He kicked up some dust when he swung around to face him. "My father once told me a night-time story when I was younger. I had to be about seven or eight. And he told me a story about a world, far off in the galaxy, that was having political problems. He described these problems as unsolvable unless someone fixed them. Little did I know that the place he was talking about was actually Discis.

"He told me that someone, a farmer, would one day rise up and help bring peace to the world. He would fight off the two empires that created the problems, and later take it upon himself to care for the planet. All would be well," Moss said.

"The Creator," Jake said, confident. "The one who wants this Pen."

"Correct. Now, after my father told me that, I asked him if that was the end of the tale. And he said that the new leader was not as he seemed. He was evil and would destroy the world if we let him. Those who put him in power, hoping for a better day, had only made things worse. This world would not be peaceful anymore. People would die, others would be exiled and the planet would go from a lush, vibrant world to an empty, dry, makeshift abyss. Thus, someone else would have to rise up and take over, restoring the planet to peace.

"That story stayed in my mind for years, and, like you'd imagine, all of it came true," Moss said, sinking his chin into his palm. "And then, once my family and my loved ones were killed during The Creator's uprising," he paused, shot a glance at Shelton, and then cleared his throat. "There was a war, and I fought to avenge my parents, but nothing worked. I lost friends and loved ones, and everything fell apart. So I went into hiding," Moss said, reflecting on his past.

"It turned out," Moss began again, "that the story my father told me was a piece of a prophecy—The Prophecy of Discis, told by five witches long ago. But he left out important parts, some of which are still unknown today. But as the story goes, or at least the story people talk about, many will try to topple the evil former. Many will fail, one will succeed. It's about one person who will get the 'ultimate power' and will wage a final war. Peace vs. terror. The Prophecy said that the prophet, the true and final Holder of The Pen, would come to Discis, not from this land, and save us all. But he wouldn't be alone. He'd come with a relative, a friend, someone who knows the land, and someone who has forgotten the land."

"You," Shelton chimed in. Jake turned his head to Shelton, who was nodding, his true intentions finally revealed. "Believe it or not, you're the Prophet of Discis. Or, well, the Holder of The Pen, as we say."

In a movie, this would have been a sweeping moment of grandeur, filled with drama, suspense, and thrill. The story they told was of seemingly Biblical proportions, built on a house of fanciful details and whimsical beliefs.

And yet all Jake could do was laugh.

"OK," he said, in a tone that sounded almost like his cousin's voice. "Yeah, OK. Sure. Right."

"Jake, this isn't a joke," Shelton said.

"Why is he laughing?" Moss asked.

"Because the story's ridiculous," Richard said, turning over from his side to face the group. "Feels like I saw that in a video game once before."

"Sure you did, Dick," Shelton replied. "Jake, come on. We're being serious."

Jake grinned, his laughter dying down. "Yeah, sure you are. Funny guys. Look. I'm going to get to bed now. Good story."

As he had promised, Jake turned over and fell asleep.

IV

When the sun came up the following morning, Moss awoke and expected to see Jake still awake, contemplating the conversation they had last night. But that's not at all what he saw.

Instead Moss's eyes only noticed Shelton laid out flat against a rock. His head was resting near a pool of blood. Moss stood up and moved like a whip. He called for Jake, but no one answered. He grabbed Shelton and rested him on his shoulders before he dashed off into the sand, leaving Richard behind. He was running forward into the desert, going the way that would lead to the Creator's Palace, hoping that Jake had gone this way.

The sand flew in the air as Moss, who had Shelton bouncing on his shoulders, dashed faster and faster, throwing his boots down with a push. The smell of the sand brushed up on Moss, yet he was already very familiar with the smell. Moss hoped to get out of the desert and find Jake, the Holder of The Pen and the true Prophet.

Moss ran so fast that within a half hour he reached the edge of the desert. He took one large jump from the sand and landed on hard rock. He tripped and fell, causing Shelton's body to sprawl on the ground.

Dust came up from the rock as Moss got back to his feet. He scanned the area of the new rocks and buttes. It was the Shatnay Lands—a seemingly never-ending spread of rocks, buttes, and cliffs.

And nearby, Moss saw a figure on the top of the closest butte. He wore a red shirt and khaki pants with skateboarder shoes. His hair was brown and covered most of his forehead. Jake.

Jake was on the top of the butte, his arms open, like a bird, ready to jump. So Moss picked up Shelton and ran over to the butte. In one motion, he wrapped his hand on a ledge and pulled himself up. It took considerable strength with Shelton still on his shoulders. He did it again. When he got to the top, he ran to the other side, dropping Shelton down on the rocky surface.

As Jake was about to go flying off, Moss grabbed him by the collar and shoved him down hard on the rock below. Jake's head bounced off the hard rock at the top of the butte.

"Wake up, you fool!" Moss screamed at Jake, who held The Pen in his hand, his eyes blood-red. Something was wrong here. Something was really wrong. "Jake, wake up!"

Jake moaned. He coughed and then spoke, but it wasn't his voice. It was a much darker one.

"Let this be a warning. Bring The Pen to me, or you will all die."

Jake shook and awoke in an instant. He threw The Pen, which rolled to the edge of the butte.

"What the hell was that?" Jake asked, feeling his body all over.

"Not sure," Moss said, searching through his mind. "I haven't seen that kind of red since . . ." Moss' words trailed off when he remembered Shelton was still on the ground nearby. He jogged over and inspected the back of Shelton's head, which had been given a once-over with red paint.

"He'll be fine," Moss said. "Unfortunately."

THE PEN

Jake sighed and turned back to Moss. "Where's Richard?"

Moss looked back towards the desert. He saw the sand that he had once been on for so long, and realized that when he ran for Jake, he didn't stop to think of Richard.

Moss shrugged. "I left Richard behind. It was either bring Richard, or watch you die."

"No. No, Richard was one of my only friends; you can't just let him live here in a world he doesn't know. This is all new to us. There isn't any way he could survive on his own," Jake said in frustration. "We have to go back and save him."

"I'm sorry," Moss said. "We can't. The Creator knows where we are now. If we don't keep moving, he'll send his guards to fetch us and give up our hope. I'm sorry, Jake, but that's the truth."

Jake shook his head. "Sorry isn't good enough. And I don't care about this stupid prophecy. I just want to find my cousin and get home, that's it," Jake looked down at The Pen that was in his hand. "Here's your stupid Pen," he said, tossing The Pen at Moss. It hit Moss' chest and fell to the rocky surface below.

Jake hopped down to the first ledge and then again onto the hard rock surface. Without saying another word to Moss, he walked away.

CHAPTER 8

I

The Creator, who went by the name Kurpo in a former life, came out of a trance. He lifted his hand off the silver goblet at the center of his desk, having just finished talking to his Master. His eyes felt heavy.

Kurpo stood up, his white cloak swaying on the stone floor at the top of his palace. He walked around to the top window and looked out at his land of Discis. He admired the pinkish-gray clouds and the patches of green lightning that struck the mountains far off in the distance. He saw The Walls of the Palace, where his guards stood holding tall black staffs to keep intruders away. They did not twitch, did not move. They stood guard, doing as they were told. But the leader of his guard, the best woman warrior he'd ever seen, Broxxi, was at the ready if he needed her and her army.

Kurpo remembered what his Master had just told him in the trance. He had a new command to follow from his Master. It was time for him to resurrect the New Blood—soldiers who had died during his wars.

He lowered his cloak's hood and ran his hand through his receding hairline.

"Yes," he said, a creepy smile erupting on his face. "The New Bloods will take back the Orb and set everything back on track," Kurpo said to himself, his anger going away into pleasure. He laughed. "For too long I've ruled without an army, and now I shall bring one back. One full of the souls of people I have killed. Perfect. And soon, I will find my Pen again."

The Creator sat down in his chair and moved his fingers like he was pressing buttons. His black glove touched the armrest of his throne. He smiled and stood back up, raising both of his arms.

"New Bloods! Rise from the ground and be mine!" he yelled.

The ground shook.

Kurpo grasped the silver goblet again and stood his ground as the

Palace rattled left and right. He watched as red spirits flowed out of the ground and soared to the top of the Creator's Palace. They swung around the tip. Many more spewed out and glided upward. The ghosts entered through The Creator's window and came to Kurpo, like dogs begging for dinner scraps.

They all stood at attention for The Creator. In an instant, they transformed into solid bodies, their heads covered by black cloaks. Their faces were cut and scarred. They all huddled around Kurpo.

"YOU CALL UPON US?" they asked in chorus. A wave of butterflies floated in his stomach. All the New Bloods fell to one knee and Kurpo stood straight again, confident now. He grabbed his black sword out from his cloak and lifted it up, looking down at his soldiers, who were dead and alive, alive but dead.

"Let it be known that the New Blood is alive!" he yelled, as lightning struck outside the Palace walls.

The New Bloods all had black swords in hand, armed to fulfill Kurpo's request.

He walked over to a door in his room—marble green, with black markings all around it. He grabbed the door handle and shut his eyes before pulling it open and stepping into a blinding white light.

II

A bright green light sprang from the open air and Kurpo stepped out, the bottom of his white cloak dragging on the rock hard surface of his Shatnay Lands. The sun shoved its way into his eyes. He wondered if he had just run a fool's errand. But then he saw what he had come for. Jake Serent was dragging his feet through the sand.

"Jake, Jake. How are things going?" asked the Creator, as Jake came closer. His eyes were squinted, his hand shielding them from the sun.

"Who are you?" the boy asked. His white shoe clunked against the rock.

The Creator smiled. He chuckled after he realized that this thin, young, and unconvincing boy was the latest Holder. He'd have his Pen back in no time.

"Remember that voice you heard awhile back? Well, that was me. Let me introduce myself. I am the Creator, the ruler, of Discis. My name is Kurpo," The Creator offered.

"You. This is all your fault. If you hadn't sent me that text then I would have never found that stupid Pen and wound up here," Jake said, after moving closer to the Creator.

"Well yes, it might be my fault, but really, isn't it Shelton's? He's the reason you're here. Or is it your cousin's fault? If he hadn't stumbled here, then you wouldn't be searching for him, would you?" The Creator reasoned. "Maybe it's your fault."

Jake sighed and ignored the accusations. "Why are you talking to me?"

"I want my Pen, Jake," Kurpo said.

"I don't have it."

"You, what?"

"I don't have your stupid Pen," Jake said.

"Then who does?"

"I'm not telling you that," Jake said.

"Excuse me?"

"Look, I may not be all-in on this prophecy thing, but I've heard enough about you to know that you're not a nice guy. There's no way I'm letting you get that Pen back," Jake replied.

Kurpo smiled. "So, you know about the prophecy. Interesting. Well, if you're not going to give me my Pen back, then there's no use for you anymore."

The Creator stepped back a few paces. He whipped a sword out from his cloak. It was black with red rubies down the middle. He pointed at the ground and another sword appeared, this one white with purple rubies. Jake, fearing his life and seeking protection, bent down and picked it up. But he already knew this sword was about more than protection. It was about battle.

The Creator tiptoed to the left and Jake moved to the right. Jake grasped the handle with two hands and swung at the Creator, who blocked the swing with one hand on his sword. Jake twirled around and tried going to the bottom of the cloak. The Creator lowered his sword to block the shot at a sloth's speed.

Jake screamed and ran toward the Creator, his sword pointed straight at his foe. The Creator's sword clanged against Jake's, and the force of Jake's run made him fly through the air, landing back first on the rock. He squirmed to his feet and held his sword with two hands.

"Last chance. Tell me. Who has my Pen?"

Jake smiled, blood dripping down his back. "It's not your Pen," he said.

Jake dropped his sword. Pieces chipped off the tip of the sword and it rattled like a snake. The Creator put his sword back under his cloak and walked over to Jake.

"Glad you see it my way," he said.

Jake didn't. He snatched his sword up and shoved it at the Creator's cloak, stabbing him.

But instead of ripping cloth, the sword went straight through. The Creator wasn't really there.

The Creator whipped out his own sword and thrust it into Jake's gut, right through to the other side. Blood poured out as Jake gasped. He put his hands on his stomach and felt the deep hole that the Creator's sword had made. Jake collapsed to his knees, and then fell face-first against the rock.

The Creator laughed in pleasure. He recreated the door, stepped through, and was gone.

CHAPTER 9

I

The sun was completely down and the black night sky emerged. The moon was blood-red. Geoff Moss stood still, his cape waving in the wind. Shelton was lying on his shoulders.

Step by step, he inched through the rocky Shatnay Lands, wondering where Jake had gone. It must have been a half hour before Moss started his journey again. Shelton was still limp as cream. Blood dripped down Shelton's face onto Moss's shoulders. He was alive, but barely.

The Pen was now floating in the water in the knapsack. He carried not one, but make that two of the most powerful weapons in the universe.

That night, Moss decided not to set up camp. He wanted to walk through the darkness of the world of Discis.

The sky was a dark gray the following morning as the sun hid beneath the clouds. Some clouds were violet until lightning struck and they were temporarily painted yellow. Water spat from the sky. Moss stopped once in a while to fill his knapsack with water. Each time he opened up his sack, he took out his map so that it wouldn't get wet. But otherwise, he let it rest.

When Moss stopped to drink and eat midway through the day, Shelton finally stirred. He woke up and Moss wondered if the two would get along now that they were alone. When Shelton stood up, he said nothing, but only sat next to a rock. He rested his head and realized that there was blood pouring out of his skull.

"What happened?" he asked.

"I don't know. I woke up a few nights ago and saw you laid out cold. I then ran to a butte to save Jake. Unfortunately, I left Richard in the desert. Jake walked away, and I haven't seen him since. It was stupid for him to leave."

"You know, Moss, if I agree with you only once, this is the time,"

Shelton said, taking a sip of water from Moss's pack. "I agree that Jake was stupid enough to walk off into this world he knows nothing of. If I read your mind right, he left because Richard was all alone now? What does it prove if he walks off?" Shelton asked.

"Jake is in trouble. With him alone, he has no power to fulfill the prophecy," Moss replied, wiping sweat off his head and peering into the distance. "That is why we have to find him." He got up and poured some water into Shelton's hands. The boy sipped it down and nodded in thanks once he had his fill. He then stood up and took a few steps forward, ready to move again. Moss grabbed his knapsack and joined Shelton.

The rock surface wore on Shelton's feet. He wasn't used to this type of environment. He was used to concrete and grass. Not rock-hard desert. His trashed skateboard shoes from the local discount store offered no help for his feet. Sweat poured from the top of his head.

While Shelton melted away, Moss locked eyes with the ground, touching it every few paces. He noticed the tracks that Jake must have made. They were foot stamps with shoes. Moss walked in the direction that the marks went so that he could keep track of where Jake went, because he—and for that matter, all of Discis—needed this boy back. Jake was the Prophet, the Holder of The Pen.

"Here," Moss said. "Jake stopped here. Then, he moved this way," Moss motioned and moved to the right. "He then moved over here and ..." Moss stopped when he saw a body laying motionless. The body's back was facing them, and there was a deep hole going through it. Moss bent down.

"Is that . . . ?" Shelton asked, as he came closer to the body. Moss nodded, picking up the body and laying it over his shoulders.

"The Prophet? Dead?" asked Shelton.

"This can't be," said Moss.

"There must be a reason. The Council of Julk should know."

"The Council of Julk?" Shelton asked. "How would they even know how to fix him?"

Moss glared to Shelton. "They're the ones who told me where you three would be in the desert. I think they know a thing or two."

"So pompous, the Council of Julk. Ugh. And I'm probably not their best friend either."

"Forget about yourself," Moss said. "They can help Jake."

Shelton scratched the back of his head. "So where are they?"

"Over the Sammack Sea. It should take us a while to get to the dock. It is a long distance away. Are you ready to continue on?" asked Moss, still holding Jake on his shoulders. Blood ran from the hole in his body down to Moss's chest. Shelton nodded. The two men moved again, not knowing they were heading into sure trouble.

II

It was night when they came to the end of the Shatnay Lands. The moons were out and were the only light to guide them. They decided not to set up camp, only because Moss was worried that Jake would die if they did not reach the Sammack Sea in time, and then all hope would be lost. There were only red stars in the sky.

"Shelton, what galaxy have you been in these last few years?" asked Moss, looking at the stars.

"It's a weird one. Planets are Earth, Jupiter, Saturn, Venus, Mercury, Mars, Neptune, and Uranus, and only one is habitable. That's where we come from."

"And what's it called?"

"Earth. That's where I was. Waiting for the next Holder. I was supposed to help him get here and meet with Kurpo."

Moss stopped and turned back to Shelton. "So is that your game, here? Get Jake to the Palace for the Creator?"

Shelton's face became blank. "I fell in love with someone on Earth. The Creator didn't like that, so he killed her. The only thing I want to do is kill him. Surely you can relate to that."

Moss definitely could.

"Look, Moss, I'm sorry for what happened all of those years ago. I was a young kid who didn't know what he was doing. I'm sorry I gave you and your family up, OK? I just hope we can move past it."

Moss inspected the rocks below. "We can for the sake of the Holder. For now."

The two journeyed forward through the rocks. After a little more walking, Moss's boot landed in grass. In front of him, he saw tall trees with branches as high as the giants he had read about from the Old Times. The trunks were double that, if not more. These trees went on for a long time. It was a forest.

"The Great Hellryo Forest," Moss said. "All we have to do is get through the forest, and we'll reach the sea. But Shelton, I feel danger, too. We must be careful." Moss stepped on some branches. He walked more, and Shelton followed. They slowly entered the Great Hellryo Forest together. "You know, this used to be have lots of berries and fruits and vegetables," Moss began. "But . . ."

"The Creator took over. Yeah, I know," Shelton said.

Moss said nothing for a while; he only walked forward. There was anger inside him, an evil hatred he had for Shelton—a traitor, a backstabber, a betrayer. Moss still couldn't warm up to him, despite his apology.

Moss felt his bag, making sure that he still had The Pen. He slipped it into Jake's pocket. The Holder should always have his Pen.

Jake lay limp in Moss's arms. Moss, though very intelligent, did not know what was going on with Jake. The Prophet could not be killed nor slain unless the ultimate power was destroyed. Was Jake even dead?

Shelton walked far behind Moss. He did not know much of the land anymore. Only Moss knew the land well enough to travel. It wasn't that Moss had been this way before, but he must have researched maps for so long and found every which way and how he could get to the Creator's Palace.

Moss and Shelton passed a lichen-covered tree. More and more trees appeared. They got bigger and bigger, thicker and thicker. When passing through trees, Moss crouched and twisted ever so delicately to make sure Jake's head wouldn't bang against the trunks or that his wound wouldn't suffer from even more pain.

Moss kept looking at Jake's face. His eyes and lips were closed. He was surely dead now.

III

A bird screeched in the distance.

When the sound reached Moss' ears, he lay Jake on the ground and snapped his head to the left. He ran to a tree and felt its vibrations. He set his head on the tree and listened. Shelton, knowing what the bird was, looked up into the sky. He smiled.

"Well, Moss, haven't you thought of everything. A Naej-Bird, wow! You totally forgot right?" Shelton asked with a grin.

"Shut up, Shelton! Listen to it; it's not a normal Naej-Bird. It's different. Not a regular ominous creature, but one that is being used. An enslaved bird."

Moss followed Shelton's eyes to the sky.

A red blast of dust shot from the air and nearby trees tumbled to the ground. Everything shook. Branches snapped and cracked as each tree toppled to the ground. Within minutes, all that was left was Shelton, Moss, Jake on the ground, a clear land, and hundreds of soldiers covered in black cloaks with black swords in their hands.

"Great," Shelton said. "New Bloods."

CHAPTER 10

I

The New Bloods didn't move. They stood with their swords up right, glaring at Moss and Shelton. They waited. The sun was rising, creating a shadow of purple mist in the sky. That purple mist was met with red clouds, hovering over the New Bloods.

A voice spoke: "Let's see you get out of this one, Moss! New Bloods!" The New Bloods all jerked their heads to the sky, hearing their leader's call. "Attack!" yelled the voice of The Creator.

The New Bloods marched toward Shelton and Moss.

Shelton shot a jagged blue electric blast from his fingertip, zapping one of the New Bloods. The soldier fell to the ground and disappeared into thin air. One down, but plenty more to go.

Shelton readied himself for a huge fight. Moss did the same as Shelton by bending down into a defensive position, and then he yelled out in anger and charged for the New Bloods.

Shelton sped forward with him, making thick electric blue energy balls, smaller than the size of a gumdrop, as he ran, and then throwing them out at the New Bloods. Some of the creatures fell and disappeared, but not enough. Moss and Shelton both ran into the marching men, whose swords were pointed outward, ready to strike.

They were outnumbered. They wouldn't last long.

Suddenly an arrow came from the sky and shot a New Blood to the ground.

More arrows rained from the sky and cut through a patch of New Bloods, one by one.

From the large boulder off to the side came a boy with spiked blonde hair. He shot another arrow before hopping down from the boulder to meet Moss.

One of the New Bloods threw off his cloak and stabbed one of his own. He sliced again and again at two others. The former New Blood ran over to the blonde kid and Moss. The New Bloods still marched on as the two new people reached their instructor.

"Moss," panted the blonde kid. "How was that?"

"Well done, Kevin, Trevor," Moss said, nodding to the boys. "You did as I told you," he answered. "All right, Jake is over there on the ground, we found him stabbed in the middle of the Shatnay Lands. We'll get to him, after we fight. Now fight!" Moss yelled.

Kevin shot a glance back at his cousin. His stomach dropped. But he knew the only way to save him was to win this battle first. So he turned around, touched the shoulder of his friend Trevor, and ran back into battle.

Now in the thick of it all, Moss noticed a spear—his all-time favorite weapon—laying on the ground. He grabbed it, smirked, charged forward, slapped one of the New Bloods with the butt end, and stabbed the next.

Moss battled each approaching New Blood as Shelton followed behind while throwing those haphazard energy balls. The New Bloods kept falling one by one. Shelton punched a New Blood, grabbed its sword, and stabbed it. Moss cut through a New Blood right next to him and did it with anger. Kevin ran with his bow and arrows, shooting every New Blood in sight. His archery gym class had paid off.

Moss sliced another two New Bloods with his spear. Those New Bloods disappeared as Moss sent a few more to their ultimate demise. Moss swerved around and saw two New Bloods standing over at Jake, about to make their move. Moss sped over, but he was too far away. So he threw his spear far up in the air. It pierced the skin of the lead New Blood. Arrows from Kevin followed, sending that New Blood to his death.

Shelton shot another and Trevor stabbed another. When Trevor stabbed one, Shelton shot the next one. Stab, shot. Stab, shot. Again and again, the two teens worked together to take down the New Bloods.

Moss and Kevin worked together, too. When Moss regained his spear, Moss stabbed, and Kevin shot. Stab, shot. Stab, shot.

The New Blood survivors, for there were only nine left, retreated into the land they had cleared. Kevin, though, shooting like he had never done before, shot three of the remaining New Bloods. Trevor threw his sword and it sliced one in half. Shelton tossed the blue energy ball, now big enough to kill four more, at the group of three. And then, the last turned around, after dodging the energy ball, and got stabbed in the gut by Moss. It fell to its knees.

Moss raised his spear in triumph. Kevin raised his arrows, Trevor lifted his sword, and Shelton shot sparks from his hands. The four of them walked over to each other, met, and smiled, now that they had conquered this New Blood attack.

II

Moss looked at Kevin and Trevor and said, "Tell me. How? How did you learn to shoot so well? And how did you disguise yourself?"

"Easy," Kevin started. "I learned how to use a bow and arrow during gym class last year. So when I found a dead warrior on the ground with these weapons, I grabbed one of the New Bloods' swords and gave it to Trevor. Since Trevor is as pale as a New Blood anyway, it was easy for him to blend in."

Moss smiled, and Shelton looked as though he had no idea how they had pulled off such a great victory. "And you were both just OK with killing people?"

Kevin and Trevor exchanged a glance when they saw Shelton.

"Oh, yeah, I'm here now," Shelton said.

"Great. Nerd's with us," Trevor said.

"Did you look for the sea?" asked Moss, interrupting the boys.

"Yes, just as you said. We saw it about a mile away, and the next boat out is in the morning," Trevor answered for Kevin. Kevin nodded in agreement.

"How did we do this?" Shelton asked. "How did we defeat one of the most decorated armies in history? The Creator once told me that no one had ever defeated this army, yet we did? I don't get it."

Kevin and Trevor exchanged a shrug, choosing not to speak with the weird boy they knew from back home. Moss remembered Jake and walked over to the boy. The rest of the group gathered by him too. Kevin dropped to his knees and inspected his cousin. He was on the verge of tears, but he looked at Trevor and held back.

Moss knelt down next to Jake. He held his hand and jerked his head to Kevin. "Can we make it to the sea by morning?" he asked. Kevin nodded. Moss then lifted Jake onto his shoulders and pointed his spear in the direction of the sea.

"TO THE SEA!"

Moss ran.

Shelton and Trevor ran together and Kevin followed close behind. Moss sped ahead with uncatchable speed. He was older than the teenagers, yet incredibly fast. When Trevor ran, his cloak waved at every turn there was, so he tossed it away. Shelton, meanwhile, hovered above the ground, flying toward Moss.

The Great Hellryo Forest, which was now just broken down trees, was coming to an end. The grass returned. Moss was the first to hit the grass, followed by Shelton, and then Trevor and Kevin. They all stopped, all four of them—five, if counting Jake—and looked out straight ahead, where the sea waited for them. After a small rest, they sped off again with Moss in the lead.

As they ran, the fewest bits of white snowflakes came down from the sky. Shelton lifted his arms and drew the snowflakes to him. He examined the flakes and realized what they were. "Moss! Stop! I have to tell you something!" he yelled. Moss did not hear and kept on running. Shelton was angry. Moss wasn't listening to anything that anyone was saying. It was all about him and no one else.

Kevin tripped over a clump of grass. Trevor pulled him up so he wouldn't fall behind. They sliced through the grass. Kevin saw Moss up ahead, carrying Jake and leading the group forward. He wouldn't even stop for a rest. Now, Kevin was angry like Shelton. It was all about Moss and what he wanted.

The flurry of snow picked up at a more rapid pace. Soon enough, it was nearly impossible to see through the snow. Neither Trevor nor Shelton or Kevin could find the green outfit Moss was wearing. Moss must be so far ahead that even the color of his clothes couldn't be seen for miles. Kevin tripped again and landed smack in water.

"Hurry" Moss yelled, appearing suddenly and hopping into a rickety old boat.

Shelton used his incredible jumping power and landed on the boat, now holding Trevor. Kevin had a harder jump. He grabbed a piece of broken wood that rested just beside the water and hopped on it. He rode it on the snow.

There was a boat turned upside down against a gate. It was covered in snow and blended right in. Kevin took this to his advantage and sailed straight for it. The cool wind cut at his face as he neared the boat. He felt his stomach disappear when he sailed up the boat and flew into the air.

When Kevin saw he wouldn't get to the boat with his friends on it, he jumped off his makeshift snowboard and sailed into the sky. He landed smack on the water, belly first, his fingers gripping on the ends of the boat. He had made it, but with a cost.

Trevor helped Kevin up onto the worn-down boat. Kevin was mad at Moss again as it was evident Moss wasn't even thinking of helping. But Kevin didn't have time to feel concern about Moss. He hurried along the boat's side and found Jake.

Kevin ran his hands through his cousin's hair and, finally, wept. Tears rolled down his cheeks. Kevin was sorry for all he did—smoking, beating up Jake, using Jake to skateboard on the highway. And more than anything, he didn't want his cousin to die, not one bit. Kevin wanted Jake to live, and hopefully one day they could go back to Earth, live their lives again, and forget about this whole mess.

Kevin's tears dripped down to Jake's shirt, making a wet stain. "I'm sorry, Jake," Kevin whispered. He hugged him and kept letting the tears fall.

The look on Jake's face never changed. He just kept looking up into the sky, his eyes open. Kevin knew that things would not change unless something extraordinary happened. He reached into his own pocket and pulled out his rolling papers. With rage, and tears still falling down his face, Kevin took the lighter he had and burned the package.

Kevin cried more before he tossed the package of papers out into the Sammack Sea, leaving his demons behind him.

CHAPTER II

I

    The group's boat slid up on the sand, water pushing against its back. Moss stepped down from the boat onto a paper-thin ladder and climbed down onto the sand. Trevor and Shelton followed, as well as Kevin, who was carrying his cousin. They walked together up the beach, the bottom of their pants getting frosted by the sand.
    Their eyes fell upon a tall yellow tower with an orange light sparkling with the new rising sun. One might mistake it for a lighthouse. The tip of the tower—a bulb of yellow—kissed the skies above.
    Everyone still carried their weapons—Moss had his spear, Trevor had his sword, Shelton had his hands, and Kevin had his bow and arrows on his back. Moss waved them all forward.
    "What is this place?" Kevin asked.
    "Council of Julk," Moss explained. "They represent all the people in the South who were banished from this land once Kurpo took over. They're the wisest of the wise, smartest of the smart. Kurpo meets with them every so often to make sure the southerners get the supplies they need."
    "Well that's nice of him," Trevor said.
    Moss shook his head. "They haven't met in a very long time."
    The group soon reached the front of the tower, the yellow brick's glare stinging their eyes. It was made of the purest marble, smooth and elegant. They saw two guards at the front, dressed in yellow cloaks with a pair of staffs, holding off any intruders who might dare to try entering without approval.
    "I am Geoff Moss. I'd like to speak with the Council."
    "For what reason?" asked one of the guards, whose rusted beard was twice the length of Moss's.

"The Holder," Moss said, pointing his hand toward Jake's limp body. The guard noticed he was dead.

"The Holder? That's not possible," one of the guards said. "The Holder cannot die."

"Which is why we need you to let us in so we may talk with the Council about it," Moss said, pulling out The Pen and holding it up to bolster his case. "If this is the Holder, then he may not really be dead. We need to wake him."

The guard glanced at Moss. "Fine, you are allowed to go to the Council. Only one of you and the boy. Choose now."

Moss walked back over to his group. They all looked at each other. Moss stepped up, slid The Pen back in Jake's pocket, and looked at the group. He turned back to the guard.

"Let us all go in. If this is the Holder, then you're making a mistake," Moss negotiated.

"Fine, all of you enter."

II

The group entered through the tower's golden yellow door. When inside, they noticed the yellow marble walls and a similarly colored glass floor. There were tall planks of wood set off toward the right, clearly a construction site of some kind. Moss guided the group down the end of the tower's lobby, where a group of chairs, nine to be exact, were fixed in a circle. Those sitting in the seats were dressed in yellow cloaks.

"Are we ever going to a see woman around here?" Trevor asked, noticing the group was all men.

"Let's hope," Kevin said.

Moss knelt to the ground and motioned for his group to do the same.

"Geoff Moss. Welcome back. How's your father?" asked one of the chairmen.

"Still in the Unknown Islands for all I know, Tyrese. You should know that." Moss answered, standing up. The group behind him followed.

"Why do you come to us?" the man named Tyrese asked. "Last time you were here, you asked for directions to the Krowian Desert. And that wasn't too long ago, as it were."

"The Prophecy, Tyrese. It's about the Prophecy."

"The Prophecy?" Tyrese asked.

"This is the Holder, I know it," said Moss, pointing over toward Jake's flimsy body.

"Bring him," said another. Shelton came forward and lay Jake before the Council. One of the Council members, whom Moss knew as Myke, knelt down beside Jake and held his wound.

"This is a hole made by no ordinary sword. Ancient steel. From the time long ago. The last known person to have a sword like this was The Creator," Myke replied.

"Obviously Kurpo attacked Jake. He didn't have The Pen, so he just tried to kill him," Shelton said. Moss looked at Shelton, nodded, and turned back to Myke.

"It's not a death wound. It's a spell, made to make you think he died. It wasn't meant to kill. Curious that he would use such a spell. Give it time and it should lift."

"We don't have time," Kevin said. He needed his cousin back. Myke eyed Kevin with a questioning look. "Please. He's my cousin and I need him back. Please."

"A relative, you say?" Myke asked. "Intriguing. Do you have his Pen?"

Kevin grabbed The Pen from Jake's pocket and handed it to Myke, who closed his eyes and looked up toward the tower's ceiling. He smiled, and then stabbed Jake in the cut that was made. Purple light flashed around and sealed up the wound.

Nothing happened at first. The world remained still and everyone was quiet. But then the world awoke. Sounds came back, light filled the darkness. And Jake's eyes, which had been locked shut since Moss found him in the rocks, lifted.

"Jake!" yelled Kevin, as he hugged his cousin. Jake laughed when his cousin embraced him. "I'm sorry, Jake. I'm sorry for what I did. So sorry!" Kevin said. Jake accepted the apology with a hug. He could barely breath though, so he slowly took some deep breaths as he found his footing.

Trevor came over.

"And I am sorry for hitting you with a bat," he said. "You're pretty cool, dude." Trevor gave Jake a high five.

Shelton walked over to Jake. "We made it here together, and we'll leave here together," said Shelton. Jake nodded and laughed.

Moss came over to Jake, using his spear as a walking stick. "Welcome back," Moss said. Jake laughed. He was glad just to be alive. "Tell us what happened."

III

The group of five was escorted to their own staying room for the night. Like the rest of the tower, it had yellow walls; yellow everything. There were five short-backed chairs, and each of the group sat in their own. The Council of Julk offered to let the group stay the night if they wished to. The group needed the rest, so they agreed.

Jake put his hands together and told his tale. "Well, as most of you know, I left Moss. I was angry with him for leaving Richard out to die. So I left The Pen and walked away.

"I ended up meeting the Creator," Jake went on. "He told me that I should be mad at Shelton and Moss. He created a sword for me and then we dueled, like, with swords. I had him beat. I know I did! Almost had him! But instead, he stabbed me right in the gut. And that's everything you know," Jake paused.

"And what was it like after you got stabbed?" Kevin asked.

"I don't remember," Jake said. "It's all pretty much a blur. It was so hot in the sun and I was frustrated. Hungry, tired, and all of that. I just don't even know. But what's been going on with you guys?"

"Well," started Shelton. "Me and Moss settled our differences. We defeated the New Bloods in a battle along with Kevin and Trevor, who came to us. And we ran all the way here to get you back to life."

Jake raised an eyebrow. "A New Blood?"

Shelton waved it off. "Long story."

"Yeah. Now the only hard part is getting back," Kevin said, switching the conversation. "How do we get home, Moss?"

Jake sat up, listening.

"Unfortunately, the only way home is to move forward," Moss explained. "The Creator's Palace is believed to have a pathway to anywhere in the galaxy. It seems that's where we have to go."

Moss looked over at Jake, who was figuring things out. "If we move north from here, then we'll reach a path that should lead us closer to the Palace. It shouldn't take us more than a month of walking to get there. Once we're there, we can figure out a way to get you home. It seems that's your only way back. I know you don't have any interest in the prophecy, and I get that. But we have to travel in that direction if you want to get home."

Jake looked around at his fellow friends. He smiled. "Let's do it."

And for the first time in a long time, they all fell soundly asleep.

IV

The group said their goodbyes to the Council the next morning in the tower's lobby. Jake stood at the front of his group, a new bag slung over his shoulder and his Pen dangling around his neck on a hemp necklace the Council had given him.

"The Council would like to make an exchange for letting you stay here for the night," Myke began. He didn't wait for anyone to answer him. "We know you plan on heading to the Creator's Palace to find your way back home, and we'd like to ask a favor of you."

Jake raised an eyebrow. He shook his head. "I'm no Holder or Prophet, or whatever."

THE PEN

Myke sighed. "You say that now, but your tune may change. But please, listen. We're unsure of what goes on at the top of the Creator's Palace, but we've heard the stories for generations now. And if you really are the Prophet, if you are the real and true Holder of The Pen, then you can help us."

Jake shrugged. "How?"

"When you get to the top of the tower, rumor has it that your Pen should morph into a sword, or at least it will if you ask it to," Myke explained. "If and when it does, you must return it to the stone, which lays in the center of the tower, as the story goes. Do that and the drought will end. Do that, and the Creator will be no more. Do that, and Discis will be saved."

Jake thought about the story. "I'll see what I can do," he replied.

After formal goodbyes, the group began their walk again. They exited the tower from the back, out into a dark, lush growth of vegetation. They found a path that led into darkness, away from the golden shine of the Council's tower. They stopped before it. There was no one in the lead, only Jake in the middle. Shelton and Moss were on Jake's left, with Kevin and Trevor on his right. They all looked up at the road that led up a mountain and over.

No one moved. They just stared up at the long road ahead of them. It was something they'd remember forever. Something that they would cherish later on in life, for this was the last moment that they stood in a line together, all with hopes of reaching their next destination. Each of them thought over what their plan was. They knew they'd have to walk for miles and miles to the Creator's Palace, and that maybe they'd never reach it. This was the final moment of calm before the storm.

Jake stepped forward. The rest of the group looked at him in surprise. Jake turned around to face them. He saw Moss' weathered and crusty face, Shelton's pale skin, Kevin's spiky hair, and Trevor's light shadow of facial hair. He smiled at the group. This was a group he would grow to love and honor in the coming adventure on the way to the Creator's Palace.

Jake turned around and looked at the paths that led up the mountain. It was then that he realized the importance of what he was about to do. The Pen had saved his life and given him ambition. His life before Discis was slow and normal. He wasn't well-liked, popular, or embraced. He was a young boy who went through the motions. All he had was his family, and though they meant a lot to him and he loved them without question, he knew there was more to life that he wasn't getting back home.

But The Pen, surely, gave him something new to fight for.

"We're going to do it," Jake said to his group. "We're going to fulfill the Prophecy. We're going to head to the Creator's Palace and finish off the Creator. We're going to save Discis. And then we're going to go home."

Jake turned back to his group, who were friends to him now. He smiled.

"This all makes so much sense," he said. "Think about it. Trevor, your bat hitting me would have never motivated me to be there to see Kevin disappear. Kevin, without your smoking and skateboarding, you would never have brought me here. Shelton, without your powers, I would never have gotten here. And Moss, you carried me through all the trouble to get me here. Don't you see, guys? This is what we're meant to do. We're meant to save this world. It all makes sense."

Jake looked back at the mountain ahead. He felt his Pen in his pocket before he turned back to his friends for a final time. Jake wanted to make this planet become peaceful again and save Discis's people. He wanted to do something important for once in his life. He smiled and looked deep into their eyes. He spoke in the softest voice.

"For Discis."

He marched forward onto the grass. Kevin followed close behind, with Trevor, Moss, and Shelton in the back. They all stepped onto the path and traveled up the incline—the first step toward the Creator's Palace.

So the group climbed and walked their way onto the path and up the mountain. Each of them stayed silent. There was a whole new world out there for them, a whole new life to live. A life that meant they could help Discis rid itself of evil.

Even though this new life seemed dangerous, not to mention life-threatening, all the group cared about was getting to the Creator's Palace, no matter how long it took.

"We're coming for you, Kurpo."

Jake did not turn around; all he did was keep on walking.

The group climbed.

V

It was hours later when Jake saw a red line shoot through the sky.

"Huh, wonder what that was," Jake said.

Shelton watched the line. "You don't want to know."

Jake nodded and walked on. The group did as well. They expected something like this to happen.

When the group reached the first ledge of the mountain, The Pen vibrated again in Jake's pocket. He stabbed his hand into his pocket and pulled The Pen out. He fumbled it like a hot potato, dancing around to avoid the heat. He fell to the ground and dropped The Pen. He saw that the first block was spinning with a golden light pulsing around it. The heat settled, and the block stopped moving completely as it turned a thick black.

Jake picked himself up and told his group that he was OK. He soldiered on with his strength of a thousand men. Jake walked forward with the group behind him, and knew that this was only the first step—the first chapter in a long story, but he smiled at it.

"Kevin," Jake said to his cousin, calling back.

"Yeah?"

"This is a lot better than a fantasy football draft," he laughed. Kevin laughed as well, and met Jake at the front of the group. They walked shoulder to shoulder, marching two-by-two into battle.

The first stage was finished, but there was much more to come.

VI

Kurpo heard Jake. He ran his fingers on his desk and wondered what he could do to stop Jake and his crew, who were now set on meeting him at his Palace and fulfilling the prophecy. That would mean war, which would be a waste of time. But what could be good enough to end Jake and his crew? Kurpo lifted his arms and put himself in a trance, asking his Master what to do.

Tell me Master, what should I do to end Jake and his group? Kurpo asked.

The Master remained silent. Kurpo was on his own.

PART II: THE BLIZZARD OF LEXINGTON

CHAPTER 12

I

The sun had risen quicker than any of them could have imagined. Grant, Thomas, Jupiter, Brent, April, and Chris all sat at the campfire, trying to relive the crash. It had been so sudden. One moment, they were cruising down the interstate and then bam—they hit a pocket of trees. The bus had exploded.

"It seems impossible," said Chris. Chris and Grant were both smoking the last two Pall Mall cigarettes they had left. Chris took a drag and blew out his smoke.

"What seems impossible?" Grant asked.

"Two moons. There are two moons," Chris said, pointing his hands as he was explaining.

"Well, today we're gonna go exploring the area. There's seven of us, so we're splitting up into groups of two, with one group of three. We might as well find out a little bit more about where we are," Grant said.

"Grant!" yelled Richelle. Grant turned around and saw Richelle running toward him.

"Yeah?" he called back.

"It's Jordan," she said, referring to the bus driver, who had gotten a flaming shard of metal in his gut during the crash. When she reached Grant, she was hunched over, panting from the run.

"Yeah?"

"He stopped crying in pain. He seems fine," Richelle said with a raised eyebrow. Grant took another drag of his cigarette. "What did you do?"

"Don't you love this place. We're not even here a week, and we're already getting miracles," he said. Richelle and Chris both raised their eyebrows. "Not only are there two moons, but Jordan's fine," Grant said. He took another drag, blew out the smoke, and threw his cigarette down to the ground. He stepped on it, putting it out completely.

"What do you mean?" asked Richelle.

"It's sarcasm, Richelle," Grant said, beginning to walk to where he had stationed Jordan at the remains of the bus. "For one thing, two moons isn't a good thing. It means we're probably not on Earth. And secondly, Jordan isn't fine," he said.

"Yes he is, Grant! Jordan wasn't in any pain at all," she said.

"Of course he isn't in any pain," Grant said, stopping and turning to Richelle. "He's paralyzed."

II

"So what do we do?" asked Richelle, following Grant as he walked closer to Jordan.

"What do you mean?" asked Grant.

"Should we stay by and help him?" she asked.

"Well, we can either leave and let him die, or we can stay and keep him alive," Grant reacted.

"Oh my God! Why are you so sarcastic!" she exclaimed.

"Who said I was being sarcastic?" he asked back in a stubborn tone. They walked through a set of trees and arrived at the clearing where the bus's remains were, as well as Jordan's paralyzed body.

"Well, what are we gonna do?" she asked.

"Give me time to think, will ya? Truth is, I noticed this whole thing yesterday. But because we were all going through something pretty dramatic—hell, traumatic—I decided not to tell anyone," Grant said.

When Grant reached Jordan, he noticed that Thomas, April, and Jupiter were all hovering around him and Richelle.

"You knew about this?" April asked.

"Yes, hunny, I did."

"How did it happen?" Jupiter asked.

"Remember how he fell out of the bus and got a concussion?" Everyone nodded. "Well, he hit his head so hard that a part of his brain or his back probably were impacted, which led to paralysis in his whole body."

"What?" Thomas said, his eyes larger than the two moons they had seen last night.

"You heard me," Grant returned.

Grant arrived at Jordan and bent down to confirm he was paralyzed. Thomas, April, Jupiter, and Richelle still hovered around Grant, who, luckily for him, was used to other doctors and concerned family members hovering around him and his patient. After Grant conducted some tests, he concluded that his assumption was correct—Jordan was paralyzed.

"No change since yesterday," Grant said, getting up.

Richelle sighed and brushed her hand across her forehead.

Later on that day, the group lounged around the logs that they planned

THE PEN

to burn later that night. They all glanced around at each other, each one trying to think of something to say. Today was the day that they were going to explore the land, but because of Jordan's sudden turn for the worse—or better yet, their own surprise at the worse—the trip had been postponed. Grant and Richelle had both come to the conclusion that today wasn't the day to go exploring anything unknown. Grant's reasoning was simple: someone who was paralyzed would suffer from delirium and he didn't want Jordan to go through that alone. Richelle's reason, on the other hand, was that she wanted to stay and just make sure that Jordan didn't suffer alone.

There was nothing to do. The group barely had any supplies to take inventory of, everyone knew each other's name so there was no need for a census, and they already knew something bad had happened. But they all wondered—how had that bus crashed? The only way to figure out the answer was for Jordan to tell them what he saw, but this was not going to happen anytime soon.

"Well, the weather's nice at least," Brent said. He was the considerably young one next to the others, which showed when everyone else ignored his statement.

"What're we gonna do?" asked Thomas, standing up and pacing around, while everyone else sat and watched. "I mean, we can't just wait for this guy to get out of his delirium."

"We're not going into an unknown land without any idea of how we got here, or even where the hell we are," Grant retaliated.

"Who put you in charge?" asked Thomas.

"No one did," said Richelle, butting in as usual, "but he's the doctor here and—"

"—not a doctor yet," Grant interrupted.

"All right, fine, whatever."

"Just 'cause this guy has his M.D., we're supposed to listen to him? Please! Just because he went to a few more years of college than me doesn't mean he gets to call the shots," Thomas argued.

Jealously loomed large.

III

Grant and Thomas were in a stare-down still, their eyes meeting with fire that was made with half anger and half jealousy. Thomas's jealousy was about how everyone thought Grant should lead this group. It seemed to Thomas that everyone thought that whoever was in control of the medicine had the power. But Thomas didn't follow that trend. Rather, he felt that the leader should be the person who gave them the best chance at survival. The instincts he had learned on his farm growing crops and during hunting trips as a child made him the ideal candidate in his eyes.

And the more Thomas came to think during this stare-down between him and Grant, the more he realized that there should be an election to prove who really should be in charge. He thought about how he would have the advantage of Grant. Sure, everyone at this point felt Grant should be the leader, but Thomas knew that the more the group got to know Grant, the more he could win back some votes. Hell, Richelle seemed to like Thomas more than Grant, and she was the most well-liked person of the group. Easy vote for him.

"What're we gonna do? Just stare at each other all day?" Grant asked. Thomas smirked. He knew exactly where he wanted to go with that comment.

"Grant, how about we have an election?" Thomas insisted. The rest of the group all exchanged glances.

"An election? What is this, *Lord of the Flies*? Does leadership mean that much to you?" asked Grant.

"I think everyone should decide who should lead us all," Thomas replied. Grant smiled.

"Well, good, now I can beat you at your own game," Grant said.

"We'll see about that." There was a brief relapse of the stare-down.

"Everyone!" Grant yelled. "We're havin' an election for this 'leadership.' So, how does this sound . . ."

Grant walked over to the campfire, where he saw a thick piece of wood that was light enough write on. He picked it up and walked over to Jordan, where Grant spotted his shirt from yesterday. He felt the dampness that the blood had made on the shirt. Grant walked to the cooler and nearly ripped the door handle off. He looked through the cans of beer, searching for a cup. He found an empty red cup at the bottom.

"Perfect," he said.

Grant knelt on the ground and held the damp shirt over the cup. He took a breath and squeezed, twisting it and letting the blood soak out of the shirt and into the cup. Red blood dripped down into the cup. When Grant realized he had enough blood for what he planned to, he rose from his knees and walked back over to the group. With the cup and wood in hand, Grant knelt again, this time in front of the group. He reached into his jeans, where he found the broken blue pen he had been carrying on the bus. He dipped it into the blood.

With a little bit of red on the tip of the pen, Grant wrote a single line on the block of wood.

Grant gave a sigh of relief, then turned toward the group. "Done."

Everyone's faces were still. Grant panicked, knowing that no one had figured out what he had written.

"This, you idiots, is a dash representing the number one. We've already finished day one, so I made a dash to keep track of how long we're here.

Now, on each morning, we put a dash, representing what day we're on. So," Grant said, as he dipped the pen again into the cup. "Since we were a little busy yesterday," Grant moved the pen to the wood. "I marked yesterday's, and now today's."

Grant brushed the blood on the wood. "And when we have five dashes, we'll have the voting for this 'leadership,'" Grant said, directed at Thomas, who smiled, but it wasn't any smile—it told Grant that Thomas knew he was going to do everything he could to win this, which made Grant feel a pinch of nerves.

"Be warned," muttered a voice.

Everyone directed their heads to the sound. And when they recognized where the sound came from, they only saw Jordan, lying in his nearly dead state. "B-b-bad th-th-th-th-things are going to h-h-happ-ppp-pen," he said.

Everyone cocked an eyebrow.

He spoke once more:

"The hut. We must avoid the hut."

CHAPTER 13

I

Explosions erupted up from the ground below, the orange and hot magma screaming at the skies. The fiery river spat up, spraying on a long black platform made of pure marble. On the platform sat a black throne with three legs supporting a round seat. And on the chair sat Igor, leader of the planet Ution. His hair was shaggy brown and padded down by a gold shield that hung around his chest. His right eye was covered by a green glass device that fed him constant information of his planet. And before him was a man dressed in a white cloak.

The steam that came from the magma swirled around the enclosed platform. This place, the Ution Headquarters, rested on lava. Igor's strategy was to place his headquarters in the most dangerous place he could think of, to ward off enemies. No one dares follow you into your personal hell.

The man in the white robe let his hood down, and his face looked into the leader's eyes.

"Why do you come to us, Kurpo?" Igor asked. His voice was raspy, as though his words were his last. Igor licked his razor-sharp teeth and waved his ragged nails. He wasn't afraid to use either of them.

"I come to you, Lord Igor, Lord of the Greybills, for some much needed aid. Now I know we've had our differences in the past—"

"Differences! What do you call attacking my home on your planet and forcing us out to find our own world?"

"Well, you were in my way," Kurpo reasoned. "You could have joined the rest of the survivors in the South. But I gave you your own planet. Plus, you did the same thing that I did to you when you arrived here. You flushed out all the humans and took over."

Igor ignored Kurpo's reasons. "Well, Kurpo, what's the problem you have? Why do you call for aid?" Igor stood up from his thrown and walked across the black platform. He waved Kurpo along, and the two strode across to the other side.

"There is a threat to my planet—a man who threatens to take my throne and ruin everything we have worked for. He and his group, he and his friends. I've come to ask you to help me keep them at bay and make sure they don't come to overtake me," The Creator said. He stopped and faced Igor, who wore an evil grin.

For a few moments, neither of the two spoke. They walked to the end of the platform and went through a door at the other end. The two found themselves before vast plains of black grass on the other side of the door. Red sparks shot up from the grass. Igor grabbed some, and handed it to Kurpo.

"You see, Kurpo, I made this planet into what it is. I used nothing but hard work, determination, and sure will, and now I have an entire army that can destroy anyone, anything, anywhere, at any place. I didn't need a Pen to help. I can take out anything that gets in my way, and at the moment, I don't feel any need to help you and your pathetic planet. I'm at peace," Igor explained. He let the grass blow away with the wind. "But I will help you because I want you to see that there's more to life than what's just handed to you. After all, we may need your help in the future. But I will not send my army, nor send anyone to your planet. But, I will send this."

Igor produced a metallic sphere in his hand. It glowed with a blue light in the center. The ball floated in thin air, right above Igor's palm. He moved it over to Kurpo's hand, where it stayed, floating and bobbing up and down. The light went out. The Creator, with wonder and unexplainable helplessness, turned the ball over with his own magic and looked into it. His eyes gleamed and sparkled to the ball. It was lovely, but a weird kind of lovely.

"What is this?" Kurpo asked.

"We call it a Time-X-Ball. Once someone gets hit with it, they remember their worst memory. All you have to do, Kurpo, is send it out to this group you speak of. When they find it, they will relive their pasts and rip each other apart. Their strength will dwindle and they will have nothing left."

The Creator slipped the ball into his pocket. He grinned and looked out into the sky of the planet of Ution, where the Greybills lived and ruled.

"It's a nice planet you have here."

||

When The Creator arrived back in his palace, he wondered if what had just happened was a dream.

He looked out his window and realized that his land was different than how he had left it. The green mountains, the ones that were so beautiful and gracious, were now purple with cream-colored snow on top.

The Blizzard of Lexington had come.

Kurpo looked out from his window and saw his guards watching over the now white land of Discis. He peered into the distance, where he saw The Walls locking everyone and anyone out of his Palace. He was well-protected. Jake and his group didn't stand a chance.

Kurpo journeyed back over to his throne, which now was rusting on the sides. No one had been looking after his Palace during his trip away. He grabbed the silver goblet, held it, and went into a trance to talk to his Master.

Master.

Master, answer me, for I have returned.

Yes, Kurpo. What do you need? asked the Master.

I need you Master, I need you to fill me in on things around my land, said Kurpo. *Has the Blizzard of Lexington arrived?*

Moss and the others will be walking into it, said the Master.

The Time-X-Ball bounced on the floor.

Kurpo was thrown out of the trance as the ball rolled around. A thin red hand came from the air. It grabbed the ball and lifted it out of Kurpo's view. Kurpo shot his eyes to the sky, wondering where his new weapon had gone. He was thrown back into the trance.

Tell me! What is this? yelled the Master.

The Greybills gave it to me as an aid for destroying Moss and his crew, Kurpo explained.

Don't you know what this ball does? When it loses all of its powers, it will explode. The explosion will be big enough to destroy an entire planet! said the Master.

I did not know this Master, I am sorry. What shall we do?

There was silence for a moment. But then, the Master spoke again: *Use it, but before it runs out of power, get it back.*

A red watch fell from the sky, made of a crimson string and connected to a sphere that clicked away with each second. It fell into Kurpo's palm. He turned it over and looked at it was wonder and discovery. This was new to him. He fell out of his trance but grasped the goblet to go back.

This will keep track of the time left. Once this watch becomes blue, the time will be gone, and the ball will explode. Make sure you get it back once it looks green. I want you to keep a close eye on this one, the Master said.

Yes Master! said Kurpo.

Kurpo left the trance. He stormed over to his big window and whispered for the ball to fly many mountains away to Moss and his crew. The Creator took the ball and, like a bird leaving the nest, let it fly out of his window. It went sailing out into the horizon. It flew far away and did not stop. It kept going. Kurpo watched until he lost sight of it.

The Creator found his throne again and laughed.

CHAPTER 14

I

"This is taking forever," moaned Trevor, who was now carrying the load of weapons and food. He had taken on this task back at the start of the mountains, and now was paying the price for it. Moss, being the most noble and sensible of the group, turned to look at Trevor and spoke with venom.

"You do not know what forever is until you experience it," Moss said, his voice echoing throughout the surrounding mountains. "Besides, Kevin and Jake should be back with tonight's food soon enough." Moss sat down on a rock.

Trevor had been complaining about Jake and Kevin and how long it had been since they set out to find dinner, even though it was only a half-day or two. In mountains with barely any sign of life, dinner was hard to come by.

Over the past few days, the group had only eaten deer and other small animals that they could find in the woods. They also ate such things as Stac, which looked like a cat but tasted a lot like chicken. The Earth-birthed boys all felt awkward about eating it. And they ate a lot of leaves, as many as they could find. Leaves here tasted different than Earth vegetation. These were like candy—sugar inside and out. Some tasted like strawberries, raspberries, or even blueberry ice cream.

The group's physical appearance changed, too. These boys barely bathed, and when they did, it was only a dip into water, which was dangerous at best due to the dropping temperatures. Without a tool to shave, Trevor's facial hair had gone way past a five o'clock expiration date. Moss' sand-colored beard went past his neck now, a giant bush that ate away his face.

From one side of the mountains, the Discis South Pass, came Jake and Kevin, holding some furry animal by the ears. They laughed along, like two brothers would. Jake was recalling memories.

The Pen danced with each step Jake took, since it was now attached to a coffee-colored hemp necklace hung around Jake's neck. The Pen swayed back and forth. The first block on The Pen turned to black not too long ago, but the others were still the same colors and shape. They had not passed the second stage yet.

"Kevin, Jake, what'd you find?" asked Moss, crossing over to them.

"We found something that looks like a rabbit, with a twist of shrimp," Kevin said with a chuckle. Trevor came over and exchanged a high five with Kevin and Jake, thanking them that they returned because the sun was beating hard on them.

"Where is Shelton?" asked Jake, who scanned the area around them.

"He went on and started looking at the road ahead. I think we'll probably get a mile or two before resting tonight. These mountains are mighty tough," Moss explained.

Jake scanned the mountains around him. He could not see over them, and they were blocking the sight of anything else. Though they kept the ground locked away from the outside world, the mountains were beautiful during the sunset. When that orange sun sailed down, it created such a picturesque portrait that only God—or some Creator—could have made it.

"Waahooo!"

Everyone turned toward the sky. Shelton soared, his arms spread like an eagle. He sped down, turning right and left with grace. He swept by the group and then flew back up. It was amazing for Jake to see someone flying through the sky, but Shelton was doing just that. His arms were his wings and the air was his fuel, pushing around and letting him flow in the air.

After doing three spins, he soared back to the ground and paused right in front of Moss, still in air.

"Seems like you're in a good mood," said Moss. "Wish I had your druid powers."

"I sure am. Only three miles away is a hill and it's just flat land from there. Once we get there, we'll have to make our way down and cross through hills, not mountains, and then it's plains from there on!" Shelton yelled in excitement.

Trevor wiped his forehead in relief. Jake found a spot on a boulder next to Trevor.

"How is it?" asked Moss, leaning on one of his knees and pointing to The Pen.

"It's fine," Jake answered. He picked it up from the hemp and stroked The Pen's side. "I just wonder when we'll hit the second stage. Any idea, Moss? Shelton?"

"Nope," they both answered at the same time.

Moss continued on. "We'll pass the second stage when we get there, Jake. Patience is a virtue."

Jake nodded and considered this. He slipped The Pen back into his shirt before clapping his hands together.

"So, what's next?" Jake asked.

Moss nodded. "Let's set up camp. Nothing more we can do tonight."

II

No one could sleep. Instead, the pack gathered around the fire to trade war stories and theories about where they were. It was easier than tossing and turning in the leaves and dirt. They knew that any sleep they got wouldn't make them feel rested anyway. They figured they might as well take the time to bond so that the journey wouldn't be as harrowing.

"You know, boys, it has been like three weeks since the fantasy draft," said Jake, who was sitting near the fire and throwing sticks into it. "So, almost a month ago, Kev and Trevor both went through the time portal. I remember that day. I cried for hours, not knowing where you guys had gone. It was strange."

"Yeah, it was weird when we first came," Kevin replied. "We got transported into the desert, and we met Moss. He explained to us why we were here, and how we could help. Eventually he sent us off to get weapons and extra things. Moss told us to stay around the woods, and for us to meet there. That was pretty fun," Kevin answered, moving around the fire. He looked over at Moss. "Thanks Moss. You didn't kill us."

Moss nodded. "If I had killed you, Jake would have surely killed me, and then you'd all be stuck here without a clue."

"Like Richard?" asked Jake, sadness filling his face with the thought of the boy.

"Yes. Like Richard," Moss said, nodding with sorrow. "But Richard was not supposed to be involved in our group. It's kind of strange. Jake, I had to make a choice. The Creator somehow put a trance on you, and he was controlling you. He was meaning to throw you off the butte, and if he had, you would be dead. Being that you, the Holder, could die, I couldn't take the chance. I left Richard behind."

"Why'd you keep me?" asked Shelton, who had been silent throughout this entire conversation.

"Because Shelton, the Prophecy calls for a group of five: the Prophet, the relative of the Prophet, a friend of the Prophet, one who knows the land, and one who has forgotten the land. Remember? I have no doubt you're one of those." Moss paused. "Or at least, that's what the Prophecy says."

"Does that mean we're all safe from death?" Trevor asked.

"Sadly, no," Moss said, turning his attention o Trevor. "See, we can always replace the relative or friend with another one, and we can replace

Shelton and myself as well. And because we can all be replaced, it means that Jake might also be replaceable."

Jake threw more twigs into the fire. It was sun-orange. Moss pulled his compass out from his still-wet sack. He moved around and tried to find the north and south. The compass wasn't working as easily as Moss expected. In fact, the compass arrow kept fidgeting — north and south were interchangeable. He knew what that meant.

"All right," said Moss, pointing forward. "That way is the way to the hills, like Shelton said. Now, since it's north, the Blizzard of Lexington will be coming from the south, meaning it will hit us hard. So, I suggest we get through the mountains before the storm arrives."

"Blizzard of Lexington?" Jake asked.

"Yeah," began Shelton. "The Blizzard of Lexington is a terrible blizzard that goes around this planet for on and on. It mainly lies in the south part of our world, which we used to call Freezlin before Kurpo took over and claimed it as the Cold South. Right now, it should be in our direction, though. Rarely does it hit in the North, but this year it looks like it will. The blizzard was first started when Kurpo's second-in-command during the World War, Lexington, set a curse on the planet of Discis. He made it so there would be only one way to stop the blizzard, which is still unknown. It is meant to make Kurpo angry for betraying Lexington."

Kevin smirked. "Looks like a lot of dudes want to make this Kurpo guy angry."

Moss nodded. "And we have to suffer for it is as well. Never have I been caught in the blizzard, but I have heard stories. Look, I know we just set up camp, but it would be better to move now," Moss answered. "I expect to run into Blinkys and Geos. Shelton, remember them?"

"Oh yeah," Shelton said, a slight smile on his face. "Jake, Kevin, Trevor, these things are horrible. The Blinkys are these fat green things that will shoot red beams at you. If you're hit, you'll be out for five minutes. And Geos are huge. They're bigger than a grizzly bear. They taste delicious when you kill them. But if you get scratched or even touched by one of them, you're dead. So be on the watch. Kevin, got your bow and arrows?" Kevin nodded. "Trevor, got your sword?" Trevor pointed to it. "Jake, got your..."

Jake pulled his weapon out from under his shirt. "I got The Pen."

III

They hobbled to the hills. Getting to the hills would take a few hours since they were far away from the camp. But soon enough, the White Hills of Shores were in view, their white tips hanging high in the sky, and their black grass resting below. Jake would normally marvel at the hills, but he knew he'd have to climb them. The things we love are never as beautiful when we have to fight them.

The wind howled. The snow that was resting on the tip of the hills floated down as the group zeroed in on them. The bitter taste of cold and snow whipped the group in the face. Snow fell and sunk into the group's bones, chilling them to their core. It wasn't cold enough for frostbite, but almost. With each passing hour, the group walked in circles, huddling, just so the warmth would stay.

IV

The group was getting hungry and they were running out of rations. It had only been less than a day and they were already having problems. But the biggest problem was not what they had, but what they didn't have.

"Moss," began Shelton, who was starving badly. "Got any beef? Maybe some-some-some steak?" he dreamed.

"I have no food left. Sorry," Moss answered. He was in the lead. Jake and Kevin had fallen back, just so they could hang out together.

"Dammit Moss! You should have this stuff! If I was leader, I would have more food then you would ever have!" Shelton yelled.

Moss stopped. He turned to Shelton. At this point, the rest of the group stopped and watched Shelton and Moss to see if things had finally reached a boiling point. A whole history was between them, going back to when Shelton betrayed Moss's family and old home. Moss looked at Shelton, and Shelton looked back. Shelton's eyes glowed red, snow hanging off his eyebrows.

Shelton jumped back a few feet and shot a jagged blue line of energy from the tip of his finger. The energy went right into Moss's upper chest, sending him down to the ground. The rest of the group jumped back. Down on one knee, Moss tried getting up. He put his hand on the ground so that he could rise, but Shelton shot two electric bullets right into Moss's torso.

"Shelton, stop!" yelled Jake.

Shelton ignored this and stormed over to Moss. Moss croaked as the air left his lungs when Shelton's hard boot nailed into Moss's ribs. Moss tried grasping something, anything. He tried to get something that could make him gain an advantage over Shelton. But it was up to instinct.

Shelton's boot came sailing down, but this time it didn't hit ribs. The boot hit Moss's palm, as he seized the boot and twisted Shelton over, landing him on his back. Moss crawled toward a tree with snow-covered twigs. He grasped some and pulled himself up.

With a yell, Moss charged toward Shelton, looking to spear him to the ground. But Shelton disappeared into thin air and swerved behind Moss.

With anger, Shelton tripped Moss over. Moss landed head first, and a spill of blood poured out. Shelton lifted Moss up and punched him in the face. He held him again and punched away.

Moss pulled a knife out of Shelton's upper pocket and struck it into Shelton's shoulder. Shelton screamed in horror. Everyone saw the steam from Shelton's body float in the cold air.

Shelton, on instinct, whaled a huge punch to Moss's face and sent the knife flying in the air. Shelton jumped high and grabbed the knife. He sailed down with the knife's point aimed at Moss, who rolled over as the knife edged his back, wounding him slightly.

Shelton looked down at Moss and kicked him again. Moss rolled over and spat blood from his mouth. He shot more energy from his fingers into Moss. The electric chaotic lines of energy hoisted Moss in the air. And what goes up must come down. Snow lifted in the air up from the grass as Moss hit the ground with a horrifying slam. Moss twisted and turned at this, and spit even more blood from his lips, which were already covered in blood.

With an ominous laugh, Shelton lifted the dagger. He pointed it down toward Moss and went to strike him.

With a cry, Jake dashed over to Shelton and pinned him to the ground with all his body weight behind him. Shelton tried weaseling his way out from under Jake, but Jake stopped him with a punch straight to the jaw. Shelton stopped twitching and trying to move and rested.

Kevin and Trevor walked over to Moss and tried waking him up. Moss began to stir. They let Moss get back up to his feet, knowing that the fight must be over now. Moss, then, having regained his strength, walked over to where Jake had Shelton pinned to the ground. And in one swift move, Moss shoved Jake off of Shelton and locked Shelton in a headlock. The knife he held was right near Shelton's cheek. Jake expected Moss to let go of Shelton, but he didn't. Rather, Moss tightened his grip around Shelton's head, squeezing the life out of him.

"No matter what you say Jake, I cannot forgive Shelton!" yelled Moss. "He killed my family. He betrayed us all! He tried to kill me! I will not let go of this betrayer!"

"He's right, Jake. He'll never let me go," Shelton managed to squeeze out.

A sound came from the distance. It was a roar.

Jake turned around, knowing the sound was coming from behind. Kevin and Trevor did as well. Shelton tried to move his eyes, but couldn't. There was a loud stomping sound. Stomp. Stomp. Stomp. The group looked toward the land they had just came from and, out from the distance, came a gigantic purple bear. Its claws extended for over a yard and as it stood high above the group, it roared once again.

"It's a Geo!" cried Shelton, his cheeks pushed together.

Jake tightened his grip on The Pen, but bent down low to pick up the fallen dagger. Trevor yanked out his sword. Kevin retrieved out his bow and arrows. Moss released Shelton, who readied himself. Moss pulled out his spear and angled it forward.

The Geo roared again and inched closer and closer to the group.

Trevor and Jake charged forward. They ran with their sharp weapons, going for the Geo's feet. And behind them, Kevin and Shelton worked together. While Kevin shot arrows at the Geo, Shelton shot spiky energy balls, both going toward the Geo's chest. When Moss got to the Geo, he took his spear and sliced it into the bottom foot of the monster. Jake did the same with his dagger. Trevor, however, swerved and waggled around the monster's feet, cutting each foot, allowing blue blood to splash out.

As Trevor reached the end of the monster, he noticed a group of obtuse green bugs approaching. They were on all four legs and stormed right for Trevor. These were the Blinkys. Trevor readied himself, bent down and aimed his sword. The first Blinky that approached, knowing if it went much further, it would die, shot a long red beam, and it struck Trevor, knocking him out cold.

Through the corner of his eyes, Kevin saw the Blinky and shot two arrows.

"Shelton, take down the Geo. I'm going for the Blinkys!"

Kevin moved through the falling snow from the hills. He hopped over to the Blinky, and shot three arrows at it. From the distance came more Blinkys.

"Oh come on!" Kevin yelled as they approached. Before the Blinkys arrived, he shot a flurry of arrows at them, not missing a single one.

Back with the Geo, Moss sliced through a leg and the beast fell. The Geo was on three legs. Jake sawed off another without hesitation. Shelton shot at the Geo's upper body, making it weak and immobile. With one last plunge, Moss threw his spear up to the Geo's head. The spear went right through the forehead and the Geo went crashing down, making the snow lift high.

Jake danced around in triumph. But his celebration was cut short when a red line zapped him right in the neck. Jake fell to the ground. He didn't feel any of the other red beams that came his way.

Trevor rushed to Jake and waved for Moss and Shelton to go and kill the Blinkys. When they came closer to the green bugs, Moss noticed Kevin had also been knocked out. Shelton ran over.

"If I attach energy to these arrows, I might be able to kill two at a time!" said Shelton. He grabbed a few arrows and the bow.

Moss charged at the Blinkys. He dodged every red beam that came toward him, and stabbed every bug that stood in his way in a fit of murderous prowess. Shelton blasted energy onto his arrows and shot them through the air. Some of the bugs exploded, which made others catch the red beam liquid, killing them.

Moss struck every last one, and before long, all the Blinkys had gone.

V

"How much longer?" asked Trevor, trying to wake Kevin and Jake.

"Should be a few more minutes. It all depends on how many times they were hit, since each beam takes away five minutes," Shelton said.

"Well," started Moss, "while Jake and Kevin are out, we should plan now. We have to get by these high hills, but how? I noticed that the side path has been blocked by piled up snow since we started to walk. And as for climbing over, well, the sides of the hills have been covered in snow, and it would be impossible to go over. So, anyone have any ideas?"

"Yeah, I got one," started Trevor, "why don't we have Shelton lift us over the hill? I mean, he could use his energy to lift us over. It could work!"

"Well, I figure I could update my strength level to red-diamond," Shelton suggested. Moss and Trevor didn't get it. "That way I could hoist you all over. Sounds good. All right. If you need me, I'll be in the corner getting my strength up."

Shelton walked off and went into the corner near a frosted-over tree. Trevor huddled in a blanket the Council had given them and tried to shake Kevin and Jake with his shoulders, but it was near impossible. Moss, his olive clothes layered with snow, moved over to Kevin and kicked him, but nothing happened. He shrugged when it proved futile. Trevor laughed, his teeth chattering as he rocked back and forth.

Moss rubbed two twigs that had not been totally covered by the snow, hoping to see flames rise against the bluish hue of the white snow. But the winds picked up and it made the snow come even fiercer. Every time a little spark shot, the snow blew it out. It blew right into his face, stinging him. But Moss kept at it. No matter the weather, he kept trying to make the fire start, even if it seemed useless.

"Oh! Damn this!" yelled Moss, eventually throwing the twigs a few feet away.

"Everything OK, Moss?" asked Trevor, still wrapped in the blanket and waiting for Kevin and Jake to wake up.

"I guess so. But this Blizzard of Lexington is the worst it has ever been. I have never heard of it being this bad. It seems as though the snow won't stop falling! And besides that, once the snow piles up, the only way to go is up."

"But Shelton will lead us out. He said he could," Trevor reasoned.

"He better do it quick, though, because the temperature is getting

THE PEN

worse and worse with each passing flake. This could get bad," Moss explained.

"You want bad, Moss? Try living where we're from. People spend way too much money on pointless things and there are all these damn wars happening at every turn," Trevor told him.

"War is not bad."

"Yes it is, if it's over finding weapons that our enemy didn't have! Now that I look at it, it's much like Discis. Our leaders don't do any good for us," Trevor mentioned.

"Do they have rules they have to follow?" asked Moss.

"Well, there is the Constitution of the United States of America, which basically shows rules and regulations, along with the amendments, but that's even left open to interpretation. Does the Creator have anything like that?" Trevor came back with.

"In a way. When Kurpo betrayed this world and took over, he wasn't alone. He had a fellow leader. They call him the Master now, but that wasn't always his name, from what I hear. The Master has all control over things, and can help Kurpo do things. He gives suggestions to Kurpo. But he is a spirit."

"Is he powerful?" asked Trevor.

"Imagine the most powerful thing you know," said Moss. Trevor nodded when he thought of it (a skyscraper falling down on a person). "And now think of the most evil thing," Moss said. Trevor thought of the New York Yankees beating the Red Sox in the ALCS 2003 when Aaron Boone hit a homerun in the 11th inning to win the game. "And multiply those by twenty. That oughta do it."

"But can he hurt us?" Trevor asked.

Moss shook his head. "He's only a spirit, now. But Kurpo lends his ear to him. And anything the Master instructs or desires gets done. And that, my friend, is evil enough. I'd hate to imagine what he'd be like in human form again."

"Can that happen?" Trevor asked.

There was a rustling sound in the snow and Kevin began to stir. He wiggled around and awoke. He was in a stupor for only a moment before he realized he had been knocked out.

"How long have I been out?" he asked.

"About five hours," Trevor answered, exchanging a high-five. Kevin raised a hand at Moss, like he was saying hello.

"Damn, it's cold. Why didn't we leave yet?" asked Kevin, rubbing his arms with his hands. Trevor handed him one of the blankets.

"Shelton is going to lift us over the mountain. He's building up his energy strength, so we're waiting for that," answered Trevor. "Of course, it may take a while, according to Moss. By the way, did you manage to see

91

how many times Jake got zapped?"

"No idea."

Trevor put his arm on his knees and tried to make himself feel warmer, but it wasn't working. He wanted to be back home with a plate of cookies and hot chocolate next to him, with marshmallows and whipped cream and a cherry on top. Usually he was a kid who didn't want be home, but he wanted hot chocolate. That was worth the price.

Kevin looked over at his cousin and brushed the light flakes of snow off of his face. It was killing Kevin to look at Jake, who, for the second time in less than a few days, looked like death. He seemed like death.

VI

Shelton finished his upgrade after a few hours, pushing himself to level black-raven, which was the strongest level of his power there was (it still made no sense to the rest of the group).

But Jake was still asleep. Maybe Kevin was wrong about how many times Jake had been hit. Kevin saw Jake get hit five times before he himself got zapped, so Kevin didn't know how much longer the zapping had gone on.

"When do you think he'll be back?" Kevin asked Shelton, who was throwing snow at the hill above.

"I can't say, really. I think we're gonna have to send some of you over the hill now. The longer we stay over here, the sooner we die. So, I'll take Moss and Trevor now. Kevin, you were a baseball outfielder for our high school, right?" asked Shelton.

"Yeah, For like a week."

"Good. I'm gonna leave you here with Jake. When he awakes, throw a snowball over that mound of snow blocking our way around, and make sure you put something on it that makes it noticeable. Then I'll come and get you guys. Okay?"

"Yeah, no problem," Kevin said. Chills climbed his spine.

Shelton got up from his cross-legged position and lifted Trevor up with a line of dark and misty purple energy that almost resembled a plume of smoke. Trevor kept trying to feel the energy, but it shocked him when he touched it. Shelton lifted him up. Up and up he went. Shelton could barely see him anymore, so he went completely raven.

While Trevor was high in the air, a raven flew by him and watched Trevor go higher and higher. When the raven saw Trevor reach the tip of the mountain, he flew to the other side and watched as Trevor lowered down. Trevor was laid flat on the snow on the other side of the large hill. He saw many lands of plains, with hills at the end, free of snow. Trevor was relieved. A few moments later, Moss came over, as well as Shelton. Now, it was up to Jake to wake up. And up to Kevin to throw the snowball.

VII

The snow picked up. Every so often Kevin dusted off Jake's face to keep his cousin warm and keep air coming and going from Jake's body. But there wasn't much more he could do. Kevin didn't rest. He just waited for that moment when Jake would wake up. Unless he froze to death first.

A few more minutes went by. The snow continued to pile up so much that Kevin could barely see anything as he tried to find Jake through the white sheets of snow. Kevin must have been taken by the wind and away from Jake.

A snowball wacked him in the back of the head.

Jake jogged over to Kevin, smiling like nothing had gone wrong.

"Woo! This snow is awesome!" yelled Jake. Kevin grasped Jake and hugged him. Kevin made a snowball and tried throwing it over the mountain, but it was shut down by the other snow and the furious wind.

"Dammit! Jake, we have to get a snowball over—"

Blackness.

CHAPTER 15

I

With a stir and a feeling of stupor, Kevin Keys awoke, his hands trapped in the snow. His pants were soaking wet. His clothes were heavy and tight. Kevin felt the burn of coldness as the wind blew. He cocked his head to the left and then to the right, looking for the group. And there they were, huddled around a fire.

Kevin stood up and limped his way over to the fire, holding the back of his head where he had been knocked out. He rubbed and massaged the huge bump that had formed there, purple and full of puss. As he came closer to the fire, Jake stood up and ran over.

"Hey man!" he yelled as he jumped on him, tackling him down to the snow. "You just got jacked up!"

Kevin laughed and found his feet. He walked over to the rest of the group and rubbed his hands near the fire. "Seems you guys found a way to get fire."

"Yeah, man. But that's not the real story. The real story is how you got this ball over here, and how you made it," answered Trevor, who lifted a ball that was made of hard silver. It was closed, with small silver locks chained around the outside, as though they were holding something inside.

"I didn't make this. It knocked me out cold," Kevin confessed, grabbing the ball and looking at it. He tossed it over to Jake, who caught it with ease.

"Uh. Looks like a futuristic baseball," Jake replied.

"You're all wrong," Shelton began. The group turned to him, except Moss, who kept warming the fire. "It's called a Time-X-Ball. I helped design them a while ago. Once upon a time, before I began my work helping Kurpo, the Greybills, old residents of this world who were flushed out by Kurpo, told me about this weird device, which is like the one you're holding. I can't remember much except that the ball has something to do with time."

"Time?" asked Moss, standing up. He snatched the ball from Jake. "What exactly to do with time?"

"Well, if I remember correctly, these make a human forget the world and instead remember their memories and get rid of them," Shelton explained. "But it has been over three years since then, so they probably made improvements or upgrades, or changed the whole thing for all I know. Hell, they might have kept my model. But now that we know Kevin didn't make it, all I'm gonna say is that we cannot even try to open this. All we should do is bury it. Right here, right now."

Shelton ripped the ball from Moss and threw it into the snow. He stomped on it again and patted the snow for good measure. Shelton bent down to one knee and punched the snow twice more just to be safe. He packed up some snow and mounted it high above the ball. He lifted his arms in the air and shot two jagged blue energy balls into the snow. Shelton gained some strength from the wind and sent it into the ground too.

He walked over to the fire and rubbed his hands near it. He sent some twigs to their final resting place. Shelton didn't care what the rest of the group thought. All he cared about was that they didn't find that ball. It was dangerous. He knew it.

Jake relaxed near the fire across from Shelton, The Pen dangling on his chest. Kevin and Trevor chilled around the fire, too. Moss stood and looked back at the hill they had passed over. He narrowed his eyes toward the plains that lay miles and miles ahead. Moss knew that this snow was fierce. But the worst part was, it was only the beginning.

Moss returned to the group and patted Jake on the shoulder.

"How's The Pen?" he asked.

"It's fine, I guess. Kind of a drag. I mean, I know I'm the 'Prophet,' or whatever, but I wish The Pen wasn't as important as it was. Having the fate of a planet around your neck isn't exactly an easy thing."

Moss began, "It's OK, Jake. We all have problems, and yours is The Pen. All I know is . . ."

"None of you—and I mean none of you—go looking for that ball," interrupted Shelton. His eyes sent daggers to the fire.

And, for the moment, no one did.

II

How am I supposed to sleep in this? Trevor thought.

It was a cold night. Even with his blanket, Trevor's arms were hills of goose bumps. Trevor needed something to do just to keep warm. Snow kept falling on his face and melting into his skin. Trevor rose and inspected Moss, who was deep in sleep, his chest moving up and down. Kevin and Shelton both lay on their stomachs, their feet buried in the snow. Jake was still awake near the fire. Trevor got up and walked over.

"Hey Jake," he said. The two exchanged a glance of unpleasantry. He noticed Jake was fiddling with The Pen.

"Hey, what's it like holding that?"

"Horrible," Jake said. "It's not heavy or anything. Just the pressure of it all."

"Really? Why?" Trevor asked. He wanted a smoke badly. But he had lost all his cigs when he had went skateboarding that night.

"It's hard, you know? There is just so much riding on The Pen," Jake said.

"Don't sweat it, bud. You got us with ya. We're here for you," Trevor reasoned.

"You can't help, Trevor. It's too impossible. There isn't a guarantee you guys will survive."

"Ah well, these things take time. Just keep going strong," Trevor said.

"You guys woke me up," Kevin said, joining the group.

"Yeah, sorry," Trevor said, patting Kevin's shoulder.

"I wonder how home's doing," Kevin said, sitting next to Jake.

"Yeah. I bet right now the summer is just about to end and we're getting our new clothes for school and everything," Jake said, remembering the life he once knew.

"You think we'll ever get back?" Trevor asked.

"Maybe. I mean, when I first got The Pen back at the library, the Creator told me that the door would lead to his room. Maybe when we get there we can go through a door that will lead us home," Jake answered.

"What would people think? Oh, we went through a portal and suddenly appeared here in Discis? We'd be committed. What did you tell them when we went skateboarding, Jake?" Kevin asked.

"I said you guys ran away. But I wonder what everyone thinks happened to me, Richard, and Shelton. Probably looks fishy that we disappeared at the same that Feona disappeared, too."

"My mom would believe us," Shelton said, walking up to the group and avoiding the subject that was his girlfriend. He brushed his hair away from his face and found a spot next to Trevor. He cracked a twig and tossed it into the fire. "She probably knows I was scrying. The only thing she doesn't know is that I was born here in Discis."

"Wait, then how is she your mom?"

"The Creator put a spell on her to make her believe she's had a child for a lot of years," Shelton explained. "Faked the whole thing so I could live on Earth."

The four boys sat alone without Moss, who was asleep. Most times Moss would accompany them by the fire and make dreams become losses, or make losses become dreams. It wasn't what most humans in the real world would do. But now, for the first time, all of them were sitting together, sharing stories and pastimes.

"Remember when Kev did that sick move off of the roof last year? Skateboarding down one and hopping onto another? Oh, that was lit," Trevor shared. Jake nodded, and even Shelton did. He was there that day when Kevin had done that move. Kevin laughed and agreed.

"So, what do you think it'll be like to go back?" asked Kevin, still wondering about that.

"Different. I mean, right now we're living in a life where we know nothing of what's going on and we don't have a clue where we are. And to go back, it would be totally weird," Jake answered.

Kevin responded, "I wonder if Vicky will still love me."

"You're lucky your girlfriend's still alive," Shelton said.

Trevor thought about saying something, but didn't. He decided to toss another twig in the fire.

"Speaking of that day," Jake remembered, "what do you think happened to Richard?" Shelton laughed. Kevin and Trevor had heard the story of how Moss abandoned Richard and everything, but didn't find it funny.

"Probably walking around the desert still. Either that, or he's dead," Shelton began. "But it would be funny if we met up with him down the road."

"You think we will?" asked Jake.

"In Discis, anything can happen."

The boys did not speak for a while, lost in their own thoughts. They thought about what was going on, and how everything would end. What would happen when they reached the Creator's Palace? Would the Creator be there to meet them? Would they get home? What happened if they succeeded and brought peace back to Discis?

"What do you guys think of Moss?" asked Trevor, breaking the ice.

"Dreadful," Shelton said; it was an unexpected answer.

"Shut up," said Jake. "How would you feel if someone took over your hometown and a friend sold you out?"

"We were never friends."

"I think Moss can be OK at times," Trevor said. "But when we think things are bad, he'll just snap back and tell us how hard his journey has been. Plus, I've been sensing some sternness in his voice. I can't tell what it is."

"He misses home," Shelton said. "He misses his home and all of its outside towns and villages. Plus, the dude's been walking through the desert for years waiting for us. Dude's lost his mind."

"Doesn't help that you were on the Creator's side," Jake reasoned. "Are you with us or him?"

"Well, he killed Feona and I guess tried killing me. So obviously I'm with you guys," he replied. "I bet Moss thinks I'm on Kurpo's side."

Even though they didn't know it, Moss was wide awake and listening.

III

The next morning was the same as the night. The sky was dark and the snow fell, getting worse and worse by the minute. The boys had not gotten one minute of rest, and neither did Moss, listening to the late-night conversation. When he awoke, he narrowed his eyes at the three boys. Moss packed up all the camp and walked over. He stomped on the fire.

The boys shouted in protest as the fire sizzled to its death.

"Let's go, we're packing lightly. Trevor, take everything out from that pile of crap and get rid of anything that looks like it can be disposed. Shelton and Jake, go fetch some twigs for the next camp. And Kevin, go get us some food. I'm starving!"

"But Moss—"

"I said now!"

The boys all stood up and shot Moss dark glances. Moss found Jake and looked searchingly into his face. Jake shrugged it off and walked away with Shelton. Kevin ventured off to his right, and Trevor stayed, fiddling through the things that Moss had given him. Shelton and Jake had no idea where to look, so they just kept walking.

"Yeah, that was weird," Jake said.

When Shelton and Jake returned to the campsite, they noticed an eerie silence. Only Kevin was there, stomping his toe. When he saw Jake and Shelton, he ran over. "He took Trevor!" Kevin cried.

"What?" Shelton and Jake exclaimed together.

"He took him! I don't know where! But Moss has gone off his edge! We gotta find him!" Kevin yelled.

The three boys galloped down a slope and slid down the snow. They saw foot markings and drag lines from Moss and Trevor. How far could they have gone in a half-hour? Shelton soared up into the air, becoming a raven yet again. He spied the area around him and soon found two black dots about a quarter mile away. He used his energy to hoist Jake and Kevin up. And within a few minutes, they found Moss, who was dragging Trevor by the throat.

"Moss! You've gone off the edge!" Shelton yelled through the snow's wicked voice as he turned back into his human form. Moss turned around. He lifted Trevor's New Blood sword into the air. He swiped the sword at Shelton and Kevin, keeping them away.

"I am not in the mood!" Moss exclaimed back.

"Stop it, Moss!" Jake yelled, but it wasn't to his benefit. Moss rushed toward Jake, holding the sword on the side.

In desperation, Jake lifted The Pen and ripped it from the hemp. "Take one step closer and I'll kill you, and I'll break The Pen!" Moss stood still. "Now, drop the sword."

Moss dropped the sword instantly.

From behind, Trevor punched Moss in the back of the knee. Moss fell to that knee, but whaled a punch into Trevor's face in retaliation. Trevor fell to the snow and his blood turned the snow pink. Moss kicked Trevor in the gut for good measure.

Shelton, now back as a raven, bit Moss's upper lip to get his attention. Moss punched the raven. Kevin attempted to take down Moss, but Moss grabbed Kevin's throat and hoisted him the air.

"No!" Jake screamed.

With The Pen in his hand, Jake stabbed Moss right in the side of the ribs. Moss yelled one loud cry and fell down. Jake was the only man standing. He looked down at Moss, who was gasping for air and holding his ribs. He saw Kevin and Trevor both down on the ground, holding their necks. Shelton was still a raven and struggled to fly. Pink snow was everywhere.

Jake found the hemp that he had thrown off of his neck. He rolled The Pen's end on the hemp and reattached the necklace to his neck. He took Trevor's sword, which Moss had used, and slid it against the snow. He pointed it around to everyone, all of them being on the ground.

"What have you all become?" Jake was hot with anger. "We can't get torn apart!"

He threw the sword down, walked away, and looked for a place to cool off.

IV

No one got up for a few minutes. They needed the rest.

Kevin was the first up, followed by Trevor. They both went over to Jake, who had no intention of speaking with them. Shelton was last to get up. Somehow he had turned back into a human and healed himself without much difficulty. Shelton rested next to Trevor and Kevin. Jake didn't speak, only listened to what they had to say.

Moss did not move. He stayed where we was, relaxed, opened-legged. He was silent and only gazed at the snow. Had he gone psycho? Was he demented? What had happened between Trevor and him? Not only did these questions run through his own head, but they ran through Jake's head as well. And after a few more minutes, Jake stood up and spoke again to the group.

"Look, guys, I don't know what happened back there, but I think we need to know. So Moss, tell us what happened between you and Trevor," said Jake. Moss stood up. He walked over to Jake, holding the small wound that The Pen had created.

"Nothing happened. I punched him a few times and brought him out here. I do not know what I was trying to do. Something made me do it."

"Like Jake and the butte?" asked Shelton, who stood up and walked over to Jake and Moss. Moss and Jake shot puzzled looks at Shelton.

"Yeah, that's exactly it. It might have been the Creator, but—"

"No," Shelton began. "It was not the Creator, but something else. Something that was driving you to come to it." Shelton lifted his boot, closed his eyes, and struck the snow. The Time-X-Ball appeared into the air. Shelton caught it with ease.

"Obviously something, or someone, wants us to look at this ball, otherwise we're all going to do something awful to one another. But I'm not sure if we should look into it or not."

"We should," Trevor answered. "It's either using this ball, or we all die."

"Well, obviously we won't be moving any more today, so I suggest we all get a good night's rest. We'll talk this over in the morning," Shelton said, taking control. He slid the ball in his pocket before Trevor interrupted.

"Why should you keep the ball? How do we know you won't use it?" he asked. Shelton, not giving an answer, buried the ball into the snow. He stomped on it.

"There!" Shelton threw an energy ball, making a blue stain on the snow. "That way, we'll all know where it is. 'Night!" Shelton walked away and fell asleep.

V

It was a cold, snowy night yet again. Each drop of snow was heavy and powerful against their bodies, which, despite the fur they used to keep themselves warm, were bitter and cold. Each of the members of the group slept on the cold snow that offered little padding. Flakes blew into their faces as they slept. Trevor could not fall asleep at all. He woke up at one point, expecting to find someone sitting at the fire they kept. But there was no fire, and no one was awake. Everyone had managed to fall asleep.

Trevor built up a pile of snow and rested his head on it. He glanced around at everyone. Moss was on his left, Jake on his right, and Kevin was behind him. Shelton was nowhere in sight.

Trevor wondered about the Time-X-Ball.

More than anything, Trevor wondered if the ball could really manipulate time. Could it take him back to before his life collapsed? Could it take him back to the good times?

Just the thought of his past inspired him.

Trevor slid out of the snow. He saw that everyone was asleep so that no one could stop him. Even in the darkness, he saw the blue stain that the ball made on the snow. He hobbled over to the spot where Shelton buried the ball and dug. It wasn't that big of a dig, the ball being only a foot or so down, but he found it. The ball was gray and solid. He cupped it with two hands.

A black raven flew around Trevor before changing into a real person. It was Shelton. "What do you think you're doing?" he whispered under his breath.

Before Shelton could stop him, Trevor opened the ball.

"Trevor, no!" yelled Shelton.

Moss heard the yell and, wide-eyed, noticed Trevor was opening the ball. A stand of blue light ignited from the ball's core. Moss leapt forward, trying to stop Trevor, but the ball of light zoomed into Trevor's head before anyone could get there. Kevin and Jake awoke and joined the others near Trevor, who was now laid out on the snow, his eyes closed.

"Wake up, buddy, wake up for me, buddy," said Kevin, jiggling the side of Trevor's face. Trevor rose up straight, his back stiff and his eyes rolled back.

He spoke. "I shall tell you my worst memory. You will hear my story, and you will hear what I have to say." The words did not seem to be his own.

"Oh boy," Shelton muttered.

The group listened to Trevor's memory.

CHAPTER 16

I

The buzzing roar of an alarm clock sounded off in Trevor McGaven's room as the bright Floridian sun slanted through his windows. Trevor was dressed in nothing but pink and lime green polka dotted boxers when his eyes first opened, so he put on his robe and went downstairs. His house—3 stories, 6 bedrooms and 4 bathrooms—was frosted over by the A/C. He hated the cold.

After eating a breakfast that included all kinds of food ranging from waffles to eggs, Trevor hopped on his skateboard and rode to school, dressed in a punk rock T-shirt and skinny jeans. Trevor couldn't be more excited to get to school and meet up with his crew.

"Hey Trevor," Amanda said, cuddling next to him when he arrived at school. Trevor smelled her brunette hair. Coconut.

"Hey," he said. Trevor put his arm around her shoulders and walked with her into the school.

"So, how was your weekend?" Kyle asked, popping up out of nowhere with his girlfriend, Sarah, wrapped around his arm.

"It was good, dude. Hey, did anyone catch that episode of—"

"That one geek show?" Amanda asked with a laugh.

"Ya know, that hurts. And your rude attitude is hurting my self-esteem," Trevor joked, holding Amanda.

Trevor walked with his batch of friends down the hallway to geometry class. After going through their first three classes, the four friends met back at the lunch room, where they would be forced to enjoy the mystery meat glop that someone had the audacity to call food.

"Don't you guys wonder what it's like to live in New England?" Kyle took a bite of mystery meat.

"No!" replied Amanda and Sarah at the exact same moment. They turned to look at each other and jinxed themselves in unison. Trevor stirred his food.

"What about you, Trev?"

"My grandma lives there, and it's not so bad. Winters can be brutal though, but I rather live here, in Tampa Bay, home of the Rays, home of the Bucs, home of all the weirdos who just don't give a . . ." Trevor let his words trail off, making some other people laugh at him. Amanda laughed too and laid her head on his shoulder.

"How'd you guys like Philips's biology test?" Sarah asked while picking at her rice, which tried to run away from the mystery meat.

"Easy! Simple! There wasn't anything wrong!" Amanda exclaimed.

"I thought the part about the tiger and penguin was a little hard, even though that's all I've been studying for the past few weeks. Not only that, but I'm also studying for Tevez's Spanish final. Two finals in one day? Crazy!" Trevor told his friends. "Seems like the school year's coming to a horrible end."

Trevor and his friends, after finishing their horrible lunch, moved on to their next classes. Before each class, Amanda and Trevor said goodbye with a kiss.

By the end of the day, the group of friends were so full of energy that they decided to go to Sloth's Ice Cream and Bar for some sweets and to hang out with the rest of their classmates. Trevor first stopped at home to change his clothes into something more comfortable—cargo shorts and a solid black T-shirt—before he got on his skateboard and rode down to the hip social scene.

Trevor's arrival didn't go as planned.

"Hey look, it's geek-boy Trevor!" yelled Tim Winthrop, the school's basketball star, who was surrounded by the rest of his broad-shouldered and tall teammates.

"Shut up, Tim!" Amanda called from the back of the ice cream shop.

Trevor acknowledged Amanda's wave and met her in the back. Sarah and Kyle were in the booth, too, cuddling, as usual. Amanda scooted over and Trevor found his place next to her. He slipped his arm around her waist and they kissed.

"How'd you guys like the Spanish final?" asked Trevor, which forced Sarah and Kyle to stop kissing.

"It sucked!" Kyle took a sip of his cherry soda.

"Yeah," Sarah said. "I didn't expect him to ask us who discovered Mexico City."

Kyle ignored this and kissed Sarah again. Trevor followed Kyle's lead and started kissing Amanda. This was a usual thing that people did in Sloth's. People would all come down, either get a soda or an ice cream, and then start making out—which is why the majority of those in the restaurant were youths. Most first and last dates between boys and girls took place at Sloth's. The occasional double-dates would happen, such as Trevor,

Amanda, Kyle, and Sarah's ongoing one. The dates between the first and last took place at the local theater across the street or the strip mall down the road.

After about three hours of kissing and getting high off sugary drinks, with a few conversations thrown in here and there, Trevor and his friends took a walk outside of Sloth's, where a lot of teens were running around playing practical jokes on each other. Trevor huddled with Amanda.

"Wanna come to my place?" Amanda asked. She raised a seductive eyebrow.

"Nah," Trevor said, trying to show he was playing it cool even though his heart, mind, and body were raging with the passion of a thousand suns. "My folks are mad enough at me. They want me to study for the U.S. History final tomorrow, and that's all! But just think about it, babe. By the middle of next month, we can be together non-stop! No school. No pressures. Nothing but Amanda and Trevor," Trevor said.

Amanda curled her bottom lip and nodded. She squinted her eyes and looked past Trevor out toward the setting sun. She knew, deep in her heart, that things wouldn't be so perfect. Not forever.

II

When Trevor got home, his father, Luke, was out cold. The air stunk of gas station beer. After turning off the Buccaneer-Vikings game, Trevor threw off his shirt and walked up to his room. He passed his mom's room and saw she was in a deep sleep, her TV blaring some sort of soap opera. An empty bottle of pills lay next to her.

Trevor's room was flooded with posters. There were a few of soccer players, like Messi, Ronaldo and a poster for Orlando City SC. There were also posters of the Halo video game, and a few pictures of the Rays. Next to some posters was his dad's old stereo, sitting next to a TV and an Xbox. He turned on his stereo and music began to play.

Trevor's stereo was on the mixed setting, so a slew of songs popped on. The first song came from a Scottish rock band that had made it big in the United States about a decade before. It wasn't a bad song, but Trevor doubted the song would be as popular in modern times. While listening to the music, Trevor took off his pants and traded them for some Nike shorts. He walked over to his Apple computer, wiggled the mouse, and checked his messages. There was a Facebook message waiting for him from Amanda.

[Hey! Phone was dead so I just thought I'd send you a message on here. Call me when you can!!]

He picked up his own cell and entered in her numbers. How weird it was to call her? Texting was usually good enough.

"Hello?" Amanda asked.

"Hey, hey, I got your message," he said.

"Oh. Yeah. Can we talk about it tomorrow? I can't get into it tonight. My phone's probably gonna die and I have some things I've got to deal with. We'll talk at lunch?" she said.

"Uh, OK, yeah, sure," Trevor said, slapping his phone shut and ending the call.

Trevor slammed his cell phone on his computer desk before shutting down his computer and turning in for the night.

III

The next day was a drag for Trevor, especially the morning as he waited for his lunchtime talk with Amanda. His first classes went by so slow that he even fell asleep in Spanish (he knew he would pay for that later). He was just waiting for lunchtime, where he would talk with Amanda, who had been avoiding him all day. He had seen Amanda standing by her locker and walking to her classes, but she totally ignored him. Confusing.

At lunch, Trevor entered the cafeteria, his lunch money rattling in his pocket. He didn't plan on spending the money because all he wanted to do was talk to Amanda and see what the big problem was. His nerves pooled in his stomach. As he sat down with Kyle and Sarah, who were busy kissing, he saw Amanda coming to the lunch table with her tray.

Butterflies migrated into his stomach when he saw her. They fluttered and flew, ready to burst out. His eyes connected with Amanda's for the first time today. She sat down next to him and began to eat her meal, like Trevor wasn't there. She didn't even see him.

"Amanda?" he asked.

"Trevor? Hey!" she said. "How has your day been?" Her face was gleaming.

"Uh, fine. I saw you earlier, going into your classes. So, what was it you wanted to talk about?" he asked, narrowing his eyes.

"Oh. Well," she grabbed his hand and held it softly. "You know I love you, and I trust you more than anyone. But I want to know what our future will be like."

"Huh?" he asked, totally confused.

"I mean, last night you said that we'd be together all summer, and it'd be Amanda and Trevor forever. But, I didn't believe you. I couldn't believe you because it seemed too perfect. And, this may hurt your feelings and I'm sorry we're doing this right now, but I have never had a boyfriend who didn't leave me for some stupid fight," she continued.

"Amanda, I would never leave you for the world. You know nothing could come between us," Trevor replied. "You mean too much to me."

"I can't trust you, Trevor. They, all guys, they all say that," Amanda said. She brushed her hair closer to her eyes so he wouldn't see the tears form. "I mean, what if this summer I go on vacation to California or something, and I make out with a guy? It's over! Or what if you get a summer job and you hang out with those people instead of me, Kyle, and Sarah? See how easy it is for things to fall apart?"

The cafeteria had emptied out. Kyle and Sarah had left. Amanda and Trevor were the only ones left in the cafeteria.

Trevor scanned the lunchroom and noticed they were alone. He could be more open and honest. He held Amanda's hand and rubbed it. He kissed her on the cheek.

"Amanda, everything's going to be OK," he said, rubbing her hand. "You don't have to worry. Whatever comes next, we'll face it together. We'll take on everything together."

But Amanda, still not believing in Trevor, pushed him aside. She looked at him, tears dripping from her eyes, her face puffy. He had never seen her cry like this before. Trevor, without words, turned back toward the door and started to make his way out of the cafeteria.

"I can't believe you!"

Trevor stopped, grunted, and turned back. "What is the point in all of this?"

"Because, Trevor, I love you too much," she said. "I don't want this to end for something stupid. Most couples in our school end in the summer! In school, we're together so much because we have classes and we're forced to see each other! What happens in the summer if we lose contact, or something worse?" she cried. "Maybe we're only together because we see each other every day."

Trevor heard the bell ring and didn't move, but Amanda did.

"Look, I'm going to class," Amanda said. She wiped tears away from her eyes. "I'll text you later."

"No! No! No, Amanda! You can't leave me without some kind of explanation!"

"It's because I love you!" Amanda shouted.

"If you really loved me, you wouldn't be talking about us breaking up!" yelled Trevor.

Amanda moved away and dumped her tray full of food into the trashcan. Trevor ran over and turned her around, wanting the conversation to continue.

She smacked him hard across the face.

Trevor's face burned. His neck went stiff and his head rock-hard. He paused and stumbled for a second from the hit, still confused about why it happened and why Amanda had done it in the first place.

He saw Amanda was about to leave the cafeteria. "What's the matter with you?"

THE PEN

Amanda looked at her boyfriend. Trevor's face was a deep red. She saw the sincere look in his eyes. She ran over and hugged him tight. Amanda whimpered on his shoulder and her mind began to change. She realized that Trevor was the one she loved, and she would never do anything to hurt him.

"I still can't believe you and I are in love," she cried. "I just don't want to lose you. I just need you forever. I'm scared."

"Hey," Trevor said, lifting Amanda's chin up. "You have nothing to be scared of, Amanda. Nothing, no one, not anything, can stop our love."

He put his arm around her waist and walked her to her next class. But he wasn't sure he believed his own words.

IV

Time went by fast in the following days. Trevor and Amanda had barely any time to realize that school was coming to an end. They spent every day together. They ate at Sloth's, saw some movies, and all the while shared buckets of kisses. Other students knew they were now the greatest couple you could find in Tampa. They were in love with each other like no one else their age. And they knew that summer wasn't going to break them up.

Trevor loved the fact that he was almost done with school. He knew that by not having to worry about tests, exams, or homework, he could be at Amanda's house, spending some very social hours with her. He could show her they weren't just together because they saw each other at school—that there was more to their relationship. Trevor couldn't wait for the summer.

Trevor and Kyle were shocked when they realized the last day of school had finally arrived. Things could only get better, for the summer would bring more parties, more things to do, and more alone time with their ladies.

Trevor received his report card on the last day, an annual tradition at the school. He slipped it into his pocket and reminded himself he would give it to his mom and dad when he got home, if they were in a good mood and sober. He knew he didn't do too well in Spanish.

After a day of kissing, conversation, and staring at the lockers, the bell rang. School was over. Trevor ran outside the school, throwing all of his papers into the wind. He met up with Amanda moments later and held her hand. They both hopped down the steps and stopped outside the school. Their souls fell into each other's eyes.

"I still can't believe this," Amanda said, putting his arms around his neck. "And now, we enter the Summer of Trevor and Amanda."

"And so it begins," he replied, before getting a kiss on the lips.

V

Anybody who was anybody at Trevor's high school went to Stevenson's house for the party of a lifetime on the last day of school. Older students carried in bottles of liquor to make the party rock. Others hung by and chatted the night away with the people they loved or newfound friends. Music boomed from the center of the party—a mix of retro 2009 jams that people thought would stand the test of time. Trevor stayed with Amanda, kissing without a break. Kyle and Sarah did the same. Ah, young love.

Before the clock struck midnight, Trevor knew he had to leave. His parents expected him home early and he didn't want to keep them waiting, especially when he knew he'd have to give them his report card.

"But you said we'd be together all the time!" she whined, kissing him on the cheek.

"Yeah, well, my parents will kill me if I don't get home and show them my report card. Look, I promise. Tomorrow we'll go to Rib City, or the Outback! Maybe Don Pablo's! I don't care where. But tomorrow is for you and me!" Trevor said, hugging Amanda. She smiled in return.

"I know it's just," making a motion with her hands that Trevor knew was really from the alcohol. "That I don't want you to break your promise or anything."

"I won't. You know I love you. I'll see you tomorrow, OK?" Trevor said, kissing Amanda on the cheek. "I'll try and text you, but I don't think my dad will let me have my phone when he sees my grade for Spanish," Trevor joked. Amanda smiled. Trevor waved goodbye and left the party. He rode his skateboard home.

When he got home, he half-expected to see his father passed out from the booze. But instead, when he opened the door to his house, his eyes fell on a lot of boxes labeled "TREVOR."

Trevor, not having a clue what was going on, called for his mom. She came down the steps and hugged him tight. A tear fell down her face. Her cheeks were puffy.

"I'm so glad you came home in time," she said, hugging him again.

"Mom?"

"It's your father. He was looking for you. We didn't want you leaving without a proper goodbye," she answered.

"Good . . . bye? What?"

"Your grandma called. She was talking with your father, and you know him. He saw your report card online and he thinks a change of scenery would be good for you. So your father packed up all your stuff today and you're going to go live with her for awhile," his mom sad.

"No. No, this can't be right. I have a life here, and a girlfriend. I can't just leave everything beh—"

"I'm sorry," she said.

The door swung open and Trevor's father came in. He looked at Trevor. Trevor shot him a stern look.

"Sorry for not telling you until now, son," he said. "But it's for the better. I packed all your things. Your computer is safe and your belongings as well. We have to get moving."

Trevor couldn't believe this. It had to be a dream. It just had to be. It was happening too fast. Unrealistically fast. "When do I leave?" he asked.

"Tomorrow morning, around 6 a.m. I'll bring you to the airport tonight. You need to leave town."

"Oh my God. Drama, Dad. This can't be right. Why would you do this to me?"

His father waved his hand. "Your grades, Kevin. I know I'm not the best role model for you, but you need to be better. You need to do better. This is no place for you. You have to leave."

Trevor realized there was no winning this battle.

But Trevor knew there was something more important for him to do. He had to tell Amanda. She was probably at the party, having a great time with everybody, readying herself for a beautiful summer of love and romance.

And now it was all gone.

Trevor pulled out his phone and quickly typed a text to Amanda. He couldn't really explain all of it easily, but he at least had to tell Amanda that he was leaving. She had to know the truth.

When he finished his text, he read it over:

[Amanda. *I can't believe it has to be like this, but I am being sent to live at my grandma's in Massachusetts. I don't wanna leave you baby but they're making me!! I just can't believe all this is happening. This was supposed to be the summer of me and you!! And now I have to go to my grams!! I'm literally crying here as I write this to you. Just remember Amanda, I love u more than anything in the world!! And I'll never forget U. I'LL FIND YOU AGAIN...*]

After a deep breath, he sent the blue bubble to Amanda's phone. He hurried into his contacts and blocked her thereafter. He couldn't bear to see her response. He would block her from Facebook, Instagram and Snapchat on his car ride to the airport.

Trevor sat in the passenger seat and did not talk again until they reached the airport.

Grabbing his suitcase, he looked at his father. Anger built inside of Trevor. Trevor didn't care about anything his father said. As far as he was concerned, this man was not his father and never could be.

"Well," said the father, putting his hand on Trevor's shoulder.

"Leave it," Trevor answered, pushing the hand away. His father looked at the ground.

"We never meant to—"

"Meant to hurt me? Meant to take me away on the best summer of my life? Take me away from my girlfriend! Never meant anything, did you Luke?" Trevor shouted.

"We never meant to hurt you," said Luke. "And I'm still your father. Treat me with respect."

"I hope you look back one day and see how much you ruined my life! What am I supposed to do? Go to a new school? New friends? Just start over?" Trevor asked. He felt a darkness growing inside of him.

Luke turned away. "I'm sorry. That's all I can say. I don't see how I can make things better."

"You ruined my life! You ruined my relationship!" Trevor shouted again. Everyone outside the airport stared at them.

"If you were a smart kid and did the great work that you could do in school, then maybe I wouldn't have been so hard on you!"

"Work! You wanna talk about work and school, Luke?" He took his report card and threw it at his father. "I worked my ass of this term. Better check those online scores, pal. Yeah, I didn't do great. But I did the best I could. And you have the idiotic heart to say that I don't work? Please, Luke. You can't do half the things I can. You can't even measure up to requirements of being a father!"

"Son, I—"

"I'm not your son and never will be." Trevor grabbed his bag and made his way to the airport's doors.

"Trevor!" yelled Luke. Trevor turned around. "We never meant to hurt you!"

Trevor thought about this. He shoved his bag down and jogged toward his father. Trevor lifted his fist and landed it right across Luke's right cheek. Luke felt his cheek and stumbled back.

Trevor scowled at the back of his father, waiting for him to leave. Luke shook his head and got back in his car.

That was the last time Trevor ever saw his dad.

"What have I done?" Trevor said, leaning back against a pillar, sweat pouring down his face.

Trevor eventually went inside the airport when his nerves had calmed. Hours later, he boarded the plane. He took a seat in the back by the window. He was alone at first, and half-expected to take this flight by himself. But a boy, he couldn't have been much older than Trevor and was dressed in a deep black trench coat, plopped down on the chair next to him.

"What's up man?" the kid said.

The engine started up. Trevor said nothing, choosing to read the survival brochure instead.

"Let me guess. You're being forced to leave Tampa?" asked the kid.

Trevor gave the boy a thumbs-up.

"Cool, cool," the boy said. "Whatever man. You'll be all right. Trust me. Same thing happened to me. Met this girl named Vicky, wonderful girl. I promised her the summer of our lives. But then, my pops threw me out because he thought I was a waste of time. So, I moved from Miami to Massachusetts," the boy said.

"What brought you back?" Trevor asked.

The boy smirked. "I found my way back. It's funny, though. You spend all this time trying to get back to the world you left behind, and then you realize you belong in a different world."

Trevor shrugged. "I don't know about that. I'm pretty sure I want to stay in Tampa."

The boy nodded. "Yeah, yeah, you do. Give it a few years, man. Come back in like, three years, and you won't want to be here anymore. Your girlfriend will be with someone else. Your best friend will have a new best friend. Restaurants will change, parties won't be the same, teachers will leave. Man, it just all changes. Life is always moving, never constant, I mean, yeah, never."

Trevor played the drums on his leg.

"You know what the worst thing about moving on is?" the boy asked. Trevor shrugged as if he wasn't sure. The boy smiled, and looked forward at the other people who were on the plane. "It's forgetting about those you loved the most."

Trevor looked out the window, high above Tampa. This was the final time that he would see the city where he grew up in—the city where he fell in love, the place he would always call home.

He fell asleep a short time after. When he woke up, he knew he had left his heart and soul behind.

CHAPTER 17

I

 The fire crackled. The twigs burned. Trevor came out of his trance and said nothing. He knew what he had just done, and he was ready for objections and criticism. But instead, he saw Shelton, just staring into the fire. Jake and Kevin tried to count the stars in the sky. Moss was bent over, spitting into the dust. They were all silent.

 Jake broke the silence. "Did you ever go back?"

 "No."

 "How long has it been?" asked Shelton, looking away.

 "When did we meet?" Trevor asked Kevin.

 Kevin shrugged. "Like, a year ago?"

 Trevor nodded. "A year ago it is. I met Kevin on my first day in town."

 "I had no idea," Kevin said. "Did she ever call or message you or anything?"

 Trevor shook his head.

 "Well, you never know. Maybe she called within the last month. I mean, you weren't around—"

 Before Jake could get his words out, Trevor put his hand up, a sign for Jake to stop. He walked away, his boots slamming into the snow. When he disappeared, the rest of the group lay back in awe. This was too deep, and something they never expected to hear from Trevor. They half expected his memory to be when he tried driving for the first time. But they were wrong.

 "So, what do you think we should do?" asked Jake, staring into the fire.

 "There isn't much we can do. I suggest we leave him to himself. He'll come around," Shelton answered.

 Time went by slowly. It seemed like an eternity. Trevor moved a few yards away and kept to himself. He held his knees. His mind raced with thoughts of his past for those two days.

And then he remembered about the Trevor he left behind in Tampa. He wouldn't let himself get so heartbroken again.

Trevor peered out toward the distance and came back over to the group. He found his place in the snow. They all looked at him, but turned away when Trevor met their eyes. Trevor, after what felt like the longest time, but was maybe only a few hours, cracked a smile.

"There's one more part I forgot to tell you," he said, remembering his past. "I tried calling her house, and the family that was there said her family moved. And then I tried her cell," he paused, and held himself from crying. "She changed her cell number, too. Couldn't find her on Facebook, either. Seemed she moved on, too."

Trevor took a deep breath. Shelton slapped his knees and patted Trevor on the back. Trevor cracked another smile and remembered Amanda, and all the fun times he had had, until his father made him move away.

"Well," started Shelton. "I have two thoughts which both contradict one another. One is that we shouldn't even touch that ball again. Look what it can do. I don't think that's the best thing for us right now. My other thought is that we should all take a chance with the ball, so that we're being fair to Trevor."

The group all looked at each other, silent, waiting for someone to speak.

"I'll do it," Kevin said. He stood up and looked at the group. "It's the best I can do for Trev."

"Kevin, once you open this ball," Shelton began, handing the ball over to Kevin. "There is no going back."

"Not yet," Kevin started. "I'll do it tomorrow. I've had enough heartbreak for one night."

Shelton nodded. The group gathered some snow and put out the fire.

II

The snow slowed that night. By morning, the sun was out, melting some of the piles of snow that had grown over the last two days. Kevin was the first person to wake up. He sat on a log that sank into the mud of the melting snow. Jake joined his cousin a moment later on the log. He fiddled with The Pen while Kevin was silent. A few minutes later, the rest of the group woke up.

"So," Shelton started. "You ready?"

Kevin nodded. "I think that just because Trevor made a mistake doesn't mean he's the only one who should suffer from it. I'll open the ball, and then none of you will do the same. I'm calling it even."

Kevin pulled the Time-X-Ball out of his pocket. Before opening it, he moved his head and looked at the group, knowing that this was the right thing to do. He smiled when he met Trevor's eyes. His smile faded when he turned back to the ball and opened it.

"Well," he began. "Here it goes."

A blue light appeared from the ball when Kevin unhinged the tip. It formed into one ball and shot into Kevin's head. He fell back, hitting his head on the snow. The group didn't do anything. Kevin sat up, his eyes rolled under his lids. He moaned like a ghost.

"I shall tell you my worst memory. You will hear my story, and you will hear what I have to say."

CHAPTER 18

I

Kevin Keys was never an average teenager. He was handsome, intelligent and, well, cruel. And, maybe above anything else, he was rich. Well, at least, his new family was rich. His new father, un-biological, collected New England sports memorabilia and made large sums selling it on eBay.

But Kevin did not like his new parents. He rarely ever did.

Kevin had moved through twelve families since he was six, and each one kept ruining his life and putting him back into a foster home when things didn't work out. And this family, the Bantams, was no different. They had two other kids besides Kevin, Tyler and Danielle, who were both in college and were working out their own lives. On top of that, Kevin's foster parents often spent months away on business trips. He wasn't sure why they adopted him in the first place. Maybe it was a charity thing or a tax write-off.

But he was sure that he was alone. Kevin had no one.

"Maybe this is good," started Kevin, laying on his sofa and talking to his best friend, Ian, who was in the corner of the room. Some Scottish rock band played in the background.

"What?" Ian asked.

"I mean, maybe if I run away I won't have anymore problems."

"True."

"But Ian, the real question is . . . what would Teddy Rossman do?"

Ian, with his red hair and thick-rimmed glasses, laughed and raised his hand high in the air. "That nerd cracks me up. Such a weirdo. It might be a while until we figure that one out!" Ian laughed again with Kevin. "So are you seriously gonna run away? Going to go back to see your own nerdy cousin?"

"Not sure, dude. I mean, I have nothing left here besides my friends," Kevin said. "No parents, as usual, and no girls and all that. I just think my best bet would be to get out of here while I still can. Come on dude, you know my history of leaving families and stuff, and this time it's no different."

"Yeah it is, Kevin, are you kidding me?" Ian said, shaking his head. "You got yourself a huge house, lots of cash, friends like me; life is great. I mean, in a month or two, you'll be able to drive your dad's Mustang," Ian answered.

Ian was right.

"All right man. I promise, I won't run away until I go to college, then I'll have the right to run away." Ian laughed and the conversation ended only a few minutes later.

II

Kevin awoke to the screeching noise of his alarm clock, and he instantly jumped out of bed, hitting the floor. He rolled over, but the side of his body went into the wheels of his computer chair. What luck. After hitting the wheel, Kevin got up and hurried down two flights of stairs to his living room.

Several famous photos and paintings hung on the walls of the taupe living room. In the center, against the back wall, was a black plasma TV screen with surround sound. Underneath the TV, there was a Blu-ray player and a number of video game systems of the past, present, and future.

A few feet away from the TV and off to the left was a mini-fridge, which Kevin filled for himself with a 6-pack of soda. There were some leftovers of the Chinese food that Kevin had eaten two nights ago on the back row.

Next to the mini-fridge was a leather couch that blended with the walls. And then across the room from the couch was a matching leather loveseat. There was also a black recliner in the middle, which was Kevin's favorite chair.

Kevin, with the notion to watch Saturday morning sports, hopped into his recliner, sprang it back, and lifted his feet in the air. He grabbed the black clicker from the nightstand next to him and flipped through the channels.

Everything just clicked for Kevin right then. It was a beautiful Saturday morning in the suburbs of Lowell, yet he was stuck to the couch watching random college football games. He had no life, no goals, and no inspiration.

Time ticked away, and his ambition to stay fell away with it.

It was then he realized that these parents, like the others beforehand, just weren't working out. He had to leave. He had to make something for himself and create a life worth living. It wasn't enough for him to have

THE PEN

money and security. He needed thrill, adventure, and risk.

Life, simply, needed to change.

III

It didn't take very long for him to get packed. He stuffed his backpack with piles of clothes and a few notepads for writing to keep him busy on the bus ride. He took his skateboard with him and left his foster parents' house without a note or phone call for them to remember him by.

The bus ride back home was normal. He listened to some throwback songs of The Killers on Apple Music and just stared out the window at the bright sun for the entire trip. Even though Kevin moved all the time and lost parents and friends all the time, Kevin felt that Ian, and the life he just had, was probably his favorite so far.

His cousin Jake and his mother Kay would likely pick him up at the bus stop in South Hills, if he called them. They were probably going to keep him overnight and then send him back to his grandma's, who wouldn't let him stay for too long and would send him back to a foster home. All of this depended on whether or not the cops were looking for him since he had just left his family.

But maybe he didn't have to meet up with Jake. Kevin realized that the cops might be looking for him since he disappeared without a trace, and the first place they'd start looking would be with family. If he could avoid Jake, he might avoid getting arrested and thrown into a group home.

The bus's first stop was at Mountain College, which was about twenty minutes away from South Hills, close to Northampton. He could walk off the bus without anyone knowing, right? He could blend in with some of the college folk, make his own way, wait for a New England season to pass, and then get back on the road on an adventure. That sounded nice.

The bus driver set the bus in park. He opened the door for anyone to leave for Mountain College. Some left to go get some coffee or chips from the snack bar at the bus stop. Others knew this was their final stop. Kevin was one of the latter.

After covering his head with his sweatshirt's hood, Kevin stepped off the bus, holding his backpack on his shoulder. He found the snack bar and became mesmerized by the sweet chocolate delights before him. He searched his pockets and saw he had a few dollars—maybe enough for a bag of Doritos or a Snapple. Not enough for anything major.

"Will that be all?" asked the cashier.

Kevin placed his bag of chips and his diet-lemonade Snapple on the counter. He nodded and rested his hand on a few Hershey chocolate bars that were below the counter and slid them into his hoodie pocket.

"That'll be $3.87."

Kevin, with his hands still in his hood pocket, pulled out a few dollar bills. He rested his crumbled dollars on the counter. The cashier raised his eyebrow when he saw only three green pieces of paper.

"Um, excuse me, sir, you do not have enough money. I suggest that you put something back." Kevin nodded and grabbed his Snapple. He walked away and went to one of the back aisles.

When he was in the back of the store, Kevin checked for cameras. He saw one in the distant corner. His mind raced. He figured there was only a 1-in-12 chance that it is fixed on him, though he was never good at math. Kevin zipped open his backpack and shoved his Snapple in. He looked over at the register, where there was a huge line now. He could sneak out, no problem.

"Too easy," Kevin said.

The sunset's glow flooded the gas station. Kevin walked closer to the window, but what he saw stopped him in his tracks. Behind the bus were a few police cars, the policemen talking to each other, turning ever so often to inspect the store. One of the cops was a chubby man who had a few chocolate stains on his cheek. The other was thin with shaggy gray hair. They both turned to the store again and walked in as if they owned the place.

Kevin felt that old nervous feeling he felt every time that he knew he would run away, and when the cops would chase him. It was the rush and adventure he had been searching for. He smiled at its possibilities.

And then he saw something behind the cashier that made everything sensible again.

Both of the cops entered the building. The large one set his arm on the counter, some of his fat resting next to it. He tipped his hat at the cashier.

"How's business today?" he asked.

"As usual, Bill," the cashier said. "Barely any costumers today. I had a few teens in here who cleaned out my donuts. They were planning on going to some road trip. They bought chips, soda, a few of your favorite donuts. And—"

"That's all well and fine," started the gray haired cop. "But did you see a kid enter, who had blonde hair, about my height, and wasn't able to pay for the things he was buying? We're looking for a young boy. Got a warrant out for him kinda thing. He's got family in this part of town."

The cashier was quiet. Everything clicked a second later. "Yeah, yeah, I think so. He came in a few minutes ago. I think he went off to the back to put back chips or something like that. How did you know—"

"We've dealt with this kid before. He goes to many adoption homes, ya know? Then, he ends up having to leave for some odd reason, and he ends up running away. We've chased this kid like five times now. Kids these days, ya know? Entitled. He usually enters stores like yours and plans to buy some things. But the kid never has enough money, obviously. So he'll run to the back and slip everything into his pockets. He does it to waste time," answered the big cop.

"Yeah," the gray-haired cop gave a short chuckle. "But this time we'll get him, as usual. By the way, Jeff, do you have any keys?"

The cashier turned his head to the hook where he kept his keys, a brown shelf with gold hooks. To his surprise, and not the cops', the keys were gone. The cops nodded at each other and ran out the door, chasing Kevin.

V

Sweat poured from his forehead as Kevin ran faster than he had ever run before. Running down the streets was a tough thing to do in the humid summer heat. Though the sun was setting, the faint rays pounded on his body with an uncontrollable rage that forced his body to break out in sweat. It was no easy task.

Kevin had a small advantage, though. The skinny cop, with the gray hair, would eventually tire because of his age. The other cop, the large one with donut stains, would slow down because of his weight.

Kevin also had the keys to the storeowner's car, a Mustang.

He found the red Mustang parked on the side of the road. He ran over to the car and clicked the "UNLOCK" button on his keys. Kevin swung open the door and jumped onto the driver's seat.

He had been taking driver's ed courses for a few weeks now, but he knew he could drive out of this one. It was only a month or two until he could get his permit. But, permit or no permit, he'd have to drive. So he switched the engine on, pressed the gas, and was off before the cops could even catch a glimpse at any passing cars.

Kevin rode away, untouched and unseen.

"Woo!" yelled Kevin, pressing a button to make his sunroof go down. He switched on the radio to the local hip-hop station and a song by a rapper and a country star played.

He drove on, not turning his head for a moment. All he cared about now was getting away from any cops. He knew there was a very real possibility they would catch him. But going to jail was better than foster care.

Kevin swerved left and went up a hill and down another over to South Hills. It was the only place he knew. Sure, the cops would be there waiting for him, but he was sure Jake would help him avoid the pigs. If there was one person who could help Kevin get out of a mess, it was Jake.

It might have been because he was alone, but everything clicked for Kevin again during his drive through the night. He thought about where he was running from and where he was running to. He thought about how he was going to ask his cousin to help him avoid a criminal scandal. He remembered that cops were on his tail, pursuing him. It was a life Kevin never thought he would live, nor one he ever really wanted to.

Kevin decided that he wasn't going to run anymore. He would get to Jake's, go to Friendly's, and hang out with some friends. It was a perfect idea. And then after going to Friendly's, he would find a police station and turn himself in. Yes, a great idea. An idea that would have Kevin become a better person was a good one.

He drove all through the night. The stars and the lights on his Mustang were the only thing that kept him going. No other cars seemed to be on the road. Kevin drove alone.

Deep into the night, Kevin decided to stop at a local taco shack to get some grub so that he wouldn't wake his grandparents up late in the night. He pulled up to the drive-thru. It didn't matter to Kevin what food he got. Anything would do.

"Welcome to Massey's Tacos. How may I help?" said the person in the drive through.

"Yeah! I'll have a—"

"Calm down, dude," she said, yawning. "It's three in the morning. Chill."

"But—"

"Ya know what? Just come inside. You seem harmless," the voice said.

Kevin nodded and drove around the drive-thru. He parked his car in the empty parking lot that matched the dark blue sky above. It seemed strange that Kevin was being invited inside the fast food chain so late at night. He swung open the door, walked his way through, and stopped at the counter to finally order his nacho pizza.

"Yo!" he yelled.

"Look," said a voice from behind the counter. A girl emerged, pale-faced with deep-set blue eyes that were mirrors of the ocean. Her nametag read Virginia. "I told you! It's three in the morning . . ." she yawned. "How may I help you?" she said before yawning again.

"I'll have a—"

Virginia woke up when she saw Kevin's face. "You're Kevin Keys, aren't you?"

"Huh?"

"Yeah! Oh my god! You're that guy that's always on TV, the one who keeps running away! Yeah, you went to my cousin's party once!" she said. "Didn't you go to South Hills?"

"For a minute. I don't doubt we've met though. Any party around here, I usually go to. That's when I'm in town."

"Are you leaving or staying this time?" Virginia began. She had filled a

THE PEN

Mountain Dew for Kevin, and handed it to him. "Have this. It'll keep you up!"

"Thanks. Yeah, no, I'm coming in this time. I just ran away."

"Oh. So if I turned you in, I'd get a handsome amount of money? Eh?"

"I guess so," he replied, sipping the Mountain Dew.

"Don't worry, I wouldn't. I have too much respect for the all-mighty Kevin Keys. Especially after that time we made out."

Kevin spit out some soda in amazement. "We what?"

"You don't remember? I was the blonde that was hanging out with that girl Kathleen who was getting drunk, and broke her foot when she was vacuuming the pool?"

"Oh yeah. I remember. Ah!" Kevin said, remembering how he left. "You're the one I spilled vodka on before I left, right?"

"Yeah. Not the best way to leave someone after making out with them," she smiled.

"Did the window get fixed?" he asked.

"Yeah. You owe me $750 for it."

"That's all? I'll give you that next time I find a home."

"And when's that?" she asked.

"Ya see, in the summer, the family I'm with will usually send me here to stay with my grandparents. I guess they're unfit to raise me. Some income stuff. So, I'll drop in and see how you're doing then. But I mean, right now, I'm in town because I ran away from some of my parents. Cops are after me, so I may lay low around here for a while. Maybe I can see you more often."

"I'd like that," the girl said with a wink. She looked up at the menu. "So, what'll it be?"

"Oh. Uh . . ." He had totally forgotten food.

"Come over the counter, it won't do much harm. That way you can pick out what you want," Virginia said, as the yawns returned.

Kevin hopped over the counter. Virginia walked beside him and they went around the kitchen. Not a lot of things were there, but there were a few good choices. He saw a case of nachos. He walked closer to them, passing by metal stoves, poles, and utensils. Everything was fresh and clean.

Virginia had snuck off somewhere else.

"Yo! Virginia—"

"Shhh," she said, coming out in front of him. She put a finger on his lips and kissed them.

"Whoa, should we be doing this?"

Virginia raised an eyebrow. "I haven't cleaned everything yet. Don't worry about it."

VI

Kevin woke up without a top. His hair was all messy and disordered. He opened his hazel eyes and found himself still in the kitchen of taco shack. He called Virginia's name, but there was no answer. He went to stand, but was pushed back down to the floor.

Kevin fully opened his eyes and saw that there were a few policemen standing over him.

"No running this time, Kevin," said one cop, who had blonde hair that was shaved on the sides. Kevin sighed and put his hands out. The cop put some cuffs around him and brought him out to his patrol car. Kevin didn't speak.

While on his way to the car, Virginia was talking with a beefy cop, who slurped down an equally beefy burrito. Kevin heard her give details on how Kevin came into the restaurant and how they spent the night.

As Kevin was being carried away, he stopped and turned to Virginia.

"Don't worry about it. I don't blame you. Must be great to take advantage of a run-away," he smirked, giving Christy a wink before being shoved into the back of the patrol car.

The police car's locks clicked.

CHAPTER 19

I

Master, hear my call, said Kurpo.

What is it, Kurpo?, said the Master.

The Time-X-Ball is weak. It is not enough, my Master, to end the group. Though they are weak in many places, they are strong in bonding, said Kurpo.

Are they? Well, they must be. No one said this would be easy. So, we must find a way to stop them before they try and take Discis back to the way it was, said the Master.

You just gave me a great idea, Master. I have the perfect plan, said Kurpo.

And what might that plan be? said the Master.

You'll see, Master. You will see, said Kurpo.

CHAPTER 20

I

Shelton woke up. The snow was still falling next to the midnight sky. He looked around at his fellow group members, who had fallen to sleep after hearing Kevin's story. He wondered if anyone else would want to use the Time-X-Ball. Shelton was one who did not want to use it, only because he felt it wasn't necessary. But there was something about the ball that terrified him. There was something that wanted to bring him back to his evil self. But for the night, Shelton ignored it and fell back to sleep.

II

Snow whipped around the group that night. The Blizzard of Lexington was at its peak. A few days ago they had been in the eye of the storm, but now they were in one of the outer and most dangerous parts of the wintry weather. The wind was faster and it carried snow around at a faster pace than before. The snow was so cold it burned.

Jake woke up. His face wasn't the only thing that burned. The Pen, oddly, was burning his chest.

To stop the pain, Jake untied The Pen from his neck and gently placed it on the snow. Jake felt his chest, panting hard. He waited for the white-hot burn to die down before he grabbed The Pen again. He looked at its edges and saw they were circled with a maroon light. Jake twisted his Pen in his fingers.

A large lime green beam shot out. It landed next to Shelton, who sprang to attention.

"What did you just do?" Shelton questioned, now standing up and snarling at Jake.

"Uh. I didn't do anything," Jake said reasonably. He eyed his Pen with bewilderment.

"Yes, you did, Jake! I saw it! You shot that beam at me and I want to know why!" yelled Shelton, awaking Kevin. Shelton grabbed Jake's arm. "Tell me or die! I swear. I'm in no mood right now, kid."

THE PEN

"What are you doing?" Jake cried, trying to wrestle out of his grasp.

"Hey! Shelton! Let the dude go!" yelled Kevin, who arrived at the scene.

"This doesn't concern you! Get out of Jake's business!" Shelton yelled as he shot a quick line of silver lightning out of his fingers. Kevin fell back a few feet. Jake took advantage, and popped Shelton right in the lips. "You filthy little—"

A massive snowball came from the sky and bruised Jake in the head. Shelton paused and stared down at his fallen friend. Trevor and Kevin ran over to Shelton and tripped him down to contain him. They held his arms and shoved his face into the snow for good measure. Moss, who had been sleeping through this whole thing, ran over to the scene. The snow stopped falling.

"What's going on here?" yelled Moss, noticing the cessation of the snowfall.

"We're not sure, Moss! All we saw was Shelton preparing to attack Jake," Trevor said.

Shelton muttered something into the snow, but no one could understand it.

"Speak again, you traitor!" Moss yelled, stomping on Shelton's back.

"Jake shot a beam at me first. He was trying to kill me."

Moss turned his head at Jake and cocked an eyebrow.

"It's not true! The Pen acted on its own!" yelled Jake.

Moss turned his head back to Shelton. He took his boot off Shelton's back and let him stand. Shelton's eyes glowed a crimson red. Trevor and Kevin backed away. Shelton's eyes were so red they expected large fiery beams to come at them from his eyes.

Moss charged at Shelton, who stopped Moss by shooting a blue light, stunning him. Shelton did the same to Kevin and Trevor, leaving only Jake standing. Shelton gathered some energy and blasted a green beam from his eyes, paralyzing Jake. Shelton moved closer, his eyes getting darker and darker.

Shelton looked over to the left and saw the Time-X-Ball. He pointed his finger at it and lifted the ball into the air, pushing it toward Jake. Shelton twisted his finger, making the ball open, the light appearing. Jake's eyes widened in fright. Shelton let out one last grin.

With force, he pushed the ball right into Jake's chest.

It bounced right off.

As the ball dropped to the ground, Shelton and Jake were at a stare-down.

"Why won't it work on me?" Jake asked.

Shelton smirked. "It must mean you don't have bad memories."

Jake didn't understand.

"Or," Moss started, standing again, unfrozen, "The Pen won't allow it."

CHAPTER 21

I

Jake rested at the campfire and watched Shelton stare into the flames. When Shelton's eyes caught his own, Jake switched his attention to The Pen and inspected it. He saw the second block, which was blue and had an axe and a bow and arrow on it, and tried to interpret what it meant, but his mind was drawing a blank. He decided that asking Shelton would be easier, for he knew more about The Pen than Jake did.

"What do the blocks mean?" Jake asked. The breaking of the silence shocked Shelton.

"I don't know," Shelton said. "I heard once before they have to do with stages of The Final Journey, which is associated with you, the Holder," Shelton paused for a moment. "I also think that the Time-X-Ball is being used to try and turn us against one another, ya know? I think it's showing us our worst memories and making us feel vengeful and angry toward one another. It makes us want to see our worst memories to make everything better, even when we know it's not. The reason I was so angry last night was because the ball wanted me to relive my memories so I would come back even worse off and want to kill all of you," Shelton spoke.

"So what does that mean?" Jake asked.

"Well, we've seen that once someone has used the ball, they've come back with some energy and we've bonded through it," Shelton said. He searched the sky for answers. All he saw were small flakes float down. "Maybe we need to finish this. Who's next?"

Moss raised his hand. "I am."

"Are you ready?" Shelton asked.

"Ready to relive the day you killed my family? I think about it every day. This should be easy," Moss replied.

II

The snowfall worsened as the day rolled on. The sun was buried under the soft gray clouds. Each pile of snow grew in size. To keep the snow from hurting the group, Shelton had made a purplish force field that encircled the group in a heated bubble full of fresh air, like an igloo made of his energy. He didn't think it would last long, but it would get them through the bad part of the storm. They built a bonfire that roared in the bubble.

None of them had slept in days. They waited for the storm's peak to pass.

Moss, though somnolent, agreed to get warped back and relive whatever tale was needed to be re-told. The group knew this was going to be about the day his family and his village were betrayed. It was a story they all needed to hear.

Moss took the Time-X-Ball and threw it to Shelton, who caught it with ease. Shelton whispered something to the ball before throwing it at Moss. The ball sprang open, igniting a blue fire that seeped into Moss's body, taking him back.

CHAPTER 22

I

Everything was gray—the water, the sky and the thick patches of fog ahead. Geoff Moss tried his best to see through the mist, but he couldn't see anything except plaster grayness. He checked his crew behind him and saw they were hard at work, rowing the nearly broken wooden boat along the sea. Moss wished he could see past the clouds, but life wasn't working in his favor. He'd have to suffer through the darkness.

The brown boat slid against the sloppy and damp sand as it reached the shoreline. Moss's leather boot sank into the watery sand below, digging a thick hole. He stepped over his boat onto the shore and saw that the village was hard at work. Commoners moved about bazaar that rested on the docks, pleading for others to buy fish or homemade trinkets. Other pirates pursued the shoreline's boardwalk, searching for the right woman to charm or ale to drink. The shore was always busy.

Moss watched his crew speed past him into the market. He waved at them behind their backs and moved onto whatever came next.

"Worst crew ever," Moss joked to himself.

Moss, his face clean-shaven yet covered with specks of seawater and dirt, rested his hands on his hips and looked out at the land around him. He smelled the seawater. He tasted crawfish and lobster.

"Well, well, well, look who came home," Moss heard from behind. He looked and there stood a blonde man, dressed in gray armor that had dings and dents all over.

"Craven!" Moss said, wrapping his arms around his friend. "It's been too long."

Craven gave a shy smile. "Says the man who's always at sea. You can stick around more often," he quipped.

Moss smiled back and then looked back toward the village. "How's our home doing?"

Craven shrugged. "Couldn't tell you. I've been away as well, helping those in northern Hellryo fend off some of the invaders. It's been bad, Moss. I'm not sure how much you hear out at sea, but the north is becoming a wasteland. I knew I had to come back to Kraill in case things get rough."

Moss nodded. "I heard things got worse."

"Did you hear what happened in the citadel? Down in Homeland?" Moss shook his head. "The president's building was attacked. No one knows what happened to him. Some say he died, others think he disappeared. Either way, Homeland's become a refuge for people who are leaving the north. We may head down there if things get bad here."

Moss set his hand on Craven's shoulder. "My dear friend, I promise you that Kraill will be fine. We're the best exporters in the north. Kurpo and his army wouldn't risk letting us fall apart. He'd lose communication with the south."

Craved nodded. "That's what I'm afraid of, Moss. That's what I'm afraid of."

II

Kraill hadn't changed much since Moss had last been there, except that the wind and rain had made the roads an unappealing muddy sludge that stained boots, shoes, and clothes. But the buildings were the same. The brownstone architecture remained intact, and the signs outside of the buildings—the alehouse, the clothing closet, the marketplace, and all of the homes—stood tall. Though war was raging in Hellryo and down in Freezlin, nothing had touched Kraill yet. Everything was still together.

Moss greeted a few people he met on his walk. He waved off the restaurant servers, who tried to pull him inside so he would eat their sugary sweets. Too much time at sea had left him uninterested in common foods like those sinful sweets. He would have thought differently if the shops were full of uncooked seafood that he'd have to season himself.

Some people gave Moss odd looks and questioning eyes. Others, especially the children, pointed and laughed at the pendant that hung around his neck. He nodded at them and kept moving. He was happy to be a pirate, and happy that everyone knew he was one.

His stroll through the village led him to his home, which rested in the back end of Kraill, close to where the farms were. His home was wooden, much like his boat, and a little unkempt for his taste. The door was guarded by a few potted flowers, which were getting their much-needed fill of rain. Moss strode past the rain-stained wooden gate and the flowers to the door. He pushed inside and he was hit with the smell of his home—freshly cooked fish and a burning vanilla candle. He saw his mother standing at the stove.

"Geoffrey! You're home!" his mother cheered. She dashed over to him, wrapped her arms around him, and tugged.

"Hi mother," he replied with a laugh. "It's great to see you."

"And you," she replied. "So happy to see you're back. I knew you'd come back."

"You did?"

His mother nodded. "Oh yes, completely. All my friends were telling me, 'No, Sierra, no, your son isn't coming back. Not ever. But lo and behold, here you are, my son, back from his journey across the sea. I'm so blessed."

Moss leaned against the back wall and crossed his arms. His pack was already on the ground and his boots were already off. He knew his mom's rules well.

"I'm glad I could be of service, Mom," Geoff said. "I should be honest with you, though. I'm only home for a couple of days. In-between jobs kind of thing."

Sierra waved him off. "I understand, I understand. It's tough living a pirate's life. That's what your father always used to say. Have you seen him lately?"

Moss shook his head. "I don't think I'll be seeing him for a while. Heard some things out at sea that he went home, back to the Unknown Islands."

His mom didn't say anything at first. She scooped some vegetables from a pot and threw them into another. "Well, to the fires with him, then."

Moss chuckled. "Do you think you'll see Brenna while you're in town?"

Moss was caught off-guard by the question. He hadn't even thought of Brenna until this point. "Brenna? Hmm. Maybe. Depends. If I run into her, I'll spend some time with her. But I won't actively go looking for her. This isn't that kind of trip. I'm in, I'm out, no harm done."

Sierra rolled her eyes. "You always say that. And yet you always find yourself with that girl. She's no good, I tell you, no good. I heard from the High Cardinals that Brenna's been skipping sessions. She won't even hear people's confessions anymore or attend services on the weekend."

Moss shrugged. "Maybe religion isn't her way."

Sierra shot a deadpan look to Moss. "You met her at service!"

Moss shrugged again and smiled at his mother. He loved joking with her. She slapped his arm and went back to peppering some of the food.

"Well, get yourself ready for dinner, Geoffrey. We'll be eating soon."

"Yes, mom."

Dinner wasn't as good as Moss remembered it. Maybe he had gotten so used to scummy fish that anything his mother made was almost too good to be satisfying. He preferred cutting up the fish himself, filleting on a roasting fire in the middle of the woods. This was almost too easy, too simple. And it just didn't taste as good.

Once dinner was finished, Moss found a pie before him made of some berry he hadn't heard of. He ate it anyway and it blew his mind. It didn't matter how much he enjoyed eating his own cooked fish—this pie was above anything he ate the last few months. The pie was almost worth staying home for.

"Thanks for dinner," Moss said, burping right after. Sierra shot him a stern look. "Sorry, Mom. Must be spending too much time with the other pirates."

Sierra waved it off. "It's OK, hunny, it's OK. Speaking of other people, your brother and sister went out yesterday on a trip with some of the others in town. They were going to stock the watchtowers with weapons and supplies. Apparently they'll be sending two watchmen there to look out for Kurpo's army."

Moss rolled his eyes. "This is getting serious, huh?"

Sierra nodded. "Yes, it is. I really do hope you go see your friends while you're here. I bet Tyrese would love to see you and talk about all of this with you. He's made some political moves recently. He'd be our senator had President Kallanon not taken that position away from our constitution. But Tyrese has been leading our town, matter of fact, with a group of people who are concerned over what's going on. You may want to speak with him."

Moss tossed his napkin down to his plate and stared at the crimson-colored remains of his pie. He turned to his mom with a smile. "I should go see Tyrese. I'll see him the morning."

Moss picked up his plate and put it in the sink. He went back to the table when his mom had finished her pie and brought that to the sink as well. He cleaned off the table and did the dishes to ease the burden of his mother. When all was finished, Moss blew out the candles and headed to his bed for a night's rest. He knew he'd have little time for rest in the coming days.

III

Moss was delighted when he woke up because the sun slapped him in the face. He rose from bed and saw his mom had already left for the day to start collecting fish from the sea. He put his clothes back on before he headed out the door, ready to meet with his friend Tyrese and learn a little bit more about the potential war.

The sun made the villagers a lot happier. Children ran amuck around town, tossing flowers into the air and screaming at the top of their lungs. Parents hung by closely, chasing after their youngsters and trying to instill order into their little chaotic worlds. Others trafficked through the village toward their various jobs. A few of the elderly hunted through the marketplace for personal items that could help their home. It was busier in the market than usual, Moss could tell. He wondered if it had anything to do with the impending doom of war.

Moss knocked three times on Tyrese's door before it opened. Tyrese answered it and greeted Moss with a hug. The two went into the house and that's when Moss saw five others seated around a conference table in high-backed chairs. He took off his dirt-stained hat and coat when he met the group, perplexed as to why they were huddled in Tyrese's room. He didn't recognize any of them.

"And who is this?" one of the women at the table asked. She had almost orange hair and wore a veil over her head.

Tyrese cleared his throat. "This is Geoffrey Moss. He's a good friend. I've known him since he was young. I hope you don't mind him being here."

One of the men at the table eyed Moss with curiosity. "Is he a pirate?"

"Yes, I am," Moss replied.

"He has no business here," the first woman said.

"Excuse me?" Moss asked back. "Do you know who I am?"

"Pirates have no business in our council. Too unreliable and too dangerous," the woman said.

Moss crossed his arms. "Scared of a little competition? Afraid I'm going to know more than you do about the world?"

The woman chuckled. "What do you know about this world? You've probably been busy spreading promiscuity across the sea and eating all kinds of fish."

Moss smirked. "You're a tough broad, I'll give you that. But I know a lot. I know that Kurpo's army is still taking cities in the high north, and I know that the citadel was destroyed not too long ago. I know all about war and battle. Like Tyrese said, I'm a pirate. Battle is my middle name."

The woman rolled her eyes. "Just shut him up and get him a chair."

Moss took a seat at the far end of the table, and now they were a council of six. Moss hadn't expected to walk into any sort of political meeting. But he figured that was bound to happen now that Tyrese had some political standing. He adjusted in the chair to make himself more comfortable. Tyrese was on the other end of the table, motioning for one of the members of the council to start talking.

"As I was saying," the woman began, sending daggers toward Moss, "the group has reached the watchtowers near Raddux, and they should be back any day now. We need to start training a few people to become watchmen, though."

An older man, his only hair a patch of thin and gray strands behind his ears, spoke up. "Is no one ready?"

The woman shook her head. "We haven't had to use those towers for years. No one knows what to look for or how to use everything that's in there. We'll have to train someone in the coming days. And we better do it quickly. Word came in this morning that Conyers was taken overnight."

The older gentleman who spoke moments ago almost collapsed. Moss didn't react at first, but then he remembered where Conyers was. Moss felt a shockwave reverberate through the group. The reverberation smacked him hard.

"Conyers? That's, what, thirty miles away? How could Kurpo make his way this far south?"

Tyrese shrugged. "No idea. It's even stranger that there's been no sign of the president, either. Not sure how Kurpo's doing this without his help. But we're hearing a lot of things. Some reports have come in saying that Kurpo's been giving northerners the chance to live in the south or be killed. Lots of people are flooding down to Freezlin."

"That's nuts!" Moss replied. "I heard from some men at sea that they're getting hit with the blizzard right now. How are they expected to survive?"

Tyrese's face turned cold. "I think that's the point."

Moss's eyes trailed off into the distance, his mind wondering about what this meant for Discis and its peoples. Kurpo had driven northerners toward the south, even though he had very little war experience and, as Moss remembered it, had once been a humble farmer outside the citadel. How was he doing this? Even if he had the president's army, Kurpo couldn't have been that good of a leader to push people toward the south. Moss knew he had to have something else in his hands—a wildcard that evened the score.

"Reports say Kurpo's army will now head to Rexem, Olsenton, and Sharon," the older woman said, flicking a piece of paper at the others at the table. "After that, there's no reason he wouldn't come all the way south and try to take us down. Without a ground army, he'll run right through us. Having a strong navy won't pay off. And since we've been sending so many supplies to Freezlin, we may not have enough food to support an army and our people."

The group fell silent. Villagers outside the building shouted and screamed in joy, happy to fall under the sun's watch after the day of rain they had just gone through. It reminded Moss that soon those exclamations would be of sorrow and unpleasantness if Kurpo's army made it this far south.

Tyrese cleared his throat. "We need to prepare for the idea that we may have to leave Kraill. If our watchmen see his army coming, we may need to head south before he can burn everything down. We may want to start thinking of an exit strategy."

The older woman nodded. "I agree. Let's recess for a few hours and come back with some ideas, OK?" Everyone nodded. The older woman slapped her hand against the table. "I, Senior Fellow Julk, hereby send council into recess. Reconvene by midday."

IV

Moss left Tyrese's home to get some fresh air. It killed him to know that Kurpo, the farm boy who grew up with nothing and had come from nothing, was now the leader of an army that was overtaking the north. It just didn't make sense. It pained him even more to know that Kraill was in danger, too. All he had lived for could be lost in a matter of days if Kurpo took the northern cities and descended to the shore. He always thought his hometown was safe from war, especially because he never expected anyone to invade from the north.

Geoff stepped out into the drying dirt and felt the rays of sun kiss his skin. There was something calming about the sun. It reminded him of the sea.

He walked into the center of his village and saw the town's church. A bell hung at the tip and rang through the town. He had an hour left until midday. It was the perfect amount of time to see if Brenna, the love of his life, was still serving the gods.

Moss pulled the wooden door open. It creaked with age. He opened up to a row of pews, with only the light from the stained-glass windows to guide him. The pews were all empty. Organs played a somber tune in the background. He saw the symbol of the gods at the front of the cathedral—a circular emblem with a crown on top. The gods were their kings.

Moss sat down in one of the pews. He spread his legs and let his hands rest. He rested his eyes on the front of the cathedral and thought about praying, but decided against it. He was afraid no one would hear him.

"Ah, my first visitor of the day," said a voice from the left. Moss followed the voice and saw a young boy dressed in a black cloak, a white string belt looped around his waist.

Moss looked back toward the cathedral. "That's not good news for the church."

The boy relaxed next to Moss. "I think the fact that I'm a cardinal shows the youth are very interested in the church."

"If you say so," Moss replied.

The boy grunted. "May I ask your name?"

"Moss. Yours?"

"Shelton."

Moss looked at the boy with astonishment. "Shelton? Little Shelton! The same boy that used to fetch us all water from the wells?" Shelton nodded. "Wow. And look at you. A cardinal, serving the gods."

"He has a plan for all of us. Mine is to serve him and help others to find him," Shelton replied.

"He?"

Shelton readjusted his cloak. "Sorry. The gods. It can get complicated. Some believers choose to follow one God, the almighty, the creator, and the strongest. Others choose to embrace many gods. It's a preference."

Moss turned his head back to the front of the cathedral. "Is Brenna around?"

Shelton stood up and fixed his cloak again. "I'm sorry. She's not."

Shelton turned to leave, but Moss pounded his hand against the back of the pew in front of him. The sound echoed throughout the cathedral. Surprised, Shelton turned toward Moss in dismay.

"That's not an acceptable answer," Moss reasoned.

Shelton smiled. "Careful, Moss. You don't want to lose your temper, especially when the gods are watching."

Moss chuckled. "You're just a boy. What would you know about anger? What would you know about loss?"

Shelton bowed his head. "I guess not much. But soon, I imagine, I'll lose everything. But for me, loss isn't necessarily a bad thing. Loss means you get to start over."

Moss considered this and nodded. He heard Shelton step away from him and leave the cathedral. When the young boy was gone, Moss fixed his eyes on the front of the cathedral to see if he felt something—to see if there was someone or something worth praying to. After a short while, Moss stood up and left the pews. When he left the church, he slammed the door behind him.

No one said a word.

V

Moss couldn't listen to the group talk about Discis's politics. His mind was too distracted. All he thought about was Brenna and how he wouldn't get to see her while he was in town. He would have to go another few months at sea without a fresh image of her in his head. He thought about how she wasn't in the church, and how she had abandoned her faithful duties like his mother suggested earlier. Knowing that the love of his life was gone from him, he felt his soul begin to blacken.

As he pretended to listen, Moss twiddled his fingers against the pale wooden table before him. He scratched the crevices on the table and tried to keep his body moving so that he didn't go completely ghost on the rest of the council. After all, he was sitting with the thought leaders and influencers of the world's most powerful northern port. That opportunity rarely presented itself.

Julk's words soon caught his attention, though. Moss's ears perked up.

"Can you repeat that?" Moss asked.

Julk looked across the table at Moss in surprise. "I said the best exit strategy may be to head south while we can. We have the naval ships and the ability to get down to Freezlin in less than a day. If we leave ahead of time, we can find some space on the shore and set up our civilization. That way Kurpo never touches us and never hurts us."

Moss pounded his fist against the table. "There's no way I'm going to stand for Kraill running away in fear!"

Julk was taken back. "I'm sorry you feel that way, Geoffrey. But it is not your decision. You are a guest at this table, nothing more."

Moss shook his head. "The people won't stand for it. Kraill is above that. We're fighters, we're warriors. We don't settle."

Julk chuckled. "Where do you think you are?" she asked. The question caught Moss off-guard. "The Kraill you left behind is not the one you've returned to. You left when Kraillians were willing to fight over a simple plot of land. In the last five years, we've all gained religion. We've all found faith. The youth have traveled to the churches and taken on the lords' guidance. We're not fighters anymore, Moss. And the only way to keep the faith alive—to keep our mission going—is to keep all of us alive and head south while we still can."

Moss couldn't believe what he was hearing. Kraill never had such religious fervor as it did now. It was a nation of fighters, brute warriors who tackled any challenge they faced. They rarely looked to the sky for help, except in the direst circumstances, when their weapons and fists didn't work.

Moss shook his head. He just didn't understand. How had everything changed so fast? How had his world flipped so suddenly? He came home thinking everything was going to be normal—business as usual. And yet, it was all about to change.

"I'm sorry, Geoffrey," Julk said. "But this is our best option."

VI

Moss didn't expect anything significant to happen that night. His day had been so full of heavy moments that he expected the night to be quiet, slow and simple. He thought he could watch the sunset and then drift off to sleep, ready to help his village travel to the south. But life never goes according to plan. Moss knew that from his adventures out at sea. So he shouldn't have been surprised when he couldn't fall asleep.

He tossed and turned on his bed. He tried counting blinkys—one blinky, two blinky, three blinky, four—but that did very little. He felt chills run up his spine when he thought of how dangerous those buggers could be. Moss rolled over on his right side and opened his eyes, staring out of his door at the living room of his former home. Nothing had changed. Funny, he thought. The more life changes, the more it stays the same.

Something burned in the distance and the smoke caught Moss's attention. He sat up straight, his back banging against the back of the couch. He darted over to his clothes and slipped on his gear. He grabbed his olive hat that rested in the corner and tightened it around his head. Before he swung out the door, he checked his mom's room and saw she was fast asleep. He dared not wake her up this late.

Moss scurried outside and his instincts were right—a fire burned on the other side of the village. Large puffs of black smoke soared into the sky. Townsfolk were already on their way over, carrying buckets and pails of water with them. Moss ran around the side of his home and collected a few buckets for himself. He filled them with the dirt below and then jogged off in the direction of the smoke.

But when he got closer to the fire, he saw the gravity of what was happening. The entire front end of the village, including the docks, was ablaze. Smoke rose from the wooden planks and meshed with the sky and sea. Moss threw his buckets onto the fire like the others around him, but it did little to calm the fire. Moss swung himself around and found some more dirt. He threw it on the docks, but nothing happened. This fire was too strong.

"The other side! The other side!"

Moss swung his head around and saw an older villager screaming at the top of his lungs and pointing wildly behind him. Moss poked his head up and that's when he saw something that made his stomach drop and his heart pound—the far side the village and the farms were on fire, too.

"No," Moss let out.

He stomped on the ground and dashed off back to where he had come from. He swerved around villagers who were trying to save the docks and pushed through bystanders as he made his way home. Moss ripped at some standing men and yelled for them to join him, and a few did, but certainly not enough. Too many people were concerned with the front of the village.

Moss skidded in his steps as he arrived at his home. But the home was different than he remembered. It was engorged by fiery embers—swallowed by dragon's spit. The fire crackled and roared as it burned down the wooden walls. He heard pops and dings as the fire burned away at everything inside.

Then he heard a scream from inside. It was his mother's voice.

Moss darted forward toward his house, ripping himself free from the men who tugged and told him to stay behind. He shouldered his way past the front door and found himself inside his village home, surrounded by intimidating flames. Sweat poured from his forehead and smoke clogged his lungs. He coughed out whatever ash he could as he searched for a way further in.

"I'm coming, Mom! I'm coming!"

Moss threw a piece of wood toward the flames and watched it get eaten up. He swerved around and found another scrap to toss at the flames. The fire gobbled that up, too. Moss could barely see over the flames in front of him. His breathing was slowing and his skin was dripping with sweat. He searched for a sight of his mother, but came up empty handed.

Her screams went quiet.

Moss didn't have time to keep looking. Hands ripped him away from the home and threw him to the ground. His face was slapped with dirt. He dug his hands into the ground below and shouted toward his mom, hoping something would change. But everything stayed the same. Wood panels from the top fell and crushed the home below. The fire roared and ate away his home. Soon all Moss could see were flames. His home, mother, and childhood memories gone.

VII

When Moss returned to the center of the village, men and women alike tried to put out the flames, but it was to no avail. He watched as buildings collapsed and burned to ashes. He heard families cry out in sorrow as their children and friends were burned alive. Moss tossed whatever water and dirt he could find onto the fires, but nothing changed in the slightest. The fire continued to rage through the village, cutting it up and burning it down.

As he tried his best to put out a fire on the docks, he was slapped on the back of the shoulder. Moss swerved around and found Craven waiting for him, his face blackened by the smoke and ash.

"Thank the gods," Moss said, hugging his friend. "You're still alive."

Craven smirked. "As are you."

"Any idea who did this?"

Craven shook his head. "Whoever it was, they did it without us knowing. The watchmen just got to the tower and said they didn't see anyone coming our way. Whoever did this did it from within."

Moss didn't have the time necessary to fully comprehend that. "What's being done?" he asked.

Craven pointed out toward the sea. "A group of us started loading women and children onto some of the boats. A few groups have already left and are headed south. We saved a few of the relics we had, but not enough."

Moss surveyed the sea and noticed the near-invisible ships slithering across the midnight blue water. He nodded at Craven. "Well, keep it going. Get everyone out of here."

Moss went to leave, but Craven tugged on his arm. "Where are you going?"

"Someone's got to warn the watchmen. My sister and brother are both there. I'll head out that way."

Craven nodded and extended his hand. "See you again soon, old friend."

Moss took Craven's hand and shook it. "Indeed you will. Until then."

"Until then."

Craven darted off toward the sea and Moss ran off toward the green plains.

VIII

The path to the watchtowers was quiet. A few animals rustled in the trees around him, and shouts from those fighting the fires back at Kraill pierced the silence. But otherwise everything was still, eerie and quiet. Moss wiped his head clean of all the sweat and ash that had masked his face. He did his best to clean his eyes of the salty sweat, but he knew some was still in there to burn away his eyes. He figured it was the least of his problems.

Moss saw a turn up ahead and knew he was close to the tower. Once around the corner, he would find the two watchtowers and be able to warn the watchmen that the village had been attacked. He may even get some insight as to how the village was attacked without anyone knowing. He paused before the turn and brushed himself to hide any damage. He adjusted his pants and shirt and made himself comfortable. After a slow, deep breath, Moss swung around the corner.

Only the towers were different than he remembered. They weren't pitch-black with ladders and scopes at the top. These were orange, yellow and red, and they screamed at him. They reeked of smoke and ash. Moss could taste the roasting human flesh in the air when he got near. He heard pops and cracks and snaps as he got closer.

He was too late.

Moss dropped to his knees and dug his fingers in the sand. He let the earth run through his fingers and back to the ground. He looked up at the sky and shouted at the top of his lungs. He screamed until his voice cracked. He swallowed and screamed again, this time with more of a punch.

His head fell and he collapsed to the ground, sobbing. Tears moved past his sweat and ash and mixed with the ground below. He cried out for answers, but none came. He cried out for reason, but there was none to see.

And then a boot appeared before his eyes.

Moss looked up. Standing there, his face consumed with an evil grin and blood-red eyes, was Shelton, still dressed in his black cloak.

"Shelton?" Moss uttered.

Shelton smiled. "I told you I would one day know what loss is like."

Moss pushed himself off the ground and sat back in the sand. He searched Shelton's face for answers but didn't find any. Instead, he shot him a desperate look.

"Why?"

Shelton lowered himself to Moss's level. He gripped Moss's chin and smiled at him. "Because Kraill's time was up, Moss. It's Kurpo's time to rule. It's the Creator's time to rule."

Moss didn't understand.

And he didn't have time to. Shelton stepped two paces back and then slammed his boot into Moss's abdomen. The pirate fell over on his side and coughed up smoke and blood. He felt another kick in the stomach and grunted. He looked up and saw Shelton there, eyeing him with hatred.

"I'm not going to kill you. Well, not tonight at least," Shelton said. "But you better disappear, Moss. Forever."

Moss once again searched Shelton's face for answers. He was left empty-handed again. So he nodded. "Yessir."

"Good boy, Moss. Good boy."

Moss watched Shelton walk past the towers and toward the rest of the north. He coughed some ash and blood out of his lungs. He took a deep breath to calm his nerves. But it didn't work. His mind raced and his body more. Anger filled his veins. Sadness flooded his eyes. Too many emotions all at once.

He found his ways to his knees and looked at the burning towers. He wept and cried, cried and wept. He laughed and giggled, giggled and laughed. He wept, cried, laughed and giggled. He found a new level of hysteria. He was finally at his breaking point.

He fell to the ground and into the dark.

CHAPTER 23

I

Kurpo's watch ticked away and signaled that the Time-X-Ball was about to explode. He hurried to his window near his desk and put his arm out. With all his power channeling to his hand, he pulled the ball back to him.

And like he planned, the Time-X-Ball soared into his hand. Everything worked just like he wanted it to. He cupped the ball and rolled it in his palms. He smiled, knowing that it had done its job.

Kurpo, still holding the ball, walked over to the door in the back of the room. He ripped it open—a piercing white light temporarily blinding him—and threw the ball inside.

When he had disposed of the ball, he turned back to his window and looked out at the world beyond.

"Well, now that they're going to tear themselves apart, I can finally unleash the final blow."

CHAPTER 24

I

The snow stopped falling, and whatever snow was on the ground melted away. The group couldn't sleep that night. Moss's nightmarish words painted a vivid picture that scared them in their sleep. But things were now out in the open, and no member of the group needed to hide anything from each other. That was the silver lining.

Shelton was the first one to wake up. He found himself by the fire and sheepishly watched his friends wake up. He hid from them for now by the trees, unsure of how Moss's words had painted him. He wasn't sure if he would be as trusted as he had been before. He reckoned he wasn't.

While cooking breakfast, Moss spoke to the group. "I don't want my memory to change anything about how you all feel about Shelton."

Shelton looked at the group with puppy-dog eyes as he emerged from the forest. "That's not necessary, Moss. I know what I did."

Moss waved his hand. "Without that moment, we wouldn't be where we are now. Loss gave me the chance to start over."

Shelton nodded. "Well, thank you. And I hope you can all forgive me in time."

No one said a word.

Shelton cocked his head to the left. He heard something. No—felt something.

"I feel something bad is going to happen, something in the air is telling me that we should move on." He listened again. His eyes perked up. "Now! Now. We need to move."

They started to pack.

II

"Get out of the way!" Shelton yelled.

Jake turned his head, drenched from the snow, and saw a flaming ball of fire coming toward him and the rest of the group. Jake dove into the mud next to Kevin and Trevor, who were already sprawled on the ground. Moss and Shelton stood tall as the flaming ball landed between them. Shelton ran to the ball and inspected it. The fire burned and crackled.

"Just what I thought," Shelton began. He cooled down the flaming ball by shooting a line of ice from his fingers. "The Creator is using his artillery powers to attack us. We need to be more careful. Or else—"

Shelton was cut off as another flaming ball crashed next to him.

Shelton turned his head back toward the sky and saw hundreds of red dots falling toward them. With a bit of anger, Shelton screamed to the group to run.

And so they did. They dipped and dodged away from the balls, which fell and shook the ground. They ran and stopped when the fire got to close. Run, stop. Run, stop. The fire came too fast.

The ground shook with each ball that hit the ground. Everyone was off balance. Fire burned the edges of their shirts. Moss felt more and more burns as the fireballs continue to soar down. It wasn't enough to hurt him, but he knew his skin was burned. Even though the snow was falling, the fireballs seemed to be protected by some type of force field. They remained untouched by the snow.

Shelton stopped. "Run! Guys, run! I'll try and stop them!"

"We won't leave you!" Jake yelled.

Shelton didn't care what the group did. He raised his arm and opened his palm, revealing a lime green ball of energy made of zigzagging lines. He closed his eyes and focused his magic in his hand. The green ball doubled in size. When it was large enough to his liking, Shelton opened his eyes and turned back toward the falling balls of fire. He threw the green ball up into the air. All the fireballs disappeared.

But it didn't stay that way.

The number of fireballs that came soaring down only increased. Some ripped through Shelton's green energy and crashed beside him. He kept his focus on the falling fireballs, hoping to stop them. He made his green ball bigger. But as the green ball got bigger, the more balls fell.

More.

And more.

And more and more and more and more and more.

"Shelton! Stop!" Jake yelled. He tried to run off to Shelton, but Moss grabbed Jake to hold him back. More fireballs crashed beside Jake and Moss, so they hunkered down on the grass to avoid the fire.

Shelton felt sweat drop from his temples. He pushed the green energy up more, hoping to stop the fireballs. But it wasn't enough. More fireballs kept falling and ripping through his green ball of energy.

"I can't!"

THE PEN

The fireballs destroyed his green ball of energy. Shelton was stuck in a field of fireballs. He kept shooting some off one by one with his gumdrop energy balls. But it wasn't enough. The fireballs increased in size and number. From the corner, he heard Jake scream his name as he dodged one

"Shelton!"

The evil force came back. The sky was gone—it was merely a sea of fire. There was no space in between any of the fireballs. Fire rained on him. Shelton's face glowed a crimson red as he yelled one last time.

With all the power in him, Shelton sent out all the energy he had. A massive explosion came from his body, soaring up into the sky of fire. Many of the fireballs disappeared, but the others roared through. Shelton's burst of energy raced through the air. Sweat poured from his face—he was mad and powerful with energy. He yelled once more as he used every single bit of energy he could find and sent it through his body up into the sky. But Shelton weakened. The last blast of energy he gave was not enough.

The fire didn't slow. Shelton had no energy left in him. He turned to the group and made sure they were safe before he succumbed.

"Goodbye, my friends."

The fire buried him.

III

The Pen had stopped burning.

Jake noticed that the second cube had turned to complete blackness. The second stage of Jake's Pen was over. Unlike the first block, this one had been a slow burn.

"Look, Jake, there was nothing you could do," Moss said to Jake that evening by the fire. Jake turned his head and saw Shelton's body, which was wrapped in a cloak, lying on a rock. They had yet to figure out what to do with it.

"You could have let me save him Moss. I could have gotten to him," Jake responded.

"Oh, so now every time someone dies it's my fault!" Moss exclaimed. Jake was about to respond, but Kevin interrupted him.

"Moss, we all know of your and Shelton's grudge. We're not saying you did this, but it kind of seems weird that you wouldn't let Jake try to save him." Kevin sat down next to Jake. The rain had ceased for the moment. "But, nothing matters now. Without Shelton, we're just lost here."

"That's not true," Trevor spoke up. He had been the silent one in the group. "Moss knows his way around here, right?"

Moss sighed. "Yes. But Shelton knew a lot about The Creator, so he knew how to survive."

Trevor, Kevin and Jake all exchanged a look of displeasure. "What are we going to do to his body?" asked Jake, twisting his Pen.

Moss nodded and walked over to Shelton's burned body. "We'll have to burn the rest of him."

And that's exactly what they did. After finishing their evening meals, the group lifted Shelton up and laid him on top of a pile of broken wood and tree bark. The sun was gone and only the stars shone down on them. Moss approached the pile of wood with a torch made from tree branch and rope. He paced over.

Moss unraveled a hood from his cape and dropped it over his head. Jake, Kevin and Trevor took some cloth, made some hoods, and donned them. They all stared at the pile of wood as Moss took the tip of the torch and let it rest on Shelton's leg.

The fire burned through Shelton's body. Jake caught one last glimpse of Shelton's face before the flames grew and covered Shelton's entire self, turning him into ash.

Trevor, Kevin and Jake left the scene moments later, only so they didn't have to watch Shelton's body burn. They moved back to the site of their gear and waited for Moss.

Moss didn't take his eyes off the fire. He watched Shelton's body become ash, and he watched the smoke rise. Moss thought about whether or not he could have saved Shelton. He supposed the boys were right—if he had let Jake go, maybe Shelton's life would have been spared.

What if Jake was right? What if we could have saved you? What if we could have been able to keep you from dying? We need you Shelton. We need you here, and now . . .

IV

Moss watched the fire burn until it was gone. Jake, Trevor, and Kevin had fallen asleep. But Moss did not care. He wanted to watch and reflect on Shelton's death. He needed to think things through, and try to see what went wrong.

Moss knew what had happened and why Shelton had paid the ultimate price. It wasn't because he was trying to help or because Moss didn't allow Jake to save him. It was for another reason.

It was because of the Orb that floated in his knapsack.

But he could right his wrong.

Moss walked over to his gear and picked up his knapsack. He opened it and saw that everything was as he left it. He threw it over his shoulder and walked over to the fire that was burning only a little. He touched the wood.

"I give you my blessing, Shelton. And now, I shall avenge your death until I see you again. Until then."

Moss tapped the wood. He looked back at Jake, Trevor, and Kevin.

He thought about waking them, and telling them what he was going to do. But instead, he walked away.

Moss left the fire and moved toward the large plains that awaited him. He knew what he had to do, and where he had to do it. The sun was just about to rise. He turned his head and looked back to the distance. He saw a thin line of black smoke and knew the boys would wake up soon. Moss smiled and kept moving.

Now, after Shelton's death and leaving Richard behind, Moss felt that he needed to make it up to the group. He was taking things into his own hands. He knew the group could survive without him. He had trained them well.

Moss was going to redeem his faults. When the sun was fully up, Moss could only wonder what the group was thinking. He looked back one last time. He didn't see anyone running after him. He smiled and turned to the sky, where he saw a thick purple cloud of an upcoming storm.

Moss thought about saying something, but instead he marched forward alone to avenge Shelton's death.

V

The Creator stood with confidence in his dark black room, where only a pair of torches kept the light. He left the room and traveled down a corridor of his Palace. He went inside a door. In this new room, there were no lights or torches, only darkness. Kurpo laughed and continued forward until he stopped and grinned.

Out from the air came a red spirit. Though a spirit, his Master was hooded, his eyes hidden but his smile showing. The Master laughed and stood next to Kurpo, who raised his face in pride. They both looked forward. Kurpo made the room visible with a flick of his fingers. Random fireballs floated in the air, making enough light for them to see. He turned to the spirit.

"Master, I destroyed the Time-X-Ball," Kurpo said.

The spirit nodded. "Good. And as for the group?"

Kurpo smirked. "Shelton has died."

The spirit smirked too. "Good. And what next?"

Kurpo laughed again. Master Kallanon smiled. They turned their heads forward and watched a wooden table rise up, creaking as it did so. When the wooden table was level with their eyes, Master Kallanon saw something he didn't expect—a human body locked by unbreakable chains made from the magical powers of the ancient civilizations long ago.

"Yes," the Master's spirit said. "You have done well, Kurpo."

Little did Kurpo know that this was the Master's plan all along.

PART III: THE HUT

CHAPTER 25

I

Grant Revel made the next dash on the block of wood.

Today was the third day, and things had gotten worse. Two men who desired to lead everybody out of the darkness had decided to run an election against each other. It had come to that. This leadership title was so important to these two that they, above all else that could be accomplished, had decided to hold an election. Thomas and Grant had already made the decision—funnily enough, they made it together without knowing it—that they were staying here. It was as if they were permanently here, and they weren't leaving.

Richelle felt that way. She believed that Thomas and Grant, both two arrogant, testosterone-filled men, had made an assumption that the group would not be home in five days and that they needed someone to lead them. Sure, the two moons seemed a bit strange, but Richelle's theory was that the group was lost somewhere in a Canadian forest, mainly because the bus was heading for Toronto. It seemed feasible to her that the bus had gone off a road and into the woods.

But maybe Grant and Thomas were right. Maybe they were stuck there—wherever there was.

"No way," said Chris, as he puffed out some cigarette smoke. He took another drag and looked over at Richelle. "There's no way we're in Canada. If you look at the trees, they're nothing like I've ever seen. There's no pine trees, no oak, no maple, no nothing. These trees . . . aren't even real trees. These trees are . . . I can't even tell you," he continued. He walked over to the nearest tree and felt the trunk. "Believe me, I know trees."

"Then where do you think we are?" asked Richelle, looking for an opinion and hope.

"We're either in some drugged-up dream state, or this is one big reality show," Chris said, before taking another drag.

"What about . . ." Richelle stopped herself. Chris turned to her.

"What?"

"What about, or what if, we're not on Earth?" Richelle asked.

"I was thinking that, but it doesn't seem like that's possible," he said.

"Chris, seriously. I remember a few summers back there was this thing going on in California or Arkansas or Arizona, somewhere like that. This guy walked right into his closet and was gone. Missing. Couldn't find him," she said. "Same thing happened in Florida about a year ago, if I'm not mistaken."

"Richelle, I heard the exact same story. That guy probably went into his closet, jumped into a secret passage, ran out the front door, and is probably in Omaha as we speak," he retaliated, taking a final drag, for his cigarette had become scarce in size.

"No, but Chris, the same thing happened a little while later. These teenagers were skateboarding on a highway and vanished—"

"By vanished you mean they jumped off the side of the road, rolled down a hill, went to Denny's, and then hopped on a train to Houston," he interrupted.

"No! One of the teen's cousins witnessed the event. He claims he saw his cousin vanish," Richelle said.

"He probably was hopped up on bath salts or something. These teens will do whatever they can get their hands on," Chris said again, not believing there was one ounce of truth in Richelle's tale.

"But Chris, that kid who witnessed it, he disappeared, too. Him and his friend," she spoke.

"Still not believing it, Richelle. He could have done the same thing," Chris said.

"The kid that witnessed it brought a friend to another kid's house. Then, something happened at that house. When the mother of the house went to see what happened, she found her son's girlfriend . . . dead. The vanishing kid's friend was her son," Richelle preached.

Grant, who was walking over to Richelle and Chris, spoke out. "Ahh, you're talkin' about Jake Serent and his buddies?"

"You've heard about this?" Richelle asked.

"Yep," Grant said with a nod. He leaned against one of the nearby trees and stuffed his hands in his pocket. "I heard all about it before I left. Something about there was a triple murder homicide thing, I dunno. I heard that this kid Kevin, his friend, and two other boys went missing. I guess this Jake kid was always living in the shadow of his cousin, so people think that he killed them all in a rage. Something like that. Made a lot of sense to me, honestly."

"Were you there? I mean, in South Hills?" Richelle asked.

Grant nodded. "Sure was. It turned the town upside down. Five young kids disappeared and another one is murdered? Made headlines for a year. No one knows anything about where they went."

"And you believe they're here? In this forest?" asked Chris, throwing his cigarette butt into the ground and then stepping on it.

"I believe," Richelle said, "there's a lot more than a forest."

II

"The hut," Jordan repeated.

"He's delirious," said Jupiter.

Brent, who was standing beside her, put his arm around her shoulders. "It'll be all right. He'll be fine," he said, rubbing her shoulder.

"What do you know about being fine? You were a Hollywood star when you were like, eight. And now look at you. Still cute, but not even Bollywood material," she said.

"Well, actually, I'm doing a movie—or was going to do a movie, I guess now—called *hQ: The Legend of Hommie Q*, which had potential to be a Collywood movie, thank you very much," Brent boasted.

"Is that the movie with the 13-year-old kid that raps as 'hQ,' then suddenly realizes that he can't rap, so his alias 'hQ' dies or something, and then later comes back a year and a half later as hQ2?" she asked. Brent nodded, ashamed. "Oh my God! Are you playing hQ?!"

"No," he said.

"Oh, are you playing K-Rich, the pyrotechnic friend who raps with harsher words?" she asked.

"Nope, I'm playing Add-Rap, the kid who tries to steal other kids' music and pretends to have talent," he said.

"Oh, sounds like a perfect role for you, especially for someone who was a child star," she said.

"Yeah," Brent answered, trying to avoid the hatred he felt of not being a star anymore.

"I loved your movies as a kid. Your *It's Fun in the Sun* film was great! You had abs like Arnold!" she exclaimed.

"That wasn't a movie of mine."

"Oh right, you were in *It's Fun to Run: Fun in the Sun 2*!" she remembered, as Brent nodded.

"Yep, that was me," he said. "I played 'Zim,' the blonde-haired Jew who said 'Bless you' all the time," he continued. Jupiter laughed. "All right, well, I'm gonna go see how April is. It was nice talking to you . . . Jennifer, right?"

"It's Jupiter," she responded.

"Right, sorry. All right, later," he said. Brent got up and walked across the open circle and over to April.

Jupiter stayed with Jordan. Ever since the bus had crashed, Jupiter felt obligated to be with the driver. She was sitting behind him that entire trip, and the two of them engaged in conversation during the bus ride. But she had fallen asleep, and woke up to see Jordan lying on the ground, bleeding. But it seemed like a lifetime ago since that had happened. And it also seemed like a lifetime before they would move past it.

"Hut. Hut. Hut. Hut," uttered Jordan, still out from the paralysis. "The hut, the hut, the hut, the hut, the hut," he uttered again. Jupiter sat beside the driver, brushing his sweaty hair with her hand. "No. No hut. No hut," he uttered more.

"How's he doing?" Grant asked, walking over from where Chris and Richelle sat. They had relocated their camp to the clearing near the bus. It helped block the sun.

"Still delirious. He's been saying strange things," Jupiter said.

"Like what?"

"Just a lot of weird stuff. The hut, hut, don't go, don't go. Weird stuff."

Grant looked at Jupiter and a light bulb went on his head. He walked over to where he had left the block with the dashes and picked it up with his right hand. He glanced down at it, seeing the three red marks already made with Jordan's blood. Grant walked back to Jupiter and handed it to her. After waiting a moment, Jupiter accepted the block of wood, wondering why she was being handed this. Grant reached into his pocket and pulled out the pen he had written with. He gave it to Jupiter.

"You deserve to be in charge with the block. I want you to make the dashes on the front, and write everything Jordan says on the back. Can you do that?" Grant asked. He didn't know if he could trust this girl or not.

"Yeah, but what'll that do?"

"It's just to keep me informed about what's going through his head. And that can be good news for his future."

III

Nightfall came. The two moons took center stage for the night. The stars hung in the sky. The late-night fire crackled and popped as the group sat around it, their hands out near the fire to gain warmth. Chris and Grant already had their cigarettes lit. Everyone in the group was silent, including Jordan, who had stopped muttering for the night.

Something struck Chris. Where was Richelle? He remembered seeing her around the camp this morning, but now couldn't see her here at the fire. He looked around at the trees, but couldn't see anything through the darkness. He turned to Thomas.

"Where's Richelle, man?" he asked.

"Not sure," Thomas shrugged before taking another drag. "Grant? You know where Richelle is?"

"Hmm, dunno scout," Grant said. He took the butt of his cigarette and tossed it into the flames.

"I'm gonna go look for her," Chris said, as he stood up.

He walked toward the trees, which were not that far away from the fire, so it wasn't like he was going to be going off into the unknown. When he was at the trees, he heard someone crying in the forest. After waiting a moment and listening, Chris realized it was Richelle.

He entered the forest and followed the weeping sounds, creeping past a tree and then another. And a little ahead of him he saw Richelle, sitting on a log with her head in her hands. Tears puddled in her palms.

"Hey," Chris said, getting over to her. Richelle wiped a tear from her eye.

"He–hey," she spoke.

"What's wrong?" Chris said, sitting down on the log next to her.

"It's what Grant said today. I mean, what if we aren't really just lost in a forest? What if we're millions of miles away from home, huh?" She wept. "I mean, things were just going to turn around for me, and now I'm here," she cried.

"Look," Chris said, putting his arm around her shoulder. He had the faintest idea of her history, but could tell it was the right thing to do. "It's going to be OK. We're going to get out of here fine. I promise."

Richelle glanced up at Chris and stared into his eyes. Those wonderful blue eyes.

Richelle found her lips attached to Chris's, and the two shared another kiss on the log. The kisses came faster as time went on.

As the kissing continued, Chris took of his shirt, as did Richelle.

They moved to the ground below, their lips still locked.

As the kissing kept increasing, the night went on.

They kept kissing all the way until morning.

IV

The mist of the early morning filtered throughout the forest area with a gray hue. A haze hung above everyone's sleeping heads. The grass was covered with dew. It was one of the mornings that smelled of a fresh rain, with an overcast sky. After what had happened yesterday, as well as the past few days, everyone needed a good rest. Everyone needed to sleep, and refuel themselves for the things to come. The group knew that the election was coming up, but they did not know of the trouble ahead.

Deep within the forest, where there was a small clearing, Richelle and Chris lay on the ground, both half naked. They slept.

Richelle's eyes opened soon enough, and at first she did not know where she was. Her eyes glanced around, trying to find where she was. She spotted Chris's arm, which was wrapped around her waist. Richelle scurried out of Chris's hold on her. Chris woke up from her move. When Richelle arose, she adjusted her clothes so they weren't as ruffled. Chris got up quickly too.

"Hey, what's wrong?" Chris asked.

"Nothing, it's just, I don't know if that was a great idea," Richelle spoke. She began walking away from Chris, heading back toward the clearing.

"Hey, wait," Chris said, as he caught up to Richelle and stood in front of her. "Last night, you were upset about what Grant said about not being lost in a forest in Canada or something like that, so when I found you crying, we got close. That's it. We don't have to make it a big deal," he said. "We kissed, and that's it. Nothing more, no harm done.

There was a rumbling in the bushes behind them. Richelle and Chris both turned around, hearing the bushes and weeds swaying back and forth. As they looked, they saw a tip of someone's head, and smoke coming from that person as well. It took a second for them both to realize that Grant was coming from the bushes.

Grant came out from the great sea of green plants, wearing a stained white T-shirt along with dirty jeans. He had a cigarette in his mouth.

"I thought you finished all the cigarettes?" Chris asked, trying to avoid a possible awkward situation.

"I saved one for myself, man. I mean, sometimes you need to do what's best for yourself, ya know?" Grant asked, as Chris and Richelle nodded their heads simultaneously. "Speaking of doing things," Richelle and Chris's faces turned to stone, "I overheard your little conversation about your night," Grant said.

"Grant," began Richelle, but he interrupted her.

"Look Richelle, I'm not gonna reveal your little secret to anyone, believe me," said Grant, taking a puff of his cigarette.

"Thanks," she said, but her eyes did not meet his.

"No problem," Grant said. He looked at Chris with scornful eyes. "Chris, you're gonna read the questions for the debate later today then?"

"Yeah man, sure," he responded.

"Good," Grant said. He took one last puff of his cigarette and then blew it out. The cigarette was nearly gone, except for the butt at the end. "Well," Grant started, staring at the remaining piece of the cigarette. "Good luck to me."

Grant tossed the cigarette to the ground and stepped on it. He rotated his foot, then took his foot off of the butt, looked down, and saw nothing but burned and crumbed pieces of tobacco.

V

Grant nodded at Richelle and Chris and gave them that mysterious smirk—the smirk that had been used by Grant many times. He walked back toward the clearing of the forest, where everyone was resting. He heard snoring from the group.

Grant stormed over to Thomas, who was lying on his stomach with his head on a great wad of grass. He grabbed a hold of the collar of Thomas's shirt and, with all his strength, lifted him up. Thomas woke up, but couldn't react when he was sent right back down to the ground. Grant hit him right in the nose with his fist. Thomas's face grew soft and tears flooded his eyes.

The chain-smoker didn't stop. Grant walked right up to Thomas and kicked him in the gut. Brent awoke from the disturbing noise. When he saw what was happening, Brent dashed over to the scene and pried Grant off Thomas, but Grant answered that with an elbow that sent Brent back about five feet. When Brent hit the ground, Jupiter and April awoke. They saw Grant's knuckles bleeding, just like Thomas's face.

Richelle and Chris came from the forest. When their eyes spotted what was going on, they didn't know how to react. Chris ran over to Grant. Unlike Brent, Chris found a way to rip Grant off of Thomas.

"What the hell are you doing?" yelled Chris, as he shoved Grant again.

"I'm just settling this," Grant answered back, as he gave Chris an even harder shove.

Chris's eyes widened as he shoved Grant once more. Grant had enough at this point. With all the power that he still had, he slugged Chris right in the jaw.

Chris went stumbling back against a tree. Richelle ran over to check on him.

"What the hell is your problem?" Richelle asked, as she began trying to see if Chris was bleeding or not.

"My problem is none of your damn business," Grant said. Thomas, who was on the ground, coughed up some blood. Somehow, he stood.

"Douchebag," Thomas said, as he coughed up one last spurt of blood.

"You're such an ass!" Richelle yelled at Grant.

"Yeah? Why don't you tell everyone about your little hookup last night?" Grant yelled.

Jupiter, April, and Brent, all said nothing, for they had nothing to say. Brent decided to speak up.

"What do you mean?" Brent asked.

"Lil' Richelle here—" began Grant.

"Don't!" yelled Richelle.

"Hooked up with Chris. Fun stuff," Grant said, staring only at Richelle with that mysterious smirk of his. Richelle's face turned red from embarrassment and anger at Grant.

"You are a real bastard, you know that?" Richelle asked, as she walked off. She stormed off toward the forest. Everyone else stayed silent.

VI

"All right," started Chris, who currently had a cigarette in his mouth. He had found it near where Grant had slept and decided to take it. Chris blew some smoke from his cigarette and then put it back in his mouth. "Aw pust queston w' be, if you're chusen leadah, den—oh hell wit it." Chris ripped the cigarette out of his mouth, and tossed it away. "Okay, first question is 'where do you think we are?' Now, Grant, you drew the short straw in this. So Thomas, proceed."

"Thank you Chris," Thomas began, standing on the left side of Chris. "Now let me start by saying that the actions of Grant earlier today have left me broken and battered," Thomas took a moment to show off his bruises from Grant's attack earlier. "He has assaulted me, insulted me, belittled all of you, and he should not be leader.

"But Chris, since you've asked such an outstanding question, I'll answer it. Yes people, stop all the talk. Stop all the rumors. We are in Canada. Yes, people, Canada. All of us were heading up to Toronto to catch a flight to you know where, and we must have gotten lost, which ultimately led us to here. Now you may be wondering why the hell would Canada have two moons? 'Cause they're damn Canadian! That's why!"

Everyone exploded with laughter, which was Thomas's plan all along. He didn't know why there were two moons, and felt that comedy was the only way out of it. Grant was the only one to roll his eyes, as everyone else laughed.

"Grant, care to respond in a non-violent way?" Chris asked. Grant waited for the laughter to die down before he spoke.

"Umm . . ." Grant said, looking around at everyone, and knowing he was losing this debate already. Grant, still silent, scanned the area around him. He gathered up the courage to speak to the non-caring crowd. "Well, I can't make you laugh like Steve Martin over here—"

"Is he Canadian?" Thomas asked. Everyone yet again burst out into laughing.

"No Thomas, I don't think he is. But wanna know who was? My ex-fiancée," Grant said. The entire group went quiet. "So, if you don't want that black eye to get darker, and the ribs that I didn't break to break, then I suggest you zip your mouth," Grant responded, as everyone's laughter ceased. "Now, we're not in Canada. Canada doesn't have two moons. Period. You all know that. Hell, nowhere in the solar system is like this," Grant said, gaining some interest from the crowd, but not enough. "Quite frankly, we're either in one of two places: (A) we're in another world entirely light years away from Earth, or (B), we're all on another planet.

"Yes, I said it. Another planet."

"A planet? Someone call the men in the white coats," Thomas said, trying to win back the crowd that he had lost to Grant's intriguing answer.

"You heard me, idiot. Now, yeah, it may seem weird and a little bit too sci-fi, but it's got to be true. What other explanations are there?" Granted asked. Everyone began whispering to each other about where they were or what other possibilities there could be. Chris, noticing a small sense of alarm beginning to creep over everybody, asked the next question.

"Uhh, uhh, Thomas, um, when do you plan on going to explore the woods?" Chris asked.

"I say that we go right after I win the election. Yes, that's right. Once I become leader of this group, we will all set out to see what is actually out there," Thomas said. Smiles came across everyone's faces, except for Grant's. They wanted to believe that they were going to go out and find civilization, or a town of some sort, instead of just sitting around.

"Grant, go," Chris said, with no enthusiasm at all.

"I'm not gonna write a fricken book on this, but we leave when Jordan gets better," said Grant.

"That's just stupid," Thomas said.

"Oh, is it? Well, let's do some math, Thomas, shall we? There's a total of seven people currently active. Now, who is the other?" Grant asked.

"Jordan," Thomas replied, not knowing at all where Grant was going with this.

"Correct. Now, that's a total of eight, Tommy-boy. So, what's eight divided by two, again?"

"Four," Thomas replied quickly.

"Very good. That means that once Jordan wakes up, we'll have two groups of four, which improves our survival rate, as well as our discovery rate," Grant finished.

Thomas had no clue what to say. Grant heard people beginning to agree with what he saying, no matter how much they didn't like him.

"All right. So, final question," Chris began. "If you are elected leader, what is one of the highest things on your 'to do' list."

"Well Chris—" Thomas began.

"Sorry, Thomas, Grant goes first in the last round," he said. Thomas nodded anyway, for he knew he was going to win this round anyway.

"Thanks, Chris. See, what I'm gonna do is, and I'm not gonna give you some half-ass answer. I'm gonna give it to ya straight. First, I'm gonna find us food and drink, besides this is awful and cheap beer. I'm also gonna get Jordan well again. And finally, I'm gonna get us outta here," Grant said.

And now, for the first time in the whole debate, Grant had won over the crowd.

"Thomas," Chris said with a nod.

"Well, uh," Thomas started, but he couldn't find any words to continue. "Um..."

Richelle, Brent, Jupiter, and April all began saying something under their breath. The noise grew louder. Soon enough, the sound became loud as the whole group began to chant:

"Grant! Grant! Grant! Grant!"

Grant answered this chant with his winning smile. He turned to Thomas, who looked on in sadness, and shrugged. Thomas, now frustrated, slammed his palm with his fist and then walked away from the campsite.

VII

Night seemed to come quicker here than it had back home. Was this home now? Were they indeed living in their new home? A campfire and a cooler with about only twenty-four more cans of beers? This was pretty much hell for all of them; living in a small clearing in a large forest, no food—aside from silver berries on the ground—and that nostalgic feeling inside all of them that created one big thought that they had all died in the crash and had gone to hell.

Chris put his arm around Richelle's shoulder as they sat on a log. She turned to him, and at first did nothing. She smiled, and turned her attention back toward the crackling flames. The crackle and pops of the flames were so loud that no one could even speak over them, so they sat in silence, like usual.

"So," Brent began. "Tomorrow's the big election, ey?"

"Yep," Grant and Thomas said at nearly the same time. This caused them to glance at each other.

"Hopefully you both win, that way there aren't any more fights," said Jupiter.

"Sorry sweetie, but there will be a winner. No ties," Grant said.

"How do you know?" asked Jupiter.

"Because there are seven of us. There is no way to tie," Thomas said, following up Grant's statement.

"You guys are forgetting someone," Richelle said. Chris turned to her with a cocked eyebrow.

"Who?" Thomas and Grant said together.

"Jordan," Richelle replied.

"Oh, like Mr. Paralysis is gonna suddenly get better in one night and have the ability to choose between Thomas and me?" asked Grant. Richelle seemed insulted.

"You're a doctor, Grant. You of all people should know that there are such things called miracles," Thomas said.

"One, I'm not a doctor yet, and now probably will never be," Grant repeated. "And two, there isn't such a thing called a miracle. People get sick and injured and get better because they do get better. The geek dates the cheerleader because they want to date. The divorced dad is no longer a hazard to the family because he chooses not to be. There's not some greater force acting on the world. We live here, and life is what you make it."

"So you don't believe in God?" Richelle asked.

"I believe in what I can see, and what can be done and proved. If something is impossible, I won't try doing it because it's a wasted effort. If I can't see a tumor even though some guy is describing one, I won't believe him," Grant said. "But even if there is a God, he doesn't have time to sort out our problems. He's given us the choice to make our own decisions. We're in control of what happens to us. He gives us the tools and the patient, we have to do the surgery."

"No wonder they don't want you to be a doctor," Thomas uttered under his breath.

"What'd you say?" Grant asked, hearing Thomas and standing up from his log to face him.

"I said, 'no wonder they don't want you to be a doctor.' You're rude, lethargic, and disrespectful of human life," Thomas explained, now standing up to meet Grant.

"I'll give you a black eye over your damn body if you don't shut the hell up," Grant said.

"I thought you don't believe in miracles?" Thomas spoke, fueling Grant with some fire.

"You son of a—"

"AHH!"

Grant, Thomas, and the rest of the group all swerved their heads in Jordan's direction. They had heard him yell. Grant ran over to Jordan's body, wondering why Jordan had just had that sudden outburst. Grant dropped to his knees and examined the bus driver.

"What's wrong?" Richelle asked, as the rest of the group came over to see.

"I don't know."

"You don't know? How can you not know?" Thomas exclaimed.

"I DON'T KNOW!"

There was silence. The pressure of everyone being on his back and wanting answers from him had finally gotten to him. Here were a group of complete strangers telling Grant what to do and what he should know. Yet Grant had only known these people for four days. This certainly was enough to drive a guy off the edge.

Jordan was still crying in pain. Grant searched his body for answers.

"Oh my God," Grant said as he began to feel Jordan's arm. He began to press on it, right where there was a big, large, bruise. As he did, Jordan yelped pain.

"What? What?" asked many in the crowd.

"He's waking up," Grant said. Everyone was glancing at each other. "All right, I need everyone to back away. I'm gonna try and revive his paralysis in the legs," Grant said.

"The legs?" someone yelled.

"Yes, the legs," Grant said, sweat dropping from his forehead. "He's only paralyzed in his legs now, which means that if I can make his body try and fix his legs, then they will be non-paralyzed. It's a long shot, but I might as well try. It ain't a miracle or impossible, but it is a long shot. So, everyone back away," Grant said.

Everyone followed Grant's instructions and backed far away from Jordan. Grant walked over to the block of wood with the dashes on it, then walked back to Jordan and held up the block.

"This is gonna hurt."

CHAPTER 26

I

Jake relaxed with his legs up on a boulder that was drenched from the melted snow. He had been sitting there for an hour. His backside was wet and damp. His palm rested on his chin, his arm on his knee. He thought about what was going on. Moss had left them, high and dry—well, maybe not so dry—without a clue of where to go next. Jake shook his head and touched The Pen. He felt its sharp tip and soft cubes. But no matter what he did, he couldn't get his mind off of things. The sun was setting, glowing a deep purple with a mix of a bright yellow. Jake found the sky and remembered the good times he used to have looking out at sunsets. He would sit with his mother outside on the porch and just watch the sunset. But now the sunset was his alone.

His best friend and cousin, Kevin Keys, wasn't too far away, sitting in the damp grass. He laid back on damp grass among bits of leftover snow, with his knees up and his face buried beneath them. Everything was dirty. His once spiked hair had grown out now and was starting to wave in the back. He raised his head for a moment and looked at Jake, who wouldn't say a word.

Trevor McGaven leaned back against a tree with his hands folded. His black hair covered his face. He brushed it away with the flick of his head. You couldn't see his deep green eyes anymore, only the top of his bottom lip. Trevor punched the tree behind him, which made Kevin turn his head to look at his friend. Trevor bent his head and spat at the ground before looking up again. He was madder than he had ever been—even more so than when his father decided to take him away from Tampa Bay.

Rain picked up again that night. The wind made the rain spin and swirl through the air. Thunder and lightning joined the party. When they awoke the next morning, Jake, Kevin and Trevor saw their campsite had become a major puddle.

Jake grabbed what remained of his Geo-skin pack and slid it on his shoulders. He slapped some mud off his pants and turned his head to see Kevin sitting on a soggy log and Trevor leaning back against a tree. Trevor walked a bit closer to Jake, who was ready for a fight, but Kevin stepped between the two and held off Trevor by putting his muscled arm in front of him. Trevor grinned.

"Gonna lead us outta here, Holder?" Trevor smirked.

Jake looked at the ground and raised his head.

"Look, I suggest we move on. It's been two days since we've been on our own. No food, no water, nothing. Maybe if we move, we'll find some more people, or a civilization maybe. I mean, we can't be the only people left here," Jake said.

"Jake, look around you. We're the only ones left. And don't you remember? The Creator drove everyone south. We're alone," Kevin responded. He let go of Trevor, who smiled again.

"Moss isn't dead, guys. He isn't dead," Jake insisted. Kevin walked a bit closer to Jake and tried to reason with his cousin and best friend.

"Jake, we haven't seen him since we burned Shelton's body. He's nowhere around here. Face it. He's—"

"Where is he? Huh, Jake? Where's your precious Moss? Huh? Where the hell is he? Face facts, Jake. Something or someone killed him. It's that easy. That old bag had it coming, and don't you dare disagree, Jake," Trevor yelled. The rain picked up. "We're the only ones left! Only us! No one else around, Jake! We're all that's left!"

"No!" Jake yelled through the rain. He stared into Trevor's eyes, which were still covered by hair.

Trevor smiled, having unwired Jake.

The sky swirled into a dark charcoal. A deep and long thunder boomed as rain dropped from the dark sky. Regular doses of electric lightning bolts flashed in front of Jake. He jumped back in fright. Trevor laughed. The thunder and lightning flashed at the same time right behind him. Kevin stepped in between the two and led them forward.

They decided to move on and find another location for their camp. Jake walked side by side with Kevin, and they weren't looking back for Trevor, who gritted his teeth behind them. Soon enough, the trio found that the ground around them was nothing but soaked mud. It was squishy and deep. Jake was going to say something to Kevin, but then there was a light crackle of lightning that led to a deep and powerful roll of thunder.

"Jake," Kevin began. He could barely see Jake through the heavy rain, so he began shouting. "Jake, we need to find shelter!"

Jake turned around and walked closer to Kevin. "Look around you,

Kevin. Nothing but grass for miles to come! We're stuck here!" He turned back around, holding on to the straps of his pack. He started moving forward again. His white shoes had turned a deep brown from the mud, and browner they would get, for there was nowhere to rest.

About a mile later, the rain ceased. The thunder and lightning also stopped, but the furious wind had kept up and increased in speed. When the wind stopped for a brief second, they ran until it picked up again.

And then, at one point, when the wind was stronger, Jake got shoved down to the ground. Kevin fell to his knees and Trevor fell on his back. They all turned, breathing heavily.

"I can't. I can't . . . do it . . ." Jake spoke.

"What are we gonna do, Jake?" Kevin said, sucking air after every word. "There's . . . There's nowhere to go . . . we're stranded in the middle of nowhere. No food . . . no shelter . . ." Kevin couldn't finish as the wind picked up.

Through Jake's wet and sweaty face, he dropped tiny tears. All he had done since he arrived here was work to bring The Pen to the Creator's Palace and make Discis a peaceful and harmonious place. But after all Jake had sacrificed, Moss had left the group for reasons that Kevin, Jake, and Trevor didn't understand. They were three Earth boys from an advanced civilization, now trying to outlast a planet that was very unknown to them—fierce storms and beasts, long plains, and a crazy Creator trying to kill them at every turn. The only thing helping them was The Pen, but even that was a pain to Jake.

Jake's emotion got the better of him and he screamed so nothing couldn't hear him.

He slammed his hands down into the damp grass. He pounded the dirt, yelling gibberish as he did so. He punched the ground again and again, feeling the rage swelling through his veins. He gave a giant scream of pain and slammed his fist again into the ground. Kevin and Trevor turned away. They didn't want to see Jake in his moment of rage.

After they couldn't take it anymore, Kevin and Trevor both stood and grabbed Jake by the shoulders. They lifted him up, but the wind pushed them all down. Jake was let loose, and once again punched the ground. Trevor grabbed the left arm and Kevin grabbed the right. Jake gave a cry of "no" and tried breaking from Trevor and Kevin. But the two were too strong for Jake to break free from.

The wind once again swirled and spun, almost knocking them down. But they stood their ground and began pulling Jake away. And then, with one last force of power, the wind pushed Kevin and Trevor off of Jake for the final time.

Jake fell to his knees and then his face. His world went dark.

CHAPTER 27

I

There was a loud bang and Jake woke up with a cotton blanket around him.

He was startled when he awoke, but relaxed when he noticed a crackling log fire in the back corner of the room he was in. He snuck over and knelt before it, moving the hot air to him. He was cold and wet from the rain, but all the more warm from the fire. He rubbed his neck.

There was another loud bang, one just like the sound that he had woken up to. Jake turned his head and saw a man who wore a cloth bandana around his head and a robe to keep him warm, watching him.

The old man, his face wrinkled and pruned, stood before Jake, who didn't move because he knew that this kind old man had given him shelter. The old man pulled out a blue box with a zipper going around the edges. Jake grabbed the box with a delicate touch and unzipped it, saying nothing.

With a sweaty hand, Jake lifted the box's top. When it was fully opened, Jake's eyes widened. He saw, inside the box, lying there perfectly aligned, was The Pen.

"I found this outside my hut," stated the old man.

"How'd you know?" asked Jake, a bit frightened and yet relaxed at the same time.

"Only one comes around holding The Pen, and especially at the Time of Discontinuance. That Pen is the only thing that can save this world," said the old man, as he took a seat in a high-backed wooden chair by the fire.

"Discontinuance?"

The old man nodded. "This is a time when this world shall come to an end, and all its people will be dead."

"The Creator, Kurpo, will do this," said Jake. With all the knowledge

Moss had given him, Jake was easily able to speak in confidence.

"Kurpo has been planning this for so long. Ever since, oh, I'd say, since he received that Pen. When he got it, he tried killing everyone on the entire planet, but failed, as many were able to hide. Since then, many of us have tried to carry this Pen, including myself, so that we can bring Discis out of discontinuance," the old man replied. Jake raised an eyebrow.

"You were a Holder?"

"How do you think you found that Pen? Hmm? You found it back on Earth, didn't you? Well, I was the one who put it there. I found that Pen about three years ago, and when I did, I carried it through the Blizzard of Lexington, the Monsoon of Tyil, and through deserts, plains, hills, and valleys, to get to the Creator's Palace, and you want to know what happened to me? I'll show you!"

The old man stood up and threw off his robe to reveal his back. There was a gaggle of tiny holes that had tiny scars scattered around them. There were bruise marks down his spinal column and whip marks aligned right down his back. The old man put his shirt back.

"The Creator destroyed me," the old man explained. "He whipped me, stoned me, hit me, destroyed me! I was beaten, battered, bloodied, and bruised by him and his Master! And then, when I got my last single ounce of strength, I took that Pen, I tell you, and threw it through a door that stands at the top of the Palace. The Pen crashed through the door and landed in the exact spot you found it! Then, something sent me back here! Something extraordinary.

"You better listen up, Jake Serent," he continued, "you're not the only one to hold that Pen, and you may not be the last."

II

Jake had thought his conversation with the old man had been a dream, but it was not. This was all real. He was really here.

The old man swung open the deerskin door after walking up the metal steps and exited without a word. Jake felt bad that the old man had left, mainly because he knew it was his fault. And somehow, after the argument, the old man had known Jake's name. Jake knew that the old man had answer for the questions Jake needed answers for.

When he gathered enough strength and energy, Jake decided to do two things. First was to find where Kevin and Trevor had gone to, and second was to find out more about the old man.

Jake wrapped the large cloth that the old man had given him around himself and cuddled inside it. He looked around the hut. All he saw were books, stacked high, and the raging fire. Jake made his way to the metal stairs and climbed up them until he opened the deerskin door. As he opened it, a huge gust of wind and rain came flying into Jake's face. He wiped off his wet face and continued right out the door. When he stepped out, he saw a huge rainstorm. Thunder, lightning, rain, and wind.

There was a small cave that was barely noticeable through the sheets of rain. But for some reason Jake had noticed it. It was familiar. Like the song Shelton had been humming days ago. Familiar, and yet unknown.

Jake moved away from the hut and reached it. When he had finished the small journey to the cave, he came to a door. The door handles were golden with models of The Pen, yet painted gold. The Pen handles hung loosely on the doorknobs. Jake grasped each Pen and pulled open the door.

And there, standing in front of Jake, were three men wearing solid black armor on each part of their body.

The old man appeared behind them.

"I'm sorry," Jake started, still looking at the new room he was in, and yet unsure about what he was seeing. It had black walls and barred windows with a tall spiral staircase that ascended for what seemed like miles, carving through the cave.

The old man stared deep into Jake's blue eyes. "No need for an apology, all is forgiven; you have passed my first test, Jake. You came after me. Your instincts called for you to follow me. Here. To the Palace," the old man spoke. He didn't look as old as Jake thought. This man had a wrinkled face, but yet such a youngish feel to him.

"Palace?" asked Jake.

The old man nodded. "Here you will find an exact replica of the Creator's Palace," the old man spoke. Jake's eyes widened.

"How? How did you do this?" asked Jake, with millions of questions rushing through his brain.

"All questions will be answered soon. But first, we must talk about your friends."

The old man touched Jake's shoulder and led him out of the door with The Pen handles. They went back through the cave and into the pouring rainstorm, leaving the men in black armor behind. Jake's red shirt, which he has been wearing since he first arrived in Discis, was soaked and damp and stained. Dirt, snow, rain, fire, and rock had all touched his shirt. Same for his khaki pants, too, which had gone from a light gray to a deep charcoal.

The old man led Jake back to the hut. After opening the deerskin door, they walked down the metal steps. Jake turned his attention to the blue oval box that held The Pen. He held it in his arms. The old man looked at Jake with a curious look and gave one great sigh before he headed for the fire.

"Are Trevor and Kevin . . . ?" Jake couldn't find the words to end the sentence.

The old man coughed. "I sent them on a mission. I'll fill you in on that later. But they're safe, I promise you."

Jake turned to the old man. "All right look, before we continue on with anything, I want to know who you are, where you came from, and how you got The Pen before me."

The old man took a slow walk over to a cloth chair in the corner. He paused before speaking. Jake wondered how long it had been since Sky had been asked these kinds of questions. "My name on Earth was Sky Slade. I used to live in Phoenix, Arizona. Had a beautiful fiancée, Shelby, a job as a corporate financial advisor, and a damn good life. But one day, I was looking around my house for a financial report and stumbled into some type of secret door. Inside, I found this Pen taped to the wall. I ripped it off and suddenly was shoved forward. I came by the cave we were just in. It was built as it is now. And I wasn't alone.

"There was a woman living there. She was young, but tired. Her face was covered in cuts and scars. She never told me her name. She said it was better that way. But she taught me everything I needed to know about The Pen, and told me to go to the palace and use The Pen when I got there. That's all I knew.

"After being mutilated by the Creator and his Master, I threw The Pen through that door and it landed before you. I then devoted all my time into preparing the next Holder of The Pen. I stacked these books in perfect order and spoke with neighboring kingdoms about having soldiers come and prepare the replica palace. And that's when I realized that we all have a part in this, before someone breaks the curse. Before someone finally kills the Creator, and makes Discis peaceful and loving again," Sky finished off. A small tear flowed down his face.

Jake looked at the floor and then back at Sky. "Did . . . did The Pen ever become a burden to you? Did you ever just want to go home?"

Sky looked up at the ceiling and then back at Jake. "Every damn day of my life. I wish I could just return home and go back to my old life. But I can't, Jake, I just can't. We all have a role in this game. This whole thing with The Pen is one big game, and we are all pawns. One of us, one of us who is unfortunate enough to hold The Pen, will strike down the king. None of us plan it, Jake. I was looking for a report, a damn report, and I wound up in an another universe."

Jake didn't know what to say, except to tell how he got here. "It all started with Kevin, my cousin. He was skateboarding this one time, on a highway, after I begged him not to. And I guess there's a portal he went through. The Creator found some way to text me. He told me to go to the town library, where I found The Pen. After he begged me to bring it back to him, I blacked out." The old man laughed at this. "When I woke up, I went to my friend Shelton's house with my other friend—"

"Shelton? Shelton the Betrayer?"

Jake shared a confused look with Sky. It was then he realized that Shelton was truly hated by many on Discis. Few knew his softer and nicer side. His sacrificial side.

"Shelton took everything that we all loved and destroyed all of it. He took everything that meant the most to those here, and destroyed it. He's the reason that people like us are working so damn hard to put this world back together. Have you seen him lately?" asked Sky.

Jake had seen Shelton as a teenager in school, always hiding in corners and being anti-social. But Shelton had repaid his debt with honor. Sure, Shelton turned his back on so many lives; however, he protected the only thing that could help save the world. In Jake's eyes, he thought Shelton had changed entirely.

Sky gave one great sigh and tapped his own legs. "I know you must have millions of questions running through your head and now I will give you all of my answers. I have waited here for you to show up so I could train you so that you will be ready for all the Creator will throw at you. How did I know you were coming? If you look all around you, these books become very friendly."

"If you say so," Jake said with a shrug.

Sky stood up and journeyed to the other side of the hut. When he came back, he had two mugs in his hand. Both had steam rising out of them.

"This is called Cly," Sky spoke after handing him a glass of what Jake thought was tea. "It's an old drink that has existed for many generations. It helps cleanse the mouth, jaw and gums at the same time."

"Man, if I learned as much knowledge of this world as you, I'd be set," Jake said, and then took a sip.

"Funny you should say that," Sky spoke. He arose from his seat and walked around to the left corner of the hut. He reached over to a box and pulled out a book that looked like a computer hard drive to Jake. Sky threw the book to the boy, who caught it in his lap. He grunted as it came flying down.

"God, Sky! You're the first person to put every translation of the Bible together," Jake grunted after slowly moving the book from his lap.

"That's no Bible, Jake. That is the book the woman wrote for me. She took notes on everything she could find. Plants, grass, mountains, tar, birds, animals, you name it." Sky smiled as he thought of this. "Your next test, Jake, is to read that book."

Jake nodded, but still felt the pain in his lap. "Why do I need to read this?"

Sky smiled. "You need to prepare for what's coming."

"And what's coming?" Jake grunted as he tried to move the book.

Sky sighed. "War."

CHAPTER 28

I

Hours earlier, Trevor and Kevin were ready to go. They had met Sky once Jake had blacked out. He had been on a return journey from somewhere and welcomed them into his home. After some brief introductions, he elected to send them on a mission—one of most importance.

Sky gave both of them backpacks full of edible plants and other things that the old man had collected over the years. When they were all ready, Sky showed them the way they had to travel. Right behind the hut were rocky hills that would require a little creativity to climb. The boys would have to climb up those hills and travel through a forest that would take them to plains of burned grass. From there, they would travel downward into a valley, where they would find the kingdom—the kingdom that would lend them an army for the coming war.

"Farewell," Sky said to Trevor and Kevin. He patted Kevin's shoulder.

Kevin nodded over toward Jake, who was still sleeping on Sky's couch. "Take care of him."

Sky nodded. "Will do."

When Trevor and Kevin heard the door shut, they stopped and looked out at the treacherous path before them. Sky's hut had an extraordinary view of the land. They saw the sun beating hard on them from the East and the soggy green grass rested like a wet dog that had had its fill. Kevin pointed to the left and the two started in that direction. Trevor followed right behind him. They went around the left bend and curved around the left side of the hut. They looked forward and saw the rocky yet climbable hills, made of charcoal-colored rocks. Trevor nodded and took his first step onto it.

Both Trevor and Kevin started up the hill with a slow and peaceful walk—a smooth yet strategic climb. The only way to fully get up the hill was to follow the hill's rules. It was obvious to Trevor and Kevin that the hill wanted them to start with a slow walk up. But that soon turned into a heavy and powerful stride as the hill got steeper. The incline slapped them in the face. Their legs grew heavy. Sweat didn't drop, but their lungs scavenged for air.

They had to stop soon after their ascent. The hill turned too steep to continue walking. They were eye-to-eye with edgy and curved rocks that showed no discernible way of climbing. The two boys were stuck. It was impossible to continue.

"Well, that's that," Kevin said, about to turn around and slide back down the hill. His breathing finally slowed.

"Wait," said Trevor, who grabbed Kevin's left arm. "There's a way to get over the mountain, but it will take some hard work. If you look, man, if one of us was to lift the other on their shoulders, we could easily hoist one of us to the tip of the hill. Then, we could use the rope that Sky gave us to have the other climb up."

Kevin nodded in agreement. He bent his shoulders down and lifted Trevor onto them. He grunted in regret when Trevor's hard boots stepped into his shoulders. Trevor reached up and grasped the top of the hill. It was a small peak, hanging over the edge. He hoisted himself up and over, and when he was done, he threw the rope down for Kevin to climb up. When he reached the top of the hill, he stood up right next to Trevor.

They both stared out to the land beyond them, now high above it. They saw a trail that went downwards back toward the hut. That would be their way home. There was a vast verdant forest that went for about three miles, maybe a bit more by Trevor's calculations—which were as good as a high school teen's could be. Kevin put his hand over his eyes and stared out, blocking his eyes from the sun. Way off in the distance and over the horizon, Kevin spotted a thin tan line. He nudged Trevor's arm with his knuckle. Trevor turned around, and his expression became cold.

"No . . . way," Trevor said.

He descended down a light slope that gave the boys a better view at the world beyond. They saw the entire valley—the mountains they had climbed before, the sandy wastelands of the Krowian Desert, the shinny shimmering Sammack Sea.

And it was all beautiful.

CHAPTER 29

I

Jake used both of his hands to pull the book into his lap. He set it right in front of him and looked at the light coffee-brown cover, which had a title written in gold letters that Jake could hardly read because of the amount of dust that lay over them. He took his hand and wiped the dust off.

The sun from the outside shone in on the book and the gold letters stung Jake in the eyes. He tried to open one eye slowly, but it was no use, for the gold's light was shooting right into his eyes. Sky came over with a mug made of Cly and sat down near Jake. He patted the book.

"By my calculations, the writer must have made it thousands of years ago. As I told you before, that woman I met when I first got here gave this to me. It's got everything you need to know about Discis, from the type of plants that grow to the most powerful weapons of the old militaries," Sky explained.

"Sky, did you ever think maybe she was planning for someone to come and find her?" Jake asked.

"What do you mean?"

"Like, what if she was put here like we were? But she didn't know where to go or what to do, so she just wrote this book to help whoever came next," Jake said.

"It is an intriguing question. One that we will discuss later on." Sky stood up. "But for now, please join me. We're going to put you through your next test. But before you do, just remember that whatever happens, it is for good."

Jake gave a questioning look as he followed Sky out of the hut. He still didn't trust Sky completely, but he trusted The Pen and everything it led him toward. If this was where he was meant to be, then he was more than willing to be there.

It was only a few seconds of walking before Jake knew where Sky was leading him—the replica of the Creator's Palace. Jake's mind spun with ideas of why Sky would take him here. His body shook with terror. Or was it the cold? Jake could not tell at this point. The heat of The Pen, the cold of the snow and the bitterness of the terror inside of him churned with such a great capacity that it almost made him topple over.

The two men reached the cave and entered into the fake palace. It was an extraordinary complex made within the cave's rock walls. Sky ran his palm over the Palace's door, smiling at Jake, who held the large door handle. It was of the exact shape as The Pen. The door opened and screamed from its age. Jake peeked in while Sky walked forward toward a spiral staircase. Jake took a step forward, the door shutting behind him.

Jake noticed a sort of den on his immediate right. The walls were covered with empty bookshelves, except for one that had a fireplace. There was also high-backed chair in one corner of the room. The fire crackled and flamed. It reminded Jake a lot of the hut, which seemed to be a much smaller version of the den. It wasn't Sky who built the hut, so Jake figured that who ever lived in the hut before Sky had built it to be like the den in the Creator's Palace.

Odd.

There was another thick concrete door on the left side of the room that had a sketch of a wolf-like creature with thick fangs. Jake swallowed as he looked at this picture, not knowing if there was an animal on the other side of the door or not. Jake moved forward a bit, trying to forget the door with the picture. As he got to the edge of the den, Jake looked to his left and right. Both directions show long narrow black brick corridors. The floor, the walls and the ceiling were all made of night shade of red stone.

A whip came sailing right at Jake's back, cracking him right across his abdomen.

Jake yelped in pain from the leather whip. His body lost all strength and he wobbled around to regain his balance. The whip came flying again and cracked Jake in the back, forcing Jake to his knees.

Sky came from the dark corner, holding the whip in hand.

"Kurpo has no remorse, nor does his Master," Sky said. He whipped Jake once more.

Jake screamed the loudest he had ever screamed, white-hot pain erupting on his back and his legs, now piles of loose muscle.

"Do not be foolish and not expect attack! Expect it! And use it to your advantage!"

Slap! Another whip right across the back, opening up his shirt and releasing blood.

THE PEN

Jake fell down on all fours, his breaths heaving. His red shirt was torn. Blood that matched his shirt color crawled out. Sky took the whip and snapped it right into the wound. Jake rolled over to stop the bleeding and the pain, but it was to no avail. The pain, the suffering, and the complete madness ruined him. Thoughts came fast to Jake about what to do next, but they were sent away with another crack of the whip to the wound.

"Never! Never reveal the side of your body that is well!" Sky yelled.

Without hesitation, Sky snapped the whip again, and more blood slipped out from Jake's body. A wound to his back and a wound to his abdomen, both with blood pouring out.

Real tears dripped from his eyes. This was more than he had ever endured, more pain then he would ever encounter.

"Kurpo will show no mercy."

Crack!

With all his strength, Sky slashed the whip right across Jake's front. The tears kept falling into Jake's mouth as he screamed in pain. The blood on Jake's front splashed all around the room and some stained the whip. Jake cried over and over again for Sky to stop, but he didn't. The words of stop turned into just cries of pain and suffering as Sky continued whipping Jake. Faster and more painful came the whips.

After enduring dozens of powerful whips across the back and front, Jake blacked out into the abyss of his mind.

II

Jake woke up hours later, wrapped in a flannel blanket near a warm fire

Oh, how badly Jake wanted to rip Sky's head off. The man was sitting right across from him, reading a piece of paper like nothing wrong had happened.

He wanted to hurt Sky for putting him through that, but he was too tired. Maybe that was Sky's plan all along.

Or maybe Jake was dreaming.

But something inside Jake told them that those tests would help him when he reached the real Palace. The sacrifice was necessary.

"What the hell was that about?"

Sky's eyebrows perked up. "How do you feel?"

Jake was about to curse out Sky for all the pain. But, funnily enough, Jake felt no pain. Everything was at ease, calm.

"What the hell?"

Sky smirked. "You're stronger now than you were."

"How is that possible?"

"Even the most ordinary things," Sky began, picking up the whip he had used on Jake, still painted blood-red, "have that little something extra."

Jake looked to his right and that's when he saw his empty mug.

"Discis is a magical place," Sky said with a wink.

Jake gave a half laugh, but he was unsure whether or not he still hated Sky for what had happened in his mind.

"Now Jake," said Sky, getting up from his seat. He passed by Jake, who was sitting on the couch. Sky lifted up the large book that he had given Jake earlier. He walked back, and handed it over. "You must now read this. After you have read this, we will return to the palace for your final task."

Jake nodded and received the book once more. He opened the cover and began reading.

CHAPTER 30

I

"So," began Trevor, walking around the mini-camp that he and Kevin had set up, which was only a small fire and their ragged backpacks. "What next?" he asked, chewing on one of the vegetables that Sky had supplied them with.

Kevin brushed off some dirt from his khaki cut-offs and thought for a moment. "Well man," he began, "Maybe we should, I dunno, find this kingdom?" he asked.

"Sounds good," Trevor said. "But the thing is, Kev, where are we gonna find a kingdom? In the middle of nowhere."

"Hmm . . ." Kevin began to think. He didn't know where the hell to find a kingdom, for he barely knew what the word meant in this world. Kevin was more into sports and activities while his cousin Jake was probably more knowledgeable about history subjects and the like. This really should have been Jake's mission.

"Well, maybe. I dunno," Trevor said, baffled as to what he was supposed to do in this situation. "Stupid Moss. Moss never told us about any of this. Moss told us that "

They had come to the edge of the forest, all of a sudden. The trees that had once choked each other thinned out within a few paces, and now the boys faced a wide open space in the middle of a small valley. And sitting there, right before them, was a pearl tower, glowing from the sun.

Before the two boys knew it, the two were standing inside a castle. There were white marble floors, ceilings, and walls, and a sparkling spiral staircase before them. Kevin and Trevor saw the spiral staircase lead up, and saw a den on their right that led to a corridor that matched another one on the opposite side of the room.

The two looked up at the castle and saw someone standing at the top of the spiral staircase. She had brunette hair and a round black mask, shielding her face and showing only a reflection. Trevor and Kevin could barely make her out when they first saw her, but that changed as she floated down from the top to come meet them.

"Your names. Speak them," she demanded.

Kevin and Trevor both exchanged a glance when they saw the masked woman.

"Uhh, well," said Kevin, searching for the person's face. "Sorry, but, do you mind taking down your mask?"

She shook her head. "Until I know who you are, I can't. Security. You understand."

"Sky sent us," said Trevor, finishing Kevin's sentences for him, trying to act all cool and slick in front of the woman.

She eyed Trevor for a moment. "Sky? Is he the old man who lives in a hut passed the Great Hellryo Forest?" she asked. Both Trevor and Kevin nodded. "What is his request?" she asked.

"There's an army of some sort he wants us to find. The . . . uh . . ." Kevin fell speechless as he forgot what Sky had requested.

"Wait," said Trevor with a questioning look.

"Hmm?" the woman asked.

"You're not Ginta, are you?" he asked.

The princess shook her head.

"Dammit," Trevor said. "Sky wanted us to get to the Castle of Ranadeau and speak to Ginta."

"This is the Castle of Ranadeau," she said. "Ginta is our king. He lives at the top of the tower. But, I'm sorry you can't see him, Trevor," the masked woman said.

"Well—wait . . . how do you—?"

Before Trevor could get out a question, a large man, dressed in steel-plated armor and covered by ginger hair appeared from the corridor, holding a bladed staff. Three soldiers joined him moments later, all of them panting.

"New Bloods!" the man yelled.

Kevin and Trevor were taken back by this as the large man came in. "New Bloods!" he yelled again. "New Bloods outside the camp!"

Hundreds of warriors came from the corridor on the right and the spiral staircase, all dressed in silver armor with the symbol of the gods on their plates. Each soldier had a silver sword in his hands with red rubies going down the sword's face.

The woman watched as all the warriors came running and blasted out the front door.

"What are those?" Kevin asked. Trevor would have asked, but he was

THE PEN

still amazed that the women knew his name.

"Those are our warriors, the Ranadeau Warriors. There are New Bloods coming. We must hide," she said. As she was about to usher Kevin and Trevor away, Kevin stopped.

"Trev and I have faced New Bloods before. Let us in on battle!" he said.

The woman shook her head. "No, I couldn't."

"We'll make a deal. If we help you win, we get a meeting with Ginta. If we don't, well, we'll wind up dead anyway," Kevin bargained. The woman looked at Kevin, then at Trevor, who still looked shock that she knew his name.

"All right! Do you need armor?" she asked.

"All I need is a bow and arrows, and all Trevor needs is a sword," he said back. She nodded and whispered to a guard behind her.

Within seconds, a sword and bow and arrows appeared in front of Kevin and Trevor, held by two of the warriors. Kevin reached and grabbed his weapons. Trevor grabbed his slowly, keeping his eye on the masked woman.

But she, too, disappeared moments later.

"Let's go!" said Kevin. He charged toward the marble door and out.

Trevor soon followed, still mind-boggled about what just happened.

II

Kevin and Trevor waited on the battlefield. They stood beside the Ranadeau Warriors and looked forward and saw the New Bloods, who they had faced so long ago, approach. Those New Bloods, with their black cloaks and swords—how had Kevin forgotten about them? They were relatively easy to defeat, and he wasn't so sure why the Ranadeau Warriors were scared of them.

"Let's go!" yelled Kevin, pumped up about fighting. Trevor stood with his sword, silent.

"Draw!" yelled the lead warrior. He lifted his sword. The other warriors followed his command. Kevin lifted his bow and set an arrow into it. Trevor didn't lift his sword, but felt its edge. "Ready!" the lead warrior yelled, watching the New Bloods walk toward them. "Go!"

The Ranadeau Warriors all charged at the New Bloods with their swords, and the New Bloods stood still with theirs. As the two groups got closer, the battle began.

The swords of the New Bloods clanged with those of the Ranadeau Warriors.

Cling, cling, clash.

Kevin was the lone man with a bow and arrows, as everyone was using swords. Kevin shot an arrow, killing two of the New Bloods. He killed another, then another, then another. It was easy for him.

Trevor was having trouble killing like he had before, only because his mind was still confused. How did the masked girl know his name?

Kevin looked out into the sea of New Bloods, all of them the exact same thing: tall, skinny, wearing a cloak, wielding a black sword. All of them marched and fought the same way. When Kevin struck one, it would fall the same way another would. It was almost as if they were programmed like robots. Kevin shot another arrow out into the New Bloods, killing one. He stabbed one up close with an arrow, and then shot the arrow as it went through another. Kevin was unbeatable with the bow and arrow. He shot another, then another, and kept firing them down. He stopped for a moment to regain energy. Kevin saw the Ranadeau Warriors fighting against the New Bloods, yet not killing a single one. How? The New Bloods were so easy to defeat. Hell, even the confused Trevor was killing some.

Trevor slashed at a New Blood, cutting it in half, then spun and sliced through another in stunning fashion. He battled with another, got advantage of that one's sword, and now had two swords in hand. Trevor sliced through one New Blood, then another, and then thrust his blade through the one he had stolen the sword from. He saw that Kevin was having the exact same luck, killing many New Bloods, unlike the Ranadeau Warriors. Why were they having so much trouble?

Trevor sliced through two more, as Kevin shot three down. Soon, Trevor and Kevin were standing back-to-back, killing off any opposing New Bloods. Kevin scoped the area and saw the Ranadeau Warriors outnumbered New Bloods by a significant margin.

"So," Kevin began before shooting down another New Blood. "What do you say we make a run for it?"

"Where?" shouted Trevor over the yelling soldiers.

"The castle. We can talk to the princess!" Kevin yelled back.

Trevor wanted to speak to the princess because she knew his name. He nodded. "Right! Let's go!" he yelled.

Trevor gutted one more New Blood, then ran back into the sea of Ranadeau Warriors, and finally out of the battle ground. Kevin followed right behind. A New Blood chased after Kevin, which made him turn around and shoot a bow in mid-air. He smiled after accomplishing this crazy move. Trevor congratulated him, and then called for Kevin to hurry up.

The two pushed past the white marble door and into the marble opening hallway. They saw the spiral staircase that led upwards, and at the bottom stood the woman, still wearing her mask. She tilted her head in a quizzical manner at Trevor and Kevin, who were panting for air after they had just gone through battle.

THE PEN

"May I help you?" she asked.

Kevin stepped up to her. "You call those guys warriors?" he asked. "They couldn't fight to save their lives!"

The woman nodded. "That's why the New Bloods keep coming back. The New Bloods are our weakness. We're the strongest army to have lived in Discis for centuries, but when we face New Bloods, we usually fall," she said. Kevin nodded, but Trevor could only stare at the princess. "Anyway, Ginta will see you now. But, only one of you," she said to them.

Kevin looked at Trevor, and Trevor looked back.

"You go, man," Trevor said.

Kevin nodded. The masked woman pointed to the spiral staircase and Kevin nodded before jogging over to the stairs and ascending toward the tip.

The woman was about to walk away, but Trevor stopped her. "Woah, woah, woah," he said to her.

She stopped and turned around. "Yes?"

"How did you . . ." Trevor stopped to catch his breath. "How did you know my name?"

"I did? I don't remember that. I must have heard your friend say it."

"Ahh nah, nah, nah, nah," said Trevor, waving his finger. "You didn't know Kevin's name," he said. He took another look at the masked woman. "Do I know you? Or do you know me?" he asked.

"Well, I," she started. "I'm the Princess of Ranadeau."

"Who are you? Why are you still wearing that mask?"

The woman removed the mask to appease Trevor.

At first, she shot him a simple glance, waving her hair across her face. But then she really saw him for who he was. Her reality disappeared for a moment, caught off guard that her heart could swell with so many emotions when their eyes locked. All the darkness in her body fell away when their eyes met. It was like waking up from a nightmare.

"Amanda?"

CHAPTER 31

I

After spending an hour reading the thick book that had everything to do with Discis, Jake glanced over at Sky, who was drinking Cly and watching Jake read. Jake's elbows dug into the book and his head rested on his palms as he continued reading the page. He was reading about someone named Serena and her amulet. Some old folktale. Not only was Jake frustrated that he was only twenty pages through the book, but he hated that the book contained information he didn't find useful. He didn't care about plants that could make you live forever, or a certain mushroom that would give birth to some kind of animal. What he did care about was completing his "training" and moving on to whatever came next.

"Sky," Jake began. "This book is so boring."

Sky laughed. "Well, Jake, if you want to succeed, you must make yourself stronger," he said, then sipped his drink. "Success won't come to you so easily. You need to make it happen."

"Sky," Jake said, shutting the book quickly. "I don't care about plants or animals. Hell, I don't care about anything here. Honestly, I just want to restore harmony to Discis. I don't think I'll need all this stuff," he said.

Sky shook his head.

"You can't go into a bar not knowing how to order a drink," Sky said.

"Sky, I could survive without these books and training. I mean, I survived weeks without training or knowledge of Discis, and look where I wound up," Jake stood and leaned against the bookcase, which had a flat rock wall on the side.

"Look where you wound up?" Sky asked. "Jake, I found you and your friends alone in the middle of nowhere. You're still miles away from the Creator's Palace. Doesn't seem like that great of a job to me."

"I survived," Jake said.

"Right. What did your friends tell me before you got here? Right. Not only did you get stabbed by the Creator, but you nearly fell off a plateau, died from fireballs, and almost got killed by your own friend Moss on several occasions."

Jake had no reply.

"Please, Jake, you need to keep reading."

"Fine," Jake said.

He walked back toward the wall. Before sitting, he slammed his hand against the rock wall.

There was a light rumble. The hut shook and Jake hopped off his chair. Rocks tumbled everywhere and dust filled the air. Jake coughed as he hit the floor with Sky. Jake's back still felt stiff. The two soon stared at each other, Jake's face still frustrated by his quest for answers. After staring at Sky, he turned his head to the right, and looked beyond where he had fallen.

And there, behind the now fallen brick wall, sat a black stone desk with a short-backed chair in front. It was pushed right up close to the desk, which had something that made Jake wonder.

It was a computer.

II

"What the?" Jake asked, getting up from the ground and walking over to the computer. He pushed the chair out of the way.

There was a black keyboard with a standard format of letters, numbers, and symbols. On the lower right corner of the screen was a little silver button with some odd symbol on it, one with a crown. On the lower left corner was a small hole that looked like it could fit a roll of quarters. Jake put his hand on the seat and pulled it back. He sat in it and looked at the computer.

"This looks brand new," Jake said, feeling the keyboard and the screen. He looked behind the desk and to the side. "That's weird, no hard-drive," Jake said. He turned his attention back to the computer screen.

He felt the panel of the screen and put his finger on the button. Jake turned on the computer, without concern for what could happen next.

The computer went from black to red to green to yellow to black to silver to white to purple to black to green to blackredpinkgreen to bluepurplebluegreenyellowred to white. The white screen had nothing on it, except for a blinking bar, which was the starting point for typing. Jake looked at the screen for a moment with a questioning eye, before it started to type some words out.

The following words appeared on the screen:

[Please insert The Pen...]

Jake nodded, reached into his pockets, and found his most prized possession. He felt its edges and curves, soft and square. He looked down at the lower left corner and inserted The Pen perfectly into it.

[PLEASE WAIT]

It was obvious to Jake, as he had used computers a lot, that the system was loading The Pen's information and trying to upload it onto the screen. He waited a few more seconds. Sky was still lying down on the floor. He hopped up to one knee and saw Jake sitting at a computer.

"A computer?" Sky asked.

"Yep," responded Jake.

"Impossible," said Sky, getting over to the computer and gazing at it.

"Not impossible," Jake said as he still watched the screen.

[PLEASE ENTER ACCESS CODE:]

"Please . . . enter access code?" Jake read aloud. Sky was also taken back by this. "What access code?"

"It's gotta be on The Pen," Sky said.

"I've checked The Pen before, Sky, and there were never any numbers or letters on it."

"Hmm, strange," he said.

"Well, let's see." He looked down at the keyboard, and started typing.

[TYEEWR34239393]

[...]

[ERROR: X]

The X moved from the middle of the screen up into the upper right corner of it. There were three unshaded X's up there, but now one was filled in. He must have three strikes to enter numbers, and he had just wasted one.

"Damn," said Jake, slapping his knee.

"Jake, it's time for your final test anyway," Sky spoke. "Let's head over to the Palace and we'll complete that. When we get back, you can try again."

Jake nodded as he slid the chair back and followed Sky through the hut and out.

III

The colossal black stone door opened for Jake and Sky. Jake wondered what task was ahead of him. Was it to walk up the stairs and into some room, where hundreds of warriors were waiting for him? He hoped not.

"OK," said Sky, putting his hands together as though in prayer. "Your final test is not physical, but mental. Your task is to climb up these stairs and walk to the right of the opening hallway. Up there, you will find a door, which in real life would be the Creator's Room. Once in there, something from your future, past or present will await you. Now please, carry on."

"Wait, how?" Jake asked.

"Excuse me?" Sky responded.

"How does this replica Palace have the ability to show me something like that?"

Sky smirked. "You'll come to learn, Jake, that some things that happen in this world can't be explained. Just believe."

Sky stepped away from the steps and off to the right as Jake took hold of the stair railing. He nodded at Sky and ascended the stairs. One by one he climbed, higher and higher up to the tallest part of the palace. Each stair was perfectly measured to be the exactly the same length and width, which made Jake wonder how Sky and a group of warriors could build this Palace.

Jake reached the top of the staircase five minutes later, and when he stepped onto the platform in the opening hallway, he felt a chilling presence. Something was inside of him, trying to scare him away from what was in the door. But Jake knew that this was his final task and he needed to complete it to get Sky off his back. He walked to the right and descended through the hallway. He saw a door on the right side of the wall. Jake held the doorknob. He pushed the door open.

He saw a room, smaller than he had imagined it would be. There was a desk right across from him, with a vast window that looked out at the world beyond. On the desk was a goblet. Jake looked around the room and saw the two doors he had learned about. There was also a stone boulder in the center of the room.

When he looked back at the desk, Jake saw someone sitting there, running his hands on the goblet. He had straight brown hair that went down to his shoulders and wide brown eyes. Only his face was visible, as he was wearing white-plated armor.

"Hello, Jake Serent," said the person sitting at the desk.

"Hello? Have we met before?" Jake asked.

"No. My name is Lexington."

"Lexington? As in the Lexington that Kurpo betrayed? As in, the Lexington who created the blizzard?" Jake asked.

"Yes, I am the one he betrayed," Lexington said. He looked to his right. "I don't have a lot of time."

"Well, why are you here? Why are we talking?" Jake asked, with many thoughts flying through his mind. Lexington handed Jake a piece of paper.

"I created a computer for you to open. Inside the computer are records and data that I created myself. Now Jake, that paper I just handed you has the access code. Once you enter it, you will be connected to my records," Lexington said.

Jake was speechless for a moment.

"Why did you decide to build it there?" Jake finally asked. "And why not leave the access code for Sky?"

Lexington smiled. "Because Sky is not the Holder, Jake, you are."

"But Sky was a prophet, right? He was a Holder of The Pen before me. What makes me any different? What about all the other prophets who came before?"

Lexington's face filled with concern. "Jake, I don't have a lot of time left. I can't visit for very long," he looked around him. "You need to believe something, Jake. You are the true Holder. You are the Holder of The Pen, the real one. Everything that happened before has led to you. We needed everyone else to hold The Pen so that you would find it and you would save all of us. I promise. You can help save Discis. And your old world too."

"Wait, what? My old world? What do you mean?"

Lexington twitched. It was then that Jake realized Lexington wasn't really there. He was a spirit, or a projection. Something not physical.

"I have to go, Jake. My time is up. But just know you can save Discis and Earth if you just believe. Believe in yourself and everything you've fought for. And that, my friend, will save everyone."

Lexington disappeared.

IV

After Jake rushed down the stairs and into the hut, leaving Sky behind, he found himself at the computer once again. The screen was still on, The Pen was still inserted, and Jake now had the access code so that he could see everything that Lexington had left him. Jake typed in the code.

[HWS21025901]

[...]

[ACCESS GRANTED]

Jake smiled. He waited a moment. The white screen zoomed away and turned into a black screen with electric blue tables, grids, and links to certain folders. Jake noticed that there was no mouse to the computer, so he would need to use the arrow keys. The link that was highlighted was *RECORDS*. Below that was *DATA, GRIDS, CHARTS, STRATEGIES,* and *MAP*. Jake pressed ENTER on the keyboard and the records page popped up. It read:

[HOLDER: These are my notes, and everything I have collected to help you discover the way to bring Discis back to harmony. Please use this to your liking. — Lexington]

Jake prepared himself for even more reading.

CHAPTER 32

I

Kevin Keys climbed up the white marble staircase and turned right at the opening hallway. On the right hand side of the wall was a room where Kevin found Ginta, meditating on a small rug that laid in the center of the room that was boxed in by balconies. He was short, bald, and had apparently spent many hours in the sun.

"Are you Ginta?" Kevin asked as he entered the room. Ginta slowly opened his eyes.

"You must be Kevin," he spoke. Kevin nodded. "Sky sent you, did he?"

"Yeah."

"Hmm, ahh yes. Sky and I are good friends. He found this kingdom like you did, and here he found me. Now I must ask, what does my good friend request?" asked Ginta.

"Well," Kevin began. "Uhh, he wanted me to tell you that we're ready?"

"Is he sure?" Ginta asked.

Kevin could only nod. Ginta nodded back. Ginta reached into a pocket of his clothing and pulled out a wooden box. He handed it to Kevin.

"You tell Sky to blow that flute when he needs my army. They will all be at the battle scene," he said.

"Thank you," said Kevin.

Kevin turned and was about to leave, but Ginta stopped him.

"Hmm. I see trouble for you, boy." he said.

Kevin turned back.

"What?"

"Trouble follows you. Nothing but trouble."

II

"Trevor?" asked Amanda, looking at her past love. The two were drawn together with a hug.

"I've missed you. I've missed you so much," he said. Amanda tugged hard.

"I've missed you, too," she said. The two released the hug. "How did you get here?"

"I was skateboarding and I appeared here, randomly. You?" he asked.

"Well, I, umm, I was trying to call you. And then all of a sudden, I wound up here," she said.

Trevor remembered how her cell phone had changed numbers and how her family had moved. He was right in his assumptions. And now he understood why they never talked to each other—she had wound up in Discis, like he had.

"And you became a leader here?" he asked.

"Yeah, I'm not really sure what happened," she said, running her hands through her long brunette hair. "I just remember they took me in and let me help them. But I didn't remember who I was or why I was here or anything like that. But you must have broken it," she answered, a cute smile on her face. Trevor smiled back. "What have you been doing?"

"Well, uhh," he began. "My friend, Jake, has this Pen, and I guess I'm helping him bring it all the way across the land to a palace where he'll be able to restore peace to the world."

"Woah. Your friend is the Holder?"

"The what?"

Amanda waved off his ignorance. "It's this major story going around in Discis. The Holder of The Pen. He's supposed to bring Discis back to the way it was—full for vegetation, water, all of that. It's major news right now, at least that's what we've been hearing from the South. Wow. I can't believe this."

"Yeah," Trevor said, having no clue of the importance of their mission. "It's pretty messed up."

"Yo Trev!" called Kevin, finishing his walk down the staircase. He high-fived Trevor and looked at Amanda. "Who's this?"

"Amanda."

"Oh," said Kevin. "Amanda? Like, the love of your life Amanda?" he asked. Trevor nodded. Kevin extended his hand. "Nice to meet you."

Amanda blushed. "Nice to meet you, too."

"All right, so, Ginta said we're all set. Wanna head back?" Kevin asked.

"Yeah sure. Uhh, wait," said Trevor. He looked at Amanda. "You wanna come with us?" he asked.

Amanda looked behind her and saw all the guards were gone.

"Sneak me out," she whispered.

Kevin, Trevor, and their new companion Amanda, ran out the door, back toward the hut.

III

There was a knock at the hut's door.

Jake, still seated at the computer, was about to go answer it, but Sky, who had just returned from the palace, got up instead.

He opened the door to see Kevin, Trevor, and Amanda, all looking awfully cold. Sky invited all of them in.

Jake's face erupted with a smile. He shoved his chair back and jogged over to Kevin and Trevor and wrapped his arms around them. He tugged hard at his two fellow teenagers.

"Thank God," Jake said. "You guys all right?"

"Easy kid," Trevor responded.

Jake let go. He locked eyes with Kevin. "What's up?"

Kevin shrugged. "Chillin."

Jake turned his attention to the girl with brown hair.

"This is Amanda," said Trevor.

Jake's eyes widened. "Hey, I'm Jake."

"You're the Holder of The Pen?" she asked. Jake nodded. "Last guy I'd expect to save the world," she joked.

They all laughed.

"Sky, Amanda. Amanda, Sky," said Trevor, introducing the two.

"Hello," responded Sky. "Kevin, how did everything go?"

"Very awesomely," said Kevin, brushing his sweating hair with a towel. "Ginta said the army will be with us, and all we'll have to do is play this flute," said Kevin, pulled out the box from his pocket. He set it down on the nearby bookshelf.

Sky nodded in happiness. "Good. Now all of your tasks are complete."

"Is that a computer?" asked Kevin, walking toward it. Jake followed.

"Yeah, dude. I found it under these walls. It's just some old-age crap," he said.

Kevin looked at the screen and saw some type of grid or table. "Whatever floats your boat, man."

Once everyone got settled, Kevin and Jake joked around with the computer, and Trevor and Amanda cuddled on the old and worn out couch. Now that the group was back together, along with a new face in

Amanda, things finally looked to be brightening for the boys.

There was another knock at the door.

Everyone turned their heads toward the door. Jake put his hand on The Pen, still inserted into the computer, and readied himself to attack the knocker. Kevin held his arrows just in case and Trevor was ready with his sword.

Sky walked up the steps inside the hut and reached the door. He pulled it open and there stood a man, bent over and coughing. He was as tall as Sky, with brown, curly hair. His face was a pale white. Sunglasses covered his eyes. He wore a black T-shirt with a skull in the middle.

"Where am I?" he asked, panicking. "Where am I? Where the HELL am I?"

"Just calm down," said Sky, patting the man on the shoulder.

Jake ripped The Pen from its place and arose from the computer chair, as did Trevor and Amanda from the couch. Who was this man? Sky snapped his fingers at the water jugs in the corner. Kevin dashed over and brought the man a glass of water.

The man sipped the glass. "What the hell happened?" he asked.

Jake, Trevor, Kevin, and Amanda all exchanged a glance, for they too had just been randomly sucked into this land. "How did I get here? Where am I?" he cried again.

"Where did you appear?" asked Sky, wondering about this man.

The man stared at the floor for a moment, as if he were mesmerized by something. He cocked his head back up and spoke.

"There was this green light. About twelve yards away," said the man. He sat down on the ground. "Can you tell me where I am? Where are we all?"

Sky scurried out the door.

"Sky!" Jake called, chasing after him.

The man sipped more water, panting and freaked, as the rest of the group joined Jake out the door.

"Uh, be right back," Trevor said to the man as he followed Jake, Kevin, and Amanda out the door.

Sky walked along the rock walls that were near his hut, trying to find the green light the man spoke of.

Trevor and Amanda, holding hands, followed close behind, as Kevin and Jake followed directly behind Sky.

Sky, a few feet ahead, came to a stop.

They all looked, and there, in front of them, was a hovering green light, encapsulated by a silver metal arch, hidden against the rocks.

"Sky? What is that?" Jake asked.

Sky looked at it with caution. "I'm not sure."

"What should we do?" Kevin asked.

Sky reached out and waved his hand at the light.

And like they had all experienced before, one second Sky was there and the next he was not. They couldn't believe it at first, unsure yet sure, but as time went by they soon realized he wasn't coming back. He had thinned into nothingness, shrank into minute particles, disappeared into the air.

He was gone, taken away by the green light.

"Oh my God!" Amanda shouted.

"What should we do, guys?" Trevor asked.

"We have to save him," Jake said. "He's the only one who knows anything about the Creator. We have to find out where he went."

Kevin held Jake back. "What if this takes us to the Creator? What if this is a portal to his room?"

"Well, then we'll save ourselves a whole lot of walking," Trevor quipped.

Jake looked at the green light and then back at Discis. The Pen was still burning, but only faintly. He held it and looked back at the light.

"We don't know where to go next anyway," Jake said. "Might as well see where this goes. And if we get to the Creator's room by going through, then so be it. We'll beat it like we've beaten everything else."

Kevin loved Jake's confidence. He smirked and patted his cousin on the back. "After you, Holder of The Pen."

Jake rolled his eyes. He inched closer to the light. Before he could touch it, he was gone. Kevin chased after him and dashed through the light. Trevor and Amanda, the lost lovers who had found each other again, took a leap of faith and hopped into the shining spinning verdant bulb.

None of them had any idea where they were going or what they had just done.

PART IV: HOME

CHAPTER 33

I

Election day.

Grant had to yet to leave Jordan's side because he wanted to know if the driver woke up again. Jordan had woken up last night — his head throbbing, his body aching, everything sore. But he had fallen unconscious because of the excruciating pain.

And because of all the drama with Grant stabbing Jordan's leg with the block of wood, Thomas was now the heavy favorite to win the election again. Everyone disagreed with Grant for they thought he was trying to kill Jordan, even though that wasn't why Grant had stabbed him. He had done it to open up the nerves and sense of touch to the legs, not to kill him.

Using the pen and blood ink, everyone had already written down whom they wanted to win the election on a piece of the white T-shirt that had been found in the wreckage. Everyone waited for the votes to be collected. This voting system was different than ones they had been exposed to in the past. Aside from writing down whom they wanted to win—Grant or Thomas—they also had to write their own names. Thomas and Grant both felt this was appropriate so that everyone knew who voted for whom. In their eyes, this would help them figure out how to fix whatever problems they had.

It came to Grant's mind while he was looking at Jordan that he needed to get this election over with so he could make another diagnosis of Jordan. Grant stood up and walked over to each individual person and collected their ballots. He dropped them on the block of wood and set them face down.

"All right," started Grant, as everyone's attention went over to him. Everyone who had been thinking about other things had forgotten about them. "With the first vote—"

"Wait . . ."

Everyone who had their attention on Grant moved their eyes on to something new. They all glanced over and saw none other than Jordan, the bus driver who had been brutally injured during the accident, standing and looking down at Grant. No one knew what to do or say when they saw Jordan, standing on his own two feet, and smiling.

II

"Jordan?" asked Jupiter, standing up to greet him.

Grant hugged Jordan immediately.

"Do I know you?" Jordan asked after Grant had released the hug.

"Uh, no. I'm Grant Revel, and I'm a, well, I was, ah forget it, I'm a doctor. I've been working on you these past four days," Grant said, as Jordan nodded along.

The entire group was at a loss for words. They didn't expect that Jordan could have been standing after Grant had stabbed hm. Jupiter, who had been by his side this whole time, couldn't find anything to say when she saw Jordan standing. Everyone was in a complete state of shock.

"Well then," Jordan said, "you get my vote."

"Wait, you know about the election?" asked Grant.

"I may have been paralyzed and nearly dead, but I wasn't deaf," Jordan stated. "Let's see, what have I heard? Oh right. Brent was a childhood star, Richelle and Chris hooked up, Thomas and yourself hate each other, and apparently you two are having election to see who the leader will be."

"Wow, you remember a lot," Thomas started. "Do you—"

"—let's get the election over with and then we'll talk. OK, let's see here," Jordan ripped the votes from the ground and began to read them. "Well, I voted for Grant, so there's one. OK, Richelle voted for Grant, so two to nothing, and April did as well. All right, it's three to nothing. Jupiter voted for Thomas, as did Thomas, obviously, of course, and Brent. All right, we are all tied up here with three to three. Next vote, Chris voted for Grant. Grant's got a four to three advantage now with one vote left, his own. And let's see here . . . Grant voted for . . ."

Jordan paused when he saw the ballot. His eyes moved over to Grant, who had that mysterious smirk again. " . . . Thomas . . . ?"

There was silence again. No one had won.

"We'll that's just stupid," said Jordan, tossing all the papers. "You guys were immature about this damn election and neither of you won! Great job!"

Thomas and Grant exchanged a glance with each other and then looked back at everyone else. Jordan was right. They had just gone through all of that for nothing.

"Why'd you vote for me?" Thomas asked through the quiet.

Grant smirked. "Because I don't want to be the one who gets blamed when this all goes to hell."

III

The silence broke a few hours after the election. Since everyone really had nothing to say after the tie, the group remained quiet. But Jordan, ever the one to get things going, decided to break the silence. While everyone was sitting in the clearing in their respective spots, Jordan stood in the middle waiting to gather people's attention.

"OK, so here's what we're going to do," he started. "We all know that there is more out there than just this little forest, that's obvious. So here's what's going to happen. First, I'm gonna tell all of you what I saw when we crashed.

"I was driving down the highway, I forget which one we were on, but I know we were on a highway. It was bright as day, but for some reason, there were no other cars on the road. It seemed strange. Just not right. But even considering that, I kept on driving. The highway was just straight road, with buildings and stuff on the outsides of it. There was no forest, or grass, or anything. We must have been going through some kind of city area.

"Then, the last thing I remember seeing is a forest area right in front of me. It went from highway road to a deep forest—this forest. We crashed into a tree, and then I blacked out," he finished.

The silence continued. No one had a clue about what to say. They had been driving on a highway, and then just suddenly crashed into a forest? Was that even possible?

"Now that you know what happened, the next logical thing to do would be to go exploring into the forest," Jordan reasoned. "We should split up into teams. I've been working on a system, and it looks like the teams will be April and Thomas, Jupiter and Brent, and Richelle and Chris. Now, I've decided that I want to go exploring on my own, so Grant will also have to go alone." Everyone nodded along.

"I know this is quick, but we have to do something, right?" Everyone nodded. "We'll be leaving in half an hour," he said. Jordan smiled at everyone and headed back over to where his stuff was.

When the time had passed, everyone gathered up their hiking needs and joined with their teammates.

Jupiter and Brent were given the order to go east, and they did so.

April and Thomas were told to go west, and they also did so.

Chris and Richelle were told to go south, and they did.

Jordan told Grant that he'd go northwest, and that Grant should go northeast.

Grant made his way in the northeast direction, and passed by many trees and brushes. He got to the edge of the side of the forest quicker than he thought, and saw some small mountains ahead of him. For a moment, he thought about turning back and telling everyone what he was seeing here. How could mountains be hidden behind the trees? Grant didn't care how, he just wondered why.

It struck Grant that he had no reason to go back. The people didn't like him, and anything he did was taken as wrong. He had saved a man's life, and yet everyone still hated him for it. No one had thanked him at all, and that hit Grant really hard.

"Good bye," Grant uttered, as he made his way to the mountains.

He was sending himself into exile.

IV

Jordan pushed his way through some high bushes. He had gone so far into the forest that he had lost all sight of the trees and could only see the high vegetation ahead. Jordan kept going through them and then saw that there was a clearing. He moved his way through the bushes and came to an open spot in the forest.

But he wasn't alone.

Jordan saw a broken down shack with pieces of the roof and walls missing. One whole wall had been blasted out. It looked old, rusted, and unused. Jordan's eyes widened when he saw all of this. Excited, Jordan made his way over to the house.

On his walk over, he noticed something that proved his assumption wrong. He saw footsteps—made from large leather boots—stepping close to the house. He saw another set had traveled back away from the house. There was what looked like a green cape on the ground. Someone had been there.

Jordan decided to glance in the cabin.

A metal orb with thin red lines of smoke flowing around it waited for him inside.

CHAPTER 34

I

Jake tripped on a pile of garbage.

When Jake's right foot crossed through the portal, it landed on a junk pile made of broken and dismantled shards of metal. Nearly slipping, Jake regained his balance atop of the hill of junk. But as he went to take another step, one of the shards caught onto the bottom of his already dirty and cut up pants. He tugged hard to loosen his pants from the jagged metal scraps, but they would not budge. Using all of his strength, Jake tugged his pants away from the metal shard. It released, but Jake's own momentum sent him flying.

He toppled down the messy hill of junk, his arms and legs getting cut up because of the jagged and rusted shards. Though he felt the cool red worms of blood trickle down his back, it was incomparable to the pain he had suffered over the last few days. Jake's body tumbled and flopped down hard onto a surface of gravel with a smack.

Jake raised his head, his eyes searching, afraid of what he might see. But Jake only saw Sky and Kevin on his left and Amanda on his right, with Trevor's arms around Amanda. Jake stood and faced everyone's backs.

"Guys?" asked Jake on his knees, groggy and half-awake. Blood dripped from his arms and legs, but no one noticed.

"Look," Kevin said to Jake, grabbing him by the shoulder and pointing outwards.

Jake glanced up and followed Kevin's finger to a rusty and torn apart sign. It was so damaged that Jake could barely make out what it said. But when he did, terror struck his heart. He rubbed his eyes with his palms to make sure what he was seeing was real. When he glanced back, the sign was still there. Jake pinched himself, but didn't wake up from the nightmare. This was real.

On the sign, that was nearly destroyed, a few letters remained. The words read:

"Welcome to South Hills."

The only thing Jake could say was, "We're home."

II

When Jake was 3 years old, 6 months after the death of his father, Jake's mother had decided to make Jake and his 5-year-old sister move, along with her, from the city of Holyoaks to South Hills, which had been his home for 12 years.

Jake's eyes scanned the area before him. It was his home, but it had been tainted by something evil and horrifying. Jake sensed darkness, which made him feel fearful about his town, which had once made him feel warm and comforted. Now, he only felt dark and cold. Aside from the sign that was under the light post, Jake could not see much else. He wanted to see what else had happened to his town in his absence, and why the sign had become rusty and destroyed.

But there were several other questions spinning through Jake's mind. Where in town were they? What happened to the town since he was gone? How long had he been gone? Was time different in Discis than it was in town? Hell, even the world? Perplexed and confused, Jake wanted—in fact, craved—answers. Answers were his drug. Another thing that bugged Jake's mind was how Kevin, Sky, Trevor, and Amanda felt about this. He already had an educated guess about Amanda. She probably had never heard of such a low-profile town as this one and—

—an evil and monstrous sound erupted from the sky, making the group jump in complete and utter shock.

A blaze of fiery embers shot down from the dark midnight sky. The flames spread across the tar road. Jake realized it was a street he crossed often—Bardwell. The library that Jake worked at so much was just down the road.

As Jake went to take another step closer, a ball made of fire came shooting down at him. The boy hopped to his right, avoiding the fireball.

"Whoa," Kevin said, backing up.

A cloaked man emerged from the sky. The man's eyes were hidden under the hood, ensuring no one could tell who he was. In his hands were two flickering fireballs, orange and yellow with a blue outline.

"Who the hell?" asked Trevor, releasing his arm from Amanda's waist for a moment.

"Who are you?" Jake shouted.

Jake noticed a small grin crack on the face of the man under the cloak.

The cloaked man threw one of his two remaining fireballs down onto the street, which he had already set ablaze. He took the other ball and threw it behind him. The ball of fire soared high and landed on a tree that then went up in flames.

Then, the man disappeared into thin air.

"Jake," said Sky, over near the blazing street. Jake, at first paralyzed over what had just happened, hurried over toward Sky.

Sky's finger pointed toward the flaming writing. His stomach turned when he read the flaming text:

"I have returned."

III

Who had returned? That question began circling through Jake's mind. Was it the Creator? His Master? Lexington? Who could it be? And why would this person feel the need to tell Jake that they had returned? Jake stood there, silent and staring. He wondered so much who this was.

"Jake?"

Jake gathered himself and turned to his cousin. "Yeah?"

"You don't think it's Shelton, do you?" Kevin asked.

"No, Kevin, we saw him die."

"But he's the only one we know that could throw fire from his hands," Kevin bargained.

Jake shook his head. "We burned him. There's no coming back from that."

"What about that nerdy kid that came with you guys? Ritchie? Richard?" Trevor asked.

"I don't know who it is!" he yelled.

Sky, who had yet to say a word, finally spoke. "Jake," he began. "Any idea who this could be? Who did you see in the tower?"

Jake bit his lips and dug his nails into his body.

"Tell me, Jake, who did you see?" Sky asked again.

"Leave him alone, man," Trevor said.

"No one was speaking to you. This is above your pay grade," Sky said.

"Whoa, whoa, what!" Trevor said, getting frustrated with Sky.

"Trev, man," Kevin said, trying to put peace between the two.

"No, Kev," said Trevor, shoving Kevin's hand away. "This idiot thinks I'm useless. I've killed more New Bloods than you could count, my man."

"You're a punk teenager who won't live to see next week," Sky said. "You're too obsessed with your girl to see clearly."

"Excuse me!" Amanda exclaimed.

Jake shook his head at the ridiculousness of it all.

"Who was talking to you?" Sky asked, sending scornful eyes to Amanda.

The camel's back broke. Trevor's hard fist swung at Sky, clubbing him right in the jaw. He had insulted his girl, and Trevor would not stand for it. Sky fumbled back, tripping over his own feet. When he regained balance, he started after Trevor.

"You silly son-of-a—"

"Jake!" Kevin called.

While Sky, Trevor, Kevin, and Amanda had all gotten involved in the argument, Jake had already walked away from the group. Where was he going?

Soon enough, Kevin chased after his cousin. Trevor, Amanda, and Sky followed.

"Jake," said Kevin, catching up and patting Jake on the shoulder. "Where are you going?"

"Back to Discis."

IV

"Whoa," Kevin said, grasping Jake's arm and turning him around to face him. The look Kevin saw on his cousin's face was one of pure determination. Jake rarely was determined. Most of the time he just went with the flow. But for some strange reason, he was determined to get back to the far-away planet. Kevin's mind was boggled as to why Jake would want to go back to Discis when they had arrived back home. After a short pause, Kevin caught himself in a state of soundless stupor.

"Uh, uh, what? Did you just say you want to go back to Discis?"

Jake nodded.

Kevin leaned in toward Jake. "Jake, don't you think you're taking this thing too serious now?" Kevin asked. "I mean, we're back home. Why should we go back? Playtime is over. We're home. That was the goal, wasn't it? Get to the Creator's Palace, help Moss, and then come home?"

Jake's face turned to stone.

"Kevin, let me put it this way: all of my life here in South Hills, I've been nothing but the loser whose cousin is Kevin Keys. I'm not a jock, I'm not popular. I'm nothing," he spoke. Kevin looked down at the road. He knew this was completely true.

"But in Discis," Jake continued, "I feel like I'm important. I'm the Savior, Kev. And even though it might be painful, I feel like I will be the one to change things. If I can get to the top of the Creator's Palace and I can finish him off and restore peace and harmony to the planet, I can make the people that live there happy again," Jake said. He paused for a moment before speaking again. "And if you, Trevor, Amanda, and Sky all want to stay here, that's fine. But I'm going back."

"Oh yeah? And how are you gonna get back there?" Kevin asked.

This stalled Jake for a moment until he realized where he was. He remembered that earlier he had noticed they were on this street. Perfect. He could just walk through the doors of the library and be at the top of the Palace like The Creator had asked him to so many days ago (though it felt like it had been years since that moment).

"All I have to do," Jake began, "is walk through the door to the library and I'm at the top of the palace."

Kevin's eyebrow raised. "Jake, think how many people have walked through that door. And where did they go to? Oh wait, yeah, the library."

Jake shook his head at his cousin. "The day I came to Discis, I was told that if I walk through the doors of the library, I would get to the top of the palace. It's our best shot to get there and finish this once and for all. I dunno about you guys, but I am sick and tired of having the weight and the pain and the stress of this entire mess on my shoulders, OK? I want to save Discis and then go back to normal."

By this point, Trevor, Amanda, and Sky had rejoined the two cousins in the center of the street, just outside of the library. Jake looked at their faces and saw some empathy, and it was as though he was noticing this for the first time. He had been so preoccupied with bringing The Pen to the Creator's Palace that he didn't even have the chance to see how much his friends cared for him and the journey.

"Look, Jake, we get that this has been a tough road. But we're home now; we don't need to go back there and battle the Creator anymore. We're safe," Kevin said, trying to reason with his cousin.

Sky stepped up to Jake and Kevin and pointed all around them at the world that had seemingly gone dark. "Are you though?" he asked. "We may be back in the real world, but this isn't the home you all left behind. Look at these buildings—they're torn to shreds, reduced to mere rubble."

"But how?" Trevor asked. "We've only been gone a little while. How could the world turn to dust so quickly?"

"Could have been a storm? Natural disasters happen, ya know," Amanda chimed in.

"Unless," Sky began, gazing out at the stars. "Something got through from the other side."

Jake didn't fully understand. "What are you talking about?"

Sky pointed to the stars and moved his hand right toward the library. "You say that door can go to the Creator's Palace. Well, then, the door must work both ways—that's how doors work. They give and take. Something, someone, could have gotten through from the other side. Maybe the Creator wanted to send something back."

All this time he had been thinking about getting to the Creator's Palace in order to destroy its host with The Pen. He had been told time and time again that he was supposed to carry The Pen across far distances in order to slay the most evil of villains. All of this—stopping the Creator, carrying The Pen, traveling the miles—was to stop the Creator from wreaking havoc.

But maybe that wasn't true at all.

"Maybe we're too late," Jake said.

V

Jake knew that aside from being the Holder of The Pen, or the Prophet, as he was once called by Moss and the council, Jake considered himself to be the leader of his group. He never had felt that way about anything in his life. Time and time again he played second fiddle to Kevin. From those moments at Friendly's to simply hanging out in the backyard, Jake was always the afterthought, the second-best, the follower. But his journey had lifted his confidence higher than it had ever been. And now, standing there before all of his comrades, back home in a world that felt unbelievably alien to them, Jake knew he had to keep his cool. He couldn't lose his mind and freak everybody out.

When Jake's mind returned to the conversation, he realized that the group had already decided what they were going to do next.

They were going to stay in South Hills.

And when they made that decision, Jake felt a twinge of something nag at his gut. He didn't want to stay.

Here he was trying to show the entire group why going back to Discis and saving that world would help. All he wanted to do was go back to the oddball world he came from so he could save the world he was from. He didn't understand why the others didn't understand. His world—Earth, the United States, South Hills—was broken, rusted down and shaved to its broken bottom. Only the skeletons of a formerly vibrant town remained. Nothing but despair, depression, and disillusionment remained here. But in Discis—in a world where Jake was a hero and his fate alone determined the outcome of not only one, but apparently two worlds—everything was just starting to comeback to life.

"I think you guys are all making the wrong choice here," Jake said. "I mean our world is gone. The life we knew is no more, ya know?"

Jake knew the argument with Kevin was going to continue, especially now that he was making his case a little more forcefully. Kevin stepped forward, ran his hand through his hair, and eyed Jake with more intensity than either was accustomed to. They made the small group pause.

"You can't be serious, Jake," he said. "We're home. We're back where we belong. We didn't want to go to Discis, Jake. None of us did. We randomly fell into that craphole of a planet and now we're finally back home. It's been too damn long since I've had a real bed to sleep in and a real cup of coffee. I'm not going back."

Jake shook his head. "You're making a mistake, Kevin. Why do you think we were brought there in the first place? Why do you think that when you were skateboarding down that highway that you were sucked into a new world? Huh?"

"What about you, Jake? Why do you think you're supposed to be there? And why the hell are you so desperate to go back there?" Kevin asked, stepping forward and ignoring the group as his eyes burned into Jake's face. "Is it because you're not the hero here, Jake? Is it because in Discis, with that stupid Pen of yours and that idea of the Holder, that you're more than you can ever be here?"

"Shut up, Kevin."

Kevin smirked. "No, I'm done defending you. Since we were little, I've been protecting you and saving you. I'm the one that brought you friends. I'm the one that brought you girls. I'm the one that got you out of fights. I'm the one who is always saving you. You aren't the hero, Jake. And any world where you are the savior, that's a world that I'd never want to be a part of because it would just fall apart and crumble."

No one said anything. No one moved or stirred. Everyone felt the emotion hanging heavily between the two cousins. Jake was broken—it was clear by the way he wouldn't say anything and shook in his stance. Kevin, after hearing his words and letting them out, was similarly broken and shattered. He didn't want to hurt his cousin, but he wanted to stay home that much more. He would do anything for real food and hospitality. And if that meant destroying his cousin's feelings in process, he was fine with it.

Trevor and Amanda huddled together on the corner of the street. If push came to shove, he'd fight for Kevin, his one and true friend. But Amanda, he knew, was sensitive about all of this, too. She wouldn't want to see the little guy—Jake, in this case—ridiculed and bullied.

But there was something Trevor knew that beat out all the reasons to not get involved in this argument: he wanted to protect Amanda. And the only way he could do that was to bring her back home to Florida and away from Discis. He couldn't risk bringing her back to a world where she was a miserable prisoner who just wanted an escape.

So Trevor stepped forward over a pile of rubble, holding Amanda's hand with his own, and found his spot next to Kevin.

"I'm sorry, Jake," he said, "but I'm staying, too."

Sky, without a word to Jake, also moved past the pile and ended up on Kevin's side. He looked down at the rubble before him before looking up at the boy he had befriended just a few short days ago. He tried to force a smile, but nothing came.

"Sorry, Jake," he said. "But I've been searching for a way home for too damn long. I can't imagine going back to a world where I felt trapped. If you want to do this, then you have to do it alone."

And that's when the lines were drawn. Kevin, Trevor, Amanda, and Sky on one side, and Jake on his own. A line of broken glass, metal and sticks lay between them. Jake swerved his head to the right, completely away from his friends, displeased by the situation.

They didn't say another word. Kevin, Trevor, Amanda, and Sky collected themselves and walked away from Jake, heading right down the street and into the darkness. Jake didn't watch them walk. He kept his head on the street behind him and let his mind race about what had just happened. In a matter of seconds, Jake lost all the friends he had gained over the last month.

He was alone.

Since this whole thing began, Jake was told he was the hero. He was the Holder of The Pen, the Prophet. He was the only one who could destroy the Creator and restore Discis. And if everything panned out the way he thought it would, he could restore his home by doing so.

Everyone—Moss, Shelton, Richard, the Creator, Kevin, Trevor, Amanda, and Sky—had all followed Jake on his quest to save the world and rescue a decaying planet from its horrible leader. He was going to ascend to the Creator's Palace, turn The Pen into a sword and finally end the Creator's time as the villainous ruler that he surely was. They had all believed in him, so he believed, too.

But now Jake wasn't so sure anymore. He felt rather hopeless. He felt like he had already failed and that he didn't have the power to do this alone.

VI

Jake sighed heavy when he finished telling the story of his short journey home, and eyed the man across the barely lit campfire—the man who had found Jake when Jake most needed finding. Silence floated between them, the sole sound of the crackling embers deafening in its subtly. Winds howled from the west. But all else around them was still and unmoving. It was as though they were the only two left in this dying world.

"Did you ever find out what happened to them?"

Jake shook his head. "Nope. I came back and that's when you found me. For all I know, they're dead in the world I left behind."

The man across the fire took his stick and poked the flames. "There's nothing you could have done, Jake. They are all meant to do things on their own. You can't push people to do what you want. Only fate can."

Jake nodded. "I know. I just wish I knew what to do next."

And that's when the man stood up and smirked.

"We know what's next," Moss said. "War."

CHAPTER 35

I

"So this is where Jake used to live?" Sky asked, stepping over the broken wooden steps on his way to the porch that overlooked the slums of South Hills. Kevin turned and surveyed the area. He saw his childhood. He saw the world he had grown up in, even though he was only here part of the time.

"Yep. Good ol' Serent Ranch. Funny to be back here," Kevin said, turning back around toward the group, stepping by Trevor and Amanda, and getting to the creaking porch. "Seems like everything's a mess."

"So where are Jake's folks?" Sky asked, clueless.

Kevin hopped up onto the porch and reached the crimson and scratched red door. "His dad died when he was young, so God knows where. And his mom, well, God help her."

He bowed his head and stared at the ground, hoping his cousin's mom hadn't suffered the worst. Trevor, Amanda and Sky all bowed just the same, worried that an innocent bystander, and a loved one of someone they all cared for and knew, was possibly on the wrong end of things. The world they were in now didn't look like it took care of its citizens. Everything looked lifeless.

"So what's the plan? Go inside and steal some goodies?" Trevor asked.

"I'm starving," Amanda responded, holding her growling stomach.

Kevin thought about knocking—it's what he would have done a month ago—but instead squeezed the doorknob and went to open the door. Nothing happened. The door didn't budge. He tried again, but it remained still and tall. He tried a shoulder tackle, but knew the door would win that fight.

"Damn," Kevin said under his breath. "It's locked."

Right at that moment, glass shattered and spewed in all different directions. Trevor covered himself and Amanda, Kevin bunkered down low, and they all turned to see Sky standing with his arm cradled by his chest. He broke the window.

"What?" he asked. He ignored the questioning looks they gave him as he stepped through the window and into the Serent home. Trevor, Kevin, and Amanda followed suit, stepping over the broken glass and into the dark pit that was waiting before them.

Everything was dark. Pitch dark. Lifeless dark. They all squinted their eyes to try and find something, as though that would help. They peered around the room, trying to make sense of anything so they could catch their bearings. But nothing came. It was too damn dark.

Within seconds, though, their eyes adjusted and they started to make out the faintest outlines of a living room and household furniture.

"Looks like someone's lived here before," Trevor said.

Sky nodded. "But when was the last time they lived here? That's the more important question, I think. The fact that the rest of the area is in the pits and this house is in good shape screams weird to me."

Trevor shrugged. "I don't think there's much to worry about. I'm betting something crazy happened—maybe it was that dude with the fireballs—and everyone had to evacuate. Jake's mom was one of those people. Doesn't mean people were hurt or anything."

Sky smirked. "The more you ignore the obvious, the more likely it is."

"What do you know about it?" Trevor asked. "What makes you think you know more than I do about any of this? Newsflash, Sky, you've been in a cave for the last decade. Me? I've been living in this world. It's moved on from your time."

Sky stepped closer to Trevor. He looked at Amanda and then back at the boy before him. "If you had seen the things I had, you'd be a lot more worried about the absence of people. When the people are gone, that's the first sign that there's trouble."

Amanda stepped closer. "What do you mean?"

Sky waved his arm around. "There are no people here. It's as though an entire civilization was wiped off the face of the planet. Does that sound familiar? Well, it should. Take Discis, for example. Besides the lone kingdom or council, the world is barren up in the northern regions. People are gone. It's a sign that things can't be right."

"You're saying what happened on Discis—all those people missing, all the emptiness—is happening here? What, so, people just disappeared?" Trevor asked. "Or did the Creator come and kill people?"

Sky shrugged. "I don't know what happened, Trevor. All I know is that the last time there was a world without people and there was a crazy man terrorizing everyone, it was in the place that we just came from. So I'm going to be as cautious as I can be."

And then there was light. A thin flickering flame rose from the darkness and lighted the room. Holding the flame, and the lighter from which it came, was Kevin.

"Enough," he said. "Let's find what we can to eat and drink, and maybe get a clue of where we're going."

Kevin, Trevor and Amanda joined together and started walking around to find things. Sky remained still. He eyed the home he was in and everything it represented. And it was at that moment, when he was alone and looking at a place that had once been a sanctuary to a family, that Sky felt as though he had done this before.

II

There wasn't any food.

Kevin knew there wasn't food after he scoured the kitchen and didn't find anything. It was unlikely his friends would find anything in the floors below, and he was right to think that. Sky, Trevor, and Amanda came back upstairs empty-handed, without any food or drink. The house, even with all of its appliances and furniture, was barren of anything that could help tie them over until they figured out what was going on and what their next step was going to be.

Kevin swung around the doorframe into the living room—which had been reduced to a shredded up brown couch and knocked-over coffee table—where the rest of the group waited for him. He shrugged at them and went to the door, ready to leave. The group didn't question his motives and followed him out the door. Jake had been the leader before, but with him gone, Kevin was in charge of their next move. They didn't really have a real next move anyway, so following Kevin, even if he didn't have a plan, was better than just waiting around.

They stepped out into the cool brisk air, the wind howling around them. It was pitch dark. The streets were empty. Lifeless.

"So, children, where to now?" Sky asked.

Kevin faced the opposite direction. "I guess we've got to find some people and find out what's going on."

"You think everyone just disappeared?"

Kevin shook his head. "No way. Everyone probably left because of the dude with the fireballs. He probably destroyed the town's electrical resources and everyone left. But until we know more, it makes sense to find someone that can explain everything to us."

Before they started moving, Amanda looked over at Sky and saw his eyes floating around between the trees and buildings next to them. He looked worried. "Sky?" she asked. He whipped his head toward her. "What's wrong?" Kevin and Trevor turned their attention to him after hearing Amanda say something.

"This is so familiar," he said. "I feel like I've done this before."

"What? Like déjà vu?" Trevor asked.

Sky shook his head. "No. It's like one of those dreams that becomes more of a memory over time. I don't think I've lived this before, not exactly. But it's definitely something I've seen before."

There was a pop and a bang. Sky's limp body fell to the pavement.

"ON THE GROUND! NOW!"

Before he could react, Kevin was shoved to the ground and felt a cold pole on the back of his head. A foot stomped on his back and held him down. He heard Amanda scream and Trevor shout. He looked over and saw Amanda was on the ground, a gun pointed at the back of her head. Trevor had a gun to his head, too, and a foot was shoving on his skull right into the pavement. Sky lay motionless just to the right.

"ON THE GROUND! SHUT UP! ALL OF YOU SHUT YOUR DAMN FACES AND LISTEN TO ME RIGHT NOW! RIGHT NOW!"

Kevin felt a jolt in his side as a boot lightly tapped him.

"TELL ME RIGHT NOW WHAT YOU'RE DOING HERE! RIGHT NOW!"

Kevin tried to speak, but his mouth only ate pavement.

"SPEAK UP! RIGHT NOW OR I'LL BLOW BOTH OF THEIR BRAINS OUT!"

Kevin heard the gun cock. Amanda yelped and Trevor shouted.

"BETTER TALK BLONDEY! TIME'S RUNNING OUT!"

Kevin pushed off the ground enough to get his mouth away from the tar. "Stop! Stop! Please! We just got here and we have no idea what's going on! Please! Stop!"

"WHERE ARE YOU COMING FROM? TELL US RIGHT NOW!"

Panting, Kevin responded, "We're from here. We just got back into town and we came to our friend's house to see if anyone is home, but no one's here."

"DON'T LIE TO ME, BOY! DON'T LIE TO ME! TELL ME THE DAMN TRUTH OR I'LL SHOOT THIS GIRL RIGHT IN FRONT OF YOU! I SWEAR! I SWEAR BOY!"

"I promise. I promise. It's the truth. We just got back."

Silence.

It felt good to hear quiet. Kevin knew the man above him was thinking everything over. The gun on the back of Kevin's head lifted and so did the boot that was shoving him down. Kevin got to his feet and faced the man before him, who was dressed in all black with a black shield covering his face. Looking around, Kevin saw three similar guards were keeping Amanda and Trevor locked to the ground. Sky still lay limp. When Kevin looked back toward his officer, he noticed a handful more emerging from the darkness, all of them clutching their rifles and aiming them right at Kevin. Bright red circles flooded his torso. He knew one wrong move would send bullets right through his body.

"Tell me, boy," the officer said calmly, "what year is it?"

"What?"

"The year. What year is it? You say you're from here. What's the year? Simple question."

"How is that going to help?"

The officer lifted a pistol and cocked it. He pointed it right at Kevin. "The year. Now."

Kevin swallowed hard. "I don't know."

The officer eyed Kevin suspiciously. He tilted his head to the left, his eyes locked on Kevin's. "You hear that, boys? He says he doesn't know the year. Guess we've got ourselves a Loyalist."

The man lowered his gun and put it back in his holster. Kevin looked around him to see what was happening. The three men still had their guns locked on Trevor and Amanda, and Sky was still laid out cold in the corner. When he swung back around, Kevin noticed the shooters who came from the darkness minutes ago were gone, and it was just him and the officer now. Kevin felt his nerves relax.

"Thank you. Thank you for believing me."

The officer extended his hand. "Pleasure's mine. I'm Bill."

Kevin shook his hand. "Kevin."

"Seems you all got yourselves into a bit of a mess here, huh? Looks like you got back into town when everyone's already gone. Man, if I were you, I'd be scared, too."

Kevin nodded. "Yeah. We have no idea what to think about what's going on. We're still trying to figure it out. We lost our friend and now we're here by ourselves and we just can't figure out what to do next. I'm not really sure what's been going on the last couple of days."

Bill nodded. "Well, hopefully we can help you get your friend back. Least we can do. And I promise you, we'll explain everything you need to know."

The butterflies that set up camp in Kevin's stomach were gone. Joy was the only thing that remained. Everything was going to be all right. The scares and torment he and his friends had gone through were about to cease. Finally they could get answers to why their home was barren and what these soldiers were doing here. It would all come to an end, and they'd finally put Discis behind them.

But then Kevin realized his friends weren't with him. He turned around and saw Sky, Trevor, and Amanda were gone, and so were the soldiers who were keeping them to the ground.

"Wait, where are my friends?"

Bill smiled. "Your friends are coming home with us."

"Wait, what?"

"And so are you."

Darkness.

III

The darkness lasted for hours. Kevin opened his eyes. The blackest black surrounded him. It was cold, damp, and soundless, wherever he was. His body shivered, the bitter cold cutting deep into his bones and slashing away as though it were the jagged edge of a knife. He couldn't see his breath; there wasn't enough light. But he knew one deep breath would fog up the room.

A drop of water cried in the distance. The walls moaned. Kevin was relieved to hear some semblance of sound, even though he couldn't make out what those exact sounds were. His teeth chattered. His body jerked in a fit from the freezing cold. Kevin was the only thing moving in an otherwise still place.

A door opened in the distance. Kevin jerked his head and saw a pale light come from far off. The door closed and all was pitch black again, but only for a moment. Lights attached to hanging lamps at the ceiling buzzed on, swinging when they did. They flickered for a second before they caught fire and illuminated the room. And then Kevin saw where he was. It was a hallway, lined with cages. Kevin, for a reason he did not know, was trapped in one of these cages, too. His cage was simple. It was just him and the floor. No blankets, no bench, nothing. Just a stain-green floor with rusted spots, and him.

Footsteps banged against the cement floor. Kevin spun his head around to try and gain some idea of who was coming to him.

"Help me," Kevin heard himself say. "Help me, please."

The boots stopped.

"Please, please help me. I don't know where I am or why I'm here. Please," Kevin said. He couldn't remember the last time he asked someone for something, but it came out as though it was second nature.

The boots moved again, and the sound of them hitting against the floor got closer. Kevin picked himself off the ground, his body sore and his legs a pair of heavy rocks. Kevin gripped onto the chain-link cage and peered through. A shadow passed through the darkness. The boots came to a stop at his cage, and that's when Kevin saw Bill, the man he had met earlier, standing before him.

"You," Kevin said.

"Me," Bill replied.

"Will you help me? Why am I here?"

Bill smirked. "That's not something for me to answer, boy. You'll have to talk to The General."

Kevin bowed his head against the fence, still gripping it. He sighed. "Where are my friends?"

Bill smiled. "Again, you'll have to ask The General."

"Great," he said sardonically. "Will you take me to him?"

"Of course," Bill said. It was only then Kevin realized Bill had a key in his hand and was twiddling it between his fingers. He put it into the lock that kept Kevin in the cage. "But before I do that, The General asked me to do something else."

The key unlocked the cage and there was a buzz. Bill slammed the cage door shut behind him and stood tall in front of Kevin. Before he could do anything, Bill drove his fist into Kevin's gut. Kevin fell to the floor. But before he could wallow in pain, Bill rose up and jammed his knee into Kevin's nose, spilling blood and sending Kevin to the floor in a daze. Kevin's eyes spun and his world floated in a circle of nausea and pain.

But it didn't end there.

Kevin felt himself being picked up by the collar and then he was thrown against the cage fence. He bounced off and smacked against the ground. He was hoping he'd go unconscious, but he didn't. He was still awake and alive and here in this reality. A boot knocked into his side and he felt a rib snap. Another kick rolled Kevin onto his back. A boot stomped onto his gut, and Kevin immediately spit up blood. Kevin felt himself get hoisted up again and, with more force than before, tossed against the cage. He fell to the ground again, broken.

Kevin spit. He coughed up blood. He slapped his hand against the pavement, his face tearing up and his body crying out in pain. Blood poured from so many places he couldn't keep track.

Bill lifted Kevin by the hair to face him. And, without a word, Bill drove his fist right into Kevin's face, breaking him.

Darkness again.

IV

When Kevin came to, it was dark again. But a bright yellow light flickered, and Kevin found himself sitting at a dark brown table with a chair on the other side. A glass of water rested on the table, as did a pair of pale pills with a note that told him to take them when he awoke. Kevin, still dazed and confused, swallowed the pills and drank the water.

Almost instantly, his body felt refreshed and the pain drifted away like a plank of wood in water.

There was another buzzing sound and the door to the room creaked open. Stepping into the room was a solider, like the ones Kevin had seen back at the house. He was dressed in an all black uniform: black shirt, camo, vest, pants, boots, gloves, and a shield mask. He sat down in the chair across from Kevin, pressed a button, and his shield lowered. Kevin stared back at a man with a square jaw, deep blue eyes, and fading brown hair with gray overtaking the sides.

"Welcome, Kevin," said the man. "I am The General. General Curtis."

Kevin looked around the room and noticed glass windows on the side—those kind of glass windows you find in the police departments, where only one person can see through them.

"It's just you and me, Kevin, no one else. Trust me, I can handle you myself," The General said, smiling a little bit. "Did you take the pills?"

Kevin nodded.

"Good. They should keep you healthy for a little while, at least long enough for us to talk about things. I'm sorry about the way my officers have been treating you, but you can't blame them, can you?"

"Where are my friends?" Kevin asked.

"Your friends are fine."

"No. Tell me, tell me right now where they are."

"They're fine. But is there something else you want to ask me?"

Kevin leaned forward. "Why? Why am I in a cage? Why are you holding me here?

The General smiled. "Why? Why not?" When Kevin didn't budge, The General smiled again. "You've identified yourself as a Loyalist." The General shrugged. "Call it protocol."

"What do you mean, Loyalist? What are you even talking about?"

"Listen to me, kid. You're young, I can see that. And whatever your motives are for being a Loyalist, I'm sure they seem right to you, or your family, or your friends, or whoever put you up to this. Whatever. But living life as a Loyalist is no way to survive. It's only going to end in pain."

Kevin didn't even know what to say. "I'm not a Loyalist."

The General shifted in his seat. The tide turned. He licked his teeth and cleared his throat. "Do you want to hear a story? I'm sure you don't, but I'm going to tell it to you anyway because, well, you're being held here and I like to talk. So, about four years ago, I was given service duty in some faraway country that you've probably never heard of. And when I went there, I noticed how grim and uncontrollable war can be. I mean, you have to make some choices that you never thought you'd have to make. And yes, I know that's very cliché of me to say and something you'd hear in the movies. But it's so true. We have to make choices, sometimes small, sometimes large, but all the time you're thinking to yourself, how did I get in this position where I have to choose something like this? It's really quite fascinating.

"Anyway, one day I'm doing my normal patrol duties. Scan the marked areas, make sure nothing crazy is happening, and get back to base. Should take, oh, I don't know, two hours to complete. Max. No one ever took more than that to complete their route. So I'm walking, doing my thing, scoping out the areas, doing what I have to do," he continued. "And this one day, of course, a little kid rolls up on my watch and he's got a grenade in his hand. He's ready to blow me sky high without a second thought. He was so young I could still smell the breast milk off his breath. So I look at him and put my hand in his face and I tell him to calm down. I tell him to put the toy away and walk away from me. And he's giving me these eyes. These devilish eyes as though I was the one person that made his life so damn terrible. Like I was the problem for all the sins his family, friends, and the entire world had committed. I mean, have you ever had somebody look at you that way? Look at you like they didn't just want to kill you, but they wanted to savor the moment and lick their lips because it gave them such satisfaction? This little boy, couldn't be older than two, was doing that for me. He wanted to blow himself up along with me, because my death was the only thing that would satisfy him in this world.

"So I had to make a choice, right then and there, what I had to do. I couldn't kill the boy, because killing him would only kill me, too. I couldn't run away because he'd throw the grenade and get me. So my only option was to talk him into putting the grenade away and saving my life. So I kept telling him, calmly, to throw the toy in the opposite direction, to stop this madness before it got crazy, to save us all from a messy situation and bring freedom back to his life," The General paused. "And I must have been pretty persuasive, because the boy turned around and walked away. He walked right back down the street where he came from and disappeared from my sight. I'm still here, ain't I? Do you want to know what happened next?"

Kevin didn't move.

"The next thing we know there's an explosion on the same road. The kid blew up his house, killing his mother, his father, his three sisters, and some friends who were over at the same," The General said, his face cold and unmoving. "Can you believe it? I could have sacrificed myself and the kid and saved about 10 lives that day. But did I? No. I took the easy route and let the kid go, thinking that was going to solve all my problems. But it didn't. It only made things worse."

The General looked down at the table, as though the past was looking back at him. He shuffled in his seat and faced Kevin. "I'm not going to make that mistake again," he continued, "Kevin."

Kevin's eyes grew wide. How did he know his name?

"See, I know who you are, and I know why you're here, and I know what you're trying to do. And it's not going to happen. I'm going to change your mind about things and stop you from destroying us," The General said, his voice deep and dark. He stood up. "Guards. Take Mr. Keys back to his cell. Let him rot in there for a few hours. And no more pills."

The door buzzed open and two soldiers came into the room. They wrapped their arms around Kevin and gripped him. Kevin shouted out in protest. "No! No! Hey! Where are my friends? Huh? WHERE ARE THEY?"

The General stopped at the door.

"You're never going to see your friends again."

He smiled as he turned the corner and left the room. Kevin tried to shove the guards off, but it was to no avail. They held on and restrained him. Kevin shouted out in anger, frustrated beyond belief. He cussed and swore and threw out words he didn't know he'd ever say.

The guards dragged him away and threw him back into the darkness.

CHAPTER 36

I

Door opens. Everything's white.

Kevin blinks. Blinks. Blinkblinkblinkblink.

Light stabs his eyes. Stabstabstab.

Where's the world? Whiteness. Pureness. Light keeps him in the dark.

He puts his head on shoulders. Lifts his head. Sees a bit more. Light dissipates. True colors come back.

He leans his head to the left. Eyes sag. Face burns.

Cuts.

Scraps.

Bruises.

Cuts.

Sees a lone figure in the light. Kevin can't move. He's stuck. Stuck against the wall.

Broken.

Battered.

Bruised.

He can't move.

Stuck. Alive, yes, but stuck.

The man says something. Kevin can't understand. Can't hear. Can't think. Man moves toward Kevin. Kevin doesn't care. He wants to move. Wants to think. Wants to want. He just exists. He breathes. He barely breathes. He waits. Waits for something.

Man says something else.

Kevin can't speak. Can't speak at all. He wants to. He wants to speak. He wants to want.

Cut to another room, and there Kevin sits. Alone. In a chair. The stained brown and green walls creak and moan. He has his sight back. He's lucid. He can see. He's returned from the dead. He's hungry. Starving. Could eat a horse. Could eat a house. Could eat himself. Himself. Kevin. Kevin Keys. Where is he? Here. Where's here? Here's home. Home is Earth. Back again. Back from Discis. Discis. Jake. His cousin. Wish he could see his cousin. Wish he could tell his cousin everything was going to be OK. But it won't be. Discis isn't OK. Earth is OK. Discis is not OK. Earth is OK. Discis is OK. Earth is not OK. What is OK anymore, anyway? OK? Discis. Earth. Neither are OK. Neither are not OK.

"Hello Kevin," he hears. Kevin turns. Neck hurts. Eyes tired. Blood all over. Scraps. Cuts. Burns. He wants out. Wants different. Wants new. Wants to be OK. But he won't be. Not yet. Maybe soon. But not now. Now is just pain. Now is just real. Now is just real pain.

Kevin looks. It's a man. Average height. Red shirt. Black vest. Glass. Young, mid-30s maybe. He's pale, plain-faced, and gawky. He has a cane. His eyebrow is raised. He walks over to Kevin, smirks, and says, "I've been waiting a long time for this."

Kevin's confused. He doesn't get it. How did this man know him? Who was this man? Where was he, again? Home?

Kevin tries speaking. Dust floats out of his mouth. "Sorry," he wheezed. "Water. Hungry."

The man smirks again. "I understand they haven't been treating you well. Understandable, since they want me to believe that you're one of us. But I know you, Kevin. I know you're not one of us. But I know who you are. Who you really are."

Kevin raises his eyebrow. He's still confused, still uncertain about this. Again, who is this man? How does he know Kevin? And, what does he know about Kevin?

"Sorry," Kevin says, his words jagged and knife-like against his throat. "You must be mistaken."

The man sits at the table. He reaches into his pocket. He throws a yellow newspaper onto the table. He bends his head and reads, "Kevin Keys, 16, has gone missing. He was last said to have been headed toward the Mass Pike. Now no one can find him. Keys was once a foster child who has moved from family to family."

The man slides the newspaper away and pulls out another sheet of white paper. "This is a police report dated September 26, almost 10 years ago. Kevin Keys, 16, has gone missing. The boy has been gone for weeks now. His family has decided to host a funeral in his honor. Keys's skateboard was found on the I-90 highway buried in the bushes, along with another skateboard belonging to Trevor McGrevor, a friend of Mr. Keys who has also gone missing."

The man reaches down and pulls out another piece of paper. It's another police report. "This one is dated January 14 of the following year," he says. Kevin's ears perk up. He knows this is after he, Jake, and Trevor had left for Discis. "The disappearance of Mr. Keys has raised some more interesting questions. Keys's best friend Trevor McGrevor is missing. Mr. Keys's cousin Jake Serent is missing, and so are Mr. Serent's friends Richard Lyons and Shelton Reclard. All five boys are believed to be a part of a conspiracy related to the death of Feona Griswold, the girlfriend of Mr. Reclard. The search goes on for the boys."

Kevin looks. He's bewildered. How could this be? He was a suspect of a murder? But how? Why?

"That was nine years ago," the man says.

Kevin's jaw drops.

"Well, soon to be 10. It's been 10 years since you went missing, Mr. Keys. And now here you are," he pauses. He looks at Kevin and smiles. "You're here just when we needed you most."

"What do you mean?" Kevin lets out.

The man smiles. "Let me explain. But first, let's get you feeling better."

II

Kevin's lucidity returned shortly after taking another one of those pills. The man, who Kevin now knew as Bennifer Lamberto, bartered his way into getting one of the pills for Kevin. The pills, Kevin learned, were an advanced form of pain reliever that returned the pain sensors in the brain to neutral, allowing one to heal without feeling any of the pain.

"So, let's talk," Bennifer said, slapping his palms down on the table. "Where was I? Right, right, OK. So it's been 10 years since you disappeared. But you're probably wondering why you're such an interesting case."

Kevin nodded. "Yeah, of course. Why do you guys know me? What's so special?"

Bennifer smirked and stroked his face before continuing. "You disappeared on a highway. And like I said, your cousin disappeared, too, as did your friend. Then they found Feona dead at one of your cousin's friend's homes. And immediately allegations went out toward you and your friends for all being co-conspirators in that murder. According to the reports I read, nothing came to light. They blamed it on Shelton Reclard, and then it kind of all fizzled away when they couldn't find any of you. The search went on for a long time, though, since it was five of you who just disappeared out of nowhere.

"But then we had to move on. Our world turned on us," Bennifer said.

"What do you mean it turned on you?" Kevin asked.

Bennifer shrugged. "The world began to eat itself. Many places became unlivable. It became too warm, and then too cold, and then too polluted. The world, simply, because a major source of concern for itself. We couldn't fix anything. So we all separated. Some of us became Loyalists, trying to save the world and keep it the way it was. We didn't set up a true government or system. Others joined The New Order to create a better Earth, one with dates, calendars and order. It's all very confusing. But the basic element is this: The world is now in utter disarray. But you, Kevin Keys, can help us save it."

Up until this point, Kevin went along with everything. He understood pretty well that the only way to get the answers he wanted was by listening and at least pretending to be the person that Bennifer wanted him to be. Kevin knew Bennifer must have his facts wrong. Kevin was merely a teenage boy who had too much fun skateboarding and hitting on chicks. Helping government agencies from the future—the present?—wasn't on his list of tricks.

"Sorry, but I have no idea how I could help you guys. I'm just a skater kid that moves from family to family and girl to girl. Not sure what value I have for you," Kevin said. And he was being honest. This wasn't his thing.

Bennifer smiled. He stroked the side of his cane and laid his hand flat on the table. "You're worth more than you know, Kevin. In fact, you're worth so much that these men are going to kill you if I don't bring you home with me. They're using you as bait. Not because you're a Loyalist, but because they think I don't know you're a Loyalist. You're a pawn in their game, but you're the ultimate chess piece in mine."

"I don't understand," Kevin said.

Bennifer cleared his throat. "Did you ever hear my name before? Did you ever hear about who I was before I became the man I am right now? Probably not. After all, I'm not someone that people really like to talk about. I was once a member of The New Order. Yes, yes, I know, how can that be? Well, it's simple. I was a soldier for these men, doing my daily job. I did as I was told. I followed orders, cleaned up messes, created new ideas, found new areas to explore, and what have you. And I was everyone's favor and errand boy. You needed something done? OK, I'm off to find it and figure it out. Everyone wanted me to do the hard work for them, so I did. This wasn't a bad gig in the slightest, and it was a great foot in the door for any future political ambitions I had. So I went along with it. Did as I was told, kept my mouth shut, and didn't get involved with anything.

"So then one day I'm on my normal routine and I stumble across a dark hallway. No one's around, so I thought I'd go on a stroll," Bennifer continued, his face looking up into the sky as though his past was resting there. "Normally I'd follow my schedule to a T and just go onto my next thing. But something seemed to be calling me from the hallway. Something wanted me to go down that dark path and find whatever was down it. Not sure what it was, nor can I explain it now, but it's as if someone was pushing me slightly to go down the hall. So I did. And there, right at the end of it, I saw a single door with the number 77 on the front. And through the small window, I saw blue lights flashing on and off."

"And what was in the room?"

Bennifer was looking far off into the distance. "It was the one thing that changed everything. It's hard to describe simply, but it's an anomaly of some sort, a hole in time and space. I won't bore you with more details, but basically someone found me in the hallway and I was put on the watch for the anomaly room. And there weren't many experiments or anything done, until one day we tried sending soldiers through. It didn't work. But we tested to see where it leads and we found it's a planet far off in the galaxy, one rich with all the things our world is missing now. A world, I hear, you may be familiar with," Bennifer said with a smile.

That's when the dots came together for Kevin. The pocket, the anomaly inside the room, was a pathway to Discis, much like Jake said the door to the library was, or the area on the Mass Pike. It was yet another entrance into this world that Kevin spent so much of his time on.

Kevin thought about it a little more and then came to understand Bennifer's plan. "You need me to help you get there."

Bennifer nodded. "Now we're talking."

III

Bennifer left the room for lunch. Kevin stayed and waited for his own food to arrive—food full of maggots, mold and mystery. But he was hungry. He was willing to chew anything.

Kevin looked back at the door, expecting to see Bennifer, but there stood Amanda, her hair flowing past her shoulders down to her ribs and her face a sight for sore eyes. She looked timid and rigid, like she had stage fright. Kevin moved in his seat, trying to stand but chains held him down.

"Amanda! Oh my God! Amanda! Amanda!"

Amanda gave a quick half smile, and it was then that Kevin realized she had a tray of food in hand. Amanda, as though she was walking on a balance beam, strode over to Kevin and rested the tray of food down on the table before Kevin. She turned back around toward the door.

"Whoa, whoa, Amanda!" Kevin shouted. "Where are you going? What's going on?"

"Can't talk," Amanda said. She did as she was told.

"What? Why? What do they have you doing? Why are you wearing a black uniform? What's going on out there? Where's Trevor? Come on, talk to me," Kevin said, pleading with her.

Amanda shook her head. "Can't. It's complicated. Trevor's fine."

She disappeared as quickly as she had arrived.

IV

By the time Bennifer came back, Kevin was full of energy. There was a kick to his step. Before Amanda came in and dropped off the food, he thought his friends were dead. He didn't know what to think. But now that he knew his friends were OK and out in the world—working for The New Order by the looks of it—he had some leverage. He had something to fight for and believe in again.

Kevin settled in his chair, slouching back and eyeing Bennifer with contempt as the man with the cane sat down across from him.

"Did you enjoy lunch?" Bennifer asked.

Kevin nodded.

"Good. Now, where were we? Ah, yeah, the room. The room with the tunnel to another world. A tunnel that only you can get through," Bennifer asked.

Kevin chuckled in his seat.

"What's so funny?"

Kevin sent venom to his opponent across the table. "I'm not doing one damn thing until you assholes let me out of here. Understand?"

Bennifer raised his eyebrow high, almost touching the hair on top of his head. "Excuse me?"

"My friend Amanda was just in here delivering food. She and my friend Trevor are out there, working for The New Order," Kevin said. He leaned forward and smacked the table. "You have them serving dishes and working for you. You're not going to kill us. None of us are going to die. So I'm not moving one damn finger until you let me out of here and let me move on with my life."

Bennifer readjusted himself in his chair. "Kevin, you must remember I don't work for The New Order anymore. We've been over this."

Kevin shook his head. "You're all lying. You're all just doing this so I can help you get through your little wormhole to Discis."

That's when Bennifer paused. He gulped. "Discis? Did you say, Discis?"

How did he not know the name of the planet already? He had been studying it. Kevin nodded to see where this was going.

Bennifer looked around the room frantically and a smile etched across his face. He was full of glee, Kevin could see that much. He was doing his best to bottle it up, to keep his feelings locked away so that nothing too important could be revealed.

"What?" Kevin asked.

Bennifer waved it off. "Nothing. Nothing yet. Just, please, don't make me into the bad guy here, Kevin, please. I told you, I'm not with The New Order."

"How can I believe that? No one here has been honest since I arrived. You've all beaten me up, and made me starve and take your precious little drugs. How am I supposed to believe any of you and have faith?"

That's when Bennifer smiled again, this time a more genuine and sincere smile. "Kevin, I'm not with The New Order because I got too obsessed with figuring out where this tunnel was heading to. I became too invested in it. The New Order is about reestablishing the world we have now. But I know the truth. The future isn't here. It's out there. It's out in the stars."

Kevin didn't know what to make of Bennifer's call out to the stars. He figured the world he was in now was much different than the one he left behind. He guessed if he were out in the real world again, he would have a very similar feeling.

"I left because I wanted to find something new, and it seems we have this entire idea of a war brewing because we all can't agree on what we want to do," Bennifer shook his head. "I need your help, son. I need you to help me this one time. Just one favor. One favor that'll help everyone here on Earth, and it'll help you see your friends again."

That piqued Kevin's interested. He wanted to see his friends again and see where that would lead him to.

"I know these men have lied to you. I know that they've put you in circumstances that I would never want to be in myself. I know that you have suffered and nearly died for just being in the wrong place at the wrong time," Bennifer started, emotion coming through and overtaking his face. "Kevin, I know that this hasn't been easy for you and things have been happening so quickly. I know no one has explained this all to you and given you straight answers. I see that you're suffering, and I am sorry.

"But you and I have an opportunity, right now, to save the entire planet. You and I have a chance to bring your home back to life. I know you've been gone for 10 years and a lot of the people you loved are no longer here. But we have a chance to make sure that your future is set in stone and that you have a place to call home. I read your files. I know you've always been searching for a home. Well, we can give you one. Help me now and you will have a home forever. You will have friends and a mass of people who care about you," he said, short of breath.

His eyes on the brink of spewing tears, Bennifer said, "Will you help me? Please?"

Kevin knew he couldn't say no. No meant death. Yes meant home.

"What do you want from me?"

Bennifer breathed hard. "I need you to trust me."

"Trust you?"

"Will you do that? Please? Trust me with what happens next."

Kevin considered this and nodded. He wanted to see his friends again. "Of course."

Bennifer walked to the other end of the room, his eyes stuck on Kevin. Time moved slowly. The way Bennifer maneuvered through the room toward the door, wrapping his hand around it, slowly turning it, making Kevin wait, making Kevin sweat it out, letting the silence take over the brown and green room that Kevin had spent too much of his time in for the last few hours. Sweat swelled on Kevin's head as he waited, patiently, for something, anything, to happen.

And that's when it all happened. Ever so quickly.

V

He's sitting, watching Bennifer. Bennifer walks to the door. He opens it. Doors open. Swings open.

Three soldiers rush in. They have guns their hands.

Guns.

Big guns.

Rifles. Rifles painted black. Rifles painted black that require two hands to hold.

Shields cover the soldiers' face.

Loud noises. Shouts and screams as the soldiers rush in. They point their guns at Kevin. Kevin screams. Screams for them to stop. Yells. Yells for them to stop. Yells for them to leave him alone. Kevin yells at Bennifer, who's shaking his head.

"He's not ours."

Bennifer leaves the room. Kevin's eyes follow him. He's gone.

The soldiers wrap handcuffs around Kevin. One slugs him in the face. Bruises begin to build. Another shot smacks Kevin. He hits the table hard. Kevin's lifted and slugged again. Kevin falls against the table. His head bounces off. World becomes blurry. World becomes different. Earth becomes blurry, weird, mixed, different.

Kevin finds himself in a hallway. His hands are in cuffs. He's walking. But he's really being shoved. Shoved to somewhere. Where oh where he'll go he does not know. He's pushed. Pushed through a dark brown and green hallway that's leaking. Sweating. Dripping. He's pushed again. Shoved through. He takes a left. Then a right. Then a leftrightleft. He doesn't know where he is anymore. He's pushed through a door and into light.

He's at the head of a room. Now, he faces a trillion soldiers. A million soldiers. Probably a thousand soldiers. He's unsure who's before him, but they're soldiers. Their shields are down. Their masks are gone. He's looking at everyone, and they're looking him.

"MEN!" he hears behind him. Kevin looks. It's The General. That damn General. The General who thinks he's everything. The General who thinks he's the man. The General the hero. "THIS MAN CLAIMED TO BE A LOYALIST. CLAIMED TO BE ONE OF OUR ENEMIES. AND GUESS WHAT? IS HE AN ENEMY?"

"NO!" Kevin hears the soldiers sing.

"IS HE ONE OF US?"

"NO!" the soldiers yell together

"SHOULD HE BE ONE OF US?"

"NO!" the soldiers yells.

"AND WHY NOT?"

"BECAUSE HE CLAIMED TO BE A LOYALIST, SIR!"

"AND IS HE A LOYALIST?"

"NO!"

"AND IS HE ONE OF US?!"

"NO!"

"AND WHAT DO WE DO WITH THOSE WHO AREN'T ONE OF US?"

"END THEM!"

"EXCUSE ME?"

"END THEM!"

"WHAT WAS THAT?"

"END THEM! END THEM! END THEM! END HIM! END HIM! END HIM! END HIM! END HIM! END HIM! END HIM! END HIM! END HIM! END HIM! END HIM! END HIM! END HIM! END HIM!"

The chants continue. Kevin looks to his left. The General walks toward him. The soldiers chant away. They shout and yell, scream and yelp. They ask The General to end him. End him, end him, they shout. Endhimendhimendhimendhim.

They're banging tables. Kevin hears the bangs. Hears the shouts. He's hearing everything. He sees the soldiers pound the table. He sees The General walk toward him. He sees everything. Kevin swallows. He tastes the meal he ate. Tastes his fear. Kevin tastes everything. Kevin struggles in his cuffs. He scrapes his wrists. Kevin feels everything. Kevin sniffs the air. Smells sweat and good food. Kevin smells everything. It all begins to swell. It all begins to mix. Sight. Sound. Smell. Touch. Taste. Soldiers. General. Bangs. Fear. Food. Cuffs. Cuts. Chaos. Shouts. ENDHIMENDHIM. It all mixes. It all becomes one. And then The General pulls out his gun. Pulls the trigger. Kevin feels nothing.

CHAPTER 37

I

"This is going to hurt."

Trevor lifted his head and saw one of the masked soldiers before him, wires in hand. He knew what was about to happen. It didn't take a genius to figure out that he was going to be electrocuted, especially because he was handcuffed to two pillars, which stretched his body out. The solider stepped toward him with the wires.

"Are you ready?"

Trevor nodded.

The pain was white-hot and it reverberated through Trevor's whole body. Jolts zoomed and zigzagged up Trevor's spine and across his neck. His body twisted and turned, the result of the extreme electric zaps that zinged out. When the first round was done, Trevor leaned his head back against the pillar and sighed. He drooled and then spat just for the sake of feeling a different emotion than electricity. Trevor looked up and saw the solider still standing there, cold and unforgiving.

"What do you want from me?" Trevor asked.

The solider stepped forward. "I've already told you. This isn't about you. This is about your friend, Kevin Keys. He's the one we want. He's the one who's going to answer our questions. And he's the only one who can save you."

"Where's Amanda?" Trevor asked, ignoring the soldier's questions.

"Let's crank up the voltage," the soldier replied, dialing up the electricity with a flick of a button.

Trevor shook his head as best he could. "No, please, no more. I can't."

"You can," the solider said. "And you will. Don't worry, Trevor. None of this will kill you. But, it will make you wish you were dead. Let's do this."

The wires touched Trevor again, and another round of the electric torture began. Before the solider was done with this round, all Trevor could think about was how he would give anything to make it all stop.

And Amanda. He was worried about Amanda.

II

Amanda didn't ask questions. She just did as she was told.

When they first came to her, she was scared beyond belief. She didn't know where Trevor was, or what he was going through, or how she was going to get out of any of this. They told her to serve the soldiers their meals—to gather plates and trays and deliver them to the soldiers as soon as she got them.

At first, she thought this would be something typical, where the soldiers sexually harassed her like a waitress from the 1950s. But not too long into the job, she realized it wasn't half bad. Each soldier was courteous and kind with her. Like well-mannered boys, the soldiers thanked her when they received meals and when they requested something else to go on the side. Each left her a tip—she had no idea what to do with the trinkets they left her, but it was better than nothing—and each soldier was exceptionally well kept. She thought things would be horrible. But the first few days of her job proved to be interesting and tolerable. It was more than she expected.

Still, she didn't know where Kevin and Trevor were. And even when she asked about them, she was told they were fine and that was the end of it. She was told not to question anything, or else she'd be given a fate worse than she could imagine.

Instead of fighting and resisting, Amanda decided to play it cool and fulfill her role. She knew the best way to defeat an enemy was to find its weakness. And by being the server and giving the soldiers their meals, she could figure out how to cut down the giant that was clearly terrorizing her friends.

"Miss, may I have another cup of coffee? Is there any left?"

Amanda smiled at the shield-less soldier, rugged with a five o'clock shadow. That was the other thing about where she was working. All the soldiers removed their shields and proved to be more than just men with armor. They were humans fighting for a cause that they called The New Order.

From general chatter and gossip between her, some soldiers, and the other waitresses, she gathered some things about the new world she was living in. She didn't want to seem too clueless, since that would only raise questions about where she was from and where she had been. But Amanda was happy to learn that not too long ago, something happened to the world she had been familiar with, and factions had risen up. The New Order was this one. Another was The United Alliance, which was more political than anything else, according to one lunch server. There were some smaller groups, too, including one that had allegiance to a new ideal that time wasn't real.

But the main political rival of The New Order was the relatively odd group called Bennifer's Army. Bennifer was a man ahead of his time, people said, and he allegedly left The New Order after a project he commissioned went horribly wrong. Since he left, though, his Army was trying to retake cities and towns at any chance they had. Soldiers called them "Loyalists."

Amanda wished she knew more, specifically about what went wrong and made the entire universe go upside down. Obviously whatever happened to South Hills was connected to whatever was happening here with The New Order. She imagined she would figure out more in the near future, and then see how she might find her way to Bennifer's Army. If The New Order was keeping her and her friends hostage, she would unite with anyone who was looking to take down the beast.

"Of course, sir, be right back," Amanda said, leaving the lunch table and heading back toward the kitchen. Soldiers waved at Amanda and smiled at her out of kindness. She was a pretty girl, so she knew what it was like to get hit on and eyed like candy. These were not those kinds of stares. These were pure niceties, pleasantries and wholesome acknowledgements. No mixed signals.

When she returned to the kitchen, Amanda saw other servers hustling about, cooks conjuring their masterpieces for soldiers to devour, and other staff members fiddling with their specific tasks. Steam floated throughout the kitchen as everyone busily shouted and called for others to help them. Amanda hurried over to the coffee machine, saw it was empty and started to brew a new pot. She had never brewed coffee until now, but she was happy to learn the skill. Very happy indeed.

Amanda saw another woman approach from the corner of her eye. The girl was sliding napkins into one of the drawers next to the coffee pot and seemed disinterested in the rest of the world.

"Hi," she said to Amanda.

Amanda was shocked to see her speak. "Hey there."

"I'm Nurse Gertrude," she said, turning and extending her hand out to Amanda.

"Hi! I'm Amanda, nice to meet you."

Gerturde shook Amanda's hand. "Nice to meet you, too," she said. "You're not from around here, are you?"

Amanda froze. Her identity had been exposed. Maybe she could hide it in someway. "What? What do you mean?"

"Well, you've got that Floridian accent," Gertrude replied.

Amanda breathed a sigh of relief. "Right, yeah, sorry. I'm not from here, I'm from Florida originally, like the Tampa area."

Gertrude raised an eyebrow. "Hmm. Florida? So how did you get all the way out here to Zion?"

Zion? What in the Hell was Zion? Amanda vaguely remembered hearing that word during history class, but otherwise she had no clue what it meant. She and her friends had started in South Hills, but after that, everything was a blur about their travels, since she had been knocked out for the trip.

"Um," Amanda paused to try and think of an answer that would go over well. "Yeah, I just felt it was the right move. I mean, I lived in Florida my whole life, and I needed a little bit of a change."

Gertrude smiled. "I feel ya. I grew up in the Midwest—Nebraska, specifically. But when I heard about all of this going on, I had to come out here. I mean, The New Order just makes so much sense in so many different ways. It's a small operation, but I think when we figure it all out, we'll be better off for it."

Amanda nodded. She had similar conversations throughout the week with people who thought The New Order was the best political faction at the moment, and that it would definitely help with the new world they were trying to build.

"Yeah, I know what you mean," Amanda said. She recognized this was her chance to find out more information. "I'm not so sure about Bennifer's Army and that whole thing. I heard they're planning something."

Gertrude raised another eyebrow. "Yeah, I haven't heard anything about that. But I wouldn't be surprised. They're always trying to shut down The New Order, it seems. I blame Bennifer for it, obviously. If he hadn't done what he'd done, he never would have tried to stop the Order."

So it seemed Gertrude knew more about Bennifer's Army than she let on. Amanda wanted to take advantage of this.

"What did he do? So many people have been telling me he did something and since then he's only wanted to take The New Order down. But no one ever tells me what he did."

Gertrude stopped fiddling with forks and knives and turned to face Amanda. "Rumor has it, he found something he shouldn't have in one of the rooms in the back. They said no one was supposed to go in the room, but he did, and since then he's had a different outlook on things. One girl said it was like a teleportation device, or time travel. Can you believe that?"

Amanda smirked and went back to the coffee. Oh, she could believe it.

"So what room was it? Maybe I should go take a look," she joked.

Gertrude laughed. "Room 77, from what I hear."

The two went back to work.

III

When Trevor came to, he was in a mostly dark room, except for the pale white light that shone down on him from the ceiling above. He bent over on his knee, his right arm chained to a pillar behind him, his left arm free. He noticed the tiled ground below and how different it was from the place he had been earlier in the day. Trevor spun his head around to try and see if there was anyone else with him, but he was alone. All the pain from earlier came rushing back to him. He surveyed his chest, seeing burn marks and cuts. He gasped at how stained his body was. These wounds would indeed become scars.

A door creaked open and boots hit the ground. Three soldiers, their shields covering their faces, stepped over to Trevor, their guns locked down at their sides. They stood still right in front of Trevor and didn't budge. The door opened again and another pair of boots stomped out the ground and entered the room. Within seconds, another soldier stepped up to Trevor and into the light. His shield was down.

"Good evening. I'm General Curtis," he said.

Trevor, drowsy and groggy, didn't say anything at first.

"Where is she?" he eventually asked.

General Curtis smiled. "Amanda is fine, Trevor."

"How do you know our names?"

The General smiled again. "Let's not concern ourselves with the mundane. I'm here to tell you what's going to happen next. If you disagree, then, well, that's your prerogative. But I want to be fair and honest with you about what's happening, seeing as a lot of what happens next is dependent on your friend, Mr. Kevin Keys."

Trevor's ears perked up and he eyed General Curtis.

The General nodded. "Yeah, I thought that would get your attention. Anyway, Mr. Keys is being held in a cell not too far from here. He's been pretty resistant to give us any information about where you're all from, what you're doing here and why you're infiltrating our camp. Now, I told Mr. Keys that if he was honest and explained everything to us, that we'd go easy on all of you. But he hasn't done that. In fact, he's been so stubborn about all this that we had to resort to more drastic measures." The General looked at all of Trevor's injuries. "You can probably understand the things we did to him."

Trevor glared at The General. "What do you want from me? Do you want me to tell you who we are? We're just like you. We're from South Hills, Massachusetts. What else do you want?"

"I wish it was so simple, Trevor. Let me be clear about what's going to happen next, OK? So, here's the thing. We're going to hurt you, Trevor. We're going to hurt you until you want to kill yourself. But you won't die. We're going to keep you alive, just so Kevin will see that we have control over your life. And I'm sorry we have to be this way because really, we have no problem with you or Amanda. It's Kevin we want. It's Kevin we need. But we're going to hurt you—hurt you real bad. Kevin will either tell us what he knows and what we want to know, or he won't. Whether he does or not, that's up to him.

"As for you," he continued, "we're going to stop hurting you. We're going to stop punishing you. And then you're going to heal, and you're going to relax. Then, you're going to join us and become one of our soldiers. You're going to join our Order and fight the good fight."

Trevor spat at The General's boot. "Never. I'll never join you. How do you expect me to join you after all this?"

General Curtis smirked. "Because your girlfriend is one of the waitresses in the food service ward. So if you want to see her again, if you want to hold her, and love her, and be with her, then you're going to do as we say. You're going to withstand all this pain. You're going to survive. And then, Trevor, you're going to join The Order."

The General didn't need to say anything more. With a spin, he went to the door, opened it, and left the room behind him.

Trevor had little time to think about what The General said before a fist came flying at him and socked him in the jaw.

Trevor's head went back as far back as the chain would let him, dazed from the one shot. He felt another rock smack him in the torso and he immediately spat out blood. He looked up and saw one of the masked soldiers right in his face. Trevor noticed the soldier's breath underneath the mask. With his eyes lowered, Trevor begged the soldier to keep going, to continue this battle without stopping. And the soldier knew it, too. That's why the fully blackened soldier stepped back and rammed his knee into Trevor's ribs. The chain rattled, Trevor's scream echoed, and the blood splatted out of his mouth and to the ground.

Before Trevor could grasp what was happening, he found himself bent on all fours, his wrists locked to the ground with new chains.

And then a whip lashed at him and slapped him in the back.

The whip cut deep. Blood exploded from his back. Another lash came and smacked his spine. He yelped in pain, but it did nothing. Three more lashes came.

Whip. Whip. Whip. Smack. Smack. Smack.

Trevor wanted to collapse to the ground and pass out. He wanted so badly to escape the world. But the chains kept his wrists upright, his knuckles pressing against the concrete. He was stuck there, stuck in this position, stuck taking the pain that the soldiers wanted to dish out.

Trevor began to fade in and out of reality. When he finally came to again, he was huddled in a corner, a blanket covering his body. A cool rush flooded him. He breathed hard and saw his breath cut through the air. Oh, how cold it was. Trevor froze despite the white-hot pain and blood that poured out of his body. His hair stiffened, the blood freezing into ice. He tried standing, but then realized his legs were glued to the ground below. Nay, not glued, but frozen. His body's sweat and blood locked him there.

Arms wrapped around him and ripped him from the ground.

The pain stabbed at him. He felt skin rip from his body. He collapsed to the ground. He shouted. He screamed. He released all the emotion he had. His body burned. His skin throbbed.

Trevor's pain faded with his consciousness. He hoped he was heading for death, knowing anything less would be something much worse.

IV

For some hours of the day, there were no soldiers in the cafeteria. Amanda hadn't seen the outside yet, but assumed many of the soldiers walked around the Zion base to keep it secure. But it was hard for her to imagine what the soldiers were doing out there when she hadn't a clue about what had happened to the world she once called home. She thought of this toward the end of her shift when the soldiers were gone and she was rolling silverware, a small yet necessary task that she'd grown to hate. She'd rather serve a million plates than put silverware into napkins in an orderly fashion.

Dishes clanged and people chatted in the kitchen. Steam soared from pots and grease spat out from the grill. Amanda twisted her silverware. Again and again she placed it in the napkin, folded the napkin's edges and rolled it into one long stem that would later become an unruly mess, serving no other purpose than to feed a hungry soldier.

Gertrude came up to her, breaking her concentration. "Boss is coming. Look sharp," she said, scurrying off toward the kitchen.

Amanda straightened herself, stiffened her back, and realigned her neck. She hadn't ever met the boss, only heard his name in passing on occasion. She thought at first it was Bill, the soldier she and her friends met back in Jake's house who had taken them into the fort. But then she had found herself serving him meatloaf one afternoon and knew he couldn't be in charge. He seemed powerful, though, or at least popular. Soldiers loved to get Bill's attention.

Amanda heard footsteps coming from her right, but she remained still. She did her work; she did as she was told. For now, that's all she could do—until she knew enough to make things hell for the soldiers and everyone under the roof.

"Amanda," she heard.

Amanda turned her head and there stood a man with a square jaw, well-groomed brown hair, and a wicked smile. He was dressed in all black soldier gear, like the rest of them, though Amanda noticed a small gold pendant attached to his hip.

Amanda swallowed. "Yes?"

"My name's General Curtis. Will you join me for a moment?"

Amanda did as she was told. She set down the rolled silverware she had been working on and followed General Curtis out of the cafeteria and out into the long hallway, which she'd only seen but never went down. She followed him down to the end of the dark hallway, reaching a pale wooden door that The General slipped open. Inside was a stained wooden table with a bench on either side. The walls were a moss green with brown stains and scars all across. The General took his place on one side of the bench and Amanda did the same. They faced each other in silence for a few seconds before The General lifted his mouth and smiled.

"I'm sorry we haven't spoken until now. Everything going all right? Everyone treating you well?"

Amanda nodded.

The General nodded right back. "Good. The second someone gets out of line, a soldier misbehaves or a nurse gets out of control, find me. I'll take care of them, OK?"

Amanda, once again, nodded. She would do as she was told.

"Part of the reason it's taken so long for me to speak with you is because I've been dealing with your friends over the last few days. And I can assure you, your boyfriend is fine," The General shifted in his seat. "Now, I'm not going to lie to you, he's been hurt pretty bad. But our doctors looked at him, and if he's as tough as he acts, he'll be back to normal in the next few days. OK?"

Amanda nodded again.

"I didn't want to hurt Trevor, to be honest. And Trevor's not who's really important to us here, OK, Amanda?" The General said. "Trevor's fine, and he's going to join the rest of our crew and become one of The Order. He will be well taken care of for the foreseeable future. As will you. You two will be free to spend your time together, live and love together, whatever you need. I promise you, no more problems for the two of you."

"What about Kevin?" she asked.

The General gave a half-smile and then killed it. "That's why I really wanted to talk to you, Amanda. See, I know the three of you aren't Loyalists. It's written all over your faces. Loyalists go for a highbrow type of person, or at least groups of people who are exceptionally against us or any other faction. Our soldiers made a mistake in thinking you were, and I apologize for that. But, in any war, there are politics involved. And this is no different. Kevin is, you could say, political leverage. One of our factions thinks we have one of their soldiers, so we can force a meeting and settle some new terms. Negotiate, if you will," he finished.

Amanda vaguely saw where this was going. "I see what you're saying. But what does that mean for Kevin?"

General Curtis bowed his head and frowned. "Well, if all goes well with the negotiation and the meeting, he'll be taken by The Loyalist camp and be treated there to be one of their soldiers, or thrown into their camp in some way."

"And if it doesn't go well?" Amanda asked, eyebrow raised.

"Then we're going to kill him."

Amanda felt tears swarm her eyes and anger zip through her veins.

"Love and war, you know the phrase," General Curtis said.

"Please, please, I'll do whatever you want," Amanda said, frantically thinking and moving her arms about the table. "I'll work every night, I'll become one of your soldiers, I'll do whatever it takes. Please! He's Trevor's best friend, and he can't be killed. Please! He's one of us!"

General Curtis shook his head. "I'm sorry, Amanda, but we all have orders, and we all have rules. For us, Kevin is political leverage. How would it make us look if we didn't kill him after he's denied by the Loyalists? Not very good. Don't worry. Life will go on, same as usual. And in a few years, you won't even realize what's happened."

Amanda couldn't think of anything to say, so she let the General continue. "See, right now you're upset, and right now you think this is all what you want. But in time, you learn to appreciate things, to like things, to become all right with things. I'm not quite sure what you've been doing over the last few years, I mean you're just a kid. But in truth, the biggest part of growing up is realizing that life passes you by. That's why they call it the past. And when it's gone, it's gone, and you have to move on to the future. You have to move on to the next thing that defines you. Right now, Trevor and Kevin define you. Three years from now, maybe you'll be defined by the killer meals you serve, or the way you kill a man, or the amount of power you have. We're all constantly in flux, looking for the next thing to make us all worthy of a legacy."

The General knocked his knuckles against the table and stood up. He straightened his uniform and gave Amanda one last smile. "I'll be in touch. We may need your help serving lunch to some important clients in the coming days."

The General left, closing the door behind him.

Amanda, scared and alone, looked around her. She heard the walls groan.

V

Days later, Amanda noticed how unbelievably crowded the lunchroom was. Soldiers came back from their morning rounds, large rifles at their sides and their boots stuffed with dirt and mud. Amanda and Gertrude both hurried about the kitchen and cafeteria, dishing out meals to the tired men and women, who smiled and complimented the waitresses as they came back and forth. It was your typical afternoon rush, something Amanda had adapted to by now. She knew how quick and efficient she needed to be so she could get her meals out on time. Everything was down to a science.

Through the chaos and mess, Amanda hurried about the middle of the cafeteria and turned to her right. As she did, she noticed the doors to the room open, meaning more soldiers were coming through. But only one came through. He took his seat at the back table, no food, no gun at his side, his face-shield lowered, his pale skin exposed. He looked scared, shattered, and sad.

Trevor lifted his head.

Amanda's eyes locked on him.

She rushed over to him and met Trevor in his arms. The two embraced tightly. The chaos of the cafeteria continued to swirl around them, but the two lovers were together again, back in each other's arms.

"I have to finish work," Amanda said when they let go.

"That's fine," Trevor said back. "We'll talk tonight."

Amanda ran back into the kitchen.

Trevor took his seat at the table. He did as he was told, too.

CHAPTER 38

I

Three years after joining The Order, Amanda was promoted.

She didn't see it coming. Gertrude called Amanda into her office one morning and said she was taking a leave of absence and she didn't know when she'd be back. She wanted Amanda to take her position. It wasn't easy from there on out. Amanda had to train hard to get the new position. From what she heard from Trevor years ago, she was doing the same training he was going through. Running through the obstacle courses, muscle-building exercising, timing drills, schooling, all of it—everything that made her into a soldier.

But here she was, standing on stage in front of the cafeteria she served for the last three years, receiving a pin of honor, making her Captain of the Watch, one of the highest ranking positions in the non-combative side of The New Order.

"And now, please honor Ms. Amanda as we announce her as Captain of the Watch!" Gertrude exclaimed from the stage.

The cafeteria erupted in applause. Thunderous shouts and claps flooded the room. Whistles and cheers spewed out from people's mouths as they applauded the now 19-year-old Amanda, who's face was cold, flat, and still. She didn't show the joy and glee she was feeling inside. She needed to remain tough—that was the only way, she knew, all of these men would respect her. The claps kept coming, but Amanda's face didn't move.

She stepped up to the microphone, leaned in, and set her mouth close to the mic. "Thank you. I'm excited to be in this new position. We will all miss Gertrude, and I could not have done any of this without her help. But today marks a new era in our history. Today, we step on a new path. With my appointment, and as my first decision as Captain of the Watch, I am putting together a small team of soldiers and staff to accompany myself on a search mission to Outer Zion. This will be the first mission The General Watch has gone on since before I even came here. I hope this will find us some new territory we can expand our borders into, and improve our stability as The New Order."

Amanda took a step back from the mic and cheers erupted again. She let out a half-smile, one that had a tinge of arrogance and acknowledged the crowd without showing that she was thrilled inside. She let the applause continue, let it swell around her, embody her and flood her all at once. She loved that she was in charge now. She loved that she had climbed so high up the ladder and become The General Watch's leader. Sure, she still had many to answer to, especially those like The General and Bill, but she had enough power now to start expeditions and get things moving. She didn't like how The New Order never left its boundaries.

They were going to find new land to conquer. The New Order could truly grow.

II

Trevor, dressed in his black soldier gear, stacked with thick pockets and weaponry from his boots to his shield, met up with Amanda minutes later right outside the cafeteria. His impressive rifle hung in his hands, lying across his chest. He was always on the defense, always on patrol. That's what they taught him back in the day. You always need to be prepared for the worst—ready to battle anyone and anything that could come your way.

The love of his life came skipping out from the cafeteria and embraced Trevor with a hug. He was happy that Amanda still embraced her quirky self, even though she was now Captain of the Watch. It was an esteemed position, one where she would be judged and ridiculed by many. But it was one she knew she could handle, and one she knew the elite, at the very least, would embrace. Some soldiers didn't like a woman in power. But others did, and the top brass of The Order especially liked her, so there was no need to worry. Trevor imagined she'd hold the position for the rest of her life, assuming she didn't die in the process. This outward expansion she planned could be a threat to her life and position, but, at the very least, it was something.

"You did great," Trevor said, smiling and kissing his girlfriend on the cheek.

Amanda returned the smile. "You think so? How do you think everyone took it?"

Trevor shrugged. "It's not easy telling everyone that we're finally going to try and find out what's going on in the rest of the world and move past the boundaries. Bold move, Amanda, bold move. But I'm sure everyone's behind you. You at least seem like you know what you're doing."

"Oh, how sweet," Amanda said. "It's like you actually believe in me!"

"Well, all I can do is try," Trevor responded.

Amanda smiled and scanned the hallways. "I just hope everyone believes in me, whether or not we find anything out there. It's taken a lot of work to get here, so, hopefully it'll be worth it."

"It will be. Three years of hard work, determination, and kissing some ass has got to get you somewhere. Plus, I'm assuming I'm on the roster to go with you?" Amanda nodded. "OK, good. Well, then you'll be fine. Even if we found nothing, I'll spin it like we found something."

"My lover," Amanda responded, kissing Trevor on the cheek. "Come on. Let's go home for a little bit."

Home. That's a word that meant many different things to them over the last three years. Amanda always thought of Florida as home, and Trevor always took a liking to South Hills as his home since he moved. But over the course of their time with The Order, they found themselves in a new kind of home. And now it was simple—this was their home now. They were members of The Order, and the Order is where they planned to stay for the rest of their lives, assuming things went as well as they hoped.

So they journeyed down the plaster gray hallways of the cafeteria's corridors before busting through a pair of double doors out into another corridor, one lined with glass that looked out upon the complex's courtyard of various vibrant flowers. The sun shone through and transformed the dull gray into a bright white. They followed a line of soldiers heading in the same direction before taking a right down another hallway, where they then found themselves at Building A's entrance. They stepped out and looked out upon the three other buildings: B, C and X.

Their boots slapped against the rocky road that led them home. Trevor always admired the crescent moon-shaped C above their building. It was one of the reasons he was happy they lived there—it reminded him that there was more out in the universe than this world. At the very least, there was a moon. Other planets existed, too, but the moon he could see every day.

And like they had done a million times before, they scanned their cards and walked into the entrance of Building C. They went down two clay-colored hallways before they found their quarters, its door decorated with notes and messages from others. They snatched all the notes off the door, went inside, and locked it behind them.

They went at each other. Trevor laid kiss after kiss upon Amanda's neck and cheeks, not caring about his aim. He simply wanted to embrace her, for she was his love today and forevermore. Amanda did the same, slipping her lips and tongue across his neck and upper chest, hoping to pleasure her love. They found their way to the bed, their gear hanging off of them. Trevor slid his hand onto Amanda's thigh, ready to make his move and start a passionate and intimate moment, like they had done hundreds of times before.

And then there was a knock at the door.

They ignored it at first, but three more knocks came. They knew what that meant. They both sighed and released from each other.

"All I wanted was 15 minutes," Amanda said.

Trevor rolled his eyes. "Trust me. All you'd get would be 5. You're looking too good today."

Amanda chuckled. She and Trevor slipped their gear back on and walked toward the door. They opened it, and standing there was The General, Bill, and three other soldiers Amanda hadn't seen in the cafeteria earlier.

"General, Bill, soldiers, to what do I owe the pleasure?" Amanda asked. Trevor stepped closer. This was odd seeing them there.

"Sorry to disturb you, especially on a day like today," The General said. "But we're going to need you. Both of you," he said, nodding at Trevor. "Will you please come with us?"

Amanda turned back to Trevor, who joined her at the door. Bill and The General swerved around with the soldiers. Amanda and Trevor followed. They left Building C and crossed through the campus's center, past the soldiers who hurriedly moved above and went right into Building B, which wasn't a surprise since this seemed to be a moment of upmost importance.

"Sorry for this," Bill said as they walked quickly to their destination. "I know it must suck having to go to work like this on your day of celebration."

Amanda brushed it aside. "It's fine. Happy to help where I can."

Bill stopped walking and put his hand out to stop Trevor and Amanda. The General and the other soldier sped forward.

"I'm going to tell you something right now," Bill said. "You kids have been with us three years now, and you're both extremely welcome members of The Order. However, there are certain things that you don't know about us and what we've been doing. Now, I need you to know, above all else, to trust us and not believe anything you might hear in the next few hours."

Trevor and Amanda looked at each other and then back at Bill.

"This could take up the rest of your day, so plan your schedules accordingly," Bill said. "Now, when we first get into the room, I need you to both stand there, shut up, and do as you're told from there on out. Do I make myself clear?"

"Yessir," they said together.

"Good."

Bill hobbled down the hallway. Trevor and Amanda followed him. When they caught up to The General and the other soldiers, they were outside one of the interrogation rooms, like the ones they had been in all those years ago. The walls were still a marsh green with copper brown stains. The General and Bill exchanged a nod and opened the door. The group of soldiers went in first, their guns raised. The General went in next. Bill waved in Trevor and Amanda, and the three followed inside.

A man waited for them in the center of the room. His skin was dark, mostly because of dirt and poor nutrition. His eyes were weighed down with bags surrounded by dark shades of purple. He had a bandana keeping his thin gray strains of hair together. His lips were cut up and bloody. He didn't look well. Not well at all.

Bill turned over to Amanda and Trevor. "Do you recognize this man? Take a look at him, talk to him, and tell me if you know who he is. And do it quick."

As Bill took a step back, Amanda and Trevor moved forward. The man looked up. He saw Trevor and Amanda, and he smiled at them. "I can't believe it," he said.

"I'm sorry, do we know you?" Trevor asked.

The man smiled again. "Of course you do."

Amanda stepped closer, crossing her arms against her chest. She stared deep into the man's eyes, searching for any clue of who he was. She didn't have a clue as to who the man was. She and Trevor went back over to Bill and shook their heads, indicating they had no idea.

"See, General, I told you they wouldn't remember," Bill said.

"Remember?" Amanda asked.

The General moved closer to them, and he gave one of his half smiles. "Amanda, Trevor, please say hello to your old friend. Someone you haven't seen in three years."

It took a minute, but then it came back to them, like a flash of lightning. Like a bad nightmare. They realized the man sitting before them at the table was the man they only knew for a few hours, but one who had helped them get home all those years ago. It was the man they thought had died all those years ago. One they didn't even know could have been alive.

Sky.

III

Trevor and Amanda finally got their 5 minutes alone, but only to talk. They left the interrogation room and went out into the long corridor. They could see Sky through the one-way window, sitting, all dirty and torn up, like a rag you just wanted to get rid of. The General and Bill fired off some questions about how Sky knew Amanda and Trevor, and how he had survived all the months since they had killed him three years ago. Those were all great questions, Amanda admitted. And it wasn't like they were necessarily hiding their identity. The Order already knew Trevor and Amanda were found in South Hills three years ago. But they never spoke to one anyone about where they had come from. They never told anyone about Discis.

"Man, that feels like a bad nightmare," Trevor said, scratching the back of his head. "I can't even remember what Sky looks like. You can barely make out his face. He looks half dead."

Amanda agreed. "I wouldn't have realized it was him if they hadn't said he died three years ago. Half of me thought it'd be your friend—what was his name?"

"Kevin," Trevor said. You never forget a friend's name.

"Right, Kevin. Anyway, I thought it'd be him. But Sky? We knew Sky for, what, a day or two?"

Trevor nodded. "He saved Kevin and me when we first got back to . . ."

Amanda stepped closer to Trevor. "We promised we'd never speak about it."

"I know. It's just hard to do that right now when someone we met there appears on our doorstep." Trevor walked closer to the window and hung on it, peering through at the helpless man at the table. "What could he possibly want?"

Amanda joined Trevor up by the window and looked through. Sky looked complacent. He seemed happy and ready to help out in any possible way. From what Amanda could tell, based on her own interrogation techniques she developed in the last few years, Sky was here by choice. But she couldn't understand why. The Order shot Sky in the back all those years ago. It made no sense for him to turn himself in, especially since he was alive and he had gotten away. And the timing didn't make sense, either. It had been three years since he was shot dead. Why wait so long before coming back to The Order?

Amanda pounded the wall. "None of this makes sense. None of it."

"What should we do, Captain?" Trevor asked. He said it with a smirk, as he always did. She was his superior, yes, but the two brought levity to their world whenever they could. Makes it easier to handle your subordinates when you have them laughing, Amanda reasoned.

"Well, Bill and The General both want our help for some reason with this," Amanda thought out loud. "They told us to plan our schedules around it. But what good can we be? We barely know the guy."

Trevor shrugged. "Maybe they want us to talk to him?"

"About what? We don't know anything that could help," Amanda said. She kept her eyes fixed on Sky, who wasn't saying anything, and yet had a courteous smile on his face. "Unless. Unless maybe he won't talk to anyone but us."

Trevor raised his eyebrow. "But what would he want to talk to us about? Like I said, we barely know the guy."

"But he must want to tell us something," Amanda said, spinning around and facing Trevor. "Why else would he give himself up so easily to the group that literally shot him in the back? I mean, it's not exactly like we're close to South Hills, either. So assuming they shot him there and left him for dead, why would he come all the way out here, unless to tell us something? There are few things that are making sense about this, but I have feeling he wants to talk to us. So maybe we should go back in there, chat it up, and then get out as quick as possible."

Trevor shrugged and offered Amanda one of his goofy smiles. "You're the Captain," he said. They kissed and then made their way to the door. It was time to find out what Sky wanted.

IV

They went into the room. Sky stared at them. Bill and The General walked over to Trevor and Amanda and stood tall before them. Bill explained that they were going to leave the room and let the three of them—Sky, Trevor, and Amanda—talk everything through. They said they'd be on the other side of the mirror in case anything happened. When Amanda and Trevor nodded in agreement, Bill and The General left the room, leaving Trevor, Amanda, and Sky together in the cold room.

Trevor and Amanda sat down in the chairs across from Sky. The three stared at each other for a few moments, waiting for someone to make a move. But no one budged. Amanda would have been more aggressive if this was a normal interrogation, but that was only when she knew the reason behind her questioning. She hadn't a clue why she was speaking to Sky right now. She hadn't the faintest idea why Sky was back in her life and what he wanted from them. She didn't know his endgame.

"You've both grown so much," Sky said.

Trevor and Amanda exchanged a glance.

"It's been three years. Three years and now we're finally reunited. Crazy how things work out, huh?" he said. Trevor and Amanda looked at each other again, unsure of what their next move should be. "I bet you're both wondering why I'm here and why I said I'd only speak to you two. But let me be honest. I only did that because I wanted to make sure the two of you were alive and that you hadn't been killed off. I wanted to make sure everything was as I was told it would be."

That struck a chord with Amanda. What did he hear things would be like? Who told him? How did Sky know to come here? Why was he being told to come here? None of it made sense.

"Sky, why are you here? Honestly," Amanda said.

Sky smiled. "I'm here because this is where I'm supposed to be."

Trevor raised his eyebrow. He looked at Amanda, whose eyebrows were also high. That could not have been more confusing.

"Wait, what?" Trevor asked. "You're not making any sense. Like, seriously, Sky. Look, I don't know why you're here, or why you need to make sure we're safe. But you need to listen to me. If you don't tell those men everything—why you're here and what your intentions are—then they will kill you, simple as that. I guarantee you. We have a very strict policy about outsiders. Trust me."

Sky smirked. "They're not going to kill me."

Silence. Amanda and Trevor didn't understand. Time stood still as they tried to figure out what it all meant, and yet they couldn't. What was Sky's deal? And why was he so confident about everything he was saying?

Sky waved his arm. "Listen, I don't want to bore you with everything. You're free to go. I just wanted to make sure you were both here, that you were both OK, and that everything is going the way it's supposed to."

Confusion set in again. Trevor and Amanda didn't have a clue what Sky meant. When they saw him raise a complacent smile, they both sighed, slid their chairs back, and got up to move toward the door.

Before they opened it to leave, they turned back to Sky.

"Don't worry," he said. "I'll be fine. And I'll be seeing you again, real soon."

Not wanting to hear another word, Trevor and Amanda opened the door and left.

V

Amanda found herself in a place she'd been before—standing before a group of soldiers awaiting her answers. She used to always give orders second-hand, mostly by relaying Gertrude's commands since the nurse was doing miles of other work. But now, Amanda gave her own instructions to the soliders. She had made it a point when she was given the Captain of the Watch position to talk to her soldiers more in person and give her own commands. She didn't want to make anyone her puppet. She knew in order to win all the soldiers' respect, she needed to appear strong and confident. Though many loved her and were proud to serve under her, she didn't want any rebellious soldiers to mutiny.

The soldiers had their shields up, masking their identities. This was how it was done with The Order. They didn't want any soldier taking credit over another or getting too much attention. When they were being given specific instructions, they went masks-up and their ears listened. No joking, no horsing around, just following orders. They did as they were told.

"When you're back from basic training this week, you'll come back to me and get approval to join the mission," Amanda said, stepping to the right with her hands behind her back. "If you're not selected on this round, we'll have another group of soldiers go out in the coming weeks. Remember, this isn't a mission to stretch your legs. We have no idea what's out there, so make sure you're aware that you could be fighting some soldiers or getting into turf disputes. This isn't a mission for the weak."

She dismissed the soldiers and they scurried off to their various posts. Amanda remained behind and glared out into the rest of the complex. She didn't know what to do next. Really, all she had to do now was wait to see what came next from her soldiers. They'd go through their training and come back ready or not to go out into the wild, and then she'd get her first official mission underway.

"Hey," she heard from behind her. She turned and Trevor was there, his shield down and his gun locked under his arm. "Nice speech."

Amanda shrugged. "I'm used to it."

Trevor rubbed her shoulder. "I'm glad I'm not one of the soldiers that has to go through basic training again for this mission."

Amanda rolled her eyes. "Don't pretend like I gave that privilege to you. You achieved top status this year. You're doing fine as one of our soldiers. I expect you to help lead this group with me when we go out into the wild."

Trevor smirked and pulled his girlfriend close. They remained still for a few minutes, letting the time pass because there were few moments where they could take a breath and hug each other.

"I don't want this to end," Trevor said.

Amanda stepped away. "What makes you think it'll end?"

Trevor shrugged. "Just with Sky being here today and talking all cryptically, I don't know what's going to happen, ya know? I just really like our lives how they are and I don't want that old piece of dirt ruining everything."

Amanda could see the worry in Trevor's eyes. She stepped on her toes and kissed him on the cheek. "We won't let this be the end. I'm sure Sky's only here because he's gone mental. Trust me, we'll be fine. We have work to do anyway. By the time you know it, we'll be out into the unknown getting new turf. We'll be laughing about all of this."

Trevor grinned and laughed a little. "Yeah, yeah, you're right. I'm sure we'll be fine."

They hugged again in the middle of the complex. They were happy that they had found each other after all those months of separation, and then added another three years together. That was the best part of all of this. They spent the last three years becoming soldiers, warriors, and leaders—together. They did it with each other in their arms, celebrating love's victory.

It didn't take much for them to be happy anymore. All they did when they were stressed was find each other, be with each other, and let the time pass. That was the beauty of their relationship. They could tackle any problems that came their way. Small, minute issues seemed like nothing when you'd spent months apart from each other in different states. They could tackle anything now.

"Captain Amanda, may I speak with you?"

Amanda turned around and standing there was Private Demak, with Private Ricardo right beside him. They looked similar to each other, except Ricardo's hair was more salt and pepper whereas Demak's was a full black.

"Surely. What seems to be the issue, soldiers?"

"We wanted to know if you planned on bringing us on this mission?" Demak asked, straightening himself to face Amanda. "Private Ricardo and myself are very valuable soldiers and we'd love to work with you on this mission to the outside world. We've always been fans of leaving the complex and finding something new."

Amanda hadn't really had time to consider all the soldiers who were going to go with her. She figured she'd send a big group of them to training, see which ones got the best scores, and then sign those soldiers up for the team. Demak and Ricardo weren't on her radar since she figured they were too busy, and they were too highly decorated to risk losing on this mission.

"Is that something you'd want?" Amanda asked.

Demak nodded. Ricardo did right after.

"Well, I'll look into it. No guarantees, but we can see. Once we get the training results back, I can let you know if there's an open roster spot. Sound good?"

Demak nodded. "Of course, ma'am. Sounds great. See you around."

And with that, the two soldiers walked away, their steps in unison.

Amanda watched Ricardo and Demak walk away and still didn't completely understand what had just happened. Her thoughts were cut off when Trevor wrapped his arms around her waist and held her tight.

"That was weird," Trevor said.

"Weird indeed."

VI

Amanda and Trevor didn't expect their lives to change forever, again, when they were awoken by a jagged alarm in their quarters.

The alarm pierced their ears. They both flopped up from the bed. It was instinctual. They had been trained to deal with these situations. They seldom experienced the alarms, though. For the most part, The Order was peaceful. But now, something had tripped the alarm. Something was amiss.

They hurried and dressed in their full suits. They grabbed their guns that hung on the walls and latched their shields to their suits. They dashed to the door, opened it up, and rushed into the hallway where a line of soldiers sped down the corridor in the direction of the cafeteria. They, too, had their guns latched onto their suits. They made way with purpose. Amanda and Trevor looked at each other and followed the soldiers in the direction they headed.

In mid-stride, someone grabbed Amanda's arm and swung her around. Trevor stopped in his tracks. Waiting there was Bill, a scowl on his face. "Follow me," he said. He jogged off down the hallway against the current. Amanda and Trevor gave each other an accepting nod and darted away with Bill.

"What's going on?" Amanda called out through the hysteria. Soldiers zoomed down the hallway across from them. Amanda, Trevor, and Bill were the only ones going against the tide.

"There's been an attack on The Order," Bill said back to them. "Can't say how, can't say who. We're sending all of our soldiers to the front of the building to defend us. We weren't ready for this."

The three swung around a corner where more soldiers were pushing their way to the front of the building to set a defense. The alarm still rang out, now joined by a computerized woman's voice shouting, "Warning! Warning! Warning!"

"Bill, sir, shouldn't we be joining the others?" Trevor asked.

"Keep quiet, kid. We've got something more important to attend to right now," Bill said.

"And what's that?" Amanda asked.

Bill spun around. "Look, you two need to shut your mouths and follow me. Questions can come later. Got it? Good. Now. Let's go."

Amanda and Trevor did as they were told and followed Bill down the hall. They reached another hallway. It was empty. No more soldiers trickled through them. The halls were filled with silence. Trevor and Amanda shot each other a glance and nodded. They were still in this together, no matter where they were headed.

Once they reached the end of the hall, they heard a shout and a scream. Bill slid to a stop and hid himself against the wall. Amanda and Trevor both armed themselves and got down on one knee, pointing their guns out to the end of the hallway. The shouting continued. Amanda heard a punch connect.

"Bill, what's protocol here?"

Bill put up a finger.

He pulled out a pistol, took a deep breath and then swung around the wall.

Amanda and Trevor waited in anticipation.

There was a shout, a pop, and a bang. Bill's shrill voice screamed in pain. And then there was another pop.

Amanda and Trevor's eyes opened wide. They didn't know what to do next. They gripped their guns and took a deep breath. They needed to make a move. Something was happening at the other end of the hall, and they needed to see what it was.

But before they could move, Sky came running up to them, a pistol in his hand and blood smattered across his face. Amanda and Trevor straightened up, part in shock, part in confusion about seeing Sky there before them.

Sky smirked at them. "Follow me."

"Hands up!" Amanda shouted, aiming the gun at Sky's heart. "Hands up now!"

"Do it Sky! Hands up!" Trevor shouted.

But Sky didn't listen. He swerved around and hurried back down the hall.

They rushed off after Sky. When they finally reached the other end of the hall with Sky, the only thing they saw was a door they had passed by many times before. Neither Amanda nor Trevor could remember what it led to, mostly because all the doors looked the same and they rarely made their way to this end of the hallway. Amanda saw it was numbered as door 77. It sounded familiar, but she couldn't quite place where she had heard it from.

Sky turned around to face Trevor and Amanda. He gripped their shoulders and smiled at them again.

"I know we haven't been in touch for a while. But it was great to see you kids grow up," he said, still smiling. "And I wish I had more time to explain what's going on, but soon the guards will be here and there won't be an opportunity to do what I need to do. All I can tell you is that you need to trust me, and know that I never stopped believing."

Trevor grabbed Sky's shoulder. "Sky, what are you talking about? What's going on? Please. Tell us and we'll make sure you're treated OK."

Sky took a step back. He reached into his pocket and he pulled out a contraption. Red and blue wires connected to different spots on what looked like a battery. A sparkplug hung on the end of it. Sky showed it to Trevor and Amanda. "Please, take a few steps back."

Trevor put one arm in front of Amanda and raised his gun with the other. Amanda already had her gun pointed at Sky.

"Whoa. Whoa. Sky, please, what are you doing?"

Sky moved the bomb closer to Trevor and Amanda. "Please. Please. Leave. Go back where you came. I need to do this. And when it's over, come back, and you will understand why I needed to do this. Please."

It was at that moment that Trevor noticed the pleading innocence in

Sky's eyes. He hadn't seen that look from anyone in The Order. It was sincere and truthful. It was honest. Sky didn't want to hurt anyone. He didn't want to blow up his friends. He needed to open the door, and this was the only way he knew how.

Trevor and Amanda backed up from Sky and went back down the hallway.

VII

When they were gone, Sky knelt beside the door and set the bomb against it. He adjusted it just right and grabbed the match he had in his pocket. He scratched it against the ground and moved it closer to the sparkplug. This was the moment he had been waiting three years for. He leaned the match in close and let the flickering flame latch onto the device.

He looked around him to catch his final glimpse at life. And then, oddly, he saw a man standing there by the door. He was dressed in a black cloak. His eyes were red with anger and he had fire in his hands.

"Thank you," the man said.

And then all Sky saw was darkness.

VIII

The sounds of the explosion pierced their ears and made everything go numb. Fire erupted from the end of the hallway. Shards of metal came shooting down the hall, scraping the rest of the corridor. Amanda was cuddled deep with Trevor's arm for shelter. Trevor peeked up and saw the fire was still flickering at the end of the hall, but it was dying down. Trevor tapped Amanda on the shoulder and the two rose to their feet. They crept toward the end of the hallway, and there they saw the remains of the explosion. Metal was everywhere, and flames burned on the edges of the door. Trevor and Amanda saw Sky's remains and walked past them. They had been trained to accept these haunting images.

When they got to the door, they saw that some metal still blocked them from entering the room. Trevor beat down the metal with the butt of his gun. The metal spewed out and a dark hallway appeared, with a blue glow at the end of it.

Before Trevor and Amanda could make their way into the room, they heard footsteps rushing up from behind. Three guards surrounded them, their guns raised and their shields covering their faces.

"Captain, what happened here?" asked one of the soldiers.

Amanda stepped closer to them. "Easy soldiers. There's been an internal attack. The terrorist was a private guest held by The General. We don't know much else, except that he was trying to get through this door and into this room."

"Have you been inside yet?" asked a solider.

Amanda and Trevor shook their head.

"Should we check it out?" the solider asked.

Amanda and Trevor both grabbed their guns. "Let's do this."

With all the force they had left, Amanda and Trevor beat down whatever shards still hung on the edge of the door. The passage was completely open now, and that midnight blue seemed to be pulsing at the end of the passage. Amanda and Trevor led the way with the three soldiers following close behind. They journeyed into the darkness toward the blue light. There was a humming and some beeping, with a faint whirr coming from the light, too. They reached a corner, and when they turned it, their eyes fell upon a breathtaking sight.

There before them was a control room. Computers beeped and whizzed one the edges of the room. A 100-inch monitor was in the center, its screen blank. Other monitors lined the room, with green lines stretched across those. Lights switched on and off. And in the center was a machine attached to a chair with wires hanging off the edge and some wires connected to the monitor. Everything pulsed and breathed. Something was going on in this room. They didn't know what, but something was happening.

"What is this place?" Amanda asked. She looked up at the ceiling, where purple and gold lines moved.

Trevor gave the room a quick glance. "It's some kind of weird control panel. I've never seen this place before. Soldiers, have you seen this place yet?"

They didn't say anything.

A few seconds went by without any words, so Trevor and Amanda turned to face the soldiers. But they weren't where they thought they'd be. Instead, the soldiers were all sitting down at the computers, typing away and working on the screens. Amanda and Trevor rushed over and it was only then they saw that two of the soldiers were ones they knew before.

"Demak? Ricardo? What are you guys doing here?" Amanda asked.

"Taking orders, just like you," Demak asked.

"Orders, from who?" Trevor asked.

The third solider, who was on the other edge of the room, stood to attention. He walked over to Trevor and Amanda and took his shield-mask off and faced Trevor and Amanda. "From me."

Kevin Keys stood there, a smirk etched across his face.

CHAPTER 39

I

Kevin Keys woke up in a stiff bed in an unfamiliar room with an IV hooked up to his arm. He was dressed in a white gown. He could feel crusted blood on the side of his face. He adjusted in the bed and shifted his eyes across the room to see if he recognized anything. But he didn't. All he saw was this turquoise room, brightened only by the LED light in the center, which flickered every so often.

There was a little commotion from the hallways, but Kevin couldn't make out what it was. It was a light banging, followed by a voice. It didn't seem significant. But in a way it was. His senses were coming back to him.

Kevin ripped the IV out of his arm and sat up in the bed. He swung his legs over the side and touched the soulless and cold floor below. He shook off the chill and walked over to the wall, opened the door, and found himself face-to-face with three doctors who were waiting outside his room. He wanted to run, but they approached him with smiles on their faces.

"Mr. Keys," said the lead doctor, whose skin was coffee-colored and whose head was a shining bowling ball. "We're glad to see you're awake. How are you feeling?"

"Where am I?" Kevin asked.

The doctor checked his chart. "You're at our station. You've been here for three days and we've been watching over you. Bennifer should be along shortly to update you on some things. But I'd like to do a few tests to make sure you're OK before we do that."

Kevin thought about protesting, but he hung back. He sat down on the edge his bed. The doctor came close to him, pulled out a light, and shone it in Kevin's eyes. He felt Kevin's neck and moved his hands across Kevin's head, putting pressure at different spots to see Kevin's reaction. Kevin felt very little pain when the doctor did this. There were one or two spots that Kevin could feel something was amiss, but he wasn't sure what it was.

"Good. Your signs look all good. I was just reviewing a lot of your blood work and that all seems good too. You should be ready to be back on your feet in no time," the doctor said.

Kevin readjusted his body on the bed. "What happened? Last thing I remember I was being brought to the center of the cafeteria or something, and everything's just black from there."

The doctor smiled pleasantly. "All I know is that you suffered some serious head trauma and you needed to be given a heavy dose of ReserX, which we've only used in a few cases. Seems you were probably a victim of a gunshot wound to the head."

Kevin cocked his eyebrow. "Wait. I was shot in the head, and now I'm fine? How does that make sense?"

The doctor turned to face Kevin and smiled one of the more pleasant smiles Kevin had seen in a while. "No, Mr. Keys. You misunderstand me. You were shot in the head, and we did have to give you some ReserX. But that's not because it was any simple gunshot wound. It's actually because, well, we had to bring you back to life."

"Huh?"

"Mr. Keys," the doctor continued. "You've been dead for almost two days."

II

Three years later, Kevin Keys looked at Trevor and Amanda, who both looked like they had seen a ghost.

And, in some ways, they had. Kevin had died years ago, and that was the last time they saw him. The three years that they were apart definitely didn't help matters. He was as dead to them as dead could be. But he was back now, in an Order soldier suit, ready to make due on the promises he made months ago.

"Well, don't act too excited," Kevin said, still smirking.

Trevor and Amanda didn't know what to say. Their mouths quivered, and their eyes were wide with surprise and shock. Kevin stepped near them, his gun still in his hands. He noticed the fear rise in both of their eyes as he approached.

"Come on," Kevin said. "Don't act like you don't know who I am."

"We know who you are," Amanda started, stepping closer to Kevin, her gun raised. "We just can't believe it."

"Well, believe it, baby," Kevin said, his teenage smile blossoming on an adult face. "You too, Trev."

Chills rolled up Trevor's spine. It had been forever since someone had called him that, let alone his best friend, who only called him that growing up.

"I just can't believe you're here. Like, right here, right now," Trevor said.

Kevin shrugged, still holding his rifle. "I know. I like to impress. Anyway, we can catch up later. Right now, we need to get moving on all of this, OK?"

"All of . . . what, exactly?" Amanda asked.

Kevin pointed for the men with him to get moving in the room. They went right back to work as they had been before—working on the computers and scrambling to input data. Kevin moved closer to Amanda and Trevor, still holding his rifle.

"We're going back."

"Back? Back where?" Trevor asked.

Kevin motioned with his eyebrows.

"No. No. No." Amanda said. "There's no way we're going back there."

"You can't be serious," Trevor said.

Kevin nodded. "We are. And we're leaving today. And you're both coming with me."

Trevor rolled his eyes. "Yeah right. There's no way we're going back there. Are you serious? Kevin. It's been three years. Three whole years since we've been to that place. And do you remember everything we went through there? All that pain? All that torment? All the long nights and days stuck in the deserts, the forests, the snow. All that death? You can't expect us to go back there."

Kevin walked right up to Trevor. "Yes, I can."

"Why?" Amanda asked.

"Because Jake's still there. And he was right. All those years ago. Do you remember that night, when we split up and we all got taken by The Order?" Trevor and Amanda shared a glance, since they both had a different understanding of The Order than Kevin probably did. "I've never forgotten it. And I remember what Jake told us all those days ago. He said we weren't done with Discis. He told us that it was our destiny to be there—that we needed to finish the job. And guess what? He was right."

"How could you possibly know that?" Amanda asked.

"Because I do, OK? And we can stand here and argue about all of this, or you can help me and skip all the drama," Kevin said.

Amanda and Trevor both shook their heads.

"Look, you guys are in this with me, whether you believe it not," Kevin said, still holding his gun and switching a few knobs and pressing a few buttons with his fellow soldiers. "We've been working for this for a long time."

"What are you talking about?" Amanda asked.

Kevin turned his head around as he typed away on one of the computers in the command center.

"I know this has got to be hard for you both, but I promise, you have to trust me," Kevin said. He wiped sweat off his forehead. "The Captain and this whole operation aren't about saving Earth or exploring the zones. It's about finding somewhere else. I promise you."

Amanda's smartphone interrupted their plans. She reached down and saw that The Captain was calling her. She showed it to Trevor, whose face was consumed by both fear and worry. Kevin stormed over and looked at Amanda's phone. He stepped back and went back to work.

"What do you want to do?" Amanda asked.

Trevor shrugged. "It's up to you, love. You're the Captain."

Amanda was silent. She looked over to Kevin, who was busy at work with the two other soldiers, who hurriedly typed away. Amanda and Trevor checked the door, where she saw four soldiers suddenly barrel their way through the metal and shards to the door. They fired a round of shots at the group. And that's when Amanda realized the horrible truth—regardless of whether she wanted to go back to Discis or not, Kevin had forced her hand. Without question, it looked like she and Trevor had killed Bill and set off the bomb. They were victims now.

Amanda, quicker than Trevor noticed, grabbed her gun and fired at the soldiers. They went flying back. She hit each on target, and then blew steam from her gun and turned back to Trevor.

"We're going with him."

III

Three years ago, Kevin had been here before—alone in a cold, dark room. He was told that Bennifer, the man who had brought him back to life, was on his way to talk with him about everything. Kevin was still coming to. He didn't fully understand how he had died and how he had suddenly come back to life. Kevin also didn't have a clue as to why Bennifer would want to revive him.

He knew he was going to get that answer when he saw Bennifer walk through the door in the corner of the room. Bennifer sported a salmon top and denim pants, which were covered with black armor. He had a beret on as well; a hat that only a captain or leader would wear. He slowly walked over to the table and plopped himself down right across from Kevin.

"Hello again," Bennifer said.

Kevin relaxed in his seat. "Hey."

"So, back from the dead, then?" Bennifer asked, a smirk on his face.

"You know it."

"Sorry for all the dramatics, Mr. Keys. You know as well as I do that they were going to kill you regardless of what I asked them to do. That's why I had to take care of your death—own it, even, so they couldn't touch you."

Kevin shrugged. "Why keep me alive?"

"I told you before that I needed your help to get to the new planet, the one that can save us."

Kevin nodded. "Yeah, Discis."

"No, not Discis," Bennifer said, wagging his finger. He stood up and walked over to one of the olive walls, stained by some brown fluids and years of aging. Bennifer touched the wall. The colors melted away quickly and were replaced with a computer screen, showing an abundance of stars and planets. Bennifer touched it and the screen zoomed in on Earth.

"Here's Earth, the planet you've known and loved and disappeared from. You'll see here that a lot of our data and analysis put the benefits of Earth in the red, meaning the planet is slowly dying," Bennifer said. He touched the screen again, zooming out. He swiped the screen a few times before reaching a similar planet in the stars, green with vegetation and blue with water. It was bigger than Earth, Kevin could tell, and it had more forests than Earth. But it looked eerily similar.

"This, this my friend, is where we want to go. It's a planet far off in the reaches of space called Tempestfield, and it's a lot like Earth. And it has resources—resources that could help us fix Earth," Bennifer said.

Kevin understood this. In fact, if he hadn't been so swept up in the fight for Discis's life all those days—years?—ago, he would have surely been on Bennifer's side and desired to find another planet. It made sense that Bennifer wanted to go and find more resources for a dying planet, especially one as valuable and amazing as Earth.

"But what do you need me for?"

Bennifer paced away from the screen. "Well, honestly, the machine I spoke to you about can bring us to Tempestfield. The problem is, it needs someone who's actually been there. Years ago, these men had a device that could only be used by memory. So they took the device and developed it a bit more into this machine so that our memories can manipulate where and when we want to go."

"But I've never been to Tempestfield," Kevin said.

"No, you haven't. The fact that you know of Discis is even better."

"Why?"

"Because it allows us to land somewhere outside of Tempestfield and make a surprise invasion," Bennifer smirked.

Kevin finally understood. This wasn't about exploring a new planet and seeing what they could find. This was about going to a new planet and invading it, sucking away its resources at all costs. Kevin shifted in his seat a little, realizing that the man he was with might be more of a villain than the others he had been taken from. So he had to play it smart.

"Will you help me, Kevin Keys?"

Kevin knew the question was rhetorical. Bennifer had killed him and given him new life, which meant he could take it away just as easily. Kevin was stuck. This was his life now. He had to play the game and help Bennifer find his planet and his way to save Earth.

IV

"Damn."

Three years later, Kevin bent down near the bottom of the machine, a wrench and other tools at his side. His gun was slung over his shoulder and he was sweating. He rose up and swung around to the other side of the black machine that resembled a car engine. He clicked a button and a door opened up at the top. Amanda and Trevor saw all kinds of lights and colors, as well as a black spot in one of the corners. Kevin slammed the door shut and stomped over to the front of the machine again.

"We've got a problem."

Kevin jogged over to his two soldiers and whispered something in their ears. They nodded and went back to their work, speedily typing away and putting in code quicker than they had been a moment earlier. Kevin joined his two friends again.

"The machine is missing its battery. We didn't anticipate the battery being gone."

"So, go get it?" Trevor said.

Kevin shook his head. "There are two problems with that. We planned on getting in, setting the code, and then getting out. Quick. That way we could avoid any battles with the guards. The time it would take to get the battery and come back will force us to engage with the guards."

Amanda crossed her arms.

"The other problem?" Trevor asked.

Kevin sighed "Only one man would know about the battery, which means he probably has it locked up in his office. They call him The General."

Amanda and Trevor shared a glance.

"That means we'd have to cross the entire campus to get the battery and come back, unnoticed."

Amanda smirked. "Not necessarily. You've got me."

"And? What will that get me?" Kevin asked.

"I've got special clearance. I can make it to The General's office and back without anyone being the wiser," she said.

Trevor nodded. "She goes there a lot to plan meetings. Wouldn't be a shocking thing for her to go over there now that they know there are intruders."

"Exactly. I can run over there, see what they want me and my team to do, and then sneak the battery out and run back over here," Amanda said.

Kevin shook his head. "It's too risky. The guards are going to keep you from him. And plus, if they see you with the battery, there will be too many of them for you to ward off."

Trevor stepped up and slapped his gun. "Good thing we're going to draw them here and hold them off."

Kevin looked at his best friend and saw the boyish look in his eyes. This was a return to form—the two troublemakers working together to make something happen. They had done this many times before—more than either of them could count. Kevin smiled at his friend and nodded. The plan was set.

V

About five hours ago, three years after he came back from the dead, Kevin checked to make sure his gun still had bullets. It did. He hit a clip on the side of it and slung it over his shoulder. He walked over to his locker, swung it closed, and turned back toward the door of the locker room. Kevin marched out the door and into the corridor, one that had once been a local town's high school but had been replaced by Bennifer's Army. He walked down the halls, past what could have easily been a math classroom, and made his way to Bennifer's office. He knocked twice, grabbed the doorknob, and entered the room.

Bennifer was working away at his computer screen that took up the back wall. Kevin caught a glimpse of what looked like a wristlet with an amulet attached to the end of it. Bennifer hid his screen and swerved around to face Kevin.

"All ready, I suppose?"

Kevin nodded. "Been waiting three years for this. To say I'm ready is sort of an understatement."

Bennifer smirked. "You've made a lot of progress, Kevin. I still remember who you were three years ago. You didn't care about this or the mission, and now here you are, embracing it all. Making our dreams into a reality."

Kevin shrugged. "If it means I can get back to Discis, I'd do anything."

"Indeed," Bennifer said with a nod. He walked over to Kevin and gripped his shoulder tightly. "You've done well, Kevin. And your reward will come. I appreciate everything you've done for us. Now, we're going to finally make due on everything."

There was a knock at the door and a woman came through, done up in her white uniform with armor covering it. She closed the door behind her and tossed a few sheets of paper on Bennifer's desk.

"Latest report you asked for," she said. "Hey, Kevin."

Kevin bowed his head. "Nurse Gertrude."

"What's the status?" Bennifer asked.

"Everything's going as planned. Amanda is now being put in charge of the group, and she'll be installed over the next few days. The Order trusts her a lot. The Captain thinks she's vitally important to the mission—he's a feminist kind of guy. Anyway, they're getting a team together to explore some of the outer regions."

Kevin crossed his arms. "Outer regions? What does that mean?"

Bennifer and Gertrude shared a glance, which was their way of asking each other if they should tell Kevin. Bennifer gave Gertrude the nod.

"The Captain really wants to go exploring the outer regions of Earth. They've been scared of exploring some of the deserted areas of Earth since the split and the war, but now he's gathering a team to head out there."

"So what does that have to do with us?" Kevin asked.

Gertrude rolled her eyes. "Come on, kid. It's simple. Once they leave, they'll keep the fortress on lockdown, so it'll be impossible to get inside. We need to act now."

Kevin shifted in his stance. "And what does Amanda have to do with this?"

Bennifer rubbed his eyes. "You need someone on the inside, Kevin. Your two friends can help you. We've already got a distraction for you, but you need to get your friends to help you use the machine. Lie if you have to, but you need them."

Kevin nodded. Bennifer held his glance with Gertrude a second longer before switching his gaze over to Kevin. He pushed back his chair when he stood up. He walked clear across the room and opened the back closet.

"Kevin, I'll notify your team that you're ready to go. Meet them down at the hangar and get going. By the time you arrive, everything will be set in motion and you should be able to slide right into room 77. We need to act now," Bennifer said.

Once the closet was open, Bennifer bent down and retrieved a small chrome safe. He brought it out to his desk, entered in a code, and watched the center door open. Bennifer swung back around toward Kevin with a little device in his hand. It was a lot like a TV remote controller, but it only had one button on it. He handed it to Kevin.

"Press this once you're in Discis. It'll help us retrieve your signal and get there."

Kevin nodded and slipped it into his pocket. He gave a nod to Gertrude and a nod to Bennifer.

"See you on the other side," Kevin said.

Kevin made it to the locker room a moment later. He saw Private Demak and Ricardo suiting up and checking their weapons. He patted them both on the shoulder and waved for them to follow. Without any words, the three soldiers walked down the corridors and out into the hanger, where a slew of other soldiers and workers operated on ships and set up other gear. Kevin and his two soldiers walked to the back off the hangar, where a simple black transport waited for them.

Before they got in, Kevin gave Demak and Ricardo a nod—a nod that signified it was time to get out there and get things accomplished. They had a specific mission and goal, and it had to be accomplished now. There was no second chance. This was all they had. They couldn't afford to lose.

The three soldiers entered the transport and shut the door behind them. It booted up and headed out of the hangar and into the world. Kevin looked down at the clock on the dashboard and saw that about three hours remained until they reached their destination. Now, all they could do was wait.

VI

Five hours later, Amanda knew she was out in the open, but she felt like hiding.

The campus was moving about as usual—the young and veteran soldiers alike traveling throughout the campus to their various meetings, like it was any other day. Clearly the bulk of the campus hadn't been informed about the intruder. Or if they had, the chaos had calmed. But Amanda knew the truth. This wasn't any other day. This was *the* day. This was the most important day in her life in a really long time, and it could change the way The Order operated forever after.

Amanda passed building A and entered Building B, where the captain's room was. She walked by some soldiers—some of whom gave her a nod, like the ones who were on her research team—and continued toward the office. Just like she predicted, no one thought differently of her walking down the corridor. They probably figured that she was going to talk to The Captain, maybe because the exploration was going to happen soon. It made sense for her to be in this building.

She reached the end of the corridor and took a left around the corner. There she saw The Captain's office, with the door shut. She paused a moment and realized that she hadn't thought of a backup plan in case The Captain was in his office. He rarely was—he was a micromanager, always wanting to control what people were doing in his building—but still. There was a very good chance that he was in the room. What was she going to do if he was in there and unwilling to leave?

THE PEN

She thought about the mission. If The Captain was in the room, she could easily talk to him and not make him think any differently of her arrival. She could try again another time, or wait outside for him to leave. Feeling confident now, Amanda walked over the door, knocked twice as was her custom, and opened the door.

The office was empty.

Amanda got to work. She tossed her backpack down to the ground and surveyed the room. She didn't know where the battery was going to be. Kevin didn't know, Trevor didn't know, and the other two soldiers didn't know, either. But Amanda could figure this out. She knew she could. She walked over to the back of the room and sat down at The Captain's desk. She opened each door and found nothing, or at least nothing that looked like the battery.

She moved over to the closet and sifted through that. Nothing. She hurried over to the other corner of the room where there was a short table of drawers. She went through those and there was nothing.

It felt like the battery wasn't there.

And then she had an idea. Amanda hopped up onto the chair at the desk and punched one of the ceiling tiles open. She gripped the sides and lifted herself up into the air vents. Shrouded in darkness, Amanda punched a button on her armor and a stark white light filled the vent. She swerved her head right and left and that's when she saw it.

The battery was just as Kevin described it. It was a tube similar to ones Amanda saw at banks as a child, covered in wires and metal. Electricity sparked inside of it, a cycle of energy rolled around some of the tubes inside. She saw the edges of it, where she knew it would connect into the machine back in the other room. With no time to spare, Amanda snatched the battery and hopped down from the ceiling onto the desk. She stepped onto the chair, and then onto the floor, and turned toward the door.

Bill, blood pouring down the right side of his face, waited there.

"Bill," Amanda said, shocked.

"You're going to want to give that back," Bill said, his hand applying pressure to his bullet wound to stop the bleeding.

Amanda looked down at the battery and then back at Bill.

"Amanda, you have three seconds to give me that, or I'll be forced to take physical action and take it from you, got it?" Bill asked.

Amanda looked at the battery again.

"One . . ."

Amanda gripped the battery tighter.

" . . . two . . ."

Bill reached for his gun.

" . . . three . . ."

Bill collapsed to the floor, a bullet lodged in his skull.

259

Amanda put her gun back into its holster, slipped the battery into her backpack, and raced out of the room.

VII

The first shots caught them all by surprise.

"GET DOWN!" Trevor shouted.

Bullets whipped past them, scratching and dinging against the walls. Kevin, Trevor, Demak, and Ricardo dived down to the ground and shielded themselves against one of the walls. Bullets whizzed by and bounced off the walls around them. The shots kept coming, fast and rapid. They were aimed to kill.

Kevin poked his heat up and fired back. He nailed one of the opposing soldiers and then another. Trevor swung his eyes around the corner and shot back, hitting no one but making some duck back down to the ground. Demak and Ricardo set up their guns against the wall and fired back down the corridor with automatic shots. Smoke filled the air as the shots kept coming from both sides.

"What are we gonna do?" Trevor shouted to Kevin.

"We better hope Amanda gets here quick. She's our escape!"

Trevor sighed. He wondered where Amanda was.

VIII

Amanda left Building B, her backpack slung over her shoulder and the battery poking out. She spied everyone around her, and it was business as usual, people milling about, everything normal. She walked across to Building C and paused. She thought for a minute about heading inside and grabbing some belongings, since she knew she wouldn't be coming back.

Unfortunately, that momentary pause hurt her.

"WARNING!" yelled the loudspeakers. Everyone around Amanda stopped in their steps and looked to the sky. "WARNING! INTRUDERS HAVE ENTERED THE CAMP! INTRUDERS HAVE ENTERED THE CAMP! SOLDIER SQUADS A, B, AND C PLEASE HEAD TO BUILDING X. ALL OTHER PERSONNEL, RETREAT TO RESERVE HANGAR D. WARNING! WARNING!"

The campus blew up into a frenzy. Soldiers in the named groups pulled out their guns and jogged off toward Building X, with everyone else retreating to some of the other spots on campus. The warning sounds kept coming and noises kept blasting. Amanda paused a second to catch her breath, waiting for the storm to slow. And it did. Once everyone was heading off in their respective directions, Amanda pulled out her pistol and armed herself. She looked around and then followed some of the soldiers toward Building X.

Amanda couldn't believe how much her life had changed today. She thought it was going to be any normal day. And then Sky showed up. And then Kevin showed up. And now she was heading back to Discis. And she had killed Bill. And now the campus was in chaos. It was all happening too fast; it was too crazy for her to handle. But she had to handle it. She needed to handle it. This was her life. This was where she ended up. This was where she had to serve.

She had to figure out, though, how she was going to get to the Project X machine and to her friends. And, if all the soldiers were there shooting at her friends, how was she going to get there and bypass all those soldiers?

And then, Amanda's phone rang. It was Trevor.

IX

"AMANDA! AMANDA! WHERE ARE YOU?" Trevor asked. He fired some shots back toward the soldiers, not knowing if he killed anyone or not. He and Kevin knew they were outnumbered. This was more about keeping the soldiers at bay so they could use the machine than winning any sort of fight.

Amanda looked around. "I'm almost in the building. What's going on?"

Trevor fired a few more shots. Kevin did the same. Demak and Ricardo used their scanners to see how many people were on the other side.

"We're under fire! We need you! We're going to use the machine to get out of here!"

X

"I'm on my way!" Amanda yelled. She shut down her phone and threw it in her pocket.

Amanda sprang into action. She rushed over to Building X and followed the soldiers in. She saw many of the soldiers she knew, waiting in line for their turn to get into the fight. As one of the senior members, the soldiers let Amanda walk past them toward the back of the room. There, right before the door that opened to the corridor where the shooting was going on, was The General, his hands behind his back and a smirk on his face.

"Ms. Amanda, thank you for coming. I've been trying to reach you all day," he said.

Amanda played her role. "Of course, General. What can I do?"

"Do you know who's on the other side of this fight?" The General asked. Amanda, playing her role, shook her head. "It's your boyfriend, Trevor. Him and three of The Loyalists' members—including your old friend, Mr. Keys."

"What?!" Amanda lied. She hoped it sounded believable.

"Yes," The General said, Amanda's nerves calming. "I need you to go in there and find out what's going on. I'll have the soldiers come back, if you go in there and set everything straight."

Amanda nodded. "Of course, sir. I'm on it."

Amanda and The General smiled at each other. She walked past him toward the room and soldiers. She knew she was off scot-free. That had been the easiest sidestep in the history of sidesteps. She was going to do it and get back to the room. She could hear Trevor shouting up ahead, firing his gun toward the soldiers down the hall.

XI

Trevor fired his shots, round after round, and finally paused. He watched the soldiers hold their retreat back behind the wall. Trevor moved forward toward the smoke. When the smoke cleared, he looked ahead and saw Amanda, an army of soldiers, and The Captain behind her.

Amanda saw Trevor smiling up ahead. She was free. All she had to do was walk up to him and close the doors and they were free to be together again.

But then from behind she heard The Captain say, "Wait."

Amanda remembered—the battery in her backpack.

"AMANDA! RUN!" Trevor screamed.

Amanda listened. She kicked off and sprinted toward Trevor.

But then a bullet pierced her leg and tripped her, sending her sailing on the ground.

She sprawled on the ground, a line of blood marking her fall. Soldiers rushed toward her and Trevor, bullets blazing. Amanda screamed in pain and in fear of what was coming.

Screaming at the top of his lungs, Trevor fired his gun wildly toward the rushing soldiers. He grabbed a scrap of metal from the earlier explosion and covered his face as he fired the shots haphazardly. He slid and slammed the metal onto the ground and propped it up. He set it up to cover him and Amanda. Shots kept firing from the soldiers, banging against the metal, as Amanda and Trevor lay on the ground.

"Are you OK?" Trevor whispered.

Amanda looked up and nodded. "Just my leg. I love you."

"I love you. And if this is how we go out, I'm fine with it."

"Me too."

There was a boom. A gigantic boom. Something erupted down the hall and there were screaming voices. Warning sounds came from all areas. Smoke filled the air and sparks sailed over Amanda and Trevor.

Amanda and Trevor heard the soldiers retreat and the bullets stopped firing. They poked their head over the middle and saw only smoke and heard screams come from all directions.

The entire hallway was engulfed with fire. The flames gobbled up the soldiers, blocking them from making their way to the room. The flames roared.

"What's going on?" Amanda shouted, buzzers beeping and people screaming as the fire raged on down the hallway.

"No time, no time!" Kevin shouted as he came running up. Kevin and Trevor lifted Amanda and rushed her into the room. They shut the door.

Trevor wrapped his arms around Amanda as Kevin took the battery and jogged over to the machine. "Come on! We've gotta go! Now!"

Kevin took the battery and shoved it into the bottom of the machine. He heard a hiss and a click. All the lights went on. It was working. Lights exploded and sparks flew everywhere. The beeps became sirens that hammered on their ears like nails to a chalkboard.

A woman's voice came over the intercom. "Warning! Warning!"

It was all a dizzy mess. Fire burned against the door of the room as more screams and shouts came from the other side.

"GO! GO!"

Demak and Ricardo entered in their last lines of code. They nodded to the group and then shot twice into the ceiling. With stealth, they climbed into the air vents and disappeared.

Kevin, meanwhile, was seated in the chair. He hooked up wires to his arms.

"EVERYONE HOOK ON!"

Trevor grabbed two wires from Kevin. He snapped one of them around his wrist and then tied the other around Amanda. All the lights on the machine went from a dark red to a bright green. The monitor at the back of the room switched on. It was white for a second.

And then, after a short fizzle, the group saw two moons, desert plains, and a midnight blue sky on the screen.

And then their world went white.

CHAPTER 40

I

Jake Serent wasn't so sure about what he was doing next. He just had to keep moving.

The streets were dark and quiet. He couldn't even hear his friends anymore. They were long gone now. It had only been minutes ago that they told him they were no longer on his side and had abandoned him. He was on his own, alone in the world he once knew—a world he didn't want to be a part of anymore.

The last time he was on this planet, he had been a loser, a nobody, and someone without a purpose who went through the motions of life. But now, having been to Discis, having gone through the trials that he faced every day, he felt like a somebody. He had a purpose. He was meant to save the world. Being back home made him feel insignificant again. It made him feel helpless. He could do little to save anyone on Earth, but he could do everything to save people on Discis. And, if what he learned earlier was true, he could save Earth, too, by doing so.

Jake wandered through the darkness until he came upon the library in all of its glory. There was trash and burned rubble around it, a victim of one of the attacks of the Man of Fire, a nickname Jake came up with in his head for the cloaked man they had seen. Jake looked around and didn't see a single soul. He took a breath and walked up to the library's stairs. Though it hadn't been too long since he had been here last—maybe a couple of months—it felt like a lifetime. The library represented another life for Jake, and it felt odd and eerie to come back to it.

He reached the doors, put his hands on the glass, and peered through. He didn't see anything. It was empty, just darkness. Books were sprawled out on the ground and computers looked destroyed and broken from whatever happened there once upon a time. Jake could barely make out the front desk, which he had spent hours at back when he was working at the library all those years ago. Jake stepped away from the glass and looked at the library from a bit of a distance. He knew he had to do something with it, he just didn't know if he had the courage to open the door. Opening the door, after all, was supposed to lead him to the Creator's Palace, as he had been told all of those months ago.

But Jake remembered how his friends didn't believe in the mission like he did. He remembered how Kevin, Trevor, and the rest of the group had denied him for wanting to open the door and go through the library to get back to Discis. He believed in his idea so much that he was willing to split up the group. He had to follow through, then, and show them that he was as dedicated as he said he'd be.

Jake grabbed the handle and pulled. The door opened and Jake stepped through, the musky smell of old books slapping him in the face.

Nothing happened.

He wasn't surprised; he almost expected it. But out of sheer anger, Jake shoved the door right back to its spot and heard it slam shut. With all of his strength, Jake swerved around and slammed his hand against the glass. It didn't break, it just wobbled and made a thud. Jake walked off the steps and onto the street. He ran his hands through his hair and sighed before screaming at the top of his lungs, letting out all the stress and pent-up anxiety that he had in him.

"Nice night for a walk, huh?" said a voice from behind him.

Jake turned and there stood a man wearing a beret and black armor. He walked over to Jake, still smiling.

"You could say that," Jake said.

The man smirked and extended his hand. "Bennifer Lamberto."

Jake shook Bennifer's hand. "Jake Serent."

Bennifer raised an eyebrow, still smiling. "Jake Serent. Now, where have I heard that name before?"

Jake shrugged.

"Are you from this town?" Bennifer asked. Jake nodded. "Yes, yes, now I remember. Friends with Shelton Reclard, cousin of Kevin Keys? You're one of the boys who disappeared, aren't you?"

Jake thought for a moment about what to say next, but then he figured it'd be best to keep things honest. "Yes, that'd be me."

"So, what are you doing back here?" Bennifer asked.

Jake thought again about how to answer. He thought of telling this man that he was just in checking on the library, or that he had been here all along. But lying wouldn't do anything. Before Jake could answer, though, Bennifer raised his hand.

"Let's stop pretending that I don't know who you are," Bennifer said.

Jake raised an eyebrow. "I just told you who I was."

Bennifer shook his head. "No, no, no, who you really are. Where you really came from. What you're really doing back."

Jake didn't fully understood what Bennifer was getting on about.

"I know you're Jake Serent from South Hills. I know you disappeared with a few other boys your age 10 years ago. And I know that you're the savior of Discis, and the Holder of The Pen."

Jake didn't say anything. His jaw didn't drop. He didn't feel shock or surprise. He kind of expected this. He wasn't sure why exactly—it wasn't that he felt cocky or arrogant about him wielding The Pen, or that he had constantly been meeting people who knew he was—but it was a feeling. Something deep in his gut told him that this was something Bennifer already knew. It was as if he had been told this beforehand, or he had always known.

Jake slid his hands into his pockets and looked back at Bennifer, who was still smirking. He was confident, Jake could tell, but not in a way that suggested he was going to win something over Jake. Rather, Bennifer looked as though he, too, had done this before. It was as though the two of them had already experienced this.

"So," Jake said, "you need me for something, then."

Bennifer nodded. "Smart kid. I do need you to do something for me. And it's really simple. I need you to go back to Discis."

Jake laughed. "Clearly you haven't been watching me for very long. I just tried walking through the library doors to get there, and nothing happened."

Bennifer shrugged. "Jake, you have The Pen, one of the most powerful tools in all of the galaxy, at your disposal. And you think that just because a door didn't take you to Discis that you're not going back? Come on. You know The Pen's power."

Jake did know The Pen's power—he had just forgotten it. He only used it when he needed to, like to help somebody. The Creator had been one to use The Pen for his own gains. He moved entire civilizations across the world so that he could have hundreds of miles of land all too himself—and he had been corrupted. Jake didn't want to go that route.

"I only use The Pen when it's to help someone," Jake said.

"You will be helping someone," Bennifer said. "See, right now, your friends—Kevin, Trevor, Amanda and Sky—are all on their way to my military base. And, truth be told, they'll live. But they'll live because they have what I need to get to Discis. And the only way they'll go back to Discis and be my key there, is if you're there waiting for them."

Jake didn't fully understand. "So you want me to go to Discis, so that they have a reason to go to Discis, so that you can go to Discis."

Bennifer nodded.

"So why don't you just use me and cut out the middle man? Wouldn't it make sense for me to just go to Discis and you come with?"

Bennifer shook his head. "That's not how it works, Jake. I need time, resources and a few other things to happen first. Use The Pen now, and it'll help your friends later on down the road. I'd say in about three years."

Jake sort of bought the logic. Bennifer wanted to get to Discis—who knew why—but he needed time before he did. By having Jake go first, he was giving his friends a reason to go back, which Bennifer could then use to get there himself. So he was helping Bennifer for sure, which more than justified him using The Pen.

More than that, though, Jake knew his friends were meant to go back to Discis. So going back would help them in that way too.

Jake walked a few paces back and made some space around himself. He gave Bennifer a quick nod before he pulled The Pen from his back pocket and pointed it toward the sky. Instinctively, he knew to point to the sky and whisper for The Pen to do its job and send him back to Discis. Everything was still at first, but his world turned a kelly green and soon Jake couldn't tell where or when he was.

That was, until Jake opened his eyes and saw the hard blue sky above him, with the faintest view of two moons dangling overhead.

He was home.

II

"What do you mean war is coming?" Jake asked, poking the fire.

Moss stood up and brushed off his hands. "You know what I mean. A battle is coming, a big one, the one that will jeopardize everything as we know it."

Jake didn't understand who the battle would be between, but it did make sense that one was coming. Moss had mentioned in the past something about war and a battle for all of Discis, and that The Pen would be at the center of it all. But Jake wasn't sure who the battle would be between, or who would show up to fight on either side. He was worried, of course, that the war would be just him and Moss against everyone who elected to be on Bennifer's side. Tackling that task seemed very daunting.

Moss stood up from the fire and made his way to the forest. He came back seconds later with a few logs, which he tossed into the fire. Jake didn't get this, either. Darkness had fallen, and it was likely time to fall asleep soon. Why was Moss keeping the fire going?

"You know, in the time that we were away from you, things made a little more sense," Jake said. Moss looked up. "When we were with Sky for those few days, I read up on the history of Discis and learned a lot. Things started to make sense. My role as the Holder started to make sense. Now I'm feeling confused again about it all."

Moss nodded. "That's understandable, Jake. I haven't been the most upfront with you about everything, mostly because I'm not a man to go around trusting people. You know my history."

Jake remembered everything he learned about Moss and Shelton and all the drama that happened when they were younger.

"But I do agree that things are probably confusing for you. And since it's just you and me for now, maybe it's better if we start being a little more open with each other."

Jake agreed. He scooted closer to the fire. Moss brushed his hands off again and looked at Jake.

"I'm here to answer any questions you have," Moss said.

Jake had so many questions, some of which were probably unanswerable. Regardless, Jake sorted through all the questions he had, trying to pick the ones that he knew Moss could answer.

"Who's the war going to be between?"

Moss smiled. "The Creator is gathering an army. They'll be facing us and whatever warriors will join us from one of the far off kingdoms in the northwest. I heard they agreed to join us."

Jake nodded. He remembered that Amanda's people were going to help them.

"Why war?"

Moss shrugged. "You know as well as I do that The Creator wants to protect himself from you and The Pen. It only makes sense that he'd amass an army to strike us down on our way there. Without us, he has no issues anymore."

"I don't get it," Jake said, shaking his head. "I don't get why he's so nervous about us and The Pen, or why he didn't just take The Pen from me all those months ago when he stabbed me. Wouldn't it make more sense for him to come down here and just take The Pen from us straight-up?"

Moss smiled again. "Have you looked at The Pen lately?"

Jake hadn't. He reached into his shirt and took out The Pen, which was still tied around the necklace around his neck. He looked at it and saw that four of the five blocks were solid black. They had once been filled with pictures and vibrant colors. Now, except for the final red one, they were black.

"That right there means The Pen is one stage from becoming one of the ultimate weapon in the universe. And the only man who can control that weapon right now is you. The Creator won't take The Pen back because it's no use to him right now. He wants you gone, dead, out of the picture—because only then will The Pen reset and be available to him again."

Now it all made sense. Jake coddled The Pen and twisted it in his hands. This was his Pen now, he was the Creator and the Holder. Kurpo couldn't do anything with it if he tried. Jake was one step away from turning it into the ultimate weapon, one that could restore order to Discis and bring balance back to the planet.

"When we climb to the top of The Creator's Palace, and we turn that Pen into a sword, and we stick that sword right into the place it belongs, everything will go back to normal. The drought will be over. Forests will flourish again. The monsters and goblins and ghosts that The Creator created will be gone. The Creator's power will be gone and people can move north again. Evil will diminish. And we will all live again."

Jake remembered all the times he had been told about that moment—about how The Pen would somehow morph into a sword, and that sword would be the ultimate saving grace for Discis. And now it all made sense. The planet of Discis would no longer be a world ruled by tyranny and one man's desires. Instead, it would go back to the peaceful and loving place that Jake had read about in his book. The world would be whole again.

Jake put The Pen back into his shirt and laid back against a tree. He looked at the fire. Thoughts came back to him of his journey and whatever steps he had to take next. He thought about what it would be like to finally reach The Creator's Palace and tackle The Creator. He thought about all the lives that had been lost on his journey here. He thought of the hours he spent stressing over the fate of a planet other than his own. He thought about how Discis, somehow, had become his planet and the one that truly needed saving. He remembered how this—all of it—was his purpose in life, his calling. And, simply, he needed to fulfill it, whether that meant he died or not.

There was a rustling in the bushes.

Jake snapped his head up as Moss rose from his log and grabbed his spear. Jake rested his hand on The Pen inside his shirt. Moss backed up few feet and cautiously spied the direction of the ruffling, ready to attack at a moment's notice.

Jake heard steps move through the bushes. It wasn't one person's steps, but a few. Jake readied himself again for a potential battle.

But through the bushes, with one torch guiding them, out stepped Kevin, Trevor and Amanda—their faces soaked with sweat, blood, and tears.

III

The whiteness dissipated, and all they could see was a hard blue sky, two moons, and few clouds.

Steam rose from their bodies. Adrenaline continued to rush through their veins. They were breathing heavily. All they could hear was peaceful silence, a drop-off from the craziness and chaos they had felt moments earlier. The whirlwind slowly died down. Balance and order settled back in.

Trevor, Amanda, and Kevin stirred. Kevin was first to his feet. Trevor crawled over to Amanda, who was still bleeding at the leg, but less than she had been moments earlier. It looked like a bullet had only grazed her. Trevor ripped off a piece of fabric from his shirt and tied it around Amanda's leg. He looked up and saw Kevin rushing about the area, using his binoculars to examine where they were.

"Did it work? Are we back?" Trevor asked.

Kevin nodded. "Oh, we're back. Two moons, a pure blue sky. Hell yeah. This is Discis, all right."

Trevor didn't let his excitement show. He helped Amanda up to her feet. The wound hadn't been as bad as they thought. The bullet had grazed her leg, but she could limp it off.

"You all right?" Kevin asked, coming closer to his two friends.

Amanda nodded. "I'll be fine. Just, please, no more firefights for a little bit. That was insane."

Kevin nodded. "Looks like we got some peace for a little bit. Until we figure out what's next."

"And what is next?" Trevor asked.

Kevin shrugged. "Not really sure. We're gonna have to make shelter for the night. There's some forest up ahead that we could probably use. Let's try and get over there before nightfall and then see what we can do next."

"Did Bennifer not give you a plan?" Amanda asked.

Kevin reached into his pocket and pulled out the tool Bennifer had given him a few days ago. "He wants me to hit this so that they can find Discis's location. Not sure if I should hit it, though."

"What would he want with Discis's location?" Trevor asked.

Kevin put the device back into one of his pockets. "He says there's a planet somewhere out in this galaxy that could restore Earth. I'm just not 100 percent sure if he was lying about it or not. Part of me wants to leave all of that nonsense behind us and focus on the now."

Amanda nodded. "I like that. We're back, we don't have to worry about all the drama happening back at home. We can just focus on what we need to do here."

"Sounds good to me," Trevor said.

The three all smiled at each other. It was good to finally be getting along. They all put their hands together and banged knuckles. It was all going to work now. They all had a plan—to find shelter before nightfall and see what happened next.

They gathered themselves, drank some water, and headed out across the plains before them. This was the Discis they remembered—flat, open, and full of conversations and travel. It was like coming home. The three walked in silence for a little bit, but then Trevor and Kevin reminisced about the memories they made the last time they were out there. They remembered running into Sky and saving Amanda. It all felt like so long ago, and it had been.

"Do you think Jake ever made it back?" Trevor asked.

Kevin shrugged. "Not sure. No one ever told me if he'd be here. All I know is that he was right, and that we were meant to come back here. I'm just not sure he was meant to come back here, too."

"Well, let's hope that wherever he is, he's safe," Trevor said.

"Aww, look at you, defending my cousin," Kevin said.

"Such a sweetie, Trevor," Amanda replied.

"Shut up, both of you," Trevor said with a smile.

They continued their journey. The forests didn't look like they'd be far away, but the trek was proving longer than they thought it'd be. Every time they took a few steps toward the forest, they felt like they were drawing farther from it. But they continued on in hopes of finding shelter. The sun began to set in the east and they realized they didn't have much time before nightfall, when the night winds and creatures howled about and gave the living chills.

They came up to the forest's edge just before nightfall. It was dark out, too dark to see anything. Kevin made the suggestion that they search for a good clearing somewhere in the woods and make shelter there for the night—that way they couldn't be seen or have to tackle any beasts during the night. They all agreed and walked through the forest, guided by moonlight. Amanda soon grabbed some sticks, roped them together and set the top on fire, bringing the three a torch they could use for the night. They set off for the forest.

"We're never going to find a clearing," Amanda said. "Maybe we should just rest here. I'm getting tired."

"Need me to carry you?" Trevor asked.

"Back off," Amanda said.

"Stop bickering," Kevin said. "We should hit a clearing soon. I can't imagine this forest is deep enough to not have a lake or body of water in it."

Trevor wiped sweat off his forehead. "Or at least somewhere comfortable to sit."

"Baby," Amanda replied.

The three journeyed past branches and twigs until they smelled fire and smoke. They smiled and, now motivated, pushed through some more lush vegetation until they could see a small fire pit glowing in the distance. Through the darkness, the trio pushed through and rushed toward the fire.

When they stepped out—finally into a clearing—they saw two men sitting by the fire. One was Moss, a face from what felt like a dream.

The other was Jake, who hadn't aged at all.

IV

When Jake's eyes opened, he was looking at the Discis he had always known. The two faint moons in the hard blue sky and the empty plains before him. But then he turned around and saw he was back at a familiar site—Sky's hut. He saw the fake Creator's Palace and the tunnel that led to Sky's underground fortress. He was right back where he had left from a few hours ago. It didn't feel at all like he had even left, except for now he was alone and aware that something was being done to bring his friends back.

Jake turned and saw the hanging green energy inside the metal arch. He looked at it cautiously, trying to see if there was anything special about the light that had brought him and his friends home those hours ago. It was nothing special. Just a glowing green light with the ability to send people back to Earth. Odd that it had been placed in such proximity to Sky's place.

Jake brushed the dust off his body and walked back to the hut proper. He opened the door and dust fell everywhere, as though it hadn't been opened in months. He walked down into Sky's hut and saw everything was just as they had left it, except that there was a man sleeping on the ground. It was the same man who had been there right before they left. He was rusty looking, like he hadn't slept in ages, but was finally getting caught up. Jake, choosing not to disturb him, walked past the man and over to the back of the room.

When the man behind him started to stir, Jake turned around. He gathered some water, drank a glass, and then set out another for the man. Jake handed it to him once he was awake.

"Hello," Jake said.

The man took the water and sipped. "You're back. Feels like it's been a while."

Jake shrugged. "I had some help."

"What about your friends? Did they walk through the green light, too?"

"Nope. Nope, just me. What's your name?"

"Grant," he said.

Jake shook his hand. "I'm Jake."

"Nice to meet you, Jake," Grant said. "Can you tell me at all about where we are right now? I've been sleeping here, trying to make sense of everything. But I can't. I mean, there are two moons in the sky, for Pete's sake."

Jake laughed. "Not from around here, huh?"

Grant shook his head. "Nope. Nope, I'm from Wisconsin. And unless Canada is a lot different than I expected, I can't say we're home anymore."

Jake laughed again. "You're right. How did you get here? Do you remember?"

The man took another sip of his water. He looked at Jake, somewhat cautiously, but then figured the youngster probably wouldn't be any harm.

"We were on a bus; there was probably more than a hundred of us. You know, one of those bus vacations everyone takes, full of old grandmas and families. We were heading off toward Canada when all of a sudden fire came raining down on us. Sent our bus off the road. Bang. There was this green light. And then all of a sudden we woke up in clearing, about three miles from here."

Jake nodded. "So there are more of you?"

Grant nodded. "Yeah, just a few. I thought I'd go look for help, but you were all the first people I found. I had no idea all of you would be so gung-ho to get out of here."

Jake understood. It was weird to him that he and his friends had been so eager to run away and get back to Earth that they had ignored the man who had shown up. Thinking back, Jake and his friends should have probably focused their attention more on this man. But instead, here they were, meeting anyway. Jake stood up and walked over toward the water and poured two more glasses. He handed one off to Grant and sipped from the other.

Grant, hunched over his cup of water, said to Jake, "I'm not sure I want to go back to my people."

Jake raised an eyebrow. "Why not?"

"Bunch of idiots, really. Can't get leadership right."

Jake stood up, rubbed his glass of water, and made his way closer to Grant. "If there's one thing I've learned from good leadership, it's that sometimes it means you have to make the hard choices. Sometimes you have to be willing to let yourself or others go for the greater good and the greater goal. Sometimes, you have to be selfish in order to be selfless."

Grant looked up at Jake. He set his water down and then rubbed his hands over his face. It was as though he was becoming someone new in the blink of an eye. He finished off his water and stood up

"You're right. You're completely right. Maybe it's time I go back there and fix the mistakes that everyone has made," Grant said.

"Not a bad idea," Jake said back.

V

Grant and Jake shook hands again. Grant walked over to the water, got his hands wet, and cleaned his face off. He gathered his bag that lay in the corner and moved over to the door. Jake followed him, and the two stepped out into the hard sun once again.

"Well, I'm back west. Would you care to join me? Maybe we could use a man like you, leading us all."

Jake shook his head. "I have my own group to lead," Jake said. "I've just got to find them first."

Grant nodded and waved goodbye. Jake watched as Grant turned around and headed back west in the direction he came from. It was an odd meeting, Jake realized, especially because Grant's arrival meant that there were more people from Earth finding their way to Discis, which meant that he wasn't the only one who was destined to be here. There was something larger at play, but he didn't know what.

Once Grant was gone from sight, Jake returned to Sky's hut and gathered whatever supplies he could. He packed some water, clothes, and weaponry that were light and wouldn't make his bag to bulky. He said goodbye to the hut thereafter and began his own journey north.

The sun began to set not too longer after Jake's departure, but he was close enough to the forest that he could find shelter. He set up a fire pit in the middle of a clearing and decided to make camp for the night. He kept The Pen and his weapons close, ready to strike or defend himself against anything that came his way.

During the middle of his sleep, Jake woke up from the sound of a snapping twig. He sat up straight and he saw a figure moving in the darkness. He grabbed his weapon—a thin dagger—and prepared for the worst, whatever that may be. That's when he saw a man he never thought he'd see again come through the forest trees.

It was Moss.

"Welcome home, Jake," Moss said.

Jake didn't know what to say at first. He was baffled, surprised even.

"Moss," Jake said, at a loss for words. "How are you here? Where did you go? How did you find me?"

Moss smiled. "I traveled to the west, had to leave something behind, and then went back east, up to the Walls of the Creator's Palace to see how far away we are. We're about 10 miles outside. What have you all been up to in the meantime? Where's Kevin? Trevor?"

Then Jake remembered that Moss had disappeared before Amanda returned and before they met Sky. There was a lot to fill him in on. Jake sighed heavily, sipped some water, and told Moss everything he could remember about the last few weeks.

VI

Jake looked at Trevor, Amanda, and Kevin. They were older than he remembered.

Trevor, Amanda, and Kevin looked at Jake. He was still young.

"Welcome back," Moss said.

The teens said very little to each other. Jake didn't know what to say. It had been only a few days since he'd last seen his cousin, but it didn't seem that way. Kevin looked older, more mature. He was scarred and covered in sweat. He looked like an adult. Trevor was the same. He was bulked up, no longer the bratty skater boy that Jake remembered. And Amanda looked tough, much tougher than the princess he remembered seeing last week. They were all grown up, all stronger, and all wiser than Jake remembered.

Jake stepped closer to his cousin, who did the same. The two met face-to-face, and then embraced in a hug. Age didn't matter, size didn't matter. They were cousins until death, and they would love each other no matter what. They started to laugh, realizing that they were together again. Trevor and Amanda joined them in an embrace, and the five youngsters embraced each other again, as though no time had passed at all.

"How are you?" Trevor said, smacking Jake's arm. "Look at you, baby face. Still haven't grown up yet, have you? Three years and you're still a little boy," he joked.

Jake raised an eyebrow. "Three years? It's been like a week."

"What?" Trevor asked, a smile on his face.

"Theory of Relativity, guys," Amanda pointed out. "Time must move a lot slower here."

It made sense now for Trevor. "Oh, that explains why when we were here before for about a month—"

"—it was like 10 years had passed back home," Kevin said.

"Wow," Jake said. "Three years. No wonder you all look like hell. What happened?"

Trevor, Kevin, and Amanda all exchanged a look. "How much time do you have?"

The three sat down and traded stories. Kevin, Amanda, and Trevor started with how they were captured and tortured and how each had found his or her own role in the new society. Trevor and Amanda spent a good part of the night talking about their own adventures together and how they still loved each other despite the struggle back home. Kevin talked about all the training, planning, and research he had to do during his three years, saying he knew more about Discis than he ever wanted to know. Moss asked Kevin questions about Discis's geography and Kevin got each of them correct. Everyone turned their attention to Jake, who recounted the last three days and his journey back.

The one constant in all of this, they realized, was Bennifer and The Man of Fire. Since they got back to Earth, Bennifer had been the one organizing their return home. The Man of Fire, meanwhile, had been causing havoc all over Earth and helping those plans move along.

"So what do you think it means? This whole Bennifer thing? He was trying to help us get back, and somehow knew about it all," Jake said.

Moss scratched the back of his neck.

"Not sure," Kevin said. "All I know is that he helped us get here. And now that everything's back together, we can start moving to the future, whatever that may be."

Moss slapped his own knees and stood up. "Indeed. Our next step is a journey. We have 10 miles until we reach The Walls that signal the border of this part of Discis and the Creator's Palace's land. Rest up tonight, and in the morning, we'll reach the walls. Should be there by sunset."

Moss waved goodbye to the youngsters and walked off into the darkness to find his resting place.

Kevin, Trevor, Amanda and Jake remained by the fire. They sat in silence for a few, letting the crackles of the fire fill the night with sound. They looked up and saw the two moons and the far-off planets in the galaxy. It was a beautiful night to gaze at the stars.

Amanda fell asleep in Trevor's arms. The two then cuddled and fell asleep off to the side of the fire.

Jake and Kevin remained looking deep into the fire. They didn't need words to express how happy they were to be back together. It was good to just finally have everything back in the right place, with everyone knowing what their true purpose was.

"So tomorrow's really the beginning of the end, huh?" Kevin asked.

Jake nodded, stoking the fire with a stick. "I guess so."

They sat in silence for a little longer, and all was forgiven.

VII

Just like old times, the group was ready at sunrise to begin their journey.

Amanda, Trevor, and Kevin were excited to get going again. The fast pace they experienced the last three years left them craving more during their downtime. Their bodies had been groomed and built over time to handle long journeys and missions. They were as ready as they could ever be to tackle the war that was coming.

Jake was excited, too. He hadn't been away from Discis as long as his friends had, but it still felt like it had been a while since he had a purpose and mission to go on. The group was back together again. And the end of their journey was in sight. Their destiny was a mere 10 miles away.

They reminisced as they walked. They talked about their stories from the past three years—or days—again and talked about some of the minute things that had happened that they hadn't covered the night before. Moss was mostly quiet, but he kept showing interest with what Kevin had learned about Discis.

"There's still a billion people on this planet," Kevin said at one point. "They're just all hiding down in the South."

They rested at points, sipping water and taking quick naps to get their energy back. No one complained the entire way. They all thought of the mission ahead. They all knew they needed to finish things and get to where they needed to go. No one was worried anymore about this mission. They finally understood their calling.

They could see the high walls of the Creator's Palace region in the distance. They had their next step in sight. They talked more with Moss about what was on the other side, and he said he had no idea. Kevin said the entire area was blacked out on maps and in books, so there was no evidence of what was on the other side.

But Jake knew what was on the other side—the end of their journey.

They reached the walls at sunset, like Moss had predicted. The pearly white walls went from the ground up into the clouds, with no way of climbing over them. There wasn't a door, either. It looked impenetrable.

Jake touched the marble walls and ran his finger around the various symbols painted across them. He would have marveled at their beauty if they weren't creations of a tyrant trying to keep people away.

"It's an old language," Jake said, remembering what he read in his books when he was at Sky's place. "It's written from the first men of Discis."

"The First Walking," Kevin explained. "Interesting."

Trevor and Amanda surveyed the walls and thought about what it would take to bust through them. They could tell bullets would do very little except disrupt the paint job and destroy some of the markings. But as far as getting inside, nothing could happen.

Kevin looked at the symbols again. "If I'm reading these correctly, it says there's no way inside the walls."

Disappointment filled everyone's hearts.

"Unless you have The Pen," Jake said.

Jake took The Pen out from under his shirt and laid it against the walls. There was a purple glow on the wall that made the outline of a door. The door crept out from the white marble and morphed into the sides. The only thing left was an entryway. They peered through and saw wheat plains and a pinkish sky beyond.

Jake, Kevin, Trevor, Amanda and Moss each looked at each other.

Everyone stepped back behind Jake. They decided to follow their leader.

Jake, clutching The Pen, walked through the door and into the Creator's Palace's realm, his followers behind him.

Survival, death, and new beginnings waited for them on the other side.

PART V: THE BATTLE OF THE PEN

CHAPTER 41

I

The Creator looked outside his window and waited.

He had been waiting for a long time. He knew Jake and his group were on their way to his palace, but they had yet to arrive. Three months had gone by, and still nothing had happened. He still felt Jake's presence, but The Pen hadn't been returned to him yet. So he knew fully well that Jake was still alive. He was just stalling, for some reason The Creator couldn't figure out.

Kurpo stood up from his seat and walked over to the balcony. He surveyed his land—the pinkish sky and the wheat plains that stretched for miles all the way to the Walls. Every time he looked out at his world, especially this part of his land, he was reminded of why he adored The Pen so much. He had found nothing but tragedy and heartbreak as a youngster. But The Pen, somehow, had brought him peace and serenity. The Pen had given him purpose and order in a world full of chaos.

Kurpo closed his eyes and went into a trance, and he remembered those days, long ago, before he was a man and had conquered Discis with his army. He thought of the days before he owned The Pen.

He was no longer at the top of his tower. He was sitting in a plush chair at the very top of an industrial building. He was younger. Not yet a full man, but not a boy, either. He looked up, and there stood a well groomed man in a suit. Chiseled chin and a shadow of facial hair. The man swung around the table and placed his hand on Kurpo's shoulder. He gripped it and apologized. Kurpo only nodded. The man swung back to the other side of the table and peered right into Kurpo's eyes.

"Kurpo, you have no idea how much this pains me," the man said.

Kurpo nodded. "I understand, Mr. President. I understand that you didn't mean to kill her. I understand."

"Please, call me Kallanon," the man said.

"*Yes, sir, Kallanon.*"

Kallanon, the charismatic man that he was, smirked at Kurpo. "Please, Kurpo. You don't have to pretend anymore. I know you're not the peaceful soul you claim to be. I know you want to jump over this table and strangle me to death for killing the only woman you ever loved."

Kurpo nodded. "You know me too well."

"But what if I could offer you something much stronger than revenge?"

Kurpo, his eyes watery, looked up at Kallanon.

"What if I said I could give you something that will give you anything you've ever wanted?"

"I'd be very interested," Kurpo said back.

Kallanon smiled. "Good. You see, young Kurpo, all of this, all of it," he said, waving his hands, "isn't pure luck or just because of manipulation. I had a lot of help."

"From who?" Kurpo asked.

Kallanon reached into his suit and pulled something out. "Not who. What."

That was the first time Kurpo ever laid eyes on The Pen.

Kurpo was back now in reality and out of his trance. He walked away from the balcony and back into his room. He moved past his chair and the back door and found his way toward the large stone in the center of the room. The slit at the top was perfect enough for a sword, and nothing else. The end of the world as he knew it was right before him. All Jake and his group had to do was make it to the top of the tower and put The Pen in the slit. That would be the end for him and everything he built.

"I won't let it happen," Kurpo said aloud. He looked up, his eyes hoping to see the heavens. "I won't let him take away everything we built together. I will destroy Jake and his group. And we will continue to rule over this world. I swear to you."

The Creator walked back over to his chair and sat down. He looked out at the rest of the world and thought about how much it would hurt to lose it. He thought about calling his Master, but decided against it. He needed to be alone and prepare for the coming war.

II

Grant Revel wasn't sure he wanted to go back.

He had enjoyed his self-imposed exile. It was just what he needed to reset his batteries and find himself again. The first few days with his team had been tough and made him question everything he thought he knew about leadership and ethics. His time away allowed him to remember who he was and what he thought was best for him and the people he surrounded himself with. Going back to camp just made him think about what life used to be—which wasn't exactly a good thing.

Grant came through the trees and into the clearing where his team's camp had been. He didn't see anyone lingering about at first. But once he made his way into the heart of the camp, things began to stir. Thomas and Jordan came from one hut, Richelle and Chris came another, and April came on her own from the back corner of the camp. Jupiter and Brent arrived moments later. They all met in the middle, where Grant stood, a backpack slung over his shoulder.

"Grant," Richelle said, reaching him and holding his arm. "You're back."

Grant nodded. "I am."

"We didn't think you were coming back," Thomas said. "It's been like, three months."

Grant nodded again. "I needed time to see where my head was at. And now that I have, I have some ideas for what's coming next."

Thomas smirked. "Oh, so now you're the leader? Did you forget about the election?"

Grant looked at Thomas. "Forget the election, I've got a plan. And if anyone else has another one, I'd love to hear it."

No one said anything.

"Good," Grant said. He took a few steps and found his way to the center of the group. "Now, when I was out there, I found a hut. It's got beds, supplies, water, and a ton of food. I carried some back with me, but it's not enough to keep us all alive. But, if we head out to the hut, we'll have shelter until we figure out where we are and how we get home."

Everyone looked around at each other. No one looked like they thought this was a bad idea, so they all turned their heads back to Grant to listen to whatever he had to say next.

It was at that moment that Grant realized he had become the leader of his group. He smirked. He remembered what the boy had told him back in the hut about being selfish. Sometimes, you had to just take control and lead your group, whether or not it made you look selfish.

"Now, let's start organizing. It's about to be nightfall. So by the morning, we should all try and head out toward the hut," Grant said. He smiled and nodded. Everyone seemed to agree with him.

Grant glanced over at Thomas, who was giving him the same devilish look he had given him all those days before. But it seemed Thomas was just showing a general dislike for Grant, not one where he would want to challenge him for power over the group. After all, Grant proved to have the strongest plan for the group. And if it meant survival for him, Thomas was more than likely to follow orders.

Richelle stood by after the rest of the group disappeared to their tents to start gathering supplies. She touched Grant's arm and smiled.

"That was a good speech," she said. "I'm excited that you have a plan now. We've been hanging out around here for way too long."

Grant smiled. "I know. And, I think I know a way to get us home, too. When I was at this hut, there was a group there. They disappeared for a few hours, but then one of the boys came back and he seemed to have just been back home. Like pow! Just came back."

Richelle raised an eyebrow. She walked Grant over to the corner of the camp where no one else could hear them.

"So we're not home?"

Grant shook his head. "No way. Have you noticed those two moons at night? There's no way this is Earth, sweetie. I saw some stuff in the hut that proved it. I read a whole bunch of stuff about where we are. A lot of it would bore you. But just know that I figured out a way to get back to where we're from and make everything A-OK, ya know?"

Richelle nodded. "I'm with you if you think it's a good idea. Everyone seems on board. Just promise us you're not going to get us into any trouble."

Grant smiled. "When have I ever started trouble?"

Richelle rolled her eyes and walked off toward her tent to begin packing.

Grant looked out as his camp and realized that he had united everyone in just a few minutes. All it took was a plan to get everyone motivated. Hopefully, his plan would become action and the group would make their way to the hut and, eventually, find a way home.

III

Jake, Kevin, Trevor, Moss, and Amanda stood in a row and looked out at the land beyond the Walls. The sky was pink and the wheat grass moved with the wind. Dust floated in the air and pink clouds hung in the sky. It was mostly silent, save for the golden strands of grass brushing together. Out in the distance, the group could see the faint outline of a tall tower, which they all believed to be the Creator's Palace.

Jake really couldn't believe that they finally were within walking distance of the Creator's Palace. His journey felt like it had gone on for forever, and now it was nearly at its end. He had lost a few of his friends, both old and new, along the way. He had been tested, physically and mentally, at great costs, too. So much had happened that it was hard to remember it all. But now, being that he was so close to his journey's end, all that mattered was finishing the task at hand and saving Discis.

"So, we're here," Jake said. He felt The Pen, which still hung around his neck, and noticed it had picked up a certain weight now that it was nearing its former home and its ultimate end.

"We're here," Moss said in agreement. "Months have gone by, but we're here."

Jake remembered what Moss had said about his past during the Blizzard of Lexington, about how since he was a little boy, all he wanted to do was become the person in the prophecy who "knew the land." Now, Moss had finally become that person. Of the five of them who remained, Moss was the one who knew the land and, if the prophecy proved correct, he would get them to the Creator's Palace.

Jake placed his arm on Moss's shoulder. "Thank you for leading us here, Moss. Couldn't have done it without you."

Moss smiled for the first time since Jake had known him. "Thank you, Jake. All we have to do is see this through and we'll save the planet. I know none of this has been easy, and the next few days won't be either. But I'm happy you've stayed with me this whole way and chosen to fulfill your prophecy."

Jake nodded. He remembered what Lexington had told him back in the fake palace—that he was the one who was going to finally fulfill the prophecy. Sky had been a prophet, but he was never meant to finish things like Jake was. All the supposed prophets had been stepping-stones to Jake.

He was the one who would end the Age of Discontinuance.

Jake walked over to Kevin and Trevor, who stared out at the land before them. "You boys ready for this?"

Trevor nodded, but Kevin stood still.

"Kevin?" Jake asked.

Kevin ran his hand through his hair. "Sorry, Jake. I'm just trying to check out this place real quick. There isn't a lot known about the land beyond the Walls. I've read some folktales though when I was with Bennifer, about Geos, Blinkys, and some other mysterious creatures out here. Rumors say this is where The Creator's experiments are all created before they're unleashed on the real world."

Amanda looked to her sides and then back at Kevin. "That means there could be some animals in here that he didn't want in the real world. And that means there could be some freaky things coming."

Kevin nodded. "We better be on guard. Things could get hairy."

Moss stepped closer to the group. "There's something else you should know about the land beyond the Walls."

Everyone turned their attention to Moss.

"This place exists in its own little bubble, free from the rest of the planet. Kurpo made it so it's sunset all the time in here. So that's all you'll see. Orange, red and pink sunsets for the rest of our days."

"Why would he pick a sunset?" Jake asked.

Moss thought back to the beginning of the war, when everything spiraled into chaos. "The love of his life died at sunset. As a testament to her, he made this place in a continual sunset. Now, he'll always remember her. It's his way of being with her without actually being with her."

"I never knew Kurpo had been in love," Jake said.

Moss nodded. "Before he was a tyrant, before he was evil, before the Master corrupted him, Kurpo was a farmer who rose through the military. And he was bound to marry a woman from his village. But she was taken from him, and slowly he became the evil man you know now."

Jake ran his hand through his hair before he buried his face in his hands. He sat down on the grass and looked out at the land before him.

He had realized Kurpo's plan.

"What is it?" Trevor asked.

"When you love something, you never let it go, no matter how much it pains you to keep it," Jake said. "The Creator's going to stop at nothing to get his Pen back."

Trevor raised one of his eyebrows. "Yeah, so? I thought we knew that."

"You don't get it, Trevor."

"What?"

Amanda walked over to her boyfriend and placed her hand on his arm. She looked out toward the Creator's Palace. "Kurpo won't stop until he gets The Pen. He doesn't want to let it go. He can't let it go. But he hasn't come after us for it, which means he can't."

"And that means he's waiting for us," Jake said.

Trevor looked out at the land. "Waiting for us?"

Moss came to the realization just then. "The only way he can get The Pen back is for us to bring it to him."

Jake almost laughed. "He needs me to deliver him The Pen. That's why he never took it from us. That's why he asked me to go through the library door. We're walking right into his trap."

Kevin sat down next to Jake and put his arm around his cousin, while Trevor and Amanda held each other close and looked out into the distance and Moss stood alone, crossing his arms.

There was no going back or forward.

IV

Grant was drinking from his bottle of water when Jordan came jogging over to him. Per Jordan's request, the pair walked over to Jordan's shelter, which was in the back corner of the camp away from many of the others. Grant stowed away his water bottle as they entered, still unsure of why they were going into this tent without anyone else knowing.

"I need to show you something," Jordan said.

Jordan squatted down and brushed sand away from the center of his camp. He reached to his right and grabbed a shovel. He started to dig and then tossed the shovel away. It was then that he pulled out the beginning of a cylinder. Once part of it was out of the ground, Jordan bent down and pulled out the rest of it. It was long and Grant thought it looked heavy.

Jordan, sweating, tossed the cylinder off to the side and grunted once he did. He then pointed to the cylinder, implying to Grant that it was time to open it.

Jordan got down on his knees and reached over to the cylinder. He pressed a few buttons on the side of it and watched as the capsule opened up. In the center was an orb, thin red lines of smoke flowing lightly around it.

Grant swerved his head over to Jordan, who shrugged in a you-know-as-much-as-me kind of way. Grant looked over at the orb again and went to touch it. He moved his hand through the smoke and stroked it. Nothing happened.

"Where did you find this?" Grant asked.

Jordan pointed out to the left. "I went northeast like we said and I found a cabin, kind of like the hut you described. It was mostly empty, except for that, which was laying right in the center. There was a green cape there, too, but no one else in sight."

Grant, wide-eyed, continued to touch the orb to measure its authenticity. "Does anyone else know about this?"

Jordan shook his head. "Please. Like I'd let Thomas get his hands on this thing. Talk about the end of civilization as we know it."

Grant nodded. "Smart thinking, ace."

"So what should we do?"

"Nothing for now," Grant said. "But we should find a way to bring it with us. It may prove to be helpful down the road. You never know when you're going to need something freaky."

Jordan nodded and put the capsule back together. Grant stood up and waited for Jordan to finish before leaving the spot. The two men left together and made their way back toward the camp, beginning to strategize about how they could get the orb to the new campsite without being noticed.

V

"We need to get moving," Moss said.

The group, now discouraged, couldn't take Moss seriously.

"If we're going to get to the Creator's Palace while we still have energy, we need to get moving now," Moss said.

"Moss," Trevor said. "There's no reason to rush. Especially now that we know that we're walking into the Creator's trap. Giving him just what he wants."

"There's got to be a way we can beat it, though," Jake said.

"I agree. He wants us in his Palace, which means he's going to leave the front door open for us. He wants us to walk in, take off our shoes and join him for dinner," Kevin started. He thought for another second. "That just means we have to find another door, another way in."

Amanda put her military mind to work. "Does anyone know what the Palace looks like?"

Jake was silent and then he remembered Sky's replica. "I do," he said, standing up. "And if I remember correctly, there's a very large window at the top that looks out at the rest of the land. We could climb through there."

Amanda shook her head. "He'd see us coming. And if it's at the front, there's no way up. We'd need to create a rope or stairs using The Pen, but by then he'd probably have guards on us."

Jake thought again about the replica. "What if we did that, just not at the front of the Palace?"

"What do you mean?" Amanda asked.

"What if we used The Pen and created a staircase in the back. We walk up those stairs and then we create a door on that side of the Palace. That way, we can make an entrance without being detected."

Trevor scratched his growing beard. "Not a bad idea."

"That works," Amanda said. "Well, it works in theory. We have no idea if it'll work in practice. But sounds good to me."

Moss moved closer to the group and put his arm on Trevor's shoulder. "So we're good to get moving again?"

Jake nodded. "Yes. Yes, we are. Let's get moving. We've got a few hours until we'll need rest. So let's get moving and see if we can get to the Palace before that happens. We'll need our brains to start working by the time we get there."

Everyone collected their things — packs, some firewood and guns — and readied for the long walk ahead. The realization that The Creator wanted them to go to the Palace was only going to be a minor speed bump in their way. They hadn't come this far to let everything fall apart and lose out on saving the world. At least now they had a plan to get into the Palace without Kurpo knowing, which meant they could sneak in and finish the job without allowing Kurpo the time to get his Pen back.

The group turned to head off toward the tower, but they halted when they saw someone standing before them.

It was The Man of Fire, dressed in his black cloak and with fireballs in his hands. They could see his orange-red eyes glowing under the cloak.

"You," Jake said.

The Man of Fire stood, his eyes fixed on the group, his hands ready to unleash fire and burn them alive.

Jake grabbed his Pen and wielded it like a warrior would. Kevin slid the safety button on his rifle to OFF and pointed it toward his new foe. Trevor and Amanda got into attack position with their rifles and aimed them at the man too. Moss readied his spear.

"Who are you?" Jake asked.

The Man of Fire smirked under his cloak.

It happened without warning. The Man of Fire disappeared into thin air, leaving only a cloud of red dust in his wake.

But he wasn't gone. The Man of Fire reappeared right behind Moss. He latched onto Moss's spear and made it begin to glow and steam. Moss yelped in pain and dropped his weapon, his palms a ruby red.

Kevin and the group turned and readied to attack The Man of Fire and finish him. But as they turned, they saw The Man of Fire, fireballs still in his hand, take Moss and roast his arms. Moss, screaming in pain, his skin so hot it was cold, backed away from his enemy. He fell to the ground and rolled on the grass, backing away from The Man of Fire, his arms and hands steaming, the smell of burning smoke filling the air.

It was time to start shooting. Kevin, Trevor, and Amanda all fired their bullets, but The Man of Fire melted them with a wave of embers. The wave's reverberation sent them flying back into the grass.

Jake, still standing, whispered an attack and pointed The Pen toward The Man of Fire.

Nothing happened.

The Pen didn't budge. Jake repeated his command, but The Pen lay dormant, void of any attacking power.

All Jake could do was watch.

The Man of Fire stomped toward Moss and reached him. His hands still full of fire, he lifted Moss up into the air and held him close. Jake saw Moss's eyes grow twice their usual size as he saw who was under the cloak. And then Moss turned away in fright as his eyes began to burn from staring too long. The Man of Fire gripped Moss tighter and more steam came from Moss's arms. He yelped in pain, screaming for help as the burns fried his arms. He watched pieces of his skin—blackened and gray—float away with the wind. The air stunk of his roasted and charred body.

The Man of Fire tossed Moss down to the ground and made another fireball. And with furious force, he picked Moss up again and shoved the fireball right down Moss's throat. Moss's screams silenced as he crisped up. Steam shot out from his body, which burned and grayed as the fire burned him. Fire shot out from his eyes. He was burned from the inside out.

The Man of Fire applied more pressure and Moss soon was just a pile of ash that flew away into the wind.

The Man of Fire rested a moment before turning back around toward the group, who were sprawled out on the grass. He shot a line of fire into the grass and disappeared.

Jake looked up and saw the fire was spreading across the grass. He grabbed The Pen from his pocket and commanded it to put the fire out, and it did easily without denial.

Jake laid his head back and passed out.

CHAPTER 42

I

The Creator stood at his window and gazed out at thousands of cloaked New Bloods and thousands more silver shielded Palace guards. They all stood with their swords at their side, patiently waiting for The Creator to give the next order. But The Creator didn't want to tell them anything yet. He wanted to look out at his soldiers and admire the army he had amassed over the last few months. He raised the New Bloods back at the beginning of this current conflict. And now he joined them with his guards, who were well-trained soldiers from the early wars who he trusted most. This was an army he could be proud of. This was an army that couldn't be beaten.

Kurpo surveyed his army and smiled. Nothing could stop it. His guards were strong soldiers who couldn't be bested by the best of warriors. And the New Bloods were all those he had trained who couldn't survive the earlier wars. But now that they were dead and reborn, they could never really be killed. Any death they suffered would be for a brief period of time, then they would be reborn again and keep coming back. As long as The Creator lived, the New Bloods lived.

The Creator passed the back door of his room and entered the side door, which led him to a dark staircase that descended from the top of the Palace to the bottom floor. Kurpo walked down each of the black cobblestone steps and then stepped out onto his land, into the faded sunlight, where he saw his army waiting patiently for battle.

One of his guards, Constable Broxxi, one of the greatest heroines of the old wars who was now the leader of The Creator's guards, stepped up to him, her neck shielded by a tan scarf that lightly blew with the wind. Her face, once perfect but now divided by a plum scar that went down the middle, perked up when she saw her leader approach.

"Hello, hello. What brings you out here, Creator?" Broxxi asked.

Kurpo crossed his arms and stared out at his army. "I wanted to get a good look at all of you—to see if you're all really ready for war again."

"We are," Broxxi replied. "Just waiting for the enemies to approach. Some of my men are worried that no war is coming."

"War is coming," The Creator replied. "Should be in a day's time. They'll come from the east, with a small army that the New Bloods themselves can easily defeat."

Broxxi raised her left eyebrow. "Then why are my men out here?"

"I like to prepare for the worst," Kurpo replied.

Broxxi nodded and stared back at her soldiers. She would never admit this to anyone, but secretly she was counting how many blades, spears, and swords her army had. She wanted to make sure everyone was well-equipped and ready to defeat any enemy that came their way.

"How much damage will there be?" Broxxi asked.

Kurpo shrugged. "Remember the Battle of Kilworth?" Broxxi nodded. It was her first battle, an easy one that secured her rank among the droves of men. It was the fight that proved to the rest that she was a competent warrior. "Like that," Kurpo replied.

Broxxi smiled at the notion. That was going to be the easiest battle ever, then, especially because the New Blood army couldn't die by the hands of men.

"Sounds like it'll be easy, then," Broxxi replied.

"It will," Kurpo said. "I have one request, though."

Broxxi turned her head to Kurpo.

"One of the boys coming this way has my Pen," he said.

Broxxi finally understand the severity of the situation. She thought it better not to ask questions about how the Creator had lost his weapon, though. She didn't want to see him angry. No one liked Kurpo when he was angry.

"You have to make sure he makes it to the tower. Tell your men to let him through," Kurpo replied.

She didn't understand that, though. Wouldn't it make more sense to just kill the one carrying The Pen and return the item to Kurpo?

"What? Why?" Broxxi asked. It was a tame version of what she really wanted to ask.

"Because the only way I can get my Pen back is if he comes up to the top of the tower. That's the only way The Pen will change hands," the Creator said. "He has to live."

"What about the others?" she asked.

Kurpo smiled wickedly. "Kill them all."

THE PEN

II

"Are we ready?" Grant called.

He looked out at his group—Jupiter, Brent, April, Thomas, Chris, Richelle, and Jordan—and they all nodded. Grant waved them forward and picked up his pack. He slung it over his shoulder and the group started to walk away from their campsite, together, for the first time.

As Grant walked ahead of the group, Jupiter and Brent hung in the back, their arms wrapped around each other, having found love in a place without hope. April and Ian walked side by side, but alone in their own eyes, not letting the other in too much. Richelle, Chris, and Jordan walked together in a line, eyeing Grant with quizzical looks, still unsure if they believed in him as a leader or not.

"This has been a crazy few months," Richelle said.

"And I missed five of the days. Can't imagine what those five days were like," Jordan said. "But the good news is that normality will return. We're going to get to this hut, and then hopefully find shelter."

"I don't know," Richelle said. "I have a bad feeling about this."

Chris didn't say anything.

"What are you talking about?" Jordan asked.

"How do we know Grant hasn't gone crazy and is leading us to some insane trap to just murder us all?" Richelle asked.

Jordan gave a half-smile. He knew Grant was trustworthy, especially because Grant was the only other person who knew of the orb and had kept it secret.

"Trust me, we'll be fine."

The group walked toward the clearing away from their camp. They soon found themselves among barren plains of green grass that swayed lightly with the wind. They could see a forest way off in the distance, along with something that looked like white-capped mountains. But otherwise, all they saw were stretches and stretches of grass. Oh, and a swarm of dark clouds in the distance that were heading their way.

Because of the clouds, Grant knew he'd have to get the group to some kind of shelter by the end of the night. Otherwise, they'd be swept up in a spectacular and dangerous storm that could hurt them and limit their chances of getting to the hut and possibly home. He knew if he lost one or two of the group, then the group's morale would drop, and he'd have to convince everyone to keep moving forward. It was imperative that they all made it to the hut and found their way home together.

About an hour later, the group rested. Grant stood by himself at first, but then Richelle came to join him. Grant was mid-sip when Richelle approached from behind. He looked over at her and smiled as she sipped from her own water bottle.

"What can I do ya for?" Grant asked.

Richelle turned to Grant, her face consumed with worry. "I'm just nervous about all of this," she said. "I mean, we're in this weird place, and we're just going somewhere we've never been before. I don't know if I can take it."

Grant smirked. "You can take it."

"Oh yeah?" Richelle asked, a light smile coming to her face.

Grant took another sip of water. "Oh yeah. You're the strongest one here."

Richelle chuckled. "The group voted you and Thomas leaders. Not me."

Grant pointed at her. "That's exactly why you're the real leader. You may not have the title, or the recognition, or whatever you wanna call it, but April, Jupiter, Brent, and Chris, hell, even me, we all look to you. You keep us straight."

Richelle didn't think of that before. She stared out at the plains.

"I'm not sure I'm meant to be a leader," Richelle said.

Grant took the bait. "Oh yeah? Why's that?"

"It's stupid, really," she began, half-laughing, "I used to play the flute in elementary school. Our school encouraged us all to be in band class, so we all joined and we all had to pick an instrument," Richelle started. She crossed her arms. "And I chose the flute. I thought it was pretty. And I fell in love with the sound. So beautiful. So simple. So easy and calming. I really enjoyed it. I enjoyed it so much that our teacher, Mrs. Simpkins, I think, asked me to do a solo. She wanted me to play all alone and be the leader of the group for our winter concert."

Richelle looked down at the ground. Grant could tell where the story was going.

"I messed up," Richelle said, rubbing the back of her neck. "I don't even remember how. My mouth slipped or my tongue got stuck, I dunno. I just remember playing the first three notes all wrong and dead air filling the auditorium. I ran off-stage crying. I was so upset."

Grant nodded. "But you joined a band, didn't you? Isn't that what you said one night? It couldn't have been that scarring."

Richelle nodded. "Yeah, I joined a band. But I never wanted to lead it, or be a part of the group. I joined a band because I like music and like the sound it creates and how calm it makes me. I didn't like my band or my friends. I mean, there's a reason we split up."

Richelle paused. "I'm selfish."

Grant smiled and cracked up.

"What?" Richelle asked. Grant didn't stop laughing. "What's so funny?"

"That is exactly why you'd make a great leader," Grant said. "Sometimes you have to be willing to let yourself or others go for the greater good and the greater goal. Sometimes, you have to be selfish in order to be selfless."

Grant took another sip of water, slung his bag over his shoulder, and called for the group to keep moving forward.

III

Jake didn't know how much time had passed when he finally opened his eyes. It was still sunset, the clouds were still a pinkish gray, and the grass still swayed with the wind. Everything was just as it was.

Except that Geoff Moss was no longer there to guide him.

Jake raised himself up to a sitting position and stared out at the burned grass before him. Kevin and Trevor stood, too, looking far out into the distance and talking things over. Amanda was putting together a fire in the center of it all, which made Jake think that it must be around nighttime. Jake shook his head, watched dust fly off, and then stood up to meet with his friends. Trevor and Kevin moved from their spot and joined Jake at the fire, which Amanda had just lit.

The four didn't say anything to each other at first. Jake knew they were all thinking the same thing—that Moss, the one man who knew the land and had guided them through much of their experience, was gone forever. He floated away into the wind, as though he had never been alive at all. Jake felt sadness creep into him and make camp by his eyes, causing water to flow out from behind the caves of his eyes. He wiped away his tears and instead focused his mind on The Man of Fire—the one who had come and killed Moss without a second thought.

"That was messed up," Trevor said.

Amanda nodded. "Didn't expect it. Especially from The Man of Fire."

"The Man of Fire," Jake said, trying to make sense of the name. "Why wouldn't you expect something like that from a man with that kind of name?"

Amanda, Trevor, and Kevin exchanged glances. Amanda looked at Jake. "Remember how we told you there was a fire that distracted the army from coming after us? No one could have started a fire as quickly as The Man of Fire. He helped us get back here, which makes it weird that he would kill our guide."

Jake nodded.

"Unless," Kevin started, "he wanted us to get back here so he could kill us."

Trevor shook his head. "If he wanted us all dead, he would have killed us all. But he didn't. He killed Moss and left us all behind."

Amanda nodded. "Which means that he wanted Moss dead, and he didn't care what happened to us."

It was all too confusing for Jake. He could tell that Amanda, Trevor and Kevin had reached another intellectual level. They could talk about a person's mindset and theories and motives, but he couldn't. As far as he could tell, The Man of Fire had just killed Moss for no apparent reason. He could have ended the rest of them, but he had chosen to simply kill Moss. Motivation and reason didn't matter. Moss was dead because of The Man of Fire.

Jake rubbed his head and pulled The Pen out of his pocket. That was another mystery to him—why had The Pen worked to put out the fire, but didn't work to attack The Man of Fire? In the past, The Pen had saved him and his friends from certain death. But for some reason, it wouldn't cause harm to The Man of Fire. How could that be? Why wouldn't it kill The Man of Fire, but it would kill the fire that he produced?

"So what do we do now?" Trevor asked.

That was a good question, Jake thought. The Man of Fire had killed their guide, their leader, the man who knew the land. Even though the directions to the Creator's Palace seemed pretty simple, Moss's guidance had always made Jake feel safe. He always knew that no matter what came their way, they'd have Moss there to back them up or enlighten them. Now, though, they were completely alone.

Alone.

"We keep moving," Jake said. "We can rest for a few minutes, but we've got to keep moving. That's the plan."

Trevor and Kevin nodded. "Sounds good."

"But what about the war?" Amanda asked.

The three boys turned toward the girl.

"Moss said that war is coming, which means he probably had some plan in mind for getting an army, right? We don't even have a clue about how to assemble an army," Amanda said.

Jake thought for a second and then remembered what Moss had told him about the war. "Weren't we supposed to meet up with your old clan? The Ranadeau Warriors?"

Amanda shrugged. "Even if we do, that's only hundreds. What kind of army would The Creator have?"

Jake thought back to the books he had read and the experiences he had faced during his time there. "If I remember correctly, about 5,000 of his most loyal troops from the early wars survived and now guard his Palace. And if he's risen all the New Bloods from his old army, that means he's got well over 10,000 soldiers, about half of which can't die completely unless he dies, too."

It suddenly came to Jake how difficult this was going to be. Even if somehow they met up with Ranadeau Warriors, the battle would still be 1,000 against 10,0000, which meant that each man in the Ranadeau tribe would have to take on ten of the Creator's. That seemed impossible. And Jake knew it was.

Jake thought about what Moss would have said at that moment. He would have encouraged the group to keep moving, because Moss always had a plan. Even if the plan was as simple as keep moving toward the Palace, it was still a plan. But Jake didn't feel optimistic, especially because he knew that the odds were stacked against them. He could see a few soldiers killing ten men each, but if a few of the Ranadeau Warriors, or even members of their four-person clan, died, then that would mean another ten would pile on top, and soon the battle would become too hard to handle.

In the past, Jake might have sulked and complained about the end of days being nigh. He would have screamed in frustration that everything was so damn difficult. But he had gotten this far on Moss's vague plans, and he wasn't going to let this be the end of it. They still had eight miles to go. And even if he died after walking those eight miles, at least he would know he willingly met his fate.

"Guys," Trevor said out of nowhere.

Kevin, Jake, and Amanda turned to Trevor, who was looking at the sky.

"What's that?" he asked, pointing.

They all looked up and saw a black spacecraft emerge from the sky, heading right toward them.

IV

The storm hit them about two hours later. It started with a sprinkle, but soon turned into a fury of raindrops, lightning strikes and thunder booms. Soon enough, Grant and his group couldn't see even a few feet ahead. All they saw was the gray mask of raindrops. The rain soaked through their clothes to their bones, chilling them and turning the day into winter.

The group passed through the muddy grass with a bit of a jog, hoping to get through the rain more quickly. Grant hoped that the rainstorm would end soon and they would find a clearing again. Or, better yet, that they would find the hut and finally have a place to rest.

But they weren't so lucky. The rain continued to pour down on them without remorse, and the lightning continued to strike and flash through the sky. Thunder rumbled louder with each step, as though the heavens above were enjoying a nice night of bowling. The rain became so loud at one point that it drowned out the thunder. It became so heavy that the group couldn't even see the lightning. All they saw was the transparent gray of the rain.

Richelle shouted through the loud rain for Grant, who stopped in his tracks when he heard her. He swerved around and she shouted into his ear that they needed to rest. Grant shouted back that there was no place to rest and that they need to keep moving through the dark and ominous rain.

V

Jake, Trevor, Kevin, and Amanda ran after the black spacecraft that landed about half a mile from where they had been standing. The dust was just settling from the ship's arrival when they took their last steps. It was a slick black chrome, dark enough that they could see their own reflections. Kevin touched the wings to get a feel for it. It seemed oddly familiar to him.

The group of four all turned their heads to the right when a hissing sound came from the ship. They looked over and saw a ramp slowly emerge and dig its way into the grass below. The group walked over to the ramp to get an eye for who was coming out. Amanda and Trevor readied their weapons, just in case the arriving person was menacing. Kevin and Jake stuck together, also ready to take on whoever came next.

Down the ramp came a man. He held a cane and his black armor covered most of his torso. He had mostly brown hair, save for streaks of gray across the sides.

Bennifer.

Kevin's head almost exploded. Amanda and Trevor felt their jaws drop. Jake had no idea what to make of it.

Bennifer, his cane pounding against the ramp platform and then settling on the grass, walked over to the group, a subtle smile on his face. Kevin felt like he needed to say something, but he didn't know what he would say. It was the same for Amanda and Trevor. They felt like they should pay Bennifer some sort of attention, but they had no clue what to even say to the man. It was a man they thought they had left behind on Earth, a man they never thought they'd see again. And yet, he was here before them on Discis, a million miles from home.

Bennifer paused before the group of four and stood there as the ramp to his ship ascended back up. He waited a moment, pausing to see if anyone responded to his arrival or had anything to say.

It was Kevin who finally spoke. "How?"

Bennifer smiled. "We followed your coordinates, of course."

That didn't make sense to Kevin. "How? I never signaled you after I got to Discis."

Bennifer waved that off. "The device was just a failsafe, in case the Project X machine didn't register your brainwaves and catch the coordinates. But it did, perfectly."

THE PEN

Kevin didn't have any other questions to answer. It made sense. He wasn't terribly upset to see Bennifer, either, since Bennifer had been his boss for the last three years while they planned their attack on The Order. It was actually refreshing to see a familiar face again.

Bennifer nodded to Amanda and Trevor. They didn't know each other too well. Amanda had met Bennifer occasionally during meetings and odd appearances, but never got the full introduction. Trevor, meanwhile, had been on guard duty when Bennifer came to visit The Order, so he had met him on occasion. He knew about Bennifer's reputation more than anything else, which painted a vivid picture of the man.

Bennifer's eyes rested on Jake. Both felt astonished that after all this time—three years for Bennifer, and merely a few days for Jake — the two were face-to-face again. Jake couldn't believe that their plan to bring everyone back to Discis had worked. Bennifer had been right the entire time, and it was because of him that Jake had his makeshift family back with him. And it was because of Bennifer that the entire group had a chance to save Discis and Earth.

"Nice to see you again," Bennifer said.

Jake nodded. "Nice to see you, too."

Amanda readied her weapon, still distrustful of the former Order member. "What are you doing here?"

Bennifer looked to Amanda's left. "Kevin?"

Kevin cleared his throat and stepped forward. "Bennifer is using Discis as a resting place before he heads to another nearby planet called Tempestfield. The other planet has some sort of minerals or something that could save Earth."

"Correct," Bennifer said. "So in the meantime, I thought I'd drop in and say hello to my favorite gang."

"Is it just you?" Jake asked.

Bennifer shook his head. "Not at all. In fact, I brought backup. I figured we'd need it."

"For what?" Amanda asked.

Bennifer smiled from ear to ear. "War."

The ground shook. More ships appeared in the sky, all black, but of different sizes. Some were triple the size of Bennifer's, and others were five times as big. Some were just small voyage vessels. Dozens and dozens of ships came down, blowing the air and shaking the ground as they did. All the ships, now on the ground, surrounded Bennifer and the group. There were too many ships to count.

Jake realized what had happened. War had indeed been coming. Bennifer and his crew were their army.

"When I was younger, I heard this story of a prophet—someone who could bring the land back from darkness and end the struggles of the world," Bennifer said. "I heard that four people were going to be with him—his relative, his friend, one who knew the land, and one who had forgotten the land," he paused and took a deep breath. "That's all I remember from when I lived on Discis, but it's enough for me to throw my hat in the ring and help make the prophecy come true."

Jake and the rest of the group smiled when they came to the realization that Bennifer planned to help them.

"We will get you to the Creator's Palace, Jake. And we will fight for you. And for The Pen."

VI

Grant tripped and slammed right into the mud. His face sank deep into the brown sludge. Mud flooded his nose. He pushed himself off the ground and shook himself off. The rain melted some of the mud off of him. He was thankful for the rain.

When he turned his head to the left, he saw the hut. Grant waved his group on and jogged over. He heard footsteps behind him and knew people were following. He grabbed the handle on the door of the hut and threw it open before diving in, finally alive with dry air and warmth. Richelle hurried down into the hut right behind him, followed by Jupiter, April, Thomas, Chris, and Jordan.

Jordan, the last one in, slammed the door shut.

Richelle was already building a fire in the fireplace off on the other side of the hut. She ran over to the towels she saw and started tossing them to everyone.

Jupiter was shivering, her red hair now a deep maroon. Brent cuddled her and tried to warm her up.

Grant lay back against one of the walls and sighed with force. Finally, they had shelter.

VII

Richelle sat alone by the fire. Everyone else was asleep.

She thought about what Grant said earlier, about her being a leader and taking on responsibility within the group. She never thought of herself as a leader, especially of this group, who had already voted for their leader and had already started taking orders from someone else. She figured she was just one of the crew. But Grant's words stuck with her. Maybe she could be a leader. Maybe she could head this group.

Richelle's thoughts were broken when she heard shuffling from one side of the room. She looked over and saw it was Grant, waking up from his slumber. With a towel wrapped around his upper body, Grant walked over to Richelle and sat down beside her.

"Evening," Grant said.

"You too," Richelle said.

"No sleep?"

Richelle shook her head. "Can't sleep. Always have trouble sleeping in new places."

Grant smirked. "Didn't take you for the drifter type."

Richelle smiled back. "It's part of my selfishness."

Grant nodded. "Speaking of which."

Richelle watched Grant reach behind him and pull a wooden box from underneath his towel. He held it before Richelle, wiped off the thick dust that rested on the box, and lifted the box's top off. Inside was a perfect silver flute, immaculate, clean, and smooth.

"Think you can still play?"

"Where did you find this?" Richelle asked.

Grant shrugged. "This place is full of weird stuff. There's a computer in the back corner, for heaven's sake."

Richelle hadn't played the flute in a long time. She knew she could still play—those $500 lessons did her some good back when she was a kid—but it scared her, almost, to play again.

And then she thought about what Grant said about leadership. Sometimes, you have to be selfish.

She grabbed the flute, held it against her lips and began to play a soft tune.

CHAPTER 43

I

Ginta, King of Ranadeau, was meditating on his rug like he did every morning when there was a knock at his door. His eyes opened in a flash, the disturbance rocking his core and sending him out of the slight trance he had found himself in. He threw off a blanket that had been covering him and stood up, his bare feet slamming against the wooden floor below. He walked over to the door and opened it, seeing one of his leading warrior, JJah, wearing beige robes and a dark black headband, standing there.

"Sorry sir, did I disturb you?"

Ginta shook his head. "No, not at all. I was in a trance, but not a deep one. Thankfully I still have my bearings. What can I do for you, JJah?"

JJah stood up straight. "Sir, the guards said they heard it."

Ginta's eyes widened.

Without a moment to lose, Ginta swung around the door and called JJah to follow him forward. The two jogged through the stone halls of the meditation sanctuary and made their way down a marble staircase into the castle's open lobby. They traveled down a white marble corridor and found a set up of stairs that led up to the watchtower. Ginta ascended on his own, telling JJah to wait and keep watch so there could be no disturbance.

Waiting for him at the top was Ritkin, the short and stubble-faced dwarf, who always carried listening and viewing scopes wherever he went. He was perched on a chair and still looking out at the world beyond.

"Did you hear it?" Ginta asked.

Ritkin nodded. "The tune of Felder's Flute indeed played this morning."

THE PEN

"Ring the bell."

That was enough for Ginta. There was no time to spare. He hopped off the perch and descended the staircase. He found JJah waiting and told him to follow. The duo scurried back to the lobby and then out to the center of the castle. The King and his most trusted warrior dodged mingling citizens and swung into the back corner of the castle, where there was open land—where the soldiers trained.

Leading the soldiers was Marko and some other advisors, like Matkin, Jerme and Cidd. Ginta saw Burko and Hartkip, his two most trusted political advisors, standing off to the side of the soldiers, dressed in purple robes. He rushed over to them and whispered what JJah had told them moments earlier. Burko and Hartkip shouted to Marko, explaining what was happening, and Marko immediately told the soldiers to reset and gather themselves. JJah stuck with the warriors and prepared for the great journey ahead.

Ginta flew off back toward the castle, letting his soldiers get to work building their attack strategy. He climbed back up to his room and slammed the door behind him. He ripped a blanket away from his center window and gazed out at his castle and citizens below. He saw everyone moving about as though everything was normal. Little did they know how their worlds were about to change.

The bell rang from the watchtower, and immediately everyone in the castle turned their attention to Ginta's window. The King saw that the people below, who had been doing their normal daily errands until now, had their eyes fixed on him. The soldiers practicing their weaponry attacks switched their attention, too. Everyone's eyes were fixed on him.

Ginta brought his hands together. "Ranadeau citizens!" he called out. "The time has come for the Age of Discontinuance to end. We have been called to help defend the Holder of The Pen in his final battle with the Creator and end the tyranny that has destroyed this land. In an hour's time, we shall journey forward and begin this war. Anyone who would like to join and fight with us, come. And anyone who stays, watch after those we leave behind. This is our moment. This is what we've all been waiting for!"

Thunderous applause rang out across the kingdom. Ginta smiled. He knew his kingdom was ready to defend the Holder of The Pen and finally finish off Kurpo's reign of terror and drought. Chants rang out from the soldiers below as Ginta raised his hands again.

It was time for war.

II

Kevin was having a field day with all the new weaponry.

Once Bennifer's army made camp, they set up tents and huts full of weapons, training gear, and beds for sleeping in a little less than an hour. Armed vehicles flew from the sky and were dropped before them, already set up to speed off toward the Palace and defend Jake and his Pen. Kevin had bounced around from the small weapons tent to the heavy artillery station to the armored vehicle selection. It was a beautiful sight for him. He hadn't seen this many weapons in his time with Bennifer, although he knew full well that Bennifer and his team had enough weaponry to destroy worlds. Now, he was finally seeing it for his own eyes.

Kevin met up with Trevor and Amanda in one of the many huts and the three of them surveyed all the weapons they could pick from. Amanda and Trevor couldn't understand the differences between the weapons they had used at The Order's camp and these ones, especially because these new weapons seemed to be years ahead of their time and contained different settings than they were used to.

"We can invert the settings with these?" Amanda asked, scoping out one of the weapons and realizing she could soon make the trigger and gun's functions fit her southpaw style.

Demak, the Head of Weaponry, polished a few of the weapons. He was in charge of making sure soldiers got the guns they wanted and that fit their style of fighting.

"Indeed," Demak said. "You can take any weapon here and invert the settings and platform to make it fit your hand style and shooting style. If you like guns on your shoulder, you could lock it on your armor and have it rest there and shoot."

Amanda's eyes widened. It seemed ridiculous that she could make her weapon fit her needs, since she had trained so long to meet the needs of the weapons. It had always been about learning how the weapon was meant to be used. This seemed like a more personalized and customizable way to use a weapon. She loved it.

To her left, Trevor swiped his hand across one of the guns. It was black chrome and didn't seem to have any slot for a magazine or bullets.

"What's up with this one?" Trevor asked.

Demak looked at it. "That's the Sure Fire. New technology. No bullets. Just energy blasts that are about the same size and shape as bullets. Energy efficient."

"Whoa. Why doesn't everyone have one of these?" Amanda asked, picking it up.

Demak shrugged. "They're not great at killing. They're good at stunning and stalling enemies, but as for an actual kill, the bullet is still king. We've had some battles where men had the Sure Fire, would shoot to kill, and would watch their enemy walk right through those shots. Some people's bodies just don't get hurt by the energy blasts."

Amanda nodded. "So why even use it?"

Demak smirked. "Because you can change the scope and length of the blast. So let's say you're about to go into full-scale battle. One shot of this could stall anywhere between ten and fifty soldiers. So, in short, it's better for neutralizing groups of soldiers rather than one-on-one fighting."

Amanda nodded again. That made a lot of sense, and characterized the Sure Fire as a weapon that would be useful in the coming battle. She would have taken it, but her weapon of choice was one that fit on her left hand and shot bullets. She remembered seeing a comic book character once who had a similar style of weapon.

Trevor, though, took the Sure Fire in his hands. "I'll take it."

"You sure?" Demak asked.

Trevor nodded. "Of course. If we're going to have the odds stacked against us, might as well take out bunches of soldiers instead of just one."

Demak nodded in approval with a smirk on his face. "I wish ya luck in the one-on-one fights buddy."

III

Kevin, Trevor, and Amanda left the hut and found Jake and Bennifer standing together nearby. Bennifer's hands moved quickly, which indicated to the group that he was explaining something to Jake about the army. As they approached Bennifer and Jake, the trio of soldiers heard Bennifer explain a little bit more about his army and how they were just the first fleet of many more back on Earth.

"How do you have so many soldiers?" Jake asked.

"Well, after Kevin's coordinates came through, we took over The Order back home and now we have their soldiers," Bennifer said with a mild amount of triumph. "So our army increased ten-fold. I brought with me just a sliver of it to tackle this battle and get us closer to our ultimate destination. A lot are back home, but we have some on the way. Should arrive in a few year's time, I'd imagine."

Jake nodded. "Makes sense. Well, I appreciate you giving us the help. God knows what we'd do without you guys."

Bennifer smiled. "It's our pleasure. This planet gets us closer to Tempestfield, so we're more than willing to throw a few punches while we figure out the next step."

Kevin, Trevor, and Amanda approached the two talking men and stood by them with their weapons. Bennifer ran a visual analysis of all the weapons that the group was holding and nodded in approval.

"You all look like you found something that'll work," he said.

"You know it," Kevin said, running his hand over his Beast Mode X93, a large yet lightweight automatic weapon that Demak recommended for anyone who was looking to shoot for defense, rather than to shoot to kill. Apparently it was good for quick fire and easy mobility, and was built strictly to help soldiers save other soldiers.

"When do we move out?" Amanda asked.

Bennifer checked the screen on his wrist and saw it was early in the morning in real time.

"We'll be at the battlefield by sunrise, so we've got a couple of hours. But Jake," Bennifer grabbed Jake's shoulder, "Jake will be leaving us early. He's going to go on his own."

Amanda, Trevor, and Kevin all protested. Kevin stepped forward and increased his voice among the rest. "Why?"

Jake stepped forward. "It makes sense, doesn't it? We made the plan that we'd go the back of the Palace and I'd build a staircase with The Pen and get into the Palace that way. Well, the Palace stands alone. There's nothing behind it or before it except for the walls. And if the soldiers are all waiting at the front, I can run along the outskirts and sneak in from the back undetected. I'll keep my distance from the soldiers at the front and go the long way out. I can reach the back of the Palace by the time you're all in battle, which will leave me enough time to create the staircase and get upstairs."

The plan made sense to Amanda from a military perspective. If the key was to get Jake to the top of the tower, they shouldn't risk his life on the battlefield. It made sense to sneak around the back and use the element of surprise for him to get into the Palace.

"No," Kevin said, still protesting. "I'm not going to let Jake go alone. We've been together these last few steps. We can't let it all fall apart now."

"We're not," Jake said.

Kevin, Trevor, and Amanda didn't understand. They turned their attention to Jake, who picked The Pen out of his pocket and held it close to his friends. "All I've got to defend myself is this Pen, but it only works if there's someone else to save." He pointed The Pen at Kevin. "You're coming with me."

Kevin smirked. "You sure about that?"

Jake nodded. "It's going to be the Vermont vacation we never got," he said. Kevin smiled at that. He remembered how much he wanted to go to Vermont three years ago and how his disappearance had destroyed that trip. But it made sense to him now—to finally make things come full circle and have the vacation he and his cousin always wanted.

Jake stepped back. "While Kevin and I go along the sides of the castle, the rest of you can take on their soldiers head-on. We'll reach the back of the Palace and make our way up together. We can take care of things from there no problem."

"Hell yeah we can," Kevin said, bumping fists with his cousin. "Let's go."

Even if they died in this fight, they would at least know that they went down together and with the help of one another. And for Jake, that brought him the biggest amount of satisfaction he could ever have.

The Pen had finally given Jake what he always wanted.

IV

Richelle lay back against one of the hut's walls, twirling the flute in her hands. Before last night, the last time Richelle remembered playing was before she was a woman. That had been before all the terrible things that had happened to her. The last time she had played, she was still innocent and untainted by the world. Now she was a darkened soul. It felt weird to play an instrument when she knew she was a different person altogether.

The rest of the group moved around the hut, trying to find different resources they could use. Brent was off in the corner reading a book that was about the size of seven Bibles. Jupiter hung by, reading a smaller book that she had found.

Thomas and April rationed out the food, mostly because somebody had to do it and no one had stepped up to the plate yet. They broke off the food and decided what packages each person in the hut would get for the next few days. They wanted to spread out the food among the group while also saving some for the next few days.

Chris lay against the wall on the far side of the hut. He couldn't fall asleep for the life of him.

Grant and Jordan entered the hut at the same time. Richelle looked over and saw that they were both holding a larger cylinder that looked like it weighed tons. The group turned and came closer to Grant and Jordan.

"Can we have your attention?" Grant asked, panting a bit. Richelle deduced that the two had been carrying the cylinder for some time. "Back when we all split off and went on our own paths, Jordan found something. We decided to keep this secret from you until we figured out what it does and until we got to safety. Now seems like the perfect opportunity to show you all."

Jordan got down on one knee and unlocked the capsule. The group stretched their necks and looked over the side of the cylinder.

A metal orb with red smoke sat in the center.

"What the hell is that?" Thomas asked.

Grant shrugged. "Beats me."

Brent bent down to look at it. "Seems like something out of a sci-fi book."

"Or something from this world," April said back.

Thomas walked up to Jordan and Grant, steam shooting out of his ears. "You two decided to hide this from the group? Does that sound fair?"

Grant shrugged. He knew now that with Jordan on his side, his decisions were untouchable. "It just made sense to hold off until we found safety."

Thomas shook his head. "No. You should have both come to us about this! What if this thing just exploded and killed us all? What if someone came looking for it? What if that person tried to kill us?"

Grant looked out at the rest of the group and saw the tide had changed. Though most of the group knew he and Jordan were justified, Thomas's latest point was a well-taken one. Someone could have come looking for the orb and killed them for it. Luckily, they hadn't. But that was beside the point. Danger could easily have followed the orb.

There was a knock at the hut's door.

The group turned their attention in the direction of the knock.

A second knock pounded on the door.

Jordan mustered up his courage and approached the door. He put his arm out, a signal for everyone to ready themselves with any weapons they could find. Richelle pulled out a pocketknife, Grant grabbed a piece of metal he found outside, and everyone else readied themselves with books and sharp objects from in the hut. Jordan waited until everyone was ready.

He swung upon the door.

There he saw a short, bald man with caramel skin. His eyes were all-knowing and his face aged with wisdom.

V

Ginta faced a charismatic young man when the door opened.

"May we help you?" the man asked Ginta.

Ginta looked at the man and peered around at the rest of the group.

"Where is Sky?" Ginta asked.

The man stood strong. "Sorry, who are you?"

"My name is Ginta," he said. "And I'm looking for a man named Sky."

The man shrugged. "There's no Sky here. You must have the wrong place."

Ginta nodded. "I guess I do."

The door shut behind Ginta.

JJah approached Ginta right after the door closed. "Orders, sir?"

Ginta looked at the door and peered out at all the soldiers there, waiting for his command. He nodded at JJah. "Sky is not here. We've been compromised. Please, make it quick."

JJah nodded.

VI

There was another knock at the door.

Jordan swung the door open again. Before he could get a word in, a spear pierced his torso and sent him flying back into the hut, painting the walls red.

Everything went into chaos.

Brent wrapped Jupiter in his arms and the two scurried toward the door. Brent used the book he had to barrel through the group of soldiers who waited there for them. He shoved past a group or two before he met another pack of men, who all held spears. Before Brent could get his last words off to Jupiter, the spears sent the lovers to their deaths, blood splashing everywhere.

But Brent's distraction had been enough for the rest of the group to make a quick escape. Chris, strong and capable, held April's hand and pushed out of the hut. They saw a swarm of soldiers take down Brent and Jupiter, and it pained them too much to look back. Thomas and April jogged forward, hoping to make it out of the chaos and get away. But before the two could even think about where they were running to, a pair of men riding horses blocked their path. One tossed a knife down and thrust it through Chris's chest, splitting his skin. Blood spat out and smacked April in the face. She screamed as one of the men hopped down to greet her. She felt the hot smoke from her body rise as a spear pierced her.

Thomas watched as the group rushed out of the hut. He bunkered down in the corner as screams and shouts erupted from outside. He covered his ears and buried himself in his arms to keep himself safe. When he picked his head up, a group of soldiers rushed toward him. He passed out in fear of what was going to happen. He was unconscious when the five blades tore his body to shreds.

As soon as Brent and Jupiter made the distraction, Grant grabbed Richelle's hand and headed right for the door. The two burst through and followed Brent and Jupiter's path. But as the two were swarmed by soldiers, Grant and Richelle took a sharp turn back toward the hut and swung around the backside. Grant shouted for Richelle to go straight, right toward the rocks in the back corner. He yelled something about the green light, but it was drowned out by the shouts and screams. As they ran to the rocks, Grant could see the greenish tinge he remembered from earlier.

This was their only escape.

Grant turned around and saw a pack of wild soldiers sprint toward them. He stopped moving and turned to face the coming soldiers.

Richelle halted her run when she noticed Grant was no longer with her.

"Grant? Grant? What are you doing?"

Grant waved Richelle forward. "Go! I'll get this!"

Richelle remembered what Grant had told her about leadership. He was doing something selfish for a greater good. He would take the heat so that Richelle could escape.

Before she ran away, Grant tossed the orb over to her. It landed in the dirt beneath her feet.

"GO!" he shouted.

Richelle picked the orb up and slid it into her pocket. She caught one last glimpse of Grant before he was gobbled up by the soldiers, who sent red fireworks of blood into the sky. She watched them toss parts of his body into the air. She didn't want to believe it, but she was sure she saw Grant's head roll.

Richelle jogged off toward the rocks, a bloody mess.

VII

When Richelle was finally alone and out of sight of all the soldiers, she collapsed to the ground and cried hard.

Her tears soaked her arms and tired her eyes, but she didn't care. The pain was too strong for her to imagine, and tears were the only way for that emotion to release. She sobbed uncontrollably, broken and destroyed by the last few minutes of her life.

"Why?" she croaked.

She didn't understand why any of it had happened. She and her group had been together for well over three months now, surviving and living together.

And then they had all been killed in a matter of seconds.

What kind of sense did that make? What was the point of surviving if death came without a moment's notice? Why did they fight so hard to live together when death was waiting for them in their ultimate place of salvation?

Richelle wiped tears off her face and looked up.

She cried for help when she saw a man, covered by a black cloak and with fire in his hands, standing before her.

"HELP! HELP! HELP!" she yelled.

The man slowly walked toward her.

Richelle cried. She cried more than she had ever cried in her life. Tears kept coming. Fear consumed her as the cloaked man reached her. He bent down, his face close to hers.

He sent a spark of fire to her pocket.

Richelle screamed in pain.

He shot another.

She yelped in agony.

And then she realized what he was shooting. It was the orb.

She reached down and pulled the orb from her pocket. She was amazed at the smoke, swirling about her hands like it was trying to find a way inside. But there was no way inside. It just continued to swirl and swing around her hand. It couldn't find its way in as though it was locked.

She placed the orb on top of the man's fire hands, giving it to him and making it his.

And then what happened next was beautiful. The orb's smoke swirled around the fire at first and then swam into it. The fire and red smoke danced around each other, intermingling and swirling together like a double-helix. The red fire combination then consumed all of the man, twirling around him and his cloak. It spun around, fast and furious, before consuming him.

There was a puff of red smoke, and he was gone.

Richelle blacked out—her last drink a mixed cocktail of fear, agony, sadness, and confusion.

VIII

Kurpo stood at the top of his palace, and once again looked out at the world beyond. He saw his soldiers lined up and ready to fight. He could tell Jake had amassed his own army in the distance. Everything was going as he expected. Within a few hours time, Jake would willingly walk himself up into the Creator's Palace and Kurpo would be able to take his Pen again and continue his run as the Creator.

"Kurpo."

Chills ran up Kurpo's spine when he heard his Master's voice.

Kurpo swung around his chair and saw his Master standing before him, dressed in a black cloak and his hands a fireball red.

"Master," Kurpo said. "You've been busy."

The Master smirked under his cloak. "Indeed I have."

"Has everything worked out the way we hoped?" Kurpo asked. "Did you finally get the Orb back?"

Kurpo watched as The Master pulled a metal sphere out from under his pocket. Red smoke hung loosely in the air around it.

"How? Kurpo asked.

The Master nodded. "Indeed. I've finally retrieved my sphere from the pirate. He hid it among a group of Arrivers."

Kurpo smiled. "How did you get it back?"

Master Kallanon walked closer to Kurpo. It felt good to walk again. "I killed the pirate. And when I did, I found where he left the sphere. And now, I have the orb back. I have my soul back."

Kurpo's smile disappeared. "You killed Moss? You killed Moss, the pirate?"

"Yes," Master Kallanon said. "He was in our way."

Kurpo slammed his hand hard against the nearby wall. "Then how in the hell is Jake going to find us? Moss is meant to lead Jake here! Jake's supposed to come here and help me get my Pen back! That's what this always been about!"

"That's never what this was about," he said.

Kurpo raised an eyebrow.

Master Kallanon pulled his cloak hood off. Kurpo wasn't staring at the Kallanon he remembered. He was looking at the Master's new body, smaller, younger, and covered in zits. He was pale and miles less charismatic than Kallanon's original body had been.

He had taken the form of another. His soul had consumed another vessel. It was the body of a boy Jake had called Richard.

"For hundreds of years, there's been this prophecy, about the boy who will save Discis with The Pen. And every generation, the story changes a little bit, and a little bit more, and a little bit more, just by way of storytelling. Someone tells one version, another tells another, and things get lost in translation after a while," Master Kallanon said, walking around the Creator's Palace slowly, working through his thoughts.

"When I became the Holder of The Pen, for example, I was told that one day a boy would come to this tower and destroy the Creator's Palace. He would come up these steps, turn his Pen into a sword and return The Pen to the stone, restoring all the balance and destroying The Pen once and for all," he said. "But as you know, I gave you The Pen. And so the prophecy changed. It became known that the boy would come, along with someone who knew the land and one who forgotten the land. Five would come to the tower. Five would save Discis."

Kurpo didn't understand what was happening.

"But five won't come to the tower. Only Jake will. Only Jake will climb these steps. I will kill each member of his five before he gets here, and I will make sure he is the only one left when he arrives," the Master said, smiling. "The written word isn't always the truest word. The prophecy everyone knows is not the real one. I told the world a prophecy so I could get my Pen and my Orb back. Now I can begin to grow again."

"Well, thank you, Master. Thank you so much! That way I can face Jake one-on-one and get The Pen back on my own! Yes! What a smart idea, Master. Thank you," Kurpo said, smiling.

This was as it was supposed to be. This is why he had revived his Master. He could help him in unimaginable ways, and this was going to help immensely. He'd finally be able to get his Pen back and take control of Discis.

The Master smirked. "Jake will come up here alone," he continued. "And he will finally be destroyed. I have more power now than you could possibly imagine. And once he reaches the top of this tower and The Pen has completed all of its stages, and it is ready to be taken again, I will kill Jake."

The Master stopped walking and turned to Kurpo. "And I," he said, "will reclaim The Pen."

Kurpo barely had time to understand the weight of Kallanon's words before he was tossed to the other side of the room by his Master's hand. He looked up at his Master, covered in a black cloak and fire raging in his eyes. Kurpo felt a white hot pain as hands wrapped around his throat. He felt himself lifted off the ground. He was face to face with his Master.

Kurpo screamed when he realized he wasn't being choked. The Master seared his throat with his hands. His Master's hands dug into him and turned his neck from white to a crisped orange. There was nothing he could do. He was filleted, crippled, and roasted without even a chance to escape.

The Master dropped Kurpo to the ground.

"Now, Kurpo, you will die."

The Master covered The Creator in a ball of red mist. The mist, though, became an army of red ants. They feasted on Kurpo. They dug away at him and ate away at his body like scavengers of flesh. Kurpo cried out, but the red ants chewed away at his lips and silenced him.

Kurpo's body withered away, and soon there was nothing left but a pile of red dust.

The Master walked over to the window and looked out at the horizon. He wrapped his cloak tightly around him and felt the breeze run through him.

The Master, finally human again, was at peace.

CHAPTER 44

I

Jake's eyes were fixed on the fields ahead of him. He saw the Creator's Palace in the distance, standing tall and mighty like a mother watching over her children. Jake, with his khakis and red T-shirt from the first day he arrived here covered by military armor, listened to the wind move through the plains, making the grass brush together ever so lightly. Coldness filled the air with an oncoming storm kind of chill. The sky stayed pink, though, it had a redder hue than in previous days. Jake could sense darkness, too, as though the happy days for him and his friends were long gone. The darkness had come, all of a sudden.

Jake turned over to his right where he saw Kevin, suited up in armor, save for his face. Kevin's blonde hair blew the wind, and he gave a sleek smile. He enjoyed the wind, and he enjoyed the excitement of a coming battle.

"You ready for this, Kevin?" Jake asked.

Kevin laughed. "Psh, of course. I'm so ready."

Jake nodded. "Good." He paused and looked around. "What made you want to come with me?"

Kevin shrugged. "You're family. Family, whether it's blood or not, always comes first. Plus, not a big fan of waiting around with Bennifer for another three years."

Jake smiled. "At least you can grow facial hair now."

"Whatever, man," Kevin said, brushing it off. "We've got more important things to worry about now."

Jake agreed. He knew this was probably the last time he and Kevin were going to speak like everything was normal. Life was about to get more hectic for them. Sure, they had a few miles to walk to get to the Creator's Palace, but they'd have to be on lookout the entire way. It was a dangerous road, one they weren't necessarily sure they could survive.

That's when Jake remembered all the other times he and Kevin had defied logic and survived. There was the early battle against the New Bloods, the Blizzard of Lexington, heading back home, and now their new adventure. But out of all their death-defying journeys, Jake remembered something he and Kevin had done when they were young.

His mind flashed back to that life-altering jump. His mind's eye showed him Kevin landing on his skateboard as the two hopped from one room to another. He remembered how popular he was for that brief moment in history, when all the girls surrounded him and shared food with him. It was the one moment, before The Pen came into his life, when he was a part of the in-crowd. He had felt real, alive, and like nothing could topple him.

"It's been a long journey to get here," Jake said. "We probably won't make it back home anytime soon."

Kevin smiled. "This is our home now, Jake. And live or die, we've got to defend it."

Jake nodded. "Maybe when we're done, and we've killed the Creator and restored everything back to the way it was before, maybe we'll find somewhere fun to hang out."

"I'm sure there are girls here somewhere," Kevin said.

Jake laughed. "Let's hope so."

Kevin looked right and left. "So, what's the plan?"

Jake had rehearsed this before. "We travel a few miles outside the Palace's perimeter. We sneak in behind, I build a staircase with The Pen, we climb up to the top of the tower, we hope this turns into a sword, we hope we can put it back in the stone, and we hope it restores all order back to Discis and finishes off the Creator."

Kevin nodded. He checked all the nobs and whistles on his new weapon. "Sounds like a damn fine plan to me." Kevin put his fist out to Jake. "Together until the end, buddy."

"Together until the end," Jake repeated.

The two cousins stepped forward toward the Palace.

||

Trevor and Amanda waited for their orders. After all, that's what they did best.

Leaning against a rock wall, the couple filled their backpacks with all the wartime essentials they would need for the coming battle. They had trained all of the last three years for a moment like this, when they could go out into an unknown land and battle against unknown forces. Amanda had expected her journey to take her out of The Order's home and into the unexplored regions of Earth. But here she was, readying to face enemies from an entirely different planet.

And they weren't exactly normal enemies, either. If she remembered correctly, the New Bloods were resurrected soldiers, and the Creator's guards were the best soldiers he had left from the earlier wars. That didn't exactly sound like an easy task.

Regardless, Amanda had learned that as a soldier, you have to sometimes prepare for the worst. In war, the best doesn't exist. She had been taught that as long as you prepared yourself for the absolute worse, then nothing bad could really ever happen to you. You have to expect death, and know that you're always knocking on its door. Sooner or later, death will come out with a shotgun and blow your head off for knocking too long or too loudly.

Trevor looked at his girlfriend and smiled, happy to see her enjoying this wartime so much. He leaned over and kissed her on the cheek.

"I love you," he said.

Amanda smiled. "And I love you, too. But if you don't pack your bag right, our asses are gonna be wheat grass."

Trevor grinned. "Clever."

Amanda smirked back. "So, are you ready for this?"

Trevor nodded. "I'm so ready," he said. He figured this was as good a time as any to get a little more serious with their conversation. "You know, Amanda, there's a good chance that neither of us will come out of this alive."

Amanda nodded. "I know the stakes."

"It's just," Trevor searched for the right words. "I want you to know that the moment I found you again, that was the happiest day of my life. I was dealing with so much pain after leaving you in Tampa, and seeing you again finally relieved it. And the last three years have just been the best three years of my life, and, I guess I don't know what I'm saying."

"Hey," Amanda said, grabbing Trevor's chin. "We don't have to do a goodbye speech, OK?"

"Yes, we do," Trevor said. "I never got to say goodbye to you in Tampa, and I didn't know you for very long back then. I've known you for three years now, and I've loved you for three years now. But I have to say goodbye."

Amanda would normally protest, but she held off. In a way, Trevor was right. The two had been separated ages ago without a real goodbye, and now they had been given another chance to say goodbye. They knew either of them could die in the coming fight, and neither wanted to leave their feelings unsaid.

"Whatever happens," Amanda said, "just know that I'll never love someone like I've loved you. You're my only one."

Trevor smiled. "And I want you to know, like I told you all those years ago, that if I die, even in death, I'll find you again."

The two kissed for the last time.

III

Bennifer sent a message out to everyone in the camp to get to their marks and prepare to fly off toward the battlefield. As soldiers scurried around him and hurried off to their respective ships, Bennifer analyzed a map on a tablet with Demak and Ricardo, two of his most trusted soldiers. Their eyes looked through the map that their technologies had made of the landscape around them, which the locals always referred to as the Creator Palace's land. The flat wheat plains sprawled about half a mile outside the Palace, where the grass subsided and it was just hard rock and sand. Most of the battle, then, would take place on that surface.

Demak handed Bennifer another tablet map, this one showing the underground schematics of the area. Bennifer saw that most of it was just normal landscape topography, nothing strange or out of the ordinary, except for two points. He noticed that the palace's stone exterior stretched like a vine from the top of the Creator's Palace all the way through the ground, so far that the chart couldn't register all of it. He also noticed some sort of odd bubble behind the Creator's Palace.

"What am I looking at?" Bennifer asked.

Demak knelt down before the maps. "You'll see the stone that goes from the Palace through the ground. If what Jake told us is true, this is the stone that The Pen is supposed to go into. We imagine that it has some connection to the planet's core. It goes down that far, possibly to the core of the planet."

Bennifer thought about what the effects of the stone could be, but he ignored it as Demak pressed on.

"This bubble," Demak said, rubbing the map with his hand, "is some sort of weird, electromagnetic anomaly. It's kind of like the readings we got back in South Hills all those years ago, like on the highway where Keys and McGaven disappeared."

Bennifer raised an eyebrow. "So it's a portal?"

Demak shook his head. "Not quite. The readings are a little different. This bubble's a little stronger. Some kind of erratic energy."

"Stronger?" Ricardo asked. "What's stronger than something that can send someone from one planet to another?"

Demak shrugged. "Beats me. The weirdest part of it all is that the anomaly begins from the top of the Creator's Palace. It seems it's sort of leaking out somehow, so we can get a reading. But whatever it is, it can only be accessed from inside."

"What do you think? Does it have to do with the stone?"

Demak shook his head. "Nope. Those have two different data patterns. The stone one is internal, meaning it only affects this planet. The anomaly seems to reach outside of just this planet. I just don't know where it leads to or what it does. I'll need to look at more info."

"Well, if Jake does what he says he's going to do, you'll have all the time you want to look around," Bennifer said.

"Thanks, boss. Either way, we should be good from our attack positions. We scoped out about 10,000 troops out that way, so we'll have to watch out for those, but other than that, we should be all right," Demak said.

Bennifer turned back to Ricardo. "What are our odds?"

Ricardo lay a sheet of paper down before Bennifer and Demak. "Analysts say we've got a five percent chance of complete victory, since much of the army we're facing is resurrected dead soldiers. But, assuming we hold our ground as we're predicted to, we have a success rate of seventeen percent."

Bennifer looked back at Ricardo in disgust. "Just seventeen percent?"

Ricardo shrugged. "Our analysts say we're really dependent on this whole Pen thing working out like Jake says it will. It's a wildcard. Plus, we don't have any clue what's going to happen in that tower."

Bennifer thought about it and realized that this made perfect sense. A victory for his army was dependent on Jake reaching the top of the Palace and finishing whatever business he had left. And that meant that his army's strategy needed to be more defensively minded than offensive. He needed to keep the battle going long enough for Jake to make it to the Palace and do his work. Bennifer reached into his pocket and pulled out his touchscreen tablet. He marked instructions and encoded them into the military strategy network, which sent signals out to all the soldiers.

"Let's get moving," Bennifer said.

Bennifer soon found himself suited up in armor with his MegaMax 1800 rifle in his hands, the supreme leader of all weaponry. He looked to his right and saw Trevor and Amanda stepping into one of the warcraft ships with Demak and Ricardo. He walked over to the ship and shook all of their hands, wishing them luck.

Bennifer waited back behind the ships as the marshals on top waited for his signal. The army's leader looked around and saw everyone was in position to get moving. He flung three fingers into the air. The ships began to rise and cast off into the sky. He watched small ships head off toward the Palace, full of soldiers and promise. He waited until the last ship went before he grabbed a one-seated airspeeder, sat on top, and sped off to battle.

IV

Broxxi counted the weapons on each of her soldier's backs once again. Each time she saw a weapon that wasn't straight, she wanted to make it so. But that was her being nit-picky. She always had a need to nit-pick and be perfect. But if her scar taught her anything, it was that sometimes the best things aren't perfect at all.

She looked down at her watch and knew the war was likely to begin. She reached into a pocket on her brown leather belt and pulled out a telescope to look out at the war field. She surveyed the lands and, in the distance, she noticed some warships coming her way. She looked to the right and left to see if anyone was coming from the other angles. Nothing was coming from her right, it was just pretty pink skies and desert plains for miles.

But when she went to her left, she saw something she wouldn't believe: two boys, the Holder of The Pen and his relative.

Broxxi reached into her belt again and pulled out her voice magnifier. She shouted for the soldiers to ready themselves and prepare for battle. She grabbed a few soldiers who were waiting by her and ordered them to rush off toward the Holder of The Pen and his relative and capture them before they made their way closer.

Seeing that the war was coming, Broxxi swerved around and looked up at the top of the tower.

"Creator! They're coming! Time to unleash the New Bloods!"

Everything stayed still.

"Creator! The New Bloods! We need them!"

Broxxi turned back to the war field and noticed all the ships approaching in a fury. She walked to the other side of the window and shouted up again for the Creator.

"Kurpo! Please! The New Bloods!"

Just as Broxxi thought nothing was going to a happen, a red line of smoke shot out from the top of the tower and sprawled out among the desert ground. The smoke started small but then crawled its way across the rocky ground, increasing in length every second. The smoke went farther and farther, quicker and quicker, before it finally stopped and disappeared.

There was a colossal flash of red. Broxxi shielded her eyes to escape the pain. But when she reopened them, there she saw the black-cloaked soldiers, their swords intact and their eyes a blood red.

Broxxi smiled. It was wartime yet again. She pulled out her weapon—a sleek blade—from behind her back and pointed it at the sky.

"FOR THE CREATOR!"

Thunderous applause and a heavy roar shot out from the guards and the New Bloods. They jogged off toward the coming ships, ready to take down the foes that approached them.

V

It didn't feel to Jake like he and Kevin had been walking that long when his eyes first saw a clear image of the Creator's Palace. Just like the replica, the Palace was made of brick and was as black as night. There was a gigantic window at the top, and no way in or out like he had always thought there would be. Kevin and Jake stopped dead in their tracks and looked up at the monstrous Palace that was still a good 15 minutes away from it.

They turned their heads back and saw that the Creator's armies were running off to battle. That's when they noticed all of Bennifer's ships coming toward the battle, too. Kevin and Jake wanted desperately to go back and help their friends, but they knew they had a more important task ahead of them. In fact, the only way they could truly help their friends was to march forward and finish the job they had been destined to do.

Jake and Kevin stopped dead when they saw five guards—covered in slick metallic chrome uniforms, with rifles lodged in their hands—and three New Bloods—floating in air, electric blue sparks sprinkling from their fingertips—rushing toward them.

Jake and Kevin exchanged a glance and gave each other a fist bump.

Jake took The Pen out from his pocket and readied it in attack position. Kevin retrieved his gun and set it for defense mode, ready to defend his cousin against these enemies.

The two cousins jogged off to meet their approaching enemies, finally engaging in the long-awaited war.

The Battle of The Pen began.

CHAPTER 45

I

Trevor remembered all those war movies he used to watch when he was a kid about how two opposing forces would line up horizontally and begin firing at each other in battle. The real thing was a lot different for him. He and his teammates were traveling in their aircraft at a moderate speed when the New Bloods started their attack. They climbed on his ship and ripped away at it, smashing windows and yanking wires out of the engine. Sparks flew everywhere, and all he could smell was burning plastic and rubber. Before long, Trevor and his team hopped off the ship and made their way onto the dusty battlefield, where Bennifer's soldiers and New Bloods alike were already engaged in battle. Trevor fired up his weapon and began shooting.

Trevor also remembered all the victories he and Kevin had before against New Bloods. They had been easy to defeat back then. One knife stab and they were killed, or at least it seemed that way. Now, in the face of this battle, Trevor realized that it wasn't the same. Each shot knocked a New Blood back, but soon the cloaked warriors were on their feet and ready to strike again. Trevor fired twice at a New Blood to knock him out, and while it sent that New Blood back for a brief moment, it was back up within seconds and ready to eat away at the army again.

Just as Trevor was thinking about the complexities of this battle, a New Blood came at him fast with one of his swords. It missed Trevor by an inch or two, striking the ground. Trevor rolled over to his right and sent a shot at the New Blood, who fell back a few steps. The New Blood took a breath and was up on his feet again. Trevor, realizing the fight he was in, reached into his side pocket and retrieved his small dagger. He slashed away at the New Blood, who ducked each blow. The New Blood grabbed Trevor's wrist and ripped the dagger away. Trevor took his gun again and fired a final shot at the New Blood, who went flying back into the crowd. Trevor figured it was good enough for now.

Having defeated that New Blood with some ease, Trevor turned around to see what the rest of the army was dealing with. He saw soldiers mowing down New Bloods as they approached. He noticed another soldier getting ripped apart by a New Blood's sword. So Trevor, wanting to avenge his falling comrade, grabbed a sword from the ground and jogged over to kill the New Blood who had just killed a soldier. The air stunk of iron.

Trevor looked up and saw more ships coming to the battlefield to help, and it was only then that Trevor realized that he wasn't even in the thick of the battle. With all these ships coming, and more than 10,000 New Bloods and guards to kill, this was just the opening stages of the battle and there was much more to come.

But, above all else, he had to make sure he did his part and kill ten of the New Blood soldiers. Before they had Bennifer's army, he thought it was going to be ten to one. And although it wasn't that way anymore, Trevor figured he had to do his part and kill ten. That way, if he died, no one could call dishonor on his legacy.

Trevor found a New Blood battling with a fellow soldier, so he went up behind him and stunned him with a shot. The New Blood fell to the ground and cried in pain. Trevor grabbed the New Blood's shoulder and buried a round of bullets in its head.

"One," Trevor said.

Almost right after, a swarm of three New Bloods came to Trevor. With his rifle in one hand and a sword in another, Trevor swung at the New Bloods and shot at the others. He sliced through one hard with his dagger and knocked another one's face in with the butt end of his gun. The third came charging at him, but Trevor ducked his blow, swept his feet below and shot decisive blows into the New Blood's skull.

"Two, three, four," he said.

Trevor went right back into the battle, where soldiers and New Bloods tangoed in a mighty dance of death. Trevor realized he was only fighting against New Bloods, and there weren't any of the Creator's guards in sight. This was indeed the early part of the war, and things could only get more difficult the longer he survived.

Trevor killed his tenth New Blood a few minutes later. It was harder than he expected. His sword proved the most useful, as the energy shots from the gun seemed to stun the New Bloods more than anything else. He thought back to Demak's comments about how he wouldn't be very good at one-and-one combat and realized Demak was right.

Sweating and panting profusely, Trevor reached into his knapsack and pulled out a bottle of water. He drank a few sips and tossed the rest of it on his face. He looked around and wondered where Amanda was, and what else was happening on the battlefield.

II

Amanda was on her own, but she often worked best that way.

She was tearing through them, and she didn't care about leaving any for the rest of the soldiers. She figured out the right combination, too, on how to kill them. Three shots to their heads and another to their hearts knocked them back to the Hell they came from. It was easy enough, especially for Amanda, who had spent the three years doing nothing but practicing and preparing for warfare.

Three ran at her, ready to cut her away, but she fired nine rounds to their heads and another three to their chests. Done, without breaking a sweat.

She hopped over a carcass lathered in red paint and took out another three New Bloods. She broke the nose of one with her elbow, stabbed another one with bullets, and then used the dead one to shield herself from a strike. She swerved around, killed two more, and then found herself standing alone without someone to fight.

She turned in the direction of the Creator's Palace and saw she had made her way closer to it. Amanda looked to her sides and saw Bennifer's soldiers pick the New Bloods apart. With swords or bows and arrows, these New Bloods might be a little tougher, but with high-grade military weaponry, these resurrected soldiers stood no chance. Amanda thought the battle would be harder.

Amanda turned around and for the first time in this battle she saw a chrome-plated soldier. He was entirely made of metallic chrome, even his rifle and his helmet. He pushed through the New Bloods and made his way right to Amanda.

This was one of the Creator's guards, Amanda knew. And she was going to be the first to kill one.

With urgency, Amanda charged at the guard and screamed while she did it. When the time was right, Amanda leaped into the air and soared over the guard. She landed on her two feet behind him and took two shots at his armor. The bullets bounced off. Not letting her failure hurt her, she knocked at the guard's armor and then retrieved a fallen New Blood sword. She went to strike the soldier, but he was back around and facing her. He ripped the sword from her hands and slugged her in the face, sending her flying back into the stand. He pulled his sword from behind his back and swung at her, but Amanda rolled out of the way. On instinct, she rolled again, dodging yet another blow from the soldier. She kicked off the ground and found her way to her feet, without a weapon, but with a foe right before her.

The guard went at her again, but Amanda ducked and ran behind him. She kicked him in the back and twice in the knees. Without a second to waste, Amanda grabbed the guard's sword and a New Blood sword and made an X, the guard's head right in the center.

Before the guard could utter his last words, Amanda dug into the soldier's neck and sliced his head clean off. Blood squirted from the body.

Amanda wiped sweat and blood off her forehead and went back into the battle. She had killed the first guard she had seen. Other soldiers probably weren't going to be as lucky.

III

Outside the main battle, Bennifer, Demak and Ricardo hung back on one of the ships. Soldiers rushed by them and went into combat, ready to give their lives for the cause. Bennifer looked out at the battlefield and saw a massive number of New Bloods and a few sporadically placed chrome guards. He couldn't tell if his side was winning or not, but he knew full well that they were giving them a fair fight.

"Demak," Bennifer started, his eyes still fixed on the battlefield, "status report."

Demak rushed over to Bennifer. "If our readings are correct, we've lost about 1,000 men already. Some of the weaker soldiers, obviously, and mostly anyone who selected energy-specific weapons."

"Bullets are king here, boss," Ricardo said.

Bennifer nodded. "How far are our soldiers? Are we gaining ground?"

Demak smirked. "Looks like our team is making good progress. Amanda's made the biggest leap of the bunch. She's already fought three chrome soldiers and killed them all, and they're all closest to the palace. She's got a few soldiers with her."

Bennifer nodded again and turned back to Demak. "Any update on Jake and his cousin?"

Demak shook his head. "We can't get a reading on them anymore, which is good news. It means they're getting close to the anomalies, which interfere with our signals."

"Good, good," Bennifer said. "How long until I lose you two to the fight?"

Ricardo slapped a magazine of bullets into his weapon. "I'm about to head out now, sir."

"Me too," Demak said. "We're going to drop in near Amanda and help push our way towards the Palace."

Bennifer nodded. "Good. I wish you good luck. I'll expect you back here by the time this is all through."

"You got it, sir," Demak said with a nod.

Bennifer watched as his two must trusted advisors jogged into battle.

IV

Broxxi hadn't been this excited about warfare since the early wars, when her face was split in two. But she loved this fight. She always considered herself a bit of a rebel, willing to tangle the strings of the strait-laced. Standing in battle, she brushed her hair out of her eyes and looked ahead at the soldiers who were coming toward her group. She knew the army hadn't made much of a gain on them, but one pack of soldiers were coming right for the Creator's guards and she wanted to stop that pack before they got too close.

She tangled with a soldier, whose gun was no match for her quick speed. She dodged a round of bullets, rolled on the ground and dug her knife deep into her foe's knee. Another guard came for her, but she struck again and knocked him right down. Her guards swarmed around her and protected her as she momentarily became vulnerable. But she was soon back on her feet, with hate in her eyes.

Another few soldiers came her direction, but Broxxi dropped them without a moment's worry. The bullets they sent her way were nothing worth worrying about. She was too quick for them; she was too deceitful for them. Just when they thought they had her and they had figured out where she'd be, she'd duck and disappear and appear somewhere else. She could move without anyone noticing.

Two soldiers came her way and she smiled. She loved the challenge of taking on two enemies at once. As they both aimed to fire, Broxxi did a backflip and charged right at them with her sword. She zigzagged past their bullets and slid on the desert floor. She sliced away at one of their knees and stabbed the other in the back. As the still living soldier stood up, Broxxi was there with her blade, digging it into his gut. She watched the blood trickle out.

"Sorry," she smirked. She kissed the guard on the forehead and sent him back down to the ground.

Broxxi paused a moment to look out at the rest of the battle, to see if there was a spot she needed to be in. She saw New Bloods slashing away at soldiers with their swords, and her chrome guards taking down even more soldiers. She could tell just with a glance that her side was winning the battle. Only a small pack of soldiers had made their way this far into the battlefield. And once they destroyed that group, there'd be no more hope for the opponents. This would put an end to them.

Broxxi looked up toward the tower and saw a hooded figure at the top, looking out at the battle. She smiled at her Creator, loving that he was watching over the battle and doing so in approval. She smiled wickedly and spun around, returning to the battle before her.

V

Chaos was everywhere.

At the back of the battle, soldiers sent their bullets out toward the New Bloods. Some deflected the bullets, while others were taken down. The battle was fierce and tight. New Bloods slashed away at their enemies and killed off solider after soldier, taking a few bullets into their bodies while they did so. But for every soldier who died, another New Blood was killed. It was back and forth, a tight battle between two sides. Neither wanted to give an inch.

The battlefield started to mesh a little bit more in the center. New Bloods fell to the soldiers, but the chrome guards who had emerged from the back of the battlefield halted the soldiers. The chrome soldiers laughed at the bullets that hit them, and took down whatever soldiers approached them with their own weaponry. They had been well-trained for battle, and had been well-prepared for a battle like this. Few soldiers made their way past the pack of chrome soldiers, who were just too tough and strong to defeat.

But there was one group who made it to the back, and it was Amanda's group. She had an easy time defeating the New Bloods, and a more difficult time with the chrome guards. But she took them down over time and led a pack into the back of the battlefield, near the Creator's Palace. This group was fierce and strong. They had found a way to take down the Creator's guards, so the combat wasn't much of a worry, at least in a one-on-one regard. It was more about the quantity. There were too many guards to fight, so they had to take their time and slowly press on, hoping that their efforts would lead them closer to the Palace.

Dust flew up into the air and swirled around the battle. The sunset sky sat stone cold up above and watched over as this messy battle, this war, over a Pen, continued on.

VI

Amanda killed another two chrome guards before she took a deep breath. She sipped some of her water and looked around to see if any foes were coming her way. Luckily, her soldiers took down the guards who approached them. The few New Bloods who had made their way that far back into the battlefield were no match for Amanda and her crew. They picked the New Bloods off one by one, not much of a challenge for them anymore.

Amanda, watching the battle unfold before her, looked back, and saw a mess of soldiers and New Bloods tangling. She thought about Trevor, wondering where he was and if he was going to make it this far up. For all she knew, he could be dead. He wasn't the greatest fighter and, from what she could tell from the battle she saw, the energy guns did very little to the New Bloods or the chrome guards. It was very possible that Trevor hadn't made his way anywhere close to the Palace and had died some time ago.

But Amanda was filled with hope. She also had a good feeling about Trevor, that he was OK and hadn't fallen yet. She had heard once that when the love of your life dies, you can immediately feel it. She hadn't felt anything of the sort yet. She knew he was still alive.

Amanda turned back toward the battlefield and was stunned at what she saw before her. It was a woman, dressed in chrome armor, without a helmet. Medals and colors filled up her chest plate, which indicated to Amanda that this woman must have some high standing with the army. The woman was beautiful, too, save for the scar that cut down the center of her face. She was covered in dust, blood, and sweat. The woman had a sleek blade in her hand.

Amanda attached her gun back to her armor and pulled out her own blade. She smiled, wiped some water off her face, and charged after the woman, who came at her just as fast.

VII

Trevor was alive, but barely. He almost died twice in this fight, when he was still relying on the energy blasts from his weapon. He switched his gun over to bullets only and that had made much of a difference. He took down many more soldiers when he openly used bullets. That's when he realized, too, that the battle against the New Bloods was as easy as he remembered it from a few years back. He just needed a better weapon.

Trevor thought about rushing up the battlefield and clearing a way toward the Creator's Palace, but he could tell that another crew was already doing that. He thought he'd hang back and do what he could from the back of the pack. If he could help take down the entire army of New Bloods, then that would leave just the chrome guards to fight. He thought it was better to take out many soldiers rather than just a few.

Just as he was finishing off another New Blood, Demak grabbed Trevor on the shoulder and told him to follow him to the back of the pack.

Trevor and Demak jogged away from the battle and found Bennifer and Ricardo waiting there. Ricardo had blood coming off the side of his head, a battle wound from earlier in the fight.

"We're making our way toward the Palace. Amanda's leading the pack," Bennifer said to Trevor. "We need you three to head out that way, too."

"Why? Wouldn't it make sense to take down some soldiers over here before heading out that way?" Trevor asked, keeping an eye on the battlefield.

Bennifer nodded. "Yes, but we have more than enough. Trevor, you're a valued soldier on this team, and you were a valued soldier back with the Order. Please, head back out that direction and finish the fight with Amanda. We can handle the back."

Trevor nodded. He did what he was told. "Yes sir."

They were off in their own ship. It landed down on the outside of the back of the battle. Trevor, Demak, and Ricardo headed off the ship and jogged toward the battlefield. Trevor nailed down a few New Bloods before he came face to face with his first chrome guard.

Trevor knocked the guard's weapon clean out of his hand and then slugged the guard in the face with his gun. The guard stumbled back, and Trevor pounced. He sent two shots right to the guard's armor. After they banged off, Trevor switched his gun back to energy mode and sent a blast to the guard. The blue bubble of energy from Trevor's gun encapsulated the guard's armor and shocked him. Trevor could hear the buzz as the guard shivered and shrieked in pain. The guard collapsed to the ground, his head bouncing hard against the rock.

Trevor looked ahead and saw Demak and Ricardo tangling with some more guards. As he took a few steps forward, he spotted Amanda, too, fighting another woman soldier, one on one.

Trevor took one step before he was knocked face first to the ground. His head smacked against the gravel and dust flew up his nose. He swung himself over and looked up.

Standing before him was The Man of Fire, his black cloak waving in the wind.

The Man of Fire stepped closer, and Trevor recognized the face. It was the nerdy kid from high school, though now he had red eyes full of hate and there was an evil darkness to him.

"Who are you?" Trevor asked, his energy gun aimed at The Man of Fire.

"They call me the Master," he said. The red in his eyes flared up.

Trevor, still on his back, looked up in fright.

"And you, Trevor McGaven, will be the next to die."

CHAPTER 46

I

Jake dodged the guard's strike and slid on his knees, scraping them against the hot rock. When he flipped back up, another guard was swinging at him, but he dodged that strike, too, and rolled around on the ground. The guard, dressed in the chrome metal armor, struck again, stabbing his sword down against the rock. It missed Jake's head by a few inches. Jake, wide-eyed, hopped back up to his feet and clashed with the guard, wrapping his hands around his foe's wrist to try and wrestle the weapon away. The guard shoved Jake off, and the Holder of The Pen went sliding back against the rock.

The guard approached. Jake knew he was defenseless. He reached into his pocket and retrieved The Pen. He whispered a command and pointed The Pen at his hand. A thick rock came to fruition in his palm, just as Jake had asked. As the guard drew near, Jake tossed the rock at the guard's helmet, and he stumbled. Jake got to his feet and charged at the guard. He struck the guard's helmet twice and then tackled him to the ground. He smashed the rock once more against the guard's helmet until the guard was limp, unconscious from the blows.

Jake, sweat pouring down his forehead, looked up and saw Kevin shooting down another two guards who had come after them. When he was finished, he clicked a few nobs on his gun and jogged over to Jake. The two fist-bumped.

"Quite the welcome party," Kevin said.

Jake nodded with a grin. He looked behind him and saw the battle unfolding. New Blood solders, covered in black cloaks with their even blacker swords, tangoed with Bennifer's soldiers. The chrome guards were sprawled throughout, some still waiting for combat while others danced with their soldiers to death's mighty and unforgiving song. Jake thought for a second about going to help, but then he remembered what he had learned earlier: the only way to help was to get to the Palace and stop all evil.

"How far have we got?" Jake asked.

Kevin looked forward to the Palace. "If we run, we should get there in like, ten minutes. Looks like about a mile or so. As long as we don't have anymore guards in our path, that is."

Jake wiped his head clean of sweat and slid The Pen back into his pocket. "Let's hope. Come on."

Jake and Kevin jogged again toward the Palace.

II

Amanda and Broxxi fell back when their daggers hit each other.

Amanda at first slid against the rock, but then picked herself up and got back on her feet. Her foe was already approaching, her weapon drawn and aimed at Amanda's heart. Amanda grabbed Broxxi's arm and twisted it, hoping the weapon would fall. It didn't. Broxxi kicked Amanda's shin, sending Amanda down. Broxxi then flipped over Amanda and slapped the back of her head, breaking free of her grasp. Amanda squirmed back to her feet, and the two were once again at a standstill.

"You're a good fighter," Broxxi said through panting breaths.

Amanda smiled. "So are you. You got a name?"

"Broxxi," she said.

Amanda nodded. "Amanda."

"Well, Amanda, you're good, but you have a lot to learn," Broxxi said.

"We'll see about that," Amanda said.

The two went at it again, this time locking with an elbow tie-up. Amanda gripped the back of Broxxi's head and tried to shove her back, but Broxxi pushed back just as hard and the two were caught. More and more they shoved, but neither budged an inch.

They released and stood toe-to-toe again.

With a yelp, Broxxi swung at Amanda with her dagger, and it connected lightly to Amanda's neck, cutting it open slightly. Dabbles of blood dripped onto Amanda's armor.

Broxxi smiled wickedly at her move.

Anger consumed Amanda.

She charged at Broxxi and tackled her straight to the ground. She laid a few fists on Broxxi's face and then one large elbow to her nose. Broxxi slid out of the position and tossed Amanda over her, and then got back on her feet. She snorted and spat to regroup.

In a furious exchange, Broxxi and Amanda traded shot attempts, but each one blocked the next. Broxxi went for two shots to Amanda, but she blocked them with her elbows. Amanda tried a head-butt, but Broxxi dropped down and kicked at Amanda's knees. Amanda went down and Broxxi hit her with two chops to her ears.

Amanda, dazed, fell on her back.

Broxxi, smiling, reached into her pack and pulled out another dagger, this one lined with gold string. She wiped off a bit of dust and went for the kill. She hopped down onto Amanda's fallen body and went right for the throat, ready to kill her foe with one final strike.

But Amanda lifted her hand and banged it against Broxxi's wrist, sending the knife flying away. She raised her knees and slammed them into Broxxi's back, which sent her foe tumbling off of her. Amanda rolled over to her right, picked up a pile of dust and tossed it at Broxxi's face, giving her enough time to rise to her feet and reset.

The two were back to where they had started, face-to-face and ready for combat on the desert floor, the ongoing battle just a few feet away. Amanda felt her pockets to see what weapons she had and what she could use to face her foe. She didn't find much, except for a few small throwing stars, a bottle of water, and some lone bullets. Amanda surveyed the area around her and saw that her dagger was buried under dust. The only weapon she had left was her gun, but retrieving it and loading it would take too much time. By the time it would be ready, Broxxi would already be full in attack mode.

Broxxi got to her two feet and wiped the dust away. She thought about her next move, trying to see what weapons she could use next on Amanda. She felt her pockets and found she had a few small daggers, which wouldn't do much damage. She used her left hand to reach behind and see how many weapons she had in her pack and it was only a few more short daggers, which, again, wouldn't do much against Amanda's combat skills. The two had already tangoed with daggers, and neither had given an inch.

They would have to wrestle it out and use their bare hands.

Amanda and Broxxi charged at each other, collided, and locked into another furious struggle. Amanda swung behind Broxxi and elbowed her in the back of the head. She went to strike again but Broxi ducked and then latched onto Amanda's arm. She bit at it, gnawed for a second, and then spat it out. Amanda, screaming in pain, was sent back even farther as Broxxi connected with a two-legged dropkick.

Amanda tumbled forward and ate some dust, her hands scraping against the rocks.

She flipped around and tossed dust right into Broxxi's face, who dove down onto her. Amanda scurried to her feet and then tackled Broxxi down again. The two rolled and tumbled on the ground, their bodies scraping against rocks and dust as they did. When they broke free, Broxxi was first to her feet. She kicked Amanda in the side. Amanda rolled over and Broxxi kicked again. She retrieved one of her short daggers and tossed it down to Amanda's body, cutting her lightly.

As Amanda tried to get up, Broxxi swung around and caught Amanda's head. Holding it, Broxxi lifted her knee and slammed Amanda's face into it. Amanda's head bent back and she rolled over onto her back again, her head in white-hot pain.

Broxxi, panting with sweat dripping from her temple, dropped to the ground and sat, catching her breath. She had just a small amount of time to do so. When she was fully rested, she lifted herself up again and kicked Amanda's face with the bottom of her boot. Amanda coughed blood and dust and found herself vulnerable yet again.

"Told you. You have a lot to learn," Broxxi said.

Amanda coughed again.

"You think you could come into my backyard and take me down? No way, sister, no way," Broxxi said. "I'm the greatest warrior this planet has ever seen. No one can touch me. Not you, not anybody."

Broxxi reached into her pocket and pulled out one of the small daggers. She jumped on top of Amanda and put the knife to her throat. Her eyes, filled with hatred, stabbed away at Amanda's.

"You're fighting a losing battle, girl," Broxxi said. "And now, you won't have to fight it any longer."

Amanda saw the blade coming toward her, and that was enough to kick things into high gear. She used the strength she had left in her legs to lift Broxxi off her. She stood up on her feet again and readied herself in a defensive position. She looked around while Broxxi gathered herself to see if there were any weapons. There weren't. She was alone.

"OK," Broxxi said, wiping some blood from her lips. "Remind me not to say anything next time."

Amanda laughed, a drop of sweat floating near her eye. "There won't be a next time."

"Oh yeah?"

Amanda nodded. "I'm going to kill you now."

Amanda once again tossed dirt from the ground up to Broxxi. She slid through the sand and rolled up to Broxxi. She wrestled the knife away from her and went to strike, but Broxxi put her arm, shielded by armor, in front to block the blow. Broxxi lifted her arm and nailed Amanda between the eyes, sending her back a few paces. Broxxi once again wiped the dust from her eyes. She kicked the sand at Amanda's face. It caught Amanda in the eyes and made her stumble back just as easy.

"Yeah! Yeah! How do you like it?" Broxxi shouted.

Once again, the two warriors locked arms and wrestled with each other, trying to make the other give an inch, but neither did. They shouted and screamed as they pushed at each other, dust filling their mouths and blood dripping from their bodies. Broxxi spat at Amanda to try and break her, but it didn't work. Amanda spat back, but Broxxi pushed back harder. The two were locked once again, unable to find a break from each other.

They both released at the same time, gathered strength and locked again. Amanda pushed and, being the thicker of the two, started to gain an advantage. Broxxi dug her feet into the ground and gave a mighty shove back, regaining her advantage. The two released again and were toe-to-toe once more.

Broxxi had had enough. Gathering all of her strength, she charged at Amanda and wrapped one hand behind her head. Quicker than Amanda could expect, Broxxi elbowed Amanda three straight times to the face. She kicked at Amanda's shin and then head-butted her across the eyes.

Amanda stumbled back, and Broxxi kept up her attack. She sent two chops to Amanda's skull and then jumped down to the ground and swept her leg under, sending Amanda face first into the ground and knocking her out.

Broxxi was about to get up and attack Amanda and finish her. But she fell back into the rock instead, trying to catch her breath.

III

Trevor looked up at pure evil, and he had no idea what to do.

The Master's hands were consumed by balls of red mist. Trevor knew an attack was coming, so he pulled out his gun and fired a blue bubble energy blast, hoping it would do something for once.

And it did. The Master went flying back into the dust.

Trevor smiled. It had worked.

"No way," Trevor said.

He clicked a few nobs on his gun and loaded it again with the energy blast. The Master was already on his feet. The two balls of mist in his hands glowed brighter this time, and The Master sent one to Trevor. It knocked him to the ground. Trevor's back slammed against the dusty rock ground and his gun went soaring back.

The Master sent another ball of red mist at Trevor and it pushed him even farther back into the sand. But it didn't pain him for some reason. The Master sent another, and Trevor took the blow. But it wouldn't pierce his armor. It wouldn't dig into his skin. The Master conjured two more balls of red mist and sent them to Trevor. They hit him, made him roll a few feet, but did little to cause agony or pain.

Trevor used the brief opportunity he had to stand up. He got to his two feet and hopped over the soaring mist ball toward his gun. He picked it up and, without aiming, fired a shot straight at The Master. The electric blue energy blast screamed as it sped forward and soon sent Trevor's enemy flying back a few feet into the dust.

"Got you now, sucker," Trevor said.

Trevor sent another to The Master, and it hit him just as hard.

The Master stood on his two feet and looked over at Trevor, who could see the shock on his face. He didn't expect to get hit this hard.

"I never liked you in high school, and I definitely don't like you now," Trevor said.

Trevor aimed at The Master.

But he didn't fire.

A purple light sprang up in the sky from about a mile away, catching the eye of The Master and Trevor together.

IV

Jake and Kevin stopped jogging when they saw the black brick outlines of the Creator's Palace.

They could hear the battle raging behind them. They heard shouts and screams, explosions and gunfire, but none of it mattered.

"We're here," Jake said.

Jake looked at Kevin and then back to the palace. He saw the black bricks climbing into the sky, much like the replica he had entered so long ago. He remembered his dreams of what this building would look like. He remembered all the ideas that popped into his mind when Moss first told him all those months ago about the Creator's Palace and how he would have to go there. He thought of the restless nights he had when he wondered if he would ever make it here, and what would happen when he finally got close to the Palace's doors. He remembered everything, from the first moment he found The Pen until now, and realized it was all, finally, coming to an end.

Kevin looked behind him to see if anyone was coming their way, and no one was. They were free to make the stairs they had planned to make. They were about fifty feet away from the side of the Palace, which gave them enough space to make their stairs and ascend to the top, just like they had planned.

But then something happened that they didn't anticipate—Jake began to scream.

Kevin turned his attention to Jake and couldn't believe what he was seeing. Jake's pocket glowed a dark purple, and it seemed to be stabbing Jake with pain. He shouted at the top of his lungs, yelping as the pain dug at him. Kevin tossed his gun to the side and slid on his knees to Jake. He reached into Jake's pocket and ripped out the source of the pain—The Pen.

THE PEN

Just as he pulled it out, The Pen hopped out of Kevin's hand and went into Jake's palm. Jake lifted his head and watched as the final cube, a wizard and a lion, spun gold and became the deepest black Jake had ever seen.

Jake examined his Pen. All the cubes were black. The stages were complete.

Jake, his pain ceasing, rolled over and sat up next to Kevin.

Before either could utter a word, The Pen hopped out of Jake's hand and crashed into the ground. A purple light surrounded it and glowed vibrantly. They watched as The Pen shook, slowly at first and then a little more quickly, its purple glow growing by the second. Jake's eyes widened as he watched The Pen shake and tumble.

The purple light grew and grew. And soon, the purple light became a single line of light that shot straight into the sky toward the pink clouds above.

Jake's attention turned to the sky. The pink clouds became a dark gray around the purple light. Thunder crackled and lightning shot out.

And then the purple line of light descended back to the ground and went right into The Pen. As it did, the ground exploded in a fury of purple, which sent Jake and Kevin ducking away from the flying rocks.

When the dust settled, Jake and Kevin looked out and saw dust everywhere. They heard the gunfire, they heard explosions, and they heard yelling and screaming and pain.

But what they saw took all of their attention.

It was The Pen, covered in all black, from the tip to the end.

And lying right beside it was a sword, purple, with six cubes in a line down its center. One was purple, then blue, then light blue, then green, then yellow, and finally red.

Jake crawled forward and snatched The Pen. He slid it into his pocket.

He bent down and grabbed the sword, making sure not to break it in the process. It was lighter than he imagined. It was about as long as his arm, with a sharp edge that could easily cut through a steak or two. He picked it up and held it tight. He rotated it in his hands to get a good look at the sword he had always heard about but never seen.

"Dude," Kevin said.

Jake smiled. "Let's go. We've got stairs to build."

CHAPTER 47

I

Jake touched the stone brick on the side of the Palace when he first got to it just to make sure it was real and that he was finally at this point. He was still surprised that he had finally arrived at this moment, the one people had been telling him about since his first day on Discis. He was finally about to achieve his goal and fulfill the prophecy. It had all been true.

Jake and Kevin darted to the far side of the Palace, away from the eyes of the warriors. They scanned the top of the tower to see if there were any openings. Jake found one. It was a ladder that went about one-quarter of the ways down from the top of the Palace. It looked like some sort of scouting tower, as though guards could look out from it and survey the land if need be. Jake tried to see past the ladder, but couldn't see anything above it. The Palace's top kissed the clouds.

Jake pointed up. "See that ladder?"

Kevin looked up. "I do."

"Not sure where it leads, but let's build the stairs up to that. We can climb into whatever room the ladder leads to," Jake said.

Kevin checked his three o'clock and his nine o'clock. "We're all clear. How does this work?"

Jake pulled The Pen, now sleek and black, from his pocket. He twiddled it in his fingers and found it was different than he remembered. This Pen had more weight to it. Jake could feel more of a presence, too. There was more power to this Pen. And, Jake could tell, somehow, that he was in more control of this Pen. It was his, and his alone.

Jake pointed toward the tower and whispered to The Pen for it to grow stairs.

Nothing happened.

He tried again, and nothing happened.

"What's the issue?" Kevin asked.

Jake shook The Pen. "It's not doing anything." He prayed it hadn't lost its power.

Kevin checked his six o'clock and then looked back at Jake. "Well, it better hurry itself. We're going to get noticed soon. Guards have got to be on their way."

Jake inspected The Pen, looking to see if the exterior offered him any clue of what to do next with the writing utensil. And then it hit him—writing. Pens are meant to write. Though they can draw and create from illustration, pens were first made to write and communicate messages. He stepped closer to the tower and, in the air, wrote out the word "steps."

Nothing changed, at first. But a puff of black smoke emerged from thin air and swirled and twirled. When it dissipated, a set of ten steps appeared, all connected to the side of the tower, made of the same material.

"That's it?"

Jake shrugged. "We know how it works, at least. Let's try this."

Jake wrote out the word "STEPS" and another ten appeared, connected to the ones he had just created. It was then Jake realized this was going to be a build-as-you-go situation. He ushered Kevin forward and the two took their first steps onto the staircase, which was still connected to the tower.

Jake, sword in hand, and Kevin, gun at the ready, jogged up the first two sets of steps before Jake created another, which appeared before his very eyes and led in just the direction he wanted to go.

Without looking back, Jake and Kevin jogged up the steps, creating them as they moved toward the top.

"How much further?" Kevin asked.

Jake's eyes flew to the sky. The ladder was at least ten more creations away. "We've got a little bit. Why?" Jake stopped moving and checked on Kevin, whose back was facing Jake.

"We've got company," Kevin said.

Jake sharpened when he saw what Kevin saw.

A swarm of the silver-armored guards rushed toward them, their weapons at the ready. They raced at the two boys, shouting obscenities as they did so. Jake could tell from the speed they were running that there was very little chance they could avoid these guards before reaching the ladder.

So the Holder of The Pen turned back toward the staircase and wrote out the words, "MORE STEPS TO LADDER."

The puff of smoke that came out looked bigger than before, covering the area from Jake's position on the steps up to the ladder above. When the smoke vanished, all Jake saw were black-bricked steps that climbed around the side of the Palace all the way to the ladder above. It had worked. The steps went all the way up to just under the ladder—a perfect path was presented before them. Jake would normally think this was too good to be true based on his recent experiences. But he ignored that thought. It was about time they won.

"Jake," Kevin said from behind. "Make a run for the ladder. I'll hold them off."

"No way," Jake protested. "We're climbing together."

Kevin shook his head. "I said I'd defend you, and that's exactly what I'm doing. Get moving."

Jake thought about rushing forward up the steps like Kevin was asking him to. But when Jake turned to face the rest of the staircase, he knew he couldn't do that. Silver guards rushed from the top of the stairs, their swords ready to attack. Jake looked down and saw that the soldiers had climbed their way up the steps from the side unattached to the Palace without Jake or Kevin noticing. Now there were two battles to be waged—two swarms to fight off.

Soldiers approached from both ends. Jake slid his Pen back into his pocket and gripped his sword tighter. He nudged Kevin in the back, who swerved around and saw the approaching soldiers.

"May the best man win," Kevin joked.

II

Master Kallanon knew something was wrong the instant he saw the purple light flash in the sky.

He ignored Trevor, the young warrior with a big heart who had bitten off more than he could chew, and watched the purple lights flash in the sky and descend back down to the ground. The Master had never seen those colors before, at least not shooting out from the sky and then back to the ground. But that purple was as familiar as the freckles on his hand. It was the same deep purple that The Pen's exterior was made from. The same purple, legend has it, that the first seas of Discis were colored. The same purple of the ice that had forged The Pen's body. It was Pen Purple.

"Freeze," said the boy from behind him.

The Master twisted his head and glared back at Trevor, not intimidated. He could feel his own eyes burning with hatred, rage, and fire. He twirled his arm in the air and shot a blast of fire to Trevor, who went soaring back onto the desert floor.

But instead of going for the kill, The Master turned his attention back in direction of the lights. He gathered energy inside him as he glanced toward the tower. And it was then that he saw the two boys, young Jake and his cousin, climbing up black steps—steps that didn't exist before today and that must have been created with The Pen itself.

The Master watched the boys, trying to see what they were up to. All was going according to plan, after all, since Jake was about to arrive at the tower's top, which is just what the Master wanted. With each passing second, he was getting closer to owning his masterful weapon again.

The Master saw Kevin and Jake thwart their enemies—guards who had come from the top and bottom of the stairs. Kevin used his automatic rifle to mow down any of the guards that came his way. He shoulder-blocked a few and knocked others clean off the steps. He was a fighter, a dogged warrior. The two boys seemed to be winning.

Jake, though, wielded a much different weapon. The Master gathered more energy to see what Jake held and it was then he noticed—it was purple with cubes going down the center, much like The Pen.

The Master felt his eyes glow even more. The Pen was in its sword stage. The prophecy was really coming true.

The Master let his rage blast out of him. Fire shot all around him and burned against the desert ground. And, in a fit of anger, he shot out red mist.

With a newly created black and red sword in his hand, The Master flew off toward the Creator's Palace to finish the fight.

III

Trevor watched Richard flee into the distance toward the tower. That's when he knew things were getting close to their end. Jake must not be far off from finishing the prophecy, which meant their mission was almost complete.

Trevor wiped his forehead clean of the salty sweat. He licked his iron blood from his lips and spat out some dust. He cracked his back and gathered himself. He switched his weapon on and prepared to head back to the battle. There was a great distance between himself and the fighting and he wondered which direction he should jog. All he saw were men dying. Some were dying by way of sword, others by bullets. The stench of piss, feces, and blood filled the air. It was a dire place, and it all seemed the same. No matter where he ran, he would only find blood.

Something caught his attention, though. He saw two female warriors slugging each other, one punch after another. Though three years ago this might have been something he watched on his own for pleasure, his heart was stricken with pain when he saw that one of the women was the love of his life.

Without a second to lose, Trevor sped off toward Amanda, hoping to save her life.

IV

After slashing a guard's arm off and tossing him over the side of the stairs, Jake finally caught a breath.

He panted and bent over himself to gather air. He looked back and saw Kevin shoot down a few more guards before he, too, rested against the side of the steps. Their thighs burned from the steps and their hearts raced from the battle.

Jake looked past Kevin and saw a herd of soldiers rushing toward them. The battle would never cease. They were closer to the ladder, but not close enough. Another round of fighting would come soon enough, and then their lives would rest in the hands of whoever was rolling death's dice.

Kevin nodded upwards. "What are we gonna do?"

Jake checked the ladder and then the ground.

"You think you can still make the jumps you did on those roofs?" Jake asked.

Kevin had to think about it a second, but nodded.

"Good," Jake said.

Jake turned back toward the steps and thought out visually what he wanted. He wrote out his command. Black smoke came and swirled around the stairs. Jake checked on Kevin before looking back at the steps.

Only the steps were gone. What remained was a steel platform attached to the side of the Palace, unreachable by any steps. Guards couldn't get there.

Jake pointed his Pen up to the ladder above and wrote out his command. Smoke climbed the side of the Palace, and it swirled and twirled like normal. Within seconds, the ladder from the top of the palace grew and extended down to just above the platform.

V

It took Kevin a few seconds to understand. But once the ladder descended to the platform, it finally made sense what Jake was planning to do.

Kevin glared at the herd of soldiers approaching and knew that he and Jake only had a minute or two before they got to the steps and they'd have to fight them again. Kevin nodded Jake forward, telling him to get moving—fast. Kevin watched as Jake backed up a few steps and leaned one of his hands against the Palace wall. For all the years he'd known his cousin, Kevin didn't remember ever seeing him act this confident. There was something special about his cousin—something that hadn't been there when they were raised but had come to him since he came to Discis.

There wasn't any warning from Jake, as he dashed up the last few steps and hopped up to the platform, reaching it with ease. He made the jump.

"Woo!" Jake shouted, smiling. "That was awesome. Come on Kev! Your turn!"

Kevin looked down at the soldiers rushing toward him and Jake. He saluted them with two fingers and bid them farewell. He climbed down three steps and rushed up the remaining ones. He kicked off the last step and soared into the air. The thrilling rush of that day long ago on those roofs came back to him. So, midair, he twisted and twirled, like he did that day.

And he landed cleanly on the platform, his feet banging hard against the metal platform.

On his feet, he stared at the warriors and guards below and saluted them again.

Kevin patted Jake on the shoulder, smiling. He pointed to the ladder, an indication to keep moving. Jake, smiling, latched onto the sides of the ladder and started to climb. Kevin let Jake get a few paces ahead before he started his ascent.

Kevin couldn't remember the last time he was tasked with climbing a ladder. It had to have been as a kid while he was on the monkey bars. But it was easy—a lot easier than some of the tasks that his military training had prepared him for. He took one step after another, pausing every so often so that he didn't mess up and drop.

When Kevin took a break, he looked up and saw that Jake was nearing the top and an open platform once again. Kevin returned his gaze to the approaching soldiers and saw that, somehow, soldiers had made the jump from the stairs to the platform and were climbing the ladder. The chase hadn't ended.

"Jake!" Kevin shouted.

Kevin watched Jake make his last few climbs and roll over onto the platform. He laid his sword down on the platform and peered over the side toward Kevin.

"We need to cut the ladder off!" Kevin said, pointing downward.

Kevin got a nod from Jake, who then began writing his next command in the air.

And then Kevin felt a drop.

"Whoa!"

Kevin latched onto the ladder's bottom handle with all of his strength. His legs flew aimlessly in the wind. It was a deadly free-fall if he let go of the ladder.

But at least the soldiers had all fallen to their death.

"Kevin! Kevin! You OK?" Jake shouted.

"Yeah! Way to make this even more difficult!" Kevin shouted, his legs dangling in mid-air and his sweaty hands gripping the ladder tightly. "You're in serious trouble when I get up there, Jake!"

Kevin gingerly reaffirmed his grip and tightened his hands. He readied his shoulders and gathered up some strength. He reached up and grabbed the next bar with his right hand. His feet still hung in the air. He had two more bars to climb before his body was back on the ladder.

And then came pain.

It was a quick and decisive pain, almost as though it hadn't happened at all.

Kevin blinked once and saw he had lost his grip from the ladder's bar and he was in a freefall. He watched the distance between himself and Jake grow before everything went black.

VI

Jake rolled over onto the Palace's top platform, still a few yards away from the tower's top. He looked to his right and saw there was a small square window, big enough to fit a young teen.

"Jake!" he heard from below.

Jake looked down and saw Kevin on the ladder, pointing down.

"We need to cut the ladder off!" Kevin yelled.

Jake eyes focused on what Kevin must have seen—troops were jumping onto the platform and beginning to the climb up the ladder. Jake, feeling there was no time to lose, wrote for The Pen to make the ladder, except where Kevin was, disappear altogether.

And then he watched in horror as the ladder disappeared and Kevin hung loosely on the last bar, his feet dangling in the air.

"Kevin! Kevin! You OK?" Jake shouted.

"Yeah! Way to make this even more difficult!" Kevin shouted. "You're in serious trouble when I get up there, Jake!"

Jake smirked, despite the nerves that consumed his entire body. He raised himself up to his knees and peered over the side of the platform, watching Kevin climb up one bar. His feet still hung in the air, but he was getting closer to being fully on the ladder.

Jake didn't see it coming.

His eyes burning a raging red and a sword in his hand, a cloaked warrior came flying through the air. He slashed away at Kevin's legs, and Kevin fell the entire length of the tower to his ultimate demise on the desert ground below.

VII

Trevor watched in horror as a brunette female warrior, her dagger sharp and sleek, stood tall above Amanda, aimed to strike for a final kill. Trevor rushed forward with a bigger stride, his rifle at the ready. He hopped over a few fallen soldiers and slid against the desert ground. He swooped to his right and came up right behind the unknown woman warrior and latched his arm around hers, holding his rifle to her head.

"Drop it!" he yelled.

Trevor glanced across from him at Amanda, whose face was a mess of brown and red. She looked at Trevor with desperation. As though she had been defeated and was only now thinking she had a chance to survive.

"I said, drop it!" Trevor yelled at the woman he held.

Amanda, as though it were her last breath, said, "Trevor, don't."

Trevor looked at the love of his life, puzzled. And then something else caught his attention. It was something in the sky. He took his eye off Amanda and his new foe and looked up toward the graying pink clouds and saw something—no, someone—fall from the top of the Creator's Palace. Trevor watched the body fall the entire length of the tower and then disappear from sight as the massive crowd of soldiers blocked his view.

And so he never saw the dagger coming.

His skin exploded in a searing roar of hot pain as the dagger's blade pierced through his gut and cut deep. He dropped his weapon and fell to his knees. Through the pain, now the world felt cold and his body almost absent from it, Trevor watched liquid ooze from his gut. He heard a shout and scream, but his vision became too glazed over to see where it was coming from.

Trevor opened his eyes wide and caught a glimpse of the scarred women coming toward him, her weapon extended. He felt another cut, this one on his neck. More ooze and red worms trickled down his body before he collapsed to the ground.

VIII

Amanda screamed in terror.

She watched the love of her life, the boy who had been taken from her but whom she had found again, get stabbed right in the gut with a hollow cut that pierced him and sent him to his knees. She could only watch as Broxxi cut her boy's throat and shoved him to the ground, to die a painful death.

Amanda crawled over to her lover and, no care for what might happen to her, lay his head in her arms. She bent down and put her head against his and sobbed. She didn't care about what he said—about moving on without the other. She cried onto him, letting the dripping blood cover her hands and body. She smelled the iron all over him and saw the life fade from his deep blue eyes. She sobbed uncontrollably, distraught that she couldn't save him and that she would never see him again.

She heard footsteps approach and looked up. Broxxi was there, her dagger dripping with blood. But her face wasn't full of menace or satisfaction or pride. It was full of sorrow, regret, and dishonor.

"I'm sorry for your loss," Broxxi said.

She dropped the dagger before Amanda and walked back toward the battle.

Amanda held Trevor tight and saw something crawl on him. It was a crab, small and out of place. Amanda slapped it away. The only life she cared about now was Trevor's.

Amanda huddled herself around Trevor and continued to weep into his arms and shoulders. She continued to hold him and cry, even when, moments later, Demak and Ricardo carried her and Trevor away, back toward the base camp.

IX

Jake could only scream as he watched his cousin fall off the ladder. He yelled even louder when Kevin, so far from Jake's sight, disappeared into the mix of dust and soldiers below. He screamed again, tears beginning to flow from the corners of his eyes. He fell back against the side of the platform, shaken by what had just happened.

Jake took a deep breath and held his own head in his hands. He pulled at his hair, thinking that he would make sense of it all, but nothing happened.

A footstep banged against the metallic platform. Jake's face, covered in tears, sweat, dust, blood, and all the torment he had been through since his first day, looked up and saw the cloaked warrior, with his black sword, standing tall above him.

Jake watched the man pull down his hood.

An old friend stood before him.

"Hello, Jake," Richard said. "This is where you story ends."

CHAPTER 48

I

"Status report."

Demak slammed a piece of paper before Bennifer, who hunched over the table and analyzed the data before him. His most trusted advisors, Demak and Ricardo, both guarded the base camp with their rifles. They had just come back from battle, bringing Amanda and the lifeless Trevor with them. It was a shame about Trevor, Bennifer thought. But even the greatest and most honorable of men die. That's why it's important to honor them just as much in death as in life.

He looked at the report totals, surveying the damage done to their army. He noticed that the battle had started rather fair, but in the last few hours, the New Bloods had gained back some ground and had taken back control of the battle. Similarly, the Creator's guards were still plentiful. In fact, their numbers were so high that a group of them had stormed toward the tower, likely chasing Jake in his quest to get to the top.

"It looks like they're gaining back some ground, sir," Demak said. "We killed off a bunch of New Bloods, but they came back with ease. We're on the third or fourth refresh for some. It's tough for our soldiers to keep shoveling while it's snowing, if you catch my drift."

Bennifer rolled his eyes. "What can we do?"

Demak spread his hands across the paper. "Like we said earlier, best thing we can do is defend and delay. We have to hope Jake is making it to the top of the tower. If he does that, then we have a real shot at this. We just have to keep them busy long enough for Jake to get inside and do what's he's got to do."

Ricardo stepped closer to the two. "But what if he fails? Then we're just stuck in this?"

Demak and Bennifer turned to Ricardo. Bennifer hadn't considered that possibility. He had been so obsessed with the idea of winning that he hadn't realized there was the potential for no victory at all, and that the group would be stuck in a tireless fight for rest of their lives, until they all died.

"We need an exit strategy," Bennifer said. "Just in case things don't work."

Ricardo laid a piece of paper on the table. "We're still keeping tabs on all exclusive personnel. We've got readers on us three, Amanda, Trevor, Kevin, Jake, that whole crew, and a few of the top soldiers out in the field. When things get too tough, I say we send a notification out for them to get back to the base, and we ship out toward another part of the planet and regroup."

"And what? Just leave the rest of our soldiers to die?" Demak asked.

Ricardo shrugged. "If it means keeping our mission of getting where we need to go, then yes, I say we do it."

Bennifer looked at both of his advisors and then back at the papers before him.

"Can we get a signal on Keys and Serent?" Bennifer asked.

"Yes, sir, right away," Ricardo said. He spun around to one of the computers in the corner of the camp. He clicked a few buttons and then came back over to Bennifer. "Both of their readers are off."

"What?" Bennifer asked. "Did they fail?"

Demak shook his head. "It probably means they're too close to the anomaly of the tower and it's interfering with our signals. We won't know what happened to them until they get back."

Bennifer picked his head up and looked out at the Palace. Nothing was different from when he first arrived. The tower still stood tall and the sky remained that grayish pink. Men and women lost their lives on the battlefield, and yet nothing had been accomplished.

"Let's hope Jake's cooking up something good in that tower."

II

Jake had finally reached the top of the Creator's Palace. Only it was much different than he thought it'd be.

He was on his knees and his hands were handcuffed behind his back by jagged silver lines of energy or magic, he wasn't quite sure. The sword—the weapon that he had been told would put an end to the Creator's reign—laid in the hands of Richard, the friend who he started his journey with that they had left behind ages ago. Richard, his cloak's hood down,

THE PEN

paced back and forth by the large window at the top of the tower.

How was this even possible?

Jake waited for Richard to say something, but he didn't. He paced back and forth, looking at the sword and twirling it in his hand. Jake looked around him to see what the room was like. It was like he remembered it from the replica. Stone-black bricks, a gigantic window in the middle that looked out at the land, a door that led to the rest of the tower, and a separate door in the back corner. The stone was in the center. The floor was covered in a red dust, which Jake didn't understand in the slightest.

He also didn't understand why Richard was here, or why he was calling himself the Master. And, Jake didn't understand why he had yet to see Kurpo, The Creator, the man who had stabbed him as a spirit all those months ago.

But Jake stayed quiet. If what Sky told him all those months ago was true, then Jake would be soon be faced with immeasurable pain. He had to keep his energy for that. So the only thing he could do to protect himself at the moment was survey the room and see if there was anything special he could eventually use to his advantage.

Richard stopped walking and turned his head to Jake with a slick smile on his face.

"Isn't this funny?" Richard asked. "I mean, you're familiar with the prophecy, I hope. About how you're supposed to climb to the top of the tower, take this sword and stab into the stone right over there, and then everything in Discis goes back to normal. Happy endings, happy endings all around. But think about this: you're in my custody, I have your sword, and the prophecy is nowhere close to being fulfilled. So close, so close, and yet in no way close enough."

Jake had already thought of all that. He didn't find it funny like Richard did, but he did find it odd that almost everything in the prophecy had come true, except not in the way he thought it would.

Richard wielded the sword well, striking the air and slashing away at an invisible opponent. "Who knew that The Pen would make such a fine sword?" he said. He stopped his slashing movements and laid it against his hands. He slid his hands along the blade. "Sharp, decisive, and beautiful. An elegant weapon, by and far. I never thought I'd be this happy to see The Pen like this."

Richard looked to Jake. "Oh, come on Jake, please, say something. Don't just be quiet. No one likes quiet people. Believe me. Richard knows all about being quiet and not having friends."

Jake closed his eyes.

"All right," Richard said, setting the sword down on the desk by the window. "Well, now we're at a crucial point in our story, Jake. See, in order for this sword to be my Pen again, you're going to need to willingly hand it over to me. Those are the rules. Blame Serena for that. So I'm going to need you to speak and tell me that this Pen is mine again. You understand, don't you?"

Jake kept his eyes shut.

"Oh, Jake, poorest, poorest, Jake," Richard said, walking around in a circle. "I'm trying to give you a chance to live, here. You give me my Pen back, I let you live, and you can become my new second-in-command. You'll be the new Kurpo! How does that sound? If that doesn't sound good to you, well, then you'll be like the old Kurpo—nothing but a pile of dust for me to walk over."

Jake thought it was a metaphor, but then he remembered the dust on the floor. If The Master was capable of killing Kurpo, what else would he be willing to do?

"Fine, Jake," Richard said. He turned toward the window and donned the hood of his cloak. He swerved back around and faced Jake directly, only now he looked different. His eyes were red and full of hate. In one motion, Richard threw his hands out into the air. Red mist filled them. He looked at Jake with a harsh glare.

"Now, Jake Serent, you will die."

III

Amanda didn't have too much time to mourn Trevor. Once she and the crew got back to the base camp, she said her goodbyes, covered his body with a sheet, and reoriented herself. Though at first she was fine with not following through on her promise to Trevor, she knew it was more important than ever to finish the mission and move on without him, just like she had to do back when he left her in Florida all those years ago.

She gathered herself, cleaned her face, and went to get patched up by the medical staff. She waited in one of the tents for about twenty minutes before the tent's flap opened and a nurse walked in. To her surprise, Amanda saw her former mentor, Nurse Gertrude, standing at the door.

"Gertrude?" Amanda asked.

"Amanda! Hi!" she said.

The two hugged. Amanda sighed in pain, and Gertrude went right to work. Instead of inspecting each broken rib or fractured bone that Amanda had, Gertrude pulled out a paper patch and set it on Amanda's shoulder. She pulled out a flat metallic pad and set it atop the bandage. Within seconds, Amanda felt the pain fly away. Her bones snapped back into place, her bruises cleared, and the cuts sealed up. Blood and dirt still painted her face a mix of red and brown, but at least she didn't feel the pain anymore. Once Gertrude took the metal pad off Amanda's shoulder, Amanda felt like she hadn't been through any kind of fight.

"What was that?" Amanda asked.

Gertrude inspected the pad. "Neat little thing we cooked up back home. Funny the stuff we hide until we're in dire need."

Amanda stretched her arms and rolled her neck. There was no more pain.

"Now, normally I'd recommend you stay put here, but, we're in the middle of a battle," Gertrude said.

Amanda smiled. "I completely agree. I take it I have your blessing to keep fighting."

Gertrude nodded. "You do."

Amanda stood up, said goodbye to her old friend, and left the tent. She jogged over to Bennifer's hut, where she found the army's leader and his two advisors mulling over information. When she stormed in, everyone in the room flashed their eyes at her, amazed to see her mobility and readiness for action. Amanda stretched her arms and cracked her knuckles to show everyone that she was ready to get back into combat.

"What can I do?" Amanda asked.

"What were you doing before we found you?" Bennifer asked.

"Battling this other woman, Broxxi. She seems pretty high in command. Like one of the leading soldiers of the army. We engaged in one-on-one combat. She was going to beat me before Trevor saved my life," Amanda said. She held back tears as she told Bennifer this.

Bennifer looked around the room. "Does she command? If we finish her off, will her army die off as well?"

Amanda shook her head. "She runs things with a flower style of leadership. Very open, everyone works together. Our best shot to stop this army is to make sure Jake completes his mission."

Bennifer rolled his eyes. "I swear, if I hear that one more time."

Amanda half-smiled and then had a thought.

"Well," she said, walking over to the store of guns in the corner of the tent. "If we're going to wait for Jake to finish, I'm going to go out there and kick some ass while I wait."

She looked through the weapons and didn't see any that fit the bill. She looked around the tent, and that's when she saw Trevor's gun, the one she left in the tent when she first got back. She bent down and picked it up, switched on all the knobs she needed to, and then left the tent, ready to get back into battle.

IV

Jake kneeled on the floor of the Creator's room now, blood tricking down the right side of his face. The room's red dust stuck to his bloody cheeks. He groaned in pain, having been hit twice in the back by Richard's energy strikes, and by another in the head. Jake wasn't dead, but he easily could have been killed.

Luckily, The Master couldn't kill Jake, since Jake had to be the one to pass The Pen over to the Master. That gave Jake somewhat of advantage. The only thing the Master could do was cause pain.

But Jake couldn't die like this, could he?

Richard looked at Jake's back, seeing the exposed wounds. He slashed at his back again with a whip of energy, and Jake called out in pain as he rolled onto his stomach. Richard struck again, and Jake screamed from the wound.

Jake was lying, though, about the pain. He wanted the Master to think he was being destroyed. But Jake had already lived through this when he went into the replica tower. Sky had made his back stronger. And he remembered his training well. He remembered not to let his healthy side show. He remembered to keep himself ready for the next strike and the next strike. He remembered how important it was to say focused on the moment and not let the pain get to him.

Jake felt another slash of pain spank his back. Another one cut into it. There was a little burn, so he bit his teeth to try and mask it.

"Come on, Jake," Richard said. He sent another line of red mist at Jake back, zapping him. "Get it over with and give me my Pen back!"

Jake spat out the dust in his mouth. "You want this Pen back? Kill me then, Richard. Kill me and it'll be all yours." But Jake knew full well that wasn't going to happen.

Jake's back spasmed as another line of mist cut into it. Red strings of blood floated near his eyes.

"I have not been working this hard to get my Pen back just to be throttled by a little Arriver kid like you," Richard said. "I did not get this far to become the ultimate power in the universe just to be put off by you. You're not the Prophet, you're not the one and true Holder. No. You are just one, Jake. One of many. And I shall make you give me what's mine. Just like I did with Kurpo, I will make you give me back my Pen."

Another slash. Blood spilled from his back. It was cool, but it hurt like hell.

"IT'S MINE!" Richard screamed.

He slashed at Jake's back again.

"MINE! MINE! MINE!"

This time three slashes.

"MY PEN! MY PEN! MY PEN!"

Three more slashes.

Another slash, and another, and another, and another. One came right after the next, and this time Jake screamed for real. His back had no shield to this. He felt as though Richard's own pain and anger came slashing across his back, breaking Jake's skin open and spilling crimson blood across the floor. The pain didn't let up, either. Another slash, and another slash, and another.

Slash slash slash slash slash slash slash slash.

"AH! MINE! MINE! MINE! MINE! MINE! AH!"

Richard stopped and collapsed to the ground. He leaned his back against the desk, tired from all the rage and anguish he had just unleashed on Jake, who had rolled over onto his back, finally revealing his healthy side, a cardinal sin during his training days. He sucked in some air to escape the pain. If he wasn't on the track toward death before, then he certainly was now.

Jake pushed his feet against the floor and scooted backwards. He leaned himself against the back wall, right next to the back door, and tried to collect his thoughts and his feelings. He watched as Richard gathered himself and stood up. Jake closed his eyes and thought about his training and all that he had learned. Was there something he was missing? Was there something someone had told him along the way that could help him in his most desperate hour? Had Moss said something to him that he could use now? Had he read anything in the books that would help him understand what he could do to stop the Master? Did he learn anything in his journey into the tower's replica that could save him now?

And then it all clicked. He couldn't explain how, but wasn't that how this had all played out? When Kevin and Trevor disappeared all that time ago, he couldn't explain it. When The Pen brought him back to Discis, he couldn't explain it.

The feeling he felt now of what to do next was something so right, so sure—and yet unsure.

Jake wearily gazed up at the Master, who held the purple sword. He felt the blade. He ran his hands across the blade's face and slashed away into the air.

This was Jake's moment.

"Fine. You want your Pen back, I give up," Jake lied. Richard looked over to Jake with a raised eyebrow. Jake sighed in relief and nodded toward Richard. "I give you that Pen in your hands. It's yours. You may be the Holder of that Pen."

Richard's confused face became one with a wicked smile.

"Now will you please unchain me and let me live?" Jake said.

The Master flicked his fingers. The handcuffs disintegrated. He turned around and saw just red dust on the floor.

"You've done well," Richard said. "I can feel The Pen's presence. I can feel the power. You have done well. You may make a great second-in-command yet. Better than anyone before me."

Jake reached into his pocket.

"You know," Jake said, watching Richard move around the room. Jake grunted when he rose to his feet. His back cracked. "There's this saying back on Earth that fits perfectly with this situation."

"Oh yeah?" Richard said, eyeing his sword as though it were the only thing in the universe that mattered. "And what do they say?"

Jake smiled. "The Pen is mightier than the sword."

As Richard turned around to face him, Jake, holding the black Pen, wrote the words: "SAVE DISCIS."

A line of black smoke crawled from The Pen's tip. It spiraled around the Master, who started to shout and scream and yelp as the smoke covered him. He dropped the sword and shot red fire from his hands and eyes and ears and everywhere, but nothing could outdo the power of the black smoke. It enclosed him, covered him, and tore away at his body and soul and skin. It ripped him apart. He began to meld with the smoke as his screams drowned and drained away. Jake leaned back against the wall and watched as the Master—a spirit, a human, and an ultimate power—broke apart and disappeared into thin air, as though he had never been there.

But when he was gone, calm didn't set in. Redness exploded from where he stood and shot out like chaos. It blew Jake back against the wall, and now he felt a powerful red wind punish him and push him against the walls of the Palace's top room. Jake heard thunder and lightning, and all he could see were waves and waves of red smoke all around him. The pipe had burst, and all that was left was red energy soaring through the air—unstoppable waves of it. Jake fell to the ground and looked around him, seeing if there was something he could do to make it stop.

And then he saw it, much like he expected to. The purple sword with its six cubes down the center was nailed to the ground, unmoved by the blazing winds. Jake scratched his way through the wind over to the sword. He crawled as the wind pushed him back, but he kept his pace. He clawed on the floor, shoving the red dust out of the way. With one last lunge, he gripped the handle of the sword, which gave him weight to stand up through the red mist and wind. Jake hopped into the air and latched onto the stone that sat in the middle of the room and wrapped his arm around it. He knew letting go would be the end of him.

He could see soldiers battling and army vehicles busting through the battlefield through the window on his right. He could see the white-capped mountains he had once climbed, way off in the distance. The verdant forests he had journeyed through. The Walls, not so tall anymore, guarding the desert sands below. The Sammack Sea, now shining with a beautiful glow. The Sluronnano Volcano, dormant, resting, off in the background. The clearing where they had found Sky's hut. The far-off wastelands where nothing but death awaited.

He saw it all, everything he had grown to love and enjoy and miss and

THE PEN

embrace and hate and distrust these last few months. And he knew this would be the last time he'd see it.

So Jake took a mental picture of everything he saw and turned away. The wind still howled and blew at his face. The red whirlwind of mist and energy continued to swirl around him. He heard a loud bang and looked behind him. The back door opened and a glowing white light came from it. Jake turned toward the stone and faced it with determination.

He took a deep breath, gathered his strength, and lifted the purple sword as high as he could. He looked down at the stone and saw the perfectly-shaped slit.

And then Jake, just like he had been told he would do, just like the prophecy had said, slammed the sword into the stone.

And everything went white.

CHAPTER 49

I

Richelle Ewings was tired, hungry, and at a loss.

She sat alone in the grass beside a brook that ran through the insignificant patch of forest she had found after she woke up from her blackout. She had eaten a few berries she found near the water, but there wasn't much else to eat. She spent the last day bathing in the muddy brook and drinking as much water as she could stomach. It gave her something to do and something to keep her alive. She could go a long time without food, she knew that, but water was important. So she drank as much as she could, and she loved every second of it.

In her downtime, Richelle lay in the sun and thought about everything that happened to her earlier in the month and especially what had happened to her just a day ago. She thought about how important the election had been to her group and all the drama that went along with that. She thought about her tension with Grant, and all the emotions she felt toward him, both negative and positive. She thought about how the cloaked man had murdered all of her friends without remorse. All of her friends, dead and gone, in a flash. She didn't even get time to say goodbye to them. Everyone had died in a quick and horrific way, all screaming, all worried, and all of them in fear.

Richelle also considered what she should do next. She was on her own, that much was clear, but she couldn't just sit around and wait to be rescued. She had to be proactive and find the next step. Whatever green light Grant had mentioned to her had faded away and was gone, so there was no hope with that. All Richelle could do now was try her best to survive and live out the rest of her years without too much pain.

A light breeze came and chilled her, but it felt refreshing against the beating heat of the sun above. She smelled the fresh air and listened to the tree leaves brushing against each other. It was pure magic. She listened to the babbling brook, and for a moment it felt like she was back on Earth, as though there weren't any different between the two planets.

And then came the thunder.

Richelle's eyes flashed open when she heard thunder erupt, especially because the sky was a clear blue and the sun was beating down hard. There wasn't a cloud in the sky, nor a scent of any sort of rain or malevolent weather. It was all perfect. So why was there suddenly thunder? Richelle stood up and looked around at the sky and saw nothing but beauty.

Thunder rolled again, and now Richelle was worried. Why the thunder?

Richelle noted that her world was getting brighter by the second. She covered her eyes, wondering why the sun's rays had picked up in strength in the last few seconds. But it wasn't a coincidence, and it wasn't the sun. The yellowish tinge of the sun's glow faded and was replaced with a blinding white light that covered everything. Richelle shielded her eyes and hid underneath a tree, but it was no use. Soon everything was white, and everything disappeared from sight.

II

Broxxi had just slain one of the enemy soldiers when she heard a thunderous boom. She swerved her head around and looked toward the Creator's Palace, where red mist shot out from the large window above. Confused, Broxxi continued to stare up and wait for answers. But none came. Soldiers rushed over to her and asked her what the thunder meant and what the red mist was all about. Broxxi, though, didn't have answers.

Broxxi saw something she didn't expect come from the Creator's tower. A piercing white light shot out from the window and sprayed the land below. Broxxi hid her eyes from the light, which continued to grow in size with each passing second. She buried herself beneath her arms and crouched low as the white light grew larger and larger, taking over the entire land and wiping everything from sight.

Broxxi looked to her right and saw soldiers, guards, and warriors alike all on the ground, hiding away from the blinding light that continue to grow and shine and glow. She wasn't alone.

Everything was white. No stone was left unturned.

III

Amanda had just shocked a few New Bloods to their core and polished off a few chrome soldiers when thunder erupted through the land. She looked up at the sky and saw the grayish pink sky, unchanged since she had last seen, which was peculiar. Why would the sky all of a sudden produce thunder if it hadn't already? What was suddenly making thunder that hadn't been there before?

Amanda looked around her to see if any warriors were coming to fight her, but they weren't. They were all looking in the direction of the tower. Amanda followed their gaze and saw the Creator's Palace standing still, except for a bright red mist seeping out and spraying the air. Wind howled and blew the mist from the top window.

Just as Amanda began trying to figure out the mist, it went away. Instead, a light came from the top of the Creator's Palace, and it was brighter than the sun. It grew in size every few seconds and started to shine out like a lighthouse beacon in the dead of night. Amanda crouched low and hid herself from the blinding light. She gazed up to see if it went away, but she was only met with pain as the light slapped her across the eyes. She hunkered down to escape and waited for the brightness to pass.

IV

Bennifer was reading over more service reports when he heard a loud boom come from the direction of the battlefield.

With Ricardo and Demak behind him, Bennifer stormed out of his tent. He jogged over to the edge of the battlefield and looked way out in the distance toward the tower. He saw red mist spray from the top window and then begin to swirl all around and come out in a fury.

The red mist went away and was replaced with an unbearable whiteness. Bennifer squinted and kept his eyes fixed to see where the light came from, and noticed it was from the tower. It grew and grew in size without stopping, wiping across the world as though to leave a clean slate.

Bennifer smiled. "Well done, Jake. Well done."

V

All Jake could see was whiteness, except for the faint outline of a door.

Jake, through the blinding hot white light, crawled toward the back door and fell through into pure white space.

CHAPTER 50

I

Amanda opened her eyes when the whiteness was gone, and she was amazed at what she saw. All of the New Bloods were gone, and all the Creator's soldiers were on their knees, surrendering. She looked around her and saw that the pinkish sky had faded and was replaced with a hard blue one. It reminded her of a beautiful Florida summer day.

Amanda took off her helmet and smelled the fresh breeze that came in and wiped away the stench of battle. She peered back toward her camp and saw, off in the distance, that the Walls of the Creator's Palace were gone, too. And the hills and forests off in the distance were a vibrant verdant color. Clear skies shone from where they were until they met the edge of the world.

She walked over to some of her soldiers, who were celebrating because they knew they had won. She patted them on the shoulder before walking back toward the base camp, where Bennifer, Demak, and Ricardo stood.

"Looks like we won," Amanda said with a smile. "You think Jake succeeded?"

Bennifer had a smile on his face. "I know he did."

"Do you think he's still alive?" Amanda asked.

"Let's go check."

Amanda led Bennifer, Demak, and Ricardo to the tower. They passed by many fallen soldiers and guards, who had all died honorably in their service for the greater cause. As they got closer to the tower, Amanda noticed the staircase that climbed to the top, the one that they had planned on building a few nights back. She smiled, knowing that Jake had stuck to the plan, which seemed to have worked.

Amanda's eyes traveled from the staircase down to the ground and that's when she noticed one fallen soldier that she didn't expect to see. His hair, she could tell, was blonde. And the markings on his uniform made it clear who he was. The four traveled over and kneeled before Kevin's body, broken and destroyed by the fall. Bennifer called for Demak and Ricardo to get a stretcher and carry Kevin away.

Shattered, Amanda watched the soldiers carry Kevin off back toward the basecamp. It was her second close friend to die within a matter of hours. She knew she could make peace with him later. She just hoped that she could find Jake, and that it wasn't too late for him, too.

She was alone now, but that didn't matter. In fact, she seemed to do better that way. She climbed the steps Jake had created, stepping over the fallen bodies of those who had been killed by sword or gunfire. She noticed a few of the guards had been hurled over the side of the stairs, too, which meant there had been an epic battle on these stairs just hours ago.

No matter what she saw, though, she had to keep going. Amanda hopped from the stairs to the open platform and looked up at the far ladder. Amanda reached into her weapons vest and pulled out a pistol that she hadn't used yet. She shot it toward the ladder and watched a rope wrap itself around the ladder's last bar. She grabbed the rope tightly and climbed up and over into open space that would kill her if she fell.

But Amanda knew what she was doing. She wasn't going to die. She had too much determination to do so. She reached the ladder and hopped onto it. She climbed to the top and rolled onto the next platform. At first, she thought it led to nowhere, but then she saw the teenager-sized hole on the side that was big enough to fit her. She climbed through and dropped.

The floor was hard and dusty. But compared to what she had been through the last few hours, it was nothing. Amanda pushed herself up and looked around the room she was in. There was a desk on the far side near a window that overlooked the lands beyond. There was a large stone in the center of the room. There was a door on one side of the room, and another toward the back. The back door was wide open and empty.

Amanda walked over to the window and looked out to see beauty and brightness shining on Discis. The sky was that magnificent blue, the trees were growing green, the walls had disappeared, and the desert was no longer in sight. The Sammack Sea shone way off in the distance.

Amanda could see the world breathe.

She turned around and swept her hand across the stone. She saw the bottom part of a sword sticking out of the top—not enough to pull the sword out, but enough to show that it was a sword that had been put in the stone.

Jake had done it.

She had seen all she needed. Amanda left the Palace the way she came—she didn't feel like going through the entire building just yet—and found Bennifer waiting for her. She smiled.

"He did it," Amanda said.

Bennifer smiled. "That's good to hear."

"I don't know where he is, or if he's even alive, but Jake did it," Amanda said, smiling with joy. "I can't believe the kid did it."

Bennifer laughed lightly. "Me neither. That kid's the last person I'd have picked to save two worlds at once."

Amanda raised her eyebrow. "Two worlds?"

Bennifer nodded. "Jake saved Discis, that's clear. But because of his journey, we found Discis. And because we found and saved Discis, we can find our next destination, which hopefully holds the key to saving Earth."

Amanda nodded in complete approval.

"And I hope, Ms. Amanda, that you'll join us."

Amanda smiled. Trevor had told her to keep going. That's exactly what she intended to do.

II

When the whiteness went away, the first thing Broxxi noticed was that her New Bloods were gone.

Wide-eyed, Broxxi hurried over to a group of her guards, who stood alone. She looked out at the rest of her warriors and saw they were severely outnumbered. The army they faced was packed with soldiers, vehicles, and weaponry more sophisticated than she had ever seen. All she had were soldiers with simple weapons, and there certainly weren't enough soldiers to make those simple weapons count for anything.

"Stand down!" Broxxi yelled out at her crowd.

The guards all looked at her in shock at first, amazed that she had given in so easily. She didn't even try to start the next round of fighting. But then, slowly, the guards followed her example and lay their weapons down. The guards lifted their helmets off their heads and got down on their right knees. They placed their right hands across their chest and admitted surrender.

Broxxi did the same. She saw soldiers rushing toward them with weapons. Vehicles and flying crafts came soaring over as well.

Broxxi knew what was coming next. They were going to be taken captive and either put to work with the military or used to help run the land in the coming years. And there was nothing she could do to stop that. The Creator was gone, after all, and Discis had begun to breathe again like it always had. So she knew that things were back to the way they were once before, which meant they could never be the same again. And there was nothing she could do about it.

To her own surprise, Broxxi wept.

Tears flowed from the corner of her eyes and cleaned away the stains of war. She buried her head in her hand and let the tears sprinkle out in droves.

It was finally over. The pain, the suffering, and all the torment. It was all over. She finally had a clean slate.

III

Richelle's environment didn't change that much once after the whiteness was gone. The green plains of grass remained, as did the babbling brook and cool breeze. All was just as she had remembered it.

But when she turned to her right, she saw bunches and bunches of vegetation. Fruits and vegetables alike were lined across the trees and plants of the forest. Fruits of the bluest blues and the reddest reds glowed among the green trees. Without a second thought, Richelle hurried over to the vegetables and plucked away. She bit hard into an apple and sucked its sweet nectar.

CHAPTER 51

I

Jake worked at a library, and he absolutely hated it.

It felt like waking up from a bad nightmare, all of a sudden. Jake blinked rapidly to see where he was, and noticed he was where he began. It was the library, the one he worked at, the one he hated. He stared at a blank screen, waiting for someone to message him. He looked around him and saw the library for what it was. Stacks of books, both for adults and children, without end. He looked forward and saw a stack of books placed corner of the walkway—new books for him to put away.

Jake stood up and walked over to the books. He picked them up and saw there were six of them. One was purple, then blue, then light blue, then green, then yellow, and finally red.

Jake didn't think twice about what to do with these books. He shelved them like he did so often over the summer. He slipped them all into a row in the back corner of the children's section. Jake looked at the books one last time and saw "HWS1125" written as one of the code numbers, but didn't think twice of it.

The boy returned to his computer desk and checked his phone, which didn't have any messages or notifications from anyone. So he leaned back and sighed. Just a normal day, without much hope. He slid his hands into his pockets, ready to relax and let the hours of the workday pass by.

But then Jake felt something in his pocket that he didn't expect to be there. He slowly pulled out a pen, black with six black cubes. The Pen's tip was silver and had black ink stains on the side.

And then it all came back to him.

He saw the day when he and Kevin went to Friendly's to grab some food, the night he saw Kevin disappear, the first time he saw The Pen, the first time he traveled to Discis, the battle in the volcano, the run through the desert, the sword fight with Kurpo, the recovery from the wound, the Council of Julk, the journey through the mountains, the Blizzard of Lexington, Shelton's death, Moss's exile, Sky's hut, the replica of the Creator's tower, Grant's arrival, the green teleporter, being home, leaving home, finding Moss, finding his friends, marching to battle, watching Moss die, fighting, surviving, battling, watching Kevin die, fighting, battling, using The Pen, saving Discis—all of it.

Jake stood up, unsure, yet sure at the same time as to why he did so. He walked to the back of the library toward an open conference room, old and constructed of a dirty brown wood. He smelled mothballs and aged paper. He looked around, searching, yet unsure of what he'd find. A sheet of paper, curled at its ends, sat at the center of the long conference table at the center of the room.

Jake walked up to the grayish-white paper with his Pen and stared at it. At first, it was blank. And then, as though a button had been hit, things switched on, like a computer screen.

Jake saw a bird's-eye view of a rooftop. Unsure of what he was looking at, Jake stared deeper and could tell it was familiar, but he didn't know why. He saw two boys appear on the rooftop. One was his cousin and the other was him. He saw Kevin rush across the rooftop and head toward the jump, the one they made all those years ago. Jake stopped on the roof and Kevin went for the jump.

Jake, out of instinct alone, took his Pen and scribbled on the piece of paper, "LANDS JUMP."

Kevin landed the jump.

The picture faded and then came another bird's-eye view picture. This time, though, it was of Kevin and Trevor skateboarding down the highway. Jake remembered that night. Jake saw himself suddenly come into the frame and realized what was happening. Kevin and Trevor continued to board down the highway.

Jake, knowing where Kevin and Trevor needed to go, wrote, "SEND TO DISCIS."

The picture went away. After a moment, it was replaced with a third person view of Jake, Richard, and Shelton in the Sluronnano volcano, falling toward their demise in the lava. He saw Shelton hold himself up by his own energy, and then he saw himself stab at the side of the volcano with his Pen and stop his death. He watched Richard fall to the lava below.

Just before he hit the lava, Jake circled Richard's body and wrote, "STAY ALIVE."

The picture flashed away and in came another, this one of Jake and the

Creator, their swords out and ready for battle. The Creator stabbed Jake in the gut and disappeared.

Jake circled his body in the picture and wrote, "STAY ALIVE."

The picture flashed again and Jake saw moments in their journey move along the pages. He saw the blizzard wreak havoc on their lives. He saw Trevor and Moss punch each other. He saw Shelton sacrifice himself for the good of the group. He saw everything twirl and move with rapid pace and then it stopped again.

This time, Jake looked down at Trevor and Kevin, standing in a large lobby at a castle. Jake remembered the story he heard about this. He saw a masked woman descend from the stairs and instruct Kevin to leave. Trevor and the woman looked at each other.

Jake smiled and circled the woman with The Pen. He wrote, "REMEMBER."

The magic flew off the girl and Amanda smiled.

The pictures flashed again. And this time it stopped on Amanda, younger, on the phone, calling her lost love. Jake circled the picture and wrote, "SEND TO DISCIS."

The pictures flashed again. Sky appeared in a closet, searching through some clothes. Jake remembered what this moment was. He circled Sky and wrote, "SEND TO DISCIS."

The pictures flashed again and again, faster this time, as though the paper was searching for something. It moved back and forth, from the early times of their journey to the latter parts. It went back and forth, from the days of the Krowian Desert to the battle they had just waged.

And then it stopped. The picture showed Jake, standing in the street with Bennifer not far off. Jake saw himself raise his Pen to the sky. Jake smiled and wrote, "SEND TO DISCIS."

One more image popped up. The group—Jake, Kevin, Trevor, Amanda and Moss—stood on the grass. He watched The Man of Fire arrive and attack Moss. Jake watched himself call for help from The Pen, call for something to stop The Man of Fire.

But Jake held off because he knew, deep inside of himself, completely sure, that Moss' death had meant something.

And so he wrote nothing. Nothing at all.

The picture faded and the paper glowed. It became that eye-piercing white, just like he remembered from moments ago. The lightness began to spread, and that's when Jake knew he was done with his writing.

Jake walked away from the paper and toward the computer. The stark white screen remained just as he had left it. He stepped past it and to the library's center. He saw the librarian working away. He saw books upon books being stacked into the back of the library.

And then he saw the front door.

Jake, with a smile on his face, walked over to the library's front door and wondered what was on the other side. He took one last look at his library before he pushed past the door and everything went white again.

II

All Jake could taste was sand and seawater.

He dug his hands into the damp sand below and pushed himself up and out of the sand. On all fours, Jake spat out whatever water and sand had pooled in his mouth. He shook his head free of the sand clumps and then stood up, his sneakers digging deep into the shoreline.

When he looked up, he wasn't alone. Standing before him, dressed in all white armor and with brown hair down to his shoulders, was a man he would normally have recognized—had he not been suffering from the world's biggest migraine. Jake looked at the man's name badge on the armor and saw "Lexington" etched across.

"Hello Jake," Lexington said. "Welcome home."

Lexington patted Jake on the shoulder and the two walked up the beach toward the sand dunes. The sky was a vibrant blue, with no clouds in sight. The air was dry and clean. A light breeze hung in the air and made everything smell fresh and calm and collected.

As Jake and Lexington walked up the beach, Jake noticed his clothes weren't dirty. The red T-shirt and khakis, the same outfit he wore the day he first went to Discis, were clean, as though they hadn't been destroyed because of blood and the journey he had been through.

Lexington led Jake up the beach and through the sand dunes. They climbed over a small hill, kicking through sand. Jake didn't ask any questions. Everything felt right. He had already been through hell and back. The last thing he wanted was more concern and strife.

Jake smiled when they reached the top of the sand dunes. Before him was a wonderful city. The buildings were glass and modern. Spacecrafts sped through the skies and soared off to destinations unknown. The streets were lined with transport trains, zooming off from one side of the city to the other. Jake saw people—real people—hurrying along busy streets. He saw beautiful buildings, some silver, some blue, some a pale yellow, ones he couldn't imagine seeing, alight and shining with the sun. Everything was plated with glass and blue pillars. It was all too real to be true.

Lexington directed Jake toward a corner spot. It was a smaller building, but it still had those glass windows that made this city breathtaking. Jake peered through and saw people, real-life people, eating food. It was a restaurant of sorts. Families joined together for meals, some ate alone, and others nervously waited for people to arrive.

Lexington and Jake walked into the restaurant, and everything changed.

Everyone in the restaurant stood on their feet when they saw Jake. Smiles spread across all of their faces. They clapped and roared and cheered as Jake entered. Girls and boys alike rushed over to Jake and applauded him, slapping him on the back and nudging him in the shoulders. They cheered for him, celebrating his arrival.

Jake soon found himself sitting in a booth in the back corner of the restaurant. All of this felt right. It felt sure. Lexington was across from him, chatting, along with a few other folks. The others hurriedly spoke to Jake, asking him a thousand questions a minute about how he had saved the planet. They asked him in droves about what it was like getting to the top of the Creator's tower, or what it was like to hold The Pen for so long. They asked him how he did what he did, why he did it, and what made him want to be such a hero. They asked him how he felt about life, if he was tired, if he was hungry, if he was interested in getting married or finding someone to love. They asked him how long he'd stay in Discis, if this was his home, and if he missed the world he left behind.

Jake didn't answer anything, at least not yet. He let the questions come to him. There were too many to answer.

He looked up, though, and smiled.

Sky sat at a nearby booth where he flapped his gums at a young boy about how to hold his chopsticks. Sky turned his head to Jake and bowed.

Just to the right, Moss guided another youngster through the menu. He passively waved at Jake and went back to teaching.

Trevor relaxed at a table with three others, one of whom was Amanda. Trevor and Amanda, their arms wrapped around each other, nodded to Jake and raised their glasses to him.

Shelton, dressed in a dark hoodie and jeans, spoke with Richard in a booth. Shelton raised his hand to Jake and nodded appreciatively. Richard gave a half smile, sorry for what he had done. Jake waved to them both.

And then Jake glanced over to his right and saw Kevin, leaning against the restaurant's door, a skateboard at his feet. Jake didn't nod or wave, and neither did Kevin. The two stared at each other for a moment, their eyes telling each other the whole story. Kevin grinned, grabbed his board, and left the restaurant. He skateboarded into thin air.

When Jake turned back to the restaurant, his friends were all gone, but it was still great to see them again that last time.

Jake turned his attention back to the ground of swarming Discis citizens, who continued to rush him and demand he answer their questions. Jake didn't know any of them, but he was sure he would over time.

The 16-year-old boy, the Prophet, the Holder of The Pen, reached into his pockets and found nothing. There was no Pen. It was gone. The one thing that made him a hero no longer existed.

But it didn't matter. The Pen wasn't what gave him strength. Not anymore. It was this group of people, the ones he had saved, the ones who cared about him and loved him. Jake leaned back against his chair and smiled, letting the questions pile up.

And even though the air reeked of bacon, it didn't bother Jake at all.

EPILOGUE

Miles away from the city, the rushing waves of the beach collided with the sand, ever eating away at the land's size. Sand and rocks and water and birds chirping away. Seashells outlined the shoreline. The blue skies didn't fade, and neither did the crisp azure color of the ocean.

Discis families ran and scurried along the beach. Some friends lay against the sand and watched the waves rock back and forth. Much of the beach was littered with people celebrating the demise of their Creator and the return to a cleaner and fresher Discis. The darkness had been destroyed and only light remained.

Belacue, a young man with thick black hair and rugged features, picked away at the seashells. He enjoyed the bigger ones, the ones that made him hear the ocean when he held them close to his ear. He also enjoyed the pinkish ones for his mom.

Belacue searched through the seashells and one caught his attention. It was black and square. He tugged hard at it, but it wouldn't come out of the sand easily. He tried again, and soon enough he pulled the black seashell, its tip silver, from the sand and held it in his hand.

Only it wasn't a seashell.

CHECK OUT THESE OTHER GREAT TITLES COMING SOON:

A Wider Universe by Allison Floyd
Clockwork by Douglas B. Speck

...and more from The Pen trilogy!

ABOUT THE AUTHOR

Herb Scribner was raised in South Hadley, Massachusetts. He's been writing since he was in first grade. He's an avid coffee drinker and soccer fan. He currently lives in Salt Lake City, Utah.

Made in the USA
Charleston, SC
08 September 2016